PRAISE FOR

The Longest Night

"This one stands apart. Williams expertly brings her beautifully written story to a tense conclusion you'll still be thinking of long after you turn the last page."

—*Entertainment Weekly*

"Think *Army Wives* meets *Serial* meets your perfect long weekend read. About an army base with a lot of love triangles, and a cover-up."

—*theSkimm*

"The tension builds heavily with each page."

—*InStyle*

"The true story of the nation's only fatal nuclear accident provides the fraught context for Andria Williams's smart and detailed portrait of a dissolving postwar marriage. . . . Williams's assured debut will remind many readers of Richard Yates's *Revolutionary Road*."

—*San Francisco Chronicle*

"Ms. Williams nicely captures the graveyard-whistling helplessness of low-ranking men performing 'a service no one would love them for' and which would cost some of them their lives."

—*The Wall Street Journal*

"With its compelling plot, richly sprinkled with reminders of 1950s and early 1960s culture, *The Longest Night* offers insight into military marriages and friendships and how far we are willing to go to protect the ones we love."

—*Napa Valley Register*

"In both Paul and Nat we find echoes of Frank and April Wheeler in Richard Yates's classic novel of late-1950s suburbia, *Revolutionary*

Road. . . . [*The Longest Night*] not only packs taut, enthralling and utterly absorbing drama, but unexpected triumph and grace."

—*Paste*

"*The Longest Night* is not only a revealing story of a community gripped by Cold War paranoia, but also an unsettling portrait of commitment and desire."

—*BookPage*

"Andria Williams's first novel evocatively captures the social and marital tensions of the early 1960s, inside a military community during the birth of nuclear power."

—*Shelf Awareness*

"Scintillating . . . [Andria] Williams keeps the narrative interest percolating with great period details and by allowing her characters' thoughts and emotions full expression. . . . A smoldering, altogether impressive debut that probes the social and emotional strains on military families in a fresh and insightful way."

—*Kirkus Reviews* (starred review)

"[A] luminous debut . . . Williams expertly builds tension between Paul and Nat as the story progresses towards the inevitable nuclear tragedy in this utterly absorbing and richly rewarding novel."

—*Booklist* (starred review)

"In *The Longest Night,* unspoken longings within a marriage trigger an emotional explosion just as intense as the nuclear accident at the novel's core. Andria Williams's debut is an intimately detailed portrait of love, trust, and guilt in a town—and an era—clouded with secrets."

—Celeste Ng, author of *Everything I Never Told You*

"*The Longest Night* is a smart and compassionate novel that offers as many fresh insights into marriage and intimacy as it does about American nuclear history. Andria Williams is a terrific writer—clear-eyed and empathetic—and this is a fantastic debut."

—Molly Antopol, author of *The UnAmericans*

"It's hard to believe *The Longest Night* is Andria Williams's debut novel. Her command of language, character, and plot—the three essential ingredients for a riveting read—is extraordinary. *The Longest Night* is about the fragility of a marriage, a Cold War nuclear accident on the plains of Idaho, and the stresses on a military family during deployment, and it takes on each of those things with all the robust storytelling energy of the great Russian novelists of the nineteenth century. This is the book I will be pressing into my friends' hands this year when they ask me what they should be reading."

—David Abrams, author of *Fobbit*

"In *The Longest Night,* Andria Williams brilliantly balances high-wire tension with heart-crushing empathy for her cast of seeking, flawed, beautifully complex characters. This debut novel effortlessly evokes the mores and signposts of an earlier era, and brings to life characters whose loneliness, longing, and dignity are rendered with an indelible vividness that transcends time. It's a hard book to put down, and an even harder one to stop thinking about."

—Suzanne Rivecca, author of *Death Is Not an Option*

"There is a kind of story about the American West that you think you know, and this book destabilizes it. Williams creates characters who challenge the protocols of the time, and are irradiated by the results. This is the West I want to read about, where landscape shapes and dislocates, where one falls and is found again. Compassionate and compelling, Williams honors the lives of her characters, and shines in this striking debut."

—Nina McConigley, author of *Cowboys and East Indians*

"In *The Longest Night,* Andria Williams demonstrates her masterful understanding of the painfully gorgeous intimacies of the human condition. The author's thrilling storyline will keep you turning the pages, while her ability to inject a sharp dose of hope, fear, and desire into the most innocent of scenes will take you captive. I loved it."

—David Gillham, author of *City of Women*

"Andria Williams writes about the challenges and struggles faced by military families in a wholly original way. As a military spouse, Williams brings every nuance of this world to life, but it's her brimming talent and startling insight into the fragility and tenacity of marriage that kept me glued to the page."

—Siobhan Fallon, author of *You Know When the Men Are Gone*

"Engrossing, witty, dynamic, and beautifully written, *The Longest Night* is a real-life literary thrill ride that unfolds in the shadow of a poorly functioning nuclear reactor. Andria Williams's characters—particularly the 1960s military wives—are portrayed with extraordinary intimacy. This is a lovely, harrowing, and original novel. You will want to read it in a single night."

—Julie Schumacher, author of *Dear Committee Members*

"Andria Williams's wonderful debut novel is a sobering yet inspiring portrait of human nature, with precisely rendered details about the early years of the nuclear power era. With exceptional characterization, serious content, graceful structure, and a storyline as gripping as a psychological thriller, *The Longest Night* is both unforgettable and impossible to put down."

—Frederick Reiken, author of *Day for Night* and *The Lost Legends of New Jersey*

"A family drama set at the dawn of the 1960s, *The Longest Night* is a smart, emotionally resonant novel that combines domestic anxiety with nuclear terror. Andria Williams writes as powerfully about the potential breakdown of a marriage as she does about the meltdown of a reactor, all while evoking the atmosphere and particulars of a time when the madmen who ran America from the sidelines might have ended us not with a whimper but a bang."

—Aaron Gwyn, author of *Wynne's War* and *Dog on the Cross*

The LONGEST NIGHT

RANDOM HOUSE | NEW YORK

The Longest Night

A Novel

ANDRIA WILLIAMS

The Longest Night is a work of fiction. Names, characters, places, and incidents are the products of the author's imagination or are used fictitiously. Any resemblance to actual events, locales, or persons, living or dead, is entirely coincidental.

2016 Random House Trade Paperback Edition

Published in the United States by Random House, an imprint and division of Penguin Random House LLC, New York.

Random House and the House colophon are registered trademarks of Penguin Random House LLC.

Random House Reader's Circle & Design is a registered trademark of Penguin Random House LLC.

Originally published in hardcover in the United States by Random House, an imprint and division of Penguin Random House LLC, in 2016.

Library of Congress Cataloging-in-Publication Data
Williams, Andria.
Longest night: a novel/Andria Williams.
Pages cm
ISBN 978-0-8129-8742-3
eBook ISBN 978-0-8129-9775-0
1. Nuclear engineers—Fiction. 2. Nuclear reactor accidents—Fiction. 3. Emergency management—Fiction. 4. Domestic fiction. 5. Psychological fiction. I. Title.
PS3623.I55627L66 2015
813'.6—dc23 2014042509

Printed in the United States of America on acid-free paper

randomhousebooks.com

randomhousereaderscircle.com

987654321

Book design by Barbara M. Bachman

For Dave Johanson

There can be no greater admiration than that of the husband . . . to return and find, as he had hoped, that his own wife has met the test of keeping up her end of things.

—*The Army Officer's Guide,* 20th Edition (1954)

The LONGEST NIGHT

PAUL

IDAHO FALLS

January 3, 1961

PAUL WAS SO LOST IN THOUGHT THAT NIGHT, DRIVING, THAT IT TOOK him a moment to notice the ambulance heading toward him on the horizon. It arced up over the road, a starry flare against the black sky until it passed him, bright and soundless. A minute later, two fire trucks and the chief's station wagon followed, traveling in a tight pack, their lights whirling yellow and white and red.

Paul's heart tightened into a fist. He tried to tell himself that the trucks could mean nothing or anything, that they could be headed to any of the reactors at the testing station, but that was bullshit and he knew it. It was bullshit just like the supervisors had been feeding them for a year: that all the CR-1's glitches were minor, that when the reactor shut down you just started it up again, when it got too hot you just did what you had to do to cool it off: *Use your heads, boys, and make the damn thing work. Keep it alive until that new reactor core arrives in spring. Then this thing'll be running so smooth, you'll be sorry you ever complained.*

So they'd waited through fall and early winter, holding out for spring.

But here it was, the coldest night in an Idaho January, seventeen below zero, and every vehicle in the fire department fleet had just blown past, headed due east for the CR-1.

Paul pulled onto the shoulder and turned his car to follow them, tires grinding on the gravel. He didn't know what he'd find when he got there. Please let them be lucky, please let it just be a false alarm so they could all endure a nice dressing-down from the fire chief, who'd had it up to here with the reactor's problems. But it was the night of the restart, the riskiest operation they performed, when they took the reactor from stone-cold nothing to full power. He sent a silent thought to the boys on shift. He thought of his wife, Nat, too, the way he'd left her at home, the awful things he'd said. If he didn't get a chance to apologize, this would be how she'd remember him, hard and cruel, driving off with a backseat full of clothing. His car bumped onto the dirt road toward the reactor and his thoughts became scrambled by fear. Here were the swirling lights of all the vehicles, the steam pumping in a white cloud into the air, Nat watching him drive away, his daughters in their beds, the fire chief waving his arms at Paul's car and calling something—and he felt the sinking sensation that he was too late for all of it, for Nat, for the boys, for his daughters, for everyone, and it was just as he had always feared: When the time came it would happen before he knew it, it would happen without him there; despite everything he had always done to be ready, he would be too late.

I

COUPE DE VILLE

NAT

June 1959

NAT WAS THE FIRST ONE OUT OF THE CAR. SHE STEPPED INTO THE dirt parking lot, her low-heeled shoes printing chevrons into the reddish dust. Ahead of them the lake shimmered blue, dancing with sun. They were somewhere in northern Utah, one day out from their final destination in Idaho Falls, and not a moment too soon.

For the past two and a half weeks they'd been driving cross-country: Virginia to Idaho in the '55 DeSoto Fireflite her husband, Paul, had bought used a couple of years before. Paul was starting his next army tour in Idaho Falls as an operator for a small nuclear reactor. You moved for Uncle Sam, he told Nat, but you still found your own transportation. So, with their two young daughters packed into the backseat they headed west, sleeping in hotels and farmhouses and even, on two regrettable nights, in the car. Nat was beginning to feel that they might be vagabonds forever, nomads wandering the rough western states, eating crackers by the side of the road in a hot wind, loitering at the edge of decent farmers' land, scrambling after barn kittens, urinating in gas stations.

Paul opened his driver's side door and stepped out. He bent to help

Liddie squeeze past the seat, a damp spot showing at the small of his back. Liddie was one and a half, and she hit the ground running, hustling toward the beach with a toddler's steady, impressive lack of hesitation or common sense, belly leading the way in pink cotton overalls. Samantha, who was three, scampered out through the passenger seat, her rumpled pale-blue dress flapping around her legs. Nat followed them, shading her eyes to the sparkle of the water and the glow of pent-up energy that seemed to rise from their daughters' small bodies like incandescence.

The round crystalline lake before them was held between mountains as if cupped in a palm. The spring air smelled sweet, and Nat was filled with a sudden stirring of hope.

She smiled up at Paul. "We just might make it," she said.

Paul's brown eyes were weary, a little bloodshot. He scratched his head, two brisk strokes over his close army haircut. "Let's hope so," he said. Then he smiled back. "How you holding up?"

"Good," she said. They trailed after the girls, Paul rolling up his shirtsleeves, Nat's shoes dangling from her fingers.

There was a faint, distant splash up the curve, followed by muted applause and whistles, and Nat turned her head. She spied a rock outcropping that jutted into the water and was surprised to see the silhouettes of people atop it. A moment later one of them sprang off the end of the rock, sailed downward in a gentle parabola, and entered the water with only the slightest sound.

"Rock divers," Nat said as the head bobbed up. She checked the girls' location—still a good distance from the water's edge, their twinlike heads of chocolate-brown hair mingling as they bent to stack rocks—and turned back to the jumpers. The dazzling water, the leap and burst were so familiar that her heart hurt. She had grown up in San Diego; swimming and diving were the things she'd loved. Some of her strongest memories were of leaping off the Sunset Cliffs in Point Loma, watching the white froth swirl before plunging in.

Paul was watching her from the corner of his eye.

"I'm going in," she said.

"Going in where?" he asked, the suspicion in his voice showing he knew her well enough.

"Up there. I want to jump in."

His forehead crimped with uneasiness, and a pulse of guilt ran through her. "That's crazy," he said. "You'll be wet on the drive."

"With this air? I'll dry in half a minute. Here, hold my shoes." Before he could argue she handed them to him and jogged through the sinking, rocky sand, pebbles coating her calves and flinging up around her knees.

"You don't know those people," Paul called.

She turned and waved. "It's okay! Be back in a second."

The girls hopped and cheered beside their father as she poked her way up the rock. Even from a distance she could see Paul's disapproval, the tenseness of his shoulders and straight line of his mouth. For that one moment she didn't care.

When she reached the top she saw the jumpers, two men and two women. They lounged on the side of the rock now, sun-warmed and serene. They seemed about Nat's age, twenty-four, and she wondered at their lives, at what had brought them to this rock midday, free from the responsibilities that regulated her own hours: children and meals and cleaning and ironing. She had been like them once, only a few years ago, and for a moment she paused as if watching grainy silent footage of herself.

"Hi," one of the men called, and Nat came to her senses and said hello. Now that she was this close to them she felt a little self-conscious, and she said, "The water just looks so alluring." As soon as she said "alluring" she regretted its dark, slightly affected tone and wished she had used a more regular word instead.

"It's wonderful," said a woman, plucking at the tight-fitting skirt of her red swimsuit. She looked up at Nat, cocking an eyebrow. "But you're going in like that?"

"I guess so," Nat said, smiling. She stepped to the edge and curled her toes. Her dress hung around her knees. This was no wild ocean but a placid, glass-smooth lake, and the water below her was clear and blue. She pointed her arms, felt the tendons behind her knees hollow and tense, her back stretch long to the tips of her fingers, and dived.

She fell through three long heart-throat seconds—one-a-thousand, two-a-thousand, three-a-thousand—before piercing the water. She could feel that it wasn't a perfect entry, feet tipped a little too far back over her head, but she didn't care. The sheer, pure cold sucked the air from her body and she surfaced, stifling a scream. Then she burst into laughter, paddling back toward her family. She hadn't done something like that in years. How could anyone not love this sensation? It slapped you in the face and shouted *You're alive!*

"Nice!" a man called above her.

Her toes reached sand and she waded toward shore. As she caught sight of Paul and the girls waiting for her, however, the excitement began to dwindle. She suddenly felt silly. Her dress suctioned squishily around her; she was forced to take small, awkward steps. By the time she got back to them Paul was fuming, her shoes clenched in his hands.

"Why did you do that?" he cried.

She squeezed out her hair, avoiding his eyes. "For fun," she said, her voice small.

Paul shook his head. "You didn't know what was under the water there. What if you dove down and hit something and never came up, right here in front of your little girls?"

"I knew it would be fine," she said. And while she'd never admit it to Paul, the relief of not striking anything—that moment of plunging into the water and feeling herself go down, down, unimpeded, the cold exploding past her face and neck and body until her own air pulled her up again—was part of the fun. It *had* to be a little scary to count for anything.

She remembered that swimming was a different thing for him than it was for her; he'd grown up poor and never learned to swim until he got to boot camp, practicing every night, he'd said, in a pond near Fort Dix. This was one of the few concrete details she had of his youth, and it was a curious, poignant image: thin teenage Paul easing himself into the shallow dark, thrashing quietly along the shoreline until he could glide two strokes alone, three, four. Even then he passed the entrance test by the skin of his teeth, just enough to fill a pair of boots destined for Korea. It was no wonder, really, that the mild risks Nat liked to take scared him: the long swims to clear her head, cliff jumping, diving. But he acted as if she were doing it just to spite him, when in fact it had nothing to do with him at all. Which maybe, from his perspective, was even worse.

What if you never came up? She always came up.

He scooped their daughters into each arm and strode ahead, and she followed, feeling contrite, wishing she hadn't been so defiant and so stupid. And yet she knew it wasn't just worry on his part: Having an audience had made it worse. He'd had to sit by and watch strangers cheer her on for something he'd not wanted her to do, as if their approval was more important than his concern.

When she got back to the car he didn't speak to her. Her dry shoes waited on her seat, side by side.

PAUL

A DAY LATER, AFTER TWO AND A HALF WEEKS ON THE ROAD, Paul and Nat and their daughters made it to Idaho Falls, where they'd been assigned to a small yellow house in a neighborhood near downtown. There was no base housing, so military personnel lived scattered among civilians. Paul began reactor training the day after they arrived, while Nat stayed behind in the empty house with the girls bouncing off the walls. He felt bad about leaving her with so much work, though slightly relieved to get out of the house, even if starting the new job made him nervous.

It took another week for their boxes to arrive, all their belongings jumbled into weird combinations. Each day when Paul got home from work, it seemed that another item or two had been put in its proper place—towels appearing in a cabinet that had, when he'd left that morning, been bare, the blender suddenly standing on the countertop—but this was moving at a slower pace than he'd expected. He tried to be patient. He knew Nat was busy with the girls.

He had three weeks of in-class training and observation, then his first week of work on the reactor itself. The CR-1 was as small and simple as everyone said, a reactor that could be run by just three enlisted men. They worked in shifts, and Paul's first shift had been the overnight with two other guys: a lead man, Franks, and a young enlisted named Webb, who was as new as Paul was. They sweated on a hot reactor floor that churned and groaned with steam, then took breaks outside in a world that felt quieter than the dawn of time. The desert at night looked endless in every direction, pitch-black at ground level with stars overhead, suspended in swaths of nebulous cream.

Now, having finished his training and his first week on the reactor, Paul stepped out into the cool morning air, breathing in the tang of sagebrush and the steamy bitterness of coffee in its paper cup. The modest promise of the weekend sat before him, two days without a lick of work. He liked thinking about it even as the sweat on his forehead began to dry from the last shift. He wedged an unlit cigarette between his lips, patted his pocket for his Zippo. Any minute now the blue government bus would pick him up for the fifty-mile ride back into town, but he couldn't yet see it on the horizon. Behind him, the CR-1 pumped clouds into the quiet sky, living its vigorous, inanimate life; ahead of him, stretched somewhere across nine hundred square miles of desert, were the thirty or so other reactors at the testing station. He saw a glint of light off a couple of them, but had never visited and did not know their crewmen. All of them were bigger than his own reactor, busier, more prestigious.

The CR-1 was the prototype for compact, portable units the army was building in the Arctic Circle, run by just two or three men. Its appearance was underwhelming: It looked like a silo. It was three stories tall, with smooth, windowless, shiny steel walls, and if it hadn't been built on testing station land, no one would have thought a nuclear reactor was housed inside. This was, from a strategic standpoint, a plus: The reactors modeled on its design would be small, cheap, easy-to-build units that could be assembled on-the-spot across the Arctic, where American soldiers would wait, able to hit pay dirt pretty much anywhere in Russia if the Soviets did anything stupid.

"Does it make you feel bad?" Nat had asked on the drive to Idaho, in a moment of reflection. "All those missiles pointed at the Russians, and none of them has ever done anything to us?"

The question had silenced him for a moment. It was just like Nat to think about the other side: sweet, and also impractical. He could still see her concerned brown eyes, the rumple in her brow when she'd asked.

Nat, who'd almost never left San Diego, a place so beautiful and floral that it hardly seemed real; Nat, whose skin was permanently divided into tan and white parts from all the teenage hours she'd spent on the beach, who was smart and funny but as apolitical as a wedding or a waterfall: The thought of their American missiles must have saddened her, or she wouldn't have put the question to Paul. This rankled him a bit because it felt like a judgment, but it also filled him with a contradictory little swish of love for her when the memory came back to him later at work.

He rarely thought about *the Soviets*. There was plenty of rhetoric going around about them: tough talk, blustery threats. He figured most Russians were probably fine and it was their government that caused problems. Starving its own people, letting the economy go to hell. It wasn't his job to analyze such things. His job was simply to do his job: to walk onto a reactor floor and keep the machine running, keep the feedwater valves pumping and the rod drive seal from leaking and the pressure from getting too high or too low.

This testing station land, they'd learned in reactor school, had once been populated by Indians, then by the Mormons who built Idaho Falls, and was later used as the Minidoka internment camp for Japanese Americans during the war. After that it spent several years as an artillery proving ground for all branches of the military, with explosives of every kind blasted across the scrub. Sometimes the operators caught Mormon kids sneaking over the chain-link fence on a dare, hunting for the six-inch slugs left from weapons trials.

Paul alternated between the steaming welcome of his coffee and the brisk lung burn of the cigarette, thought of Nat home without him, sleeping on the floor because they still didn't have a damn bed. The cross-country move and the start of his new job hadn't made for an easy time. He felt they'd just performed some marathon stunt, like climbing Mount Everest together, only to roll down the other side and land in a dusty pile of their own belongings. His new career as a nuclear operator, after eight often dull and frustrating years in petroleum supply, was supposed to offer all manner of benefits: more prestige, pay bonuses, endless opportunities. So far most of these had not materialized, and he certainly didn't feel that he and Nat were growing closer. He had no idea if his great personal gamble would work, and, finally in Idaho with reactor school behind him and his young family in tow, no going back, did the gravity of what he'd risked wash over him.

DUST ON THE HORIZON caught Paul's eye, but it wasn't the slow plume the government bus always made; it was a lower, faster-traveling cloud, and as it got closer he saw it was pulled by a flashy cream-colored car. The car was the only eye-catching thing on the whole barren desert. It looked almost like a mirage the way it gleamed, speeding along the flat highway.

Behind Paul the door to the reactor building opened and his shift leader, Specialist Franks, stepped out. He stood beside Paul and lit his own cigarette, watching the approaching car from beneath heavy eyebrows.

"Who's that?" Paul asked, pointing with his cigarette.

Franks looked surprised. "You haven't met Master Sergeant Richards? He's the day-shift supervisor."

"I've only worked the night shift," Paul said. The car grew louder now as it came closer, its engine a steady, throaty rumble. *This* was their Master Sergeant, this man in the unexpectedly beautiful car? Paul had been told that Richards, who supervised the day shift, worked next door to them in the Admin building but spent most of his time drinking in his office. Supervisors were notorious for boozing their days away on remote assignments like the CR-1; to be stuck in a leadership position on this tour was considered something of a punishment.

But the car was a showstopper, a pearly Cadillac Coupe de Ville, '57 or '58. It pulled up in front of the chain-link gate, front-loaded and pristine as a palomino. Didn't seem like Richards was feeling *too* sorry for himself.

Paul said, "I thought we were all supposed to ride the bus."

"We are," said Franks. "But that does not deter Sergeant Richards from driving his own car when he damn well pleases. He's not shy about it, either, as you can see."

"No kidding."

Franks strode over to let the car in the gate. Paul tried not to betray too much curiosity as Richards parked and stepped out, waggling his khaki cap down onto his head. He had assertive blue eyes and early graying hair that gave him an air of authority beyond his rank.

When Richards reached them, Paul and Franks stood a little straighter, echoing one after the other, "Good morning, Master Sergeant," "Master Sergeant."

"'Morning," Richards said, looking up at the steam that pumped from the reactor into the chilly morning air. "How was the night, fellows? Will I go in there and find a logbook that agrees with me?"

"Yes, Sergeant. Nothing out of the ordinary," said Franks.

"Glad to hear it. Where's the young guy?"

"Webb? Latrine, I guess."

As if on cue, the door opened and Specialist Webb, the last of their three-man crew, flew out. He was a tall, jointy, young-looking fellow with a missing tooth on one side that hollowed his cheek in. He spotted Richards and pulled up crisply. "Good morning, Master Sergeant."

"That john on fire, son? You came out of there like a bat out of hell."

"No, Sergeant. It wasn't on fire, Sergeant. I thought I'd missed the bus."

Richards chuckled. "Well, don't get your knickers in a twist about it."

"Yes, Sergeant."

"Say, Collier," Richards said with a smirk, "why don't you come inside with me? We've never had our little welcome-aboard chat."

Paul hesitated. There was the matter of the bus: He could see it on the horizon now, a blue dot wending its way toward them. It was eight A.M. and another one wouldn't be by until the end of the next shift, eight hours away. Of course the master sergeant knew this. But it was their first meeting, and Paul didn't think he had much choice other than to say "Yes, Sergeant" and follow Richards into the administration building.

The Admin building seemed an even lonelier place to work than the reactor itself; it was a long, low wooden portable left over from WWII, with tall, narrow windows. Inside, a hallway divided two rows of thin-walled offices, five on each side. Richards's rank and name had been typed onto a small manila square and tacked to a door on the right, which he pushed open to reveal a modest desk piled with endless disheveled papers. Behind the desk was a file cabinet and a dusty American flag that sagged slightly along the back wall. Richards stepped behind the desk and sat down on a small, creaky black folding chair. He linked his fingers behind his head and leaned back a little, watching Paul, who settled into an identical chair opposite.

"So, we finally get a chance to talk," Richards said, as if he'd been pursuing Paul unsuccessfully for days. "What do you think of this place? The CR-1, is it like you expected?"

"Just about," Paul said. "Things are going fine. Thank you for asking."

"Good. And how's your family? Your wife like it here?"

"She seems to."

"Excellent. You've got to keep your wife happy, you know."

Paul nodded uncertainly. On Richards's desk he spotted a framed photo of an elegant red-haired woman holding a child. With the woman's curled hair, pearl earrings, and soft, cultivated smile it could have been a picture cut from a magazine, but the toddler on her lap wore the unfocused expression and irregular eyebrows of a normal, non-movie-star child. "Your family?" Paul asked, pointing.

Richards flashed his self-regarding, deep-dimpled smile. "So I'm told."

"It's a nice photo."

"Thank you." The sergeant stretched in his chair. "So, do you go home and brag to your wife that you work on the smallest reactor the army's got?"

"I don't really mind it," Paul said, unsure why his wife, whom Richards had never met, kept coming up. The CR-1's size didn't bother him. He'd rather work in a quiet building than in one of the big-name operations on-site, with all the lab men and scientists around, asking the operators for coffee and treating them like janitors.

Richards leaned forward. "*I* wouldn't mind a touch more prestige around here, I'll tell you that." His arm snaked into a desk drawer and he pulled out two tumblers and a bottle of bourbon, which he poured neat, passing one to Paul with a grin that was somehow both friendly and challenging. "What is it you like to do, Collier? Do you ski? The skiing's amazing around here."

"I've never been skiing," Paul admitted.

"Never have—" Richards swatted his knee, breathless with disbelief. "Why, that's something. Well, do you fly-fish?"

"I've—I've fished. I don't fly-fish."

"What are you into? Cars? Sports?"

Paul stared at him, drawing a blank, suddenly horrified—nothing. He was into nothing. What was there to be into? He worked, he went home, he fixed things and sat with his wife while she listened to the radio. He'd never had much time or money to spare. The awareness of this seemed to come crashing down upon himself and Richards at the same time.

"What are you, Collier? Some kind of bumpkin?" Richards laughed, baring his teeth. He held up a hand. "No, no. Don't worry about it."

"I just—"

"Never mind. You're a quiet, studious one, I could tell the moment I saw you." He glanced away as if he'd already lost interest: Paul's poverty of leisure was not compelling.

Paul shifted in his seat and looked again at the woman in the photo on Richards's desk. Her expression seemed almost condescending to him now.

Richards sucked on his drink, bored; then a thought came to him and he leaned forward. "Well, listen," he said, almost brightening. "We have a certain way of doing things around here—you've probably noticed."

"All right," Paul said, relieved by the change of topic though he wasn't quite sure what Richards was talking about.

"Deke Harbaugh—you'll meet him, he's our lead man from Combustion Engineering," Richards said. "He's a civilian, but he understands where we're coming from better than the other pricks they've got up there. Pardon me." Richards raised a hand again and grinned. "Anyway, Harbaugh's on our side when things come up."

Paul absorbed this, wondering: *What comes up?*

"What we try to do around here," Richards said, "is keep things close, keep things army. I like to say that the buck stops here. We're *operators.*" He made eye contact to check that Paul was following. "If there's an . . . irregularity, a concern, you can bring it to me before you even write it in the log. It's a can-do attitude kind of thing. If we fix it before it hits paper, all the better. Otherwise, we're always having to go to the Combustion Engineering guys, asking permission for every last thing, like teenage babysitters."

Paul nodded. This was not how he'd been trained; in reactor school they were taught to document any occurrence, large or small, to the point that it seemed overdone. But Richards was Paul's new boss, and Paul had found it was best to listen awhile before you talked, so he did.

"Excellent," said Richards, as if Paul had agreed to something complex. "Just a can-do culture around here. I could tell you were exactly the right kind of guy for this."

Paul wanted to ask what *exactly the right kind of guy for this* meant but decided to take the praise at face value. So he stood; they shook. Paul hoped Richards would decide to head home around midday, as his reputation suggested he liked to do, and offer Paul a ride to compensate for making him miss the bus. Maybe Richards would even use him as an excuse to leave early—*I made this poor Joe stay late, so I'd better get him on home now.*

But if Richards had such a plan, he didn't mention it. "Collier, you go on and have a good day now," he said. "Close that door for me, will you?" He tossed his feet onto the desk, stretched his chair back so that it creaked, and closed his eyes. Paul hesitated, clicked shut the door.

He'd encountered master sergeants like Richards before and knew his type: men who silvered into maturity, enjoying the flirtations of women and the subordination of men, who remained athletic in that lazy way where, despite the small potbelly nudging the bottom of their brass-buttoned shirts, they could still trounce you in horseshoes or twenty-one at a division barbeque and laugh heartily about it. These were not men Paul generally liked.

He wandered into the lounge and settled onto the small, hard couch, pulling his knees up; might as well make himself comfortable. He wondered if it were admirable that he'd refrained from mentioning the missed bus, or if he'd just been a patsy. Probably a little of both.

He must have dozed, because the next thing he knew he heard a soft noise in the parking lot outside: the distinct sound of a classy car clearing its throat.

He got up and went to the window. His eyes widened when he realized it was Richards's car leaving without him. Before Paul could even get to the door, he heard the propulsion of tires against gravel.

"What the hell," he cried. He jogged into the parking lot, waving his hands above his head. "Master Sergeant!"

There was no way Richards could hear him; the car was through the gate now, heading for the highway.

Surely Richards would stop. *Surely* he'd remember that he'd stranded Paul fifty miles from home in the desert, and turn back. Paul called out again, even gave a pathetic little jump, hoping he'd be spotted in the rearview mirror. But the car glided down the road, shiny as a pearl in the afternoon sun. Richards was headed home to relaxation and family and comfy slippers, leaving Paul outside the goddamn reactor in his uniform.

Do not chase your boss's car down the road. You are not going to act desperate.

He shuffled back toward the building. Was this some kind of power play? Was Richards drunk, did he just not give a shit, what? Nat was going to ask why Paul was eight hours late, but if he told her this sad little tale she'd pepper him with all sorts of further questions. It would be better just to keep it to himself, but the thought made him feel like a lonely fool. He kicked the doorframe and stalked back inside to wait for the bus, to let Richards's dust settle on the ground and rocks, which, if nothing else, seemed better than standing there and letting it fall on him.

—

Back in the lounge he paced, agitated, humiliated almost out of proportion. Being made to stay eight extra hours for a ten-minute meeting seemed an infuriating absence of consideration, or an act of outright hostility. Richards had shown no respect in assuming Paul would stay, and even less in leaving him there, fifty miles from home with no ride.

He was too steamed up to sit still. Richards's smug questions dogged him: *What are you into? Skiing? Fly-fishing? I knew you were exactly the right kind of guy for this.* Whether it was logical or not he felt that Richards had somehow seen right through him, deduced in minutes that he was a man who could be dismissed, no repercussions.

Paul was used to being snubbed; he was from people with no money and learned early on that this made him easy to brush aside. All the tokens and symbols he used to armor himself—his uniform, operator's badge, wedding ring—meant nothing to Sergeant Richards, who blew them off in an instant and made Paul feel groveling and worthless. He didn't want to be angry now, didn't want to knock around hostile, pessimistic thoughts for the next few hours, but he had never found a way to fight that train of thought once he got on it.

He had grown up in a rural Maine cabin as quiet as a deep snow, punctuated by outbursts of inexplicable and embarrassing violence. More than once he could recall standing flat against the log wall, breathing shallowly as if he could avoid being noticed while his father, drunk, swished past in an itchy rage like some creature from the zoo. When his pa did address Paul it was mockingly, making Paul stammer and squirm, squelching his hate. His mother was not much better. She'd taken to drink as far back as Paul could remember, and one of his earliest memories was of sitting by her bed, playing with her limp fingers as she snored.

The lack of control people showed repelled him. They brought their trouble upon themselves, one person after another, and it was impossible to feel sorry for them. He wasn't surprised when his mother sought relief in bars and men; he wasn't shocked, either, when she was brought home one cold morning on a wooden sled, her eyes punched in, and left in the shed for the ground to thaw and the serviceberries to bloom.

At sixteen he stole his father's boots, hitchhiked to Portland, and enlisted in the army. When he first joined up he trusted everyone, all these people he'd dreamed about for years who were not his family, who'd decided to live upstanding and useful lives. These, finally, were his people! But he learned, to his disappointment, that they were often just as flawed as his own family had been; that even with all the military did to raise them up, they settled back into their character defects like a dog curling into a round bed.

That first spring away from home, still in boot camp, he'd received news of another nonsurprise: His father had been discovered by hunters a few miles from home, having fallen through the ice on one of his weaving walks back from town. Paul was an orphan, and he was relieved.

It turned out that his parents' deaths neither cured nor worsened things. Paul embarked on a program of self-control and betterment. In his locker he taped a Robert E. Lee quote: *"I do not trust a man to control others who cannot control himself."* Amazingly, as the years went by, he won the job, the girl, and an amount of respect that seemed neither stingy nor extravagant: It seemed just right. But like many hard-forced things his veneer was delicate, and he found that he became easily panicked. He'd fought so hard for what he had that he could imagine countless ways it might be taken away.

Which brought him back to Sergeant Richards, this day, this room. This disastrous blowing-off, this bitter, stupid stranding. Maybe Richards was just an asshole who would've left anyone at the reactor; maybe he had simply stayed in his office, gotten mildly drunk and let Paul slip his mind easily as any other minor chore. But Paul could not stop it from driving him crazy. There was something satisfying about the way an obsession fired up every spot on his brain all at once: pain, pleasure, anger, desire, defiance. Fuck everyone who had treated him like he was nothing; fuck Richards for treating him like nothing now. He would revel in this small torment, his mind churning cycles of concession and resistance, anger and acquiescence until he wore himself out.

He knew better than to fight it. There was only one thing that could soothe him and that would be walking in his front door, calmed by the golden kitchen light like a violent, rogue archangel. Nat would smile at him, knowing exactly who he was, the man he'd made himself to be, good provider and husband, father of the two little girls who would be skipping toward him, kissing him with their little crumb-covered faces: All this goodness he'd made for himself out of nothing, scaring his old self right back from where it came.

JEANNIE

Jeannie Richards examined the centerpiece for the dining room table and put her hands on her hips in disgust. The Shasta daisies looked big and coarse, the baby's breath too delicate in contrast. The red-and-white-checked tablecloth was garish, like a hillbilly picnic.

She plucked the vase from the table, marched it into the kitchen, and shoved it inside the bread hutch where she could deal with it later. The tablecloth she folded and returned to the linen cabinet, though she had an urge to stuff it into the garbage. She couldn't; it was an heirloom, if a tasteless one, from her husband's grandmother. Mitch had a reverence for extended family that bordered on unseemly. He had aspired to be something of a patriarch himself, eventually: wanted a dozen children, but in the end they had only one, conceived after a decade and a half of trying, when Jeannie was thirty-seven years old.

She looked at the gold watch on her fine-boned wrist. This evening she was hosting a small dinner party for a few of the operators who worked with her husband, and their spouses. As the master sergeant's wife it was her role to reach out to them, but she was losing steam. She was tired of giving pep talks, tired of playing perpetual den mother to the earnest, flustered women who drummed her for tidbits of advice. (*Do you think we should register to vote here in Idaho? When can I expect my husband to be promoted? Where do ladies shop in Idaho Falls?*)

"But you have so much to offer them, Jean," her friend Patty had said that morning, when Jeannie confessed her waning enthusiasm for mentorship. "You've been an army wife for sixteen years. You've had so many different *experiences*."

"Well, I don't know about that," Jeannie had said, bothered by the thought that experience was linked with age.

"World War Two, Korea," Patty listed them off. "The wives coming up don't have your background. You're *seasoned*."

Jeannie had thought on this throughout the day, her admirable seasoning. Mitch *had* served in WWII, but he'd been stationed on the remote island of Nanumea and spent most of those years playing beach volleyball, helping dump busted American equipment into the ocean, and absorbing the endless gifts of coconuts, taro, and chickens from the locals. He'd been on leave in Brisbane with his buddies during the one major attack on the island, in which seven Americans and a Nanumean died.

Upon coming home he'd slid into a long, uninspiring career. Over time Jeannie learned that her dashing army husband was not exceptionally intelligent nor principled, but somehow he hung in the game, gradually getting assigned to roles of minor leadership. He assigned himself a handful of minor affairs: a townie typist in Alabama, an immunization tech in Nebraska. If *this* was what Patty meant by "experiences," then, yes, they'd had a few. Jeannie figured she eventually learned of most of them. None resulted in children, thank God; she took solace in the fact that her fertility was not the likely culprit in their underpopulated marriage, though this, of course, was never discussed.

Jeannie's sole aspiration was for Mitch to stick it out just four more years with the army, stubborn and dumb as a barnacle, until he hit his twenty-year mark; then his pension would be generous, family healthcare insured. But his career, she feared, was approaching lethal stagnation just short of the finish. Each of his recent tours had seemed a little more sluggish, like he was being parked somewhere, a placeholder, a relic. The CR-1 rubbed it all in, this remote, ridiculous reactor, a mere prototype, at a testing station full of prestigious groundbreakers. No one checked up on Mitch, which was how he liked it, but that meant that no one cared. He had fallen off the radar.

Hence tonight's party, with Jeannie pulling out all the stops, all her tricks and charms. She'd had her hair freshly styled, the grays touched up at the salon just yesterday. Her outfit was laid out on the bed: apricot-colored organza dress, high heels, silk stockings, a bra that would catapult her little ladies upward like rocket boosters. For the guests there was a daunting cut of roast beef, gleaming silverware, a white lace tablecloth (yes, she could see now, it was much better than the red-and-white check).

She dusted off one of Mitch's wartime photos from WWII and propped it near the wet bar, beside his canteen from Korea and a mother-of-pearl box he'd brought back from Pusan. This was the Highly Selective Museum of Mitch Richards, curated and tended by Jeannie; she was sick of it. Their army life felt like an endless parade in which Mitch was a large, slow-moving float and Jeannie every other performer, running alongside, cheering, shooting off confetti, waving banners and flags, calling attention to his every move as if it were fantastic and exciting and rare. She wondered how well this worked, how well people believed it, if they saw what she intended or only bore witness to her exhausting efforts.

She smoothed the tablecloth with her palm and arranged the gravy boat, the place cards, a better selection of flowers (roses in red, pink, and white). Returning to the bread hutch she grabbed the daisies, which lolled like idiot clowns, carried them to the waste bin, and snapped their necks one by one.

THE GUESTS BEGAN TO arrive at six. Her house smelled of gravy and roast beef; she'd swapped her cooking apron for her company apron, white and smooth down her hips. Baby Angela was in the nursery with the nannies—Martha, their usual, and Martha's sister Lupe, who would help watch the guests' children during the party—and Mitch had just come home from a day of golf. Jeannie could hear him washing his face in the bathroom, which he always did with no comprehension of how much water he threw onto the sink and mirror. He left the room as if he had just sprayed it down with a hose, and glibly turned off the light.

Thank God he was tucked away in the master bath, where he could splash around like some oversized happy otter and none of the guests would have to witness the mess.

The doorbell rang and she gave an inner jump. She checked her hair and lipstick one last time, smoothed her apron, and went to answer it, smiling broadly before her fingers even touched the doorknob.

It was Lennart and Kath Enzinger, the bunco champions. "Come in!" Jeannie beamed, though the Richardses' Wednesday loss to the Enzingers was still fresh.

The Enzingers helloed: Lennart, as always, was squinty with cheerfulness, while Kath was as solemn as a bloodhound. German-born Len had spent time in an American internment camp at the outbreak of World War Two. No one held it against him now, since it had only been because of his nationality and because he had handled it graciously. Rather recently he'd married Kath, who was an enigma to Jeannie. Kath never used a dab of makeup and on weekends wore Len's shirts, which Jeannie knew because she had once stopped by on a Saturday to drop off a sweater Kath had forgotten at bunco. Kath wore her husband's shirts not in a sexy sort of swapping way, but tucked into her pants, as if that were just what she was wearing that day.

Lupe poked her head up the hallway but Jeannie waved her back; the childless Enzingers required no nanny.

The Frankses arrived—an unstylish but friendly couple, dressed in matching brown—and then the Kinneys, classy dark-haired Patty and her husband, who just went by Kinney, and their three children. There were Minnie and Deke Harbaugh: Deke, the supervisor from Combustion Engineering, who Mitch said had some awful disease from insulation work he'd done years ago and who spent most of his time whooping into a handkerchief; and Minnie, who enjoyed the fact that her husband, though weakened by his illness, was everyone else's boss. Next came the unattractive man, Slocum. He was followed by the startlingly young Webb, who seemed to give off a glow of awkward goodwill and who stood by the wet bar, sucking in one cheek a little. Franks called him over and got him to talking. Soon folks were mingling and men helped themselves and their wives to drinks. Mitch appeared from his extensive freshening, red-faced and shiny; he looked as if he had just been steamed. The hair at his temples was wet and he grinned at everybody. He would complain for weeks in advance of any gathering Jeannie planned, but once there he enjoyed himself tremendously.

The men gathered to talk baseball: Early Wynn's good season for the White Sox; the recent integration of the Boston Red Sox, the last professional baseball team to allow black players. Few things interested Jeannie less than baseball or integration, so she returned to the couch and love seat where the women had settled.

Brownie Franks was, unfortunately, subjecting the women to another discussion of her love for paint-by-number kits. The woman was obsessed with crafts. She had probably made the wooden necklace that hung around her neck like an infant's teething beads. However, watching Brownie attempt to draw Kath Enzinger into a discussion of paint-by-numbers could prove amusing. It was like watching her try to sell Girl Scout cookies to a telephone pole.

Patty Kinney leaned in toward Jeannie, her green eyes flashing beneath a crop of bottle-black hair. "Look at you, Jeannie! Every inch the lady. Are all the guests here?"

Jeannie scanned the room, sipping her mai tai. "The new couple is missing," she said. "That man Collier and his wife."

"Have you met them yet?"

"I haven't."

"Hm," said Patty, as if this lack of information were somehow information. She was Jeannie's closest friend in attendance; their husbands had gone through Belvoir at the same time.

The doorbell rang. "That could be them now," Jeannie said.

Patty's lined black eyebrows shot up with interest. "Stay here, you," Jeannie said with a laugh, and Patty made a face.

Jeannie picked her way delicately past the legs of the seated women over to the group of men who stood with their drinks.

"Mitch," she whispered. He turned from whatever chuckly conversation he'd been having and looked at her, puzzled. "The door," she said, taking his arm.

"Oh." He sighed and turned with her down the hall. He had told her once that he did not understand why they had to answer their door linked arm in arm like young lovers on a twilight stroll, but she explained that it simply set a tone: for their household, for the gathering. Jeannie believed in gentility. Everything a person did set forth an impression about them, and first impressions, of course, mattered more than any other. That was why her hand towels were ironed, her soap dispensers polished, the vacuum marks freshly ridged into the carpet like paths to righteousness. She tapped her hair as she passed the hall mirror—surely it couldn't move, it was hair sprayed within an inch of its life—and opened the door.

"You must be the Colliers," Jeannie beamed, as she sized up the couple before her. Mr. Collier had dark hair, dark eyes, and a quiet bearing. His wife was no great beauty—her face narrow and a little asymmetrical—but there was a prettiness to her, nonetheless. She wore a navy blue collared shirtdress (not quite dressy enough for an evening party) with a strand of pearls (better), and her hair was up. She was holding a large platter with a brick of meatloaf in the center, covered in cellophane wrap. Jeannie caught herself staring at it and diverted her gaze. The party was not a potluck; Mrs. Collier must have been confused. Jeannie found this both irritating (her invitation had been quite clear) and also mildly pitiable, but she would be gracious about it.

"Master Sergeant," Paul Collier said, shaking Mitch's hand.

Mitch grinned at Collier's wife. "And *Mrs.* Collier, so glad you could join us."

"Please, call me Nat," she said. "These are our daughters, Samantha and Liddie." She nudged her children forward with one hand. They were cute dark-haired girls, the little one round faced and bright eyed, the older leaner and long haired, a spitting image of Nat. "Say hello," she urged.

"Hello," said the older child. The younger one stood frozen.

On cue, Lupe appeared. "I will take you, girls," she said, smiling and holding out her hand. The nannies had been well supplied with several boxes of Cracker Jack, an RCA Victor to listen to, and a stash of increasingly sticky dolls.

For a moment it seemed Nat's younger daughter might burst into tears, but seeing her older sister trot down the hall she tripped along after her, looking back just once. Nat gave her an encouraging wave and turned back to Jeannie, shifting the plate in her arms. "Where should I put this?" she asked.

Mitch looked at it. "What do we have here?" he asked jovially, as if to a child.

"It's a meatloaf."

"How nice of you to bring something," Jeannie said. "Let's go set it down."

Nat followed her to the kitchen and paused. Jeannie saw her take in the smorgasbord on the countertops—a foil-covered platter of roast and carrots, tomato aspic, red Jell-O salad studded with marshmallows and pretzel bits like an ocean after a shark-thronged shipwreck—all in Jeannie's matching orange Pyrex.

"Oh," Nat said, "I thought we were supposed to bring something."

Jeannie smiled. "Don't worry about it," she said, gesturing for Nat to set her burden on the counter. Nat nudged aside a bowl and shifted the platter heavily down. For a moment both women studied the oily, olive-studded brown loaf.

"I was sure I'd read it was a potluck," Nat said. "I'm so embarrassed."

Jeannie laid one manicured hand on her arm and caught Nat glancing at it. "It's always nice to have variety. Come, let's meet all the wives." She led Nat around the wet bar, past the knee-high stone panther Mitch had brought back from Korea, to the couch and love seat where the women had congregated.

"This is Nat Collier," Jeannie said. She stepped back, fingers linked at waist level.

"She looks like June Carter!" Minnie Harbaugh pealed.

Jeannie could see the resemblance: It was Nat's dark hair and open expression, pretty but slightly toothy mouth; the almost playful tomboyish figure she cut in her belted shirtdress.

"Well, I sure wish I could sing," Nat said.

The wives were curious about Nat: Where had she moved from, when did she get to Idaho Falls, would she be having more children? This last question was asked right out of the gate and left Nat stammering a bit, but it was fair game, after all, as they were women and their business was babies.

Nat said she was happy, for now, with her two.

"I'm finished at three," Patty confessed, and the other women let out a near hiss of disappointment.

"I have four," said Brownie, "but if God let me I'd have a million!"

In such conversations, Jeannie was always passed over (her one, late child hinting at years of resentment or a sexless marriage, neither of which encouraged inquiry) as was Kath Enzinger (who was just strange). Resentment was, indeed, a large part of Jeannie's personal history: It had taken her sixteen years to become pregnant with Angela. By that time she had bitterly mourned and resigned herself to a life without children, throwing herself into wives' committees and charity work. Then one winter evening, having enjoyed a six-course meal with some friends and plenty of vino to wash it down, she came home and vomited the night away while Mitch slept on the couch. Eight months later Angela came to join them: a chunky black-haired babe who sucked her left thumb until it resembled the striated landscape of a fictional planet. Jeannie loved her in a puzzled sort of way; sometimes she feared she'd so desired a child that she'd used up all her passion on the wanting. And her mind, long accustomed to envy, still blazed at pregnant women, women with prams full of babies, women with twins, women with toddlers tumbling out of their shopping carts, all this fecundity where she had been so silent. Wanting something that badly for that long had turned an odd key in her, and she felt that she might never be entirely normal.

She cleared her throat. "Do you have any hobbies, Nat?"

"*Besides* having children?" Nat laughed. "Well, not really." She thought a moment, then brightened. "Oh, I like the beach. I used to enjoy hiking. Does that count?"

"Have you met many other wives yet?" This from Patty.

"Not really," Nat said. "I don't get out a lot with the girls so small." She looked down at her drink with a shy, bobbing nod, and Jeannie wondered if this self-deprecation were overplayed.

"Maybe people don't need as many friends as they think they do,"

Kath Enzinger said. This seemed oddly mystical, and no one picked it up for examination.

"Join a cards club," Patty suggested.

Brownie pushed on through this distracting commentary to resume her discussion of paint-by-number kits. "I started with Sarah's," she said, invoking her teenage daughter, "but I ordered some more sophisticated ones. Nat, you would love them," she added, a diagnosis made with remarkable speed.

"She just said she liked hiking," Kath complained.

"There are nature scenes," said Brownie. "Beach scenes. I prefer still lifes and dolls, teddy bears. There's almost no way you can make a mistake. You can work on them while your babies are sleeping," she said to Nat.

"She's not going to make friends *that* way," Patty said.

"Jean, this is just *ideal*," Minnie Harbaugh said, her southern accent looping like cursive. She waved an arm to encompass the drawing room, the drinks, the starched doilies and bright arching flowers. "How do you do it? What's your secret?"

Jeannie laughed, but everyone looked at her expectantly, as if she were supposed to have an answer. "It's just what I do," she finally said.

"Some people are blessed," Minnie said with a sigh.

"Some people are *perfect*." Brownie rolled her eyes. She removed a handkerchief from her breast pocket and dabbed the shine from her forehead and chin.

Jeannie sat back, watching the women talk. She found her drink and sipped it several times in quick succession, the ether flaring soothingly beneath her nose. Things were going well. Brownie and Patty and Kath had arrived in Idaho Falls over a year ago, so in army wife terms they were practically townies, and their relative comfort made conversation easy.

Eventually she remembered that the roast was cooling, even under its foil tent, so she moved everyone to the table. She had set up name cards to disperse the couples, an icebreaker she'd read about in *Woman's Day*. If any of her guests blanched at the realization of this avant-garde setup, they carried on admirably. Nat Collier sat at the far end of the table, three seats away from her husband, Paul, who stared at his blank plate with intensity.

Mitch settled into the seat next to Nat. She gave him a bright smile, which seemed to turn on some switch in his brain, and in a moment he was leaning in on her, holding forth on some topic or another with buzzed animation.

Now, wait a minute, Jeannie thought. Had she really placed Mitch next to Nat? She froze, halfway to the table, thinking. No, she had most certainly put Mitch next to Kath Enzinger, as a little inside joke to herself, and arranged Nat on the other end of the table. Now Nat was on the very end, next to Mitch. How could the place settings have been switched? The only explanation was that Mitch had switched them, wanting to sit next to pretty young Nat.

Jeannie squirmed with a visceral irritation. Mitch, that idiot, thought he was so smart, thought she wouldn't notice. Well she'd figured it out in two seconds but she was still trapped, because people were seated now. There was no way she could make them get up and move again.

Patty rotated in her seat and tapped Jeannie's arm. "Are you all right?" she whispered.

Jeannie shook herself and smiled. "Yes. Thank you. I was just lost in thought." She cleared her throat. "Mitch, the roast."

Mitch held up one finger while he finished his speech to Nat.

Jeannie felt her face purple. Holding up his finger, without even looking at her! She smoothed her apron, teeth gritted. Nat was nodding, leaning slightly back in her chair as Mitch leaned forward, his hand draped over the top rung.

Finally, Mitch wrapped up whatever insight Nat was lucky enough to hear to completion, flapped his hand in Jeannie's direction without looking, and went into the kitchen for the roast. He always carved the roast when they had company, but never would have remembered to fetch it himself; he would have sat there at the table, grinning and blinking, and wondering where dinner was. Oh, she was hard on him, she knew. He did look handsome, walking back with the broad orange platter. Tall and barrel-chested, with that silver-streaked hair; all the women smiled at him. Everyone nodded and twittered as Mitch pulled out the carving knife as if he had felled the beast, skinned it, and cooked it himself.

Jeannie fetched the side dishes and Nat's ungainly meatloaf. Some part of her knew that she was using Nat as a foil to her own superior domesticity. And yet, Nat had brought the thing! It would have been rude to leave it parked alone in the kitchen. She arranged each dish on the table, sliding in spoons at an angle for easy self-service. The food represented hours of work and would be devoured in a matter of minutes.

"Please," Jeannie said to the eyes watching her around the table, "enjoy."

Everyone ate and drank, with patters of conversation here and there. This part Jeannie enjoyed: watching the baking dishes pass, hearing the contented murmurs and the light scrapes of silverware against china. The candles flickered and grew shorter, bit by bit. The voices of the children could be heard faintly at the back of the house, singing along to a record of nursery rhymes the nannies had brought.

The north wind does blow
And we shall have snow
And what will poor Robin do then, poor thing?

He'll sit in the barn
And keep himself warm
And hide his head under his wing, poor thing,
And hide his head under his wing.

They sang this over again and sounded so innocent—their lisped, stumbling words—that Jeannie felt almost tender, sitting there at her table. It was dusk now and toads were calling outside. If this finished well, she would host an outdoor dinner party later in the summer. The air was so pleasant here, not like in St. Louis where she had grown up, where the summer evenings felt like breathing through wet cloths.

"Everything's delicious, ma'am," said Webb. Brownie Franks's laugh rang across the table at something Kinney had said. Things were going so well. Then Slocum, always an instigator, blurted roughly, "Did you all hear about the latest dog-and-pony show up at Test Area North?"

"Don't get me started," said Deke Harbaugh, raising both his hands. Jeannie averted her eyes from his fingertips, which were clubbed at the ends, like melted candles. She suspected this was part of his disease from the insulation work.

"Got a tour this morning," Slocum was saying. "Have an old buddy from Belvoir who went private, works for General Electric now. He took me up there and showed me around. General Electric and the air force are building a hangar for an atomic plane, to the tune of eight million. Don't have a nut or bolt of that craft yet, but they sure have a lot of pretty drawings."

"Whole thing's a crock of shit," said Harbaugh.

"Well, now," cried Jeannie.

Len tried to soothe them: "It will never take off. Eisenhower himself says it's hogwash."

"That's almost worse, 'cause then all that money will have been a waste! It just drives me crazy," said Harbaugh, his voice wheezy and full of air, "that we have real, working reactors in the army, and we have to beg for every penny. The CR-1 is falling apart—"

"Whoa, whoa," people said from around the table; the women turned to their husbands in dismay.

"With all due respect, Deke," Mitch began.

"I'm sorry. I'm sorry." Harbaugh coughed lightly, struggling to cover it. His eyes watered with the effort. "I take it too personally. It's just—the money that's been pumped their way for ten years! To build this plane that'll be too heavy to even fly! The army has a track record, but they still make us beg. Our reactor could use some help, but we have to pretend everything's going fine and dandy and just wait for them to dole out the most meager little scraps so we can fix one thing at a time."

Brownie Franks turned to her husband. "Is there something wrong with your reactor?" she cried.

"No, no," Franks said.

"But Mr. Harbaugh makes it sounds like—"

"We have a few things that could be improved. He's a little worked up, is all."

"I'd like another Scotch, that's what I'd like," said Harbaugh, bumping his fist on the table. "I'd like one on the rocks—" but before he could say any more he was gripped by a coughing spasm and fumbled for his handkerchief, opening it with those froglike fingers. Jeannie saw in horror that the cloth was covered with small gray slugs. He turned his back to them and hacked another one into it.

"Mr. Harbaugh," she said, "can I get you anything? A cough drop or some Father John's? A glass of water?"

He held up a hand. "No, no. I'll be fine, thank you. I didn't mean to become so inflamed. Minnie tells me I get too stirred up these days—fuck it," he said, by way of apology, as the cough overtook him again. He got up and headed for the back porch, the door banging behind him on the way out.

Jeannie's mind clanged *Mayday, Mayday.* Grave profanities had been uttered *at her dinner table!* How had she let things devolve? It had happened so suddenly, all thanks to that idiot Slocum. She didn't know if she should stay to manage the table or follow Harbaugh; after a moment's inner struggle she stood to go after him, but Minnie shook her head. "Leave him be," she said. "He's been doing this more and more. I'm so sorry, y'all. Don't listen to a word he says. It's humiliating." She put a hand to her mouth and gave one big sob right into it.

"Oh, God," said Kath Enzinger quietly.

"Minnie, dear," cried Patty, "it's all right. It's nothing. He just has an opinion."

"And don't you ladies worry for a bit," Mitch said. For once, Jeannie felt grateful to him. "I can tell you everything is fine at the reactor. I oversee everything that happens personally on the day shift, I read every line in the logbook. Just because people are over the moon about the atomic plane doesn't mean things are *bad* at the CR-1."

"Okay," Brownie said, nodding, her eyes annoyingly large with worry.

"Well," said Jeannie, "seeing as it's a gorgeous summer night, why don't we enjoy ourselves?" She went to the bar for another bottle of wine. "And let's talk about something lighter, shall we? Remembering," she fluttered her eyelashes at Slocum, "that we're in mixed company?"

"I'm sorry. I bored the ladies," Slocum said, grinning broadly as if he thought he were cute.

"I'm impressed that Mr. Harbaugh feels so fervently," said Nat Collier from her end of the table. She had not spoken yet so everyone turned, and their eyes made her instantly blush and shrink back in her chair, as if she hadn't expected that people would actually hear her. Forced to say something more she stammered, "I mean, he sounded like he was speaking before *Congress,* defending the little old CR-1!"

"The little old CR-1?" Patty laughed, her eyes flashing *Can you believe that!* Jeannie's way. Jeannie stiffened. Did Nat think this was funny, downplaying the reactor where these men worked? Even if the *little old CR-1* were not some elite destination tour, it was completely out of line for a newly arrived wife to mock it. And what did Nat Collier know, anyway? Her husband was a peon.

"Of course, I've never even been there," Nat said, as if reading Jeannie's thoughts. "I'm just going off how Paul describes it."

Paul squirmed at his opposite end of the table. Nat, seeming to realize she'd said too much, lowered her eyes.

"Should we keep passing around those potatoes?" Jeannie managed. "And we have this meatloaf that Nat *so* kindly brought, but no one's even taken a slice of it yet." She held it aloft; one whole olive had slid greasily to the side of the loaf, where it jutted like a wayward nipple.

"I'll take more potatoes," said Franks cheerfully.

Jeannie could still hear Deke outside, and she thought that, as the hostess, she should take him something. Why wouldn't he just drink a glass of water? When conversation normalized and the party seemed back on track she slipped from the table—smiling around in case anyone noticed, but all she got was a blank stare from Webb—and out the back door.

Deke's back was to her; he stared across the yard, clutching his handkerchief and watching the sunset as if overcome by sentimentality. *The man's dying,* she remembered Mitch saying. *Combustion Engineering just keeps him on so he won't raise a stink; it was pipe work he did for them years ago that caused it. With all his bills, he's going to die a pauper.*

"Deke, may I get you something?" she asked.

He turned quickly. She averted her eyes from the gore of his handkerchief, which he'd retched into a grotesque paisley. He shook his head until his face finally relaxed and he was able to smile wetly at her. "It's a glorious night," he said. "I'm sorry if I got a little hot in there."

"Please, don't waste another thought on it."

"This has been a wonderful party. You sure know how to throw 'em."

"Thank you," she said, genuinely touched. "I'm delighted you and Minnie could come."

"Well, I'm just glad Mitch felt up to it."

She cocked her head.

"You know," Deke said, "that there weren't any hard feelings."

"Hard feelings? Of course not." She felt a familiar sinking dread coupled with an almost morbid curiosity: What had Mitch gotten himself into this time? *Please don't let it be one of the other operators' wives. At least make it some townie none of us know.* Her fingers twitched against her apron.

"I'm sorry to even bring it up. I imagine you'd want to forget about it, at least during your dinner party."

"Really, it's all right." She reached into her gold case for a cigarette and handed him one by the tip. "They're Virginia Slims," she added, flicking her lighter.

"I'm not picky," he grinned, and let her light it. Then he inhaled, wincing in three separate, wheezy stages—it didn't look enjoyable at all—and finally exhaling with palpable relief. "It's always hard to be passed over for promotion," he said. "But you know they'll give him another look a year from now."

Jeannie nodded as the whooshing sound of her own panicky blood filled her ears. So it wasn't a woman; it was worse. Deke looked at her curiously. She stammered, "Yes, next year, that's what I've been telling myself."

"I think he was close, but the reactor hasn't been shipshape. It's not entirely his fault, but that sort of reputation rubs off on you. And then the last workplace-drinking citation did him in."

In her mind's eye, Jeannie saw herself placing a lily-white hand to her bosom and gasping, *"Workplace drinking?"* But she wasn't twenty anymore. She took a drag on her cigarette, trying to keep her fingers from shaking. "He said the reactor was just fine," she said. "Just now, at the table, he said he looks over every report himself."

"He does," Deke said.

"So—"

"Listen, Jeannie. A few drinking citations aren't insurmountable—"

"A *few*?" she blurted before she could stop herself.

For a moment Deke looked surprised. "We all love a drink," he said, "but we can't partake while we're at the reactor, right?" He shrugged and tried to smile. His teeth showed like a mouthful of corn but his eyes were handsome, hazel, and it dawned on her that he had once been healthy and young. "If it happens again, though," he said, more seriously, "Mitch could face a reduction in rank, or lose his security clearance."

Jeannie's face burned. She could handle talk of a not-shipshape reactor, whatever that meant; she could even tolerate the workplace drinking. There was something kind of manly and Wild West, if a bit stupid, about that. But to think of Mitch losing his security clearance or being pushed back a rank—no. That was too much.

"I'm sorry," he said. "This really isn't the time to talk about it. Anyhow, it doesn't reflect on you. Everybody knows that."

She took a deep breath and exhaled as slowly as she could, to calm herself. How could it not reflect on her? But she was the hostess; she still had this party to finish. She could castrate her husband later. "Thank you," she said. "That's a consolation." She tapped her cigarette into the celluloid ashtray she kept on the porch. "Well, I'd better not let things get out of hand in there," she said, and she could tell the smile she threw over her shoulder just about made Deke Harbaugh's day. She clicked back into the house, wringing her apron once, hard, in her hands.

Back inside, serving bowls were being scraped clean and conversation was puttering along here and there in the more successful pockets of the table. Patty Kinney and Minnie Harbaugh laughed and patted each other's arms. Franks and Kinney were pouring another. Brownie sang some kind of jingle to a completely unresponsive Kath Enzinger; Webb, slack-mouthed, examined the ceiling; Paul Collier was attempting to ignite the lace tablecloth with his gaze. Jeannie didn't dare glance at her husband and Nat until she had steeled herself first.

She slid into her seat. Her appetite had left her entirely, and what remained on her plate looked awful. The pretzels from the Jell-O salad had swollen to twice their original size; the tomato aspic looked like a botched medical procedure.

"How is Mr. Harbaugh?" Patty asked.

"He's fine," Jeannie assured her. "He'll be back in a moment."

There was a glass-meets-carpet *thunk* from the far end of the table, and a "Sorry," from Webb, who disappeared below. "It was almost empty anyway," his muffled, disembodied voice said.

"Webb is drunk," Patty whispered.

"I know," Jeannie said. Why hadn't Mitch been keeping on top of him? Why was Webb even there? She didn't like unattached men at her parties. Look at Slocum, starting the whole thing about the atomic plane and nearly ruining everything.

Her eyes went to Mitch, who was grinning at Nat with sloshy interest. Jeannie wanted to hurt him, somehow, right under the table. A sharp kick in the shin, a safety pin sunk in the thigh.

"I'm going to set up the desserts," she announced. She pushed back her chair and strode for the kitchen where she poured herself a vodka, tipped back the tumbler, and gulped the liquid burn *one, two, three,* then wedged a cigarette between her lips and turned her furious sights on the desserts in the corner. An angel food cake sat, vacant white; she snatched a small can of blueberry pie filling, ground it open with the can opener, and slopped it into the center. A few tiny drops of blue liquid spattered onto the countertop and the bosom of her dress, but she didn't stop: went for the next can and attacked it with the opener, pulling back only when she felt the ragged edge of the lid slice into her finger.

"Oh, god*damn*it," she cried. Blood oozed to the surface, breached the slit, and dribbled down her hand. She held her finger shakily under the faucet, rinsed it; peered close to examine the cut, moved its two halves like the mouth of a fish, and cursed again, shaking off the water droplets. It was disgusting to have a slit in your skin! It hurt and throbbed and the sensation of the skin pulling open and smooshing invisibly shut gave her the heebie-jeebies. After wrapping her finger in paper towels like a big white club she poured herself a little more vodka, jammed her cigarette back into her mouth, and returned to the angel food cake, working the can carefully open and slopping the gelatinous cylinder of deer-pellets-in-goo atop its liquidy, dispersing predecessor. Ash fell from her cigarette into the filling and she tried to scoop it out with her left index finger, then gave up and swirled it to blend in. She pulled another paper towel off the roll, wadded it, and dabbed at the drops of blue on her dress; they lightened but did not disappear.

"Are you all right?" a voice asked, and she jumped to see Nat Collier coming toward her, brow furrowed. "You've hurt yourself."

"Oh, yes, fine. Kitchen mishap. Even the best of us," Jeannie giggled with an exaggerated shrug, and Nat peered at her a moment and then nodded.

"I was just going to peek in on the kids," she said, pointing toward the back of the house.

"I'm sure they're doing well. Did you hear them singing a little while ago? Precious."

"You're right, I probably shouldn't distract them if they're doing fine. May I cut that pie for you?"

Jeannie hesitated, then stepped back and pushed an uncut key lime pie across the countertop. Nat set to work, diligently and ineptly.

"Start with quarters," Jeannie coached, unable to stop herself. "If you just cut a bunch of little slices they'll be uneven—well, it's all right. It'll be fine."

"I don't have your skill in the kitchen," Nat apologized. Jeannie granted her this with a respectable silence. "Thank you for inviting us tonight," she went on. "You're a wonderful hostess."

"I think I'll need to sleep for about three days after this." Jeannie smiled to show that she was being self-deprecating, that of course she'd be up with the birds tomorrow, dusting the Hummel figurines and polishing the doorknobs. She sipped her vodka. "How's your husband liking his new job?" *At the little old CR-1.*

"Oh, fine."

"I think you both could be very happy in Idaho Falls."

"I hope so! We're meeting more people now."

"The key to happiness is friends. Women friends," Jeannie said, pointing her cigarette at Nat. Her cut finger throbbed as if it had grown its own small heart. "Women you can count on when the chips are down."

"Yes," said Nat, with emphasis. "That's so true. I haven't had good girlfriends since high school, and I miss it so much. There are just things only a girlfriend can understand, you know?"

"I'm going to hold a party just for you," Jeannie said. She felt herself sway a little and put one hand on the countertop. "Right here at the house. You'll be the guest of honor. It'll be like your debutante ball."

"Oh my goodness, thanks," Nat said, looking nervous.

"You can borrow one of my dresses. I have a green one that would be just perfection on your figure. Of course, I might need to have the waist taken in. We can't all have a twenty-two-inch waist like you, can we?"

Nat glanced down at her waist as if it might have changed dimensions without her noticing. "I certainly don't have a waist that small!" she said.

"You could get your hair done."

"That would be fun! I never have."

"Really?" Jeannie feigned incredulity. "You've never had your hair professionally done?"

"Not for an occasion, no. I mean, I've had a *haircut* before. How are these slices?" She gestured to the pie.

"Oh, fine." Jeannie couldn't bring herself to look. She leaned a little closer to Nat. "Since we're talking just girls here, may I ask you a question? Something a little bit delicate?"

Nat nodded, eyes wide.

"This evening right before dinner, did you happen to see my husband switching the name cards on the dining room table?"

Nat froze. Jeannie could see a fib gearing up across her face, struggling to materialize. "I . . . ah . . . I wasn't really looking."

Jeannie tilted her head to the side and smiled. "You're too sweet to lie."

"I'm not sure why he would do a thing like that."

"Aren't you darling."

"Maybe . . . maybe I saw him fiddle with them. I'm not sure. He might have knocked some over and needed to right them again."

"Yes, I'm sure that's it. Mitch is always righting things."

"I feel like I'm tattling," Nat said. "Please don't tell your husband I said anything."

"Of course I won't, dear. This is between us. I can promise you that Mitch will hear nothing about it."

Nat looked relieved. "Thank you," she said. "Here, let me start carrying these out."

Jeannie waved her off with her giant injured finger. "No, no. You go sit down. I'll take everyone's orders first and then bring out what we need."

Nat nodded, gave an uncertain smile, and returned to the dining room. Jeannie leaned against the countertop, peeking inside the layers of paper towel on her finger and noticing with relief that the red spread had slowed. She rewrapped her finger with tunneled, tipsy focus. *No more vodka for you, ma'am!*

The blueberry juice on her bodice was driving her to distraction, so she fetched a small, pearl-trimmed bolero jacket from her bedroom and slid her arms into that, hurt finger first. Changing her whole dress would be far too noticeable, even among this group of clowns. Her mood was becoming quite foul. Gathering a small piece of notepaper and a dull golf pencil, she went into the dining room to take down the dessert orders.

Her guests chatted and lounged and readjusted their napkins. Brownie Franks looked at her brightly, as if Jeannie were about to lead them verbally through a long and elaborate procedure.

She forced her gaze to her husband and saw that, surprise, surprise, Mitch had turned his high beam of attention back onto Nat Collier posthaste. He was leaning against the poor woman, telling her that there was something on her shirt while he brushed imaginary lint from her collarbone. "That's better," he said. Then he clucked, "Let's tuck this in here," took the napkin on her lap by two corners and, like a perverted maître d', nestled it down on either side of her thigh as if her leg were a sleeping infant. Nat's face reddened; she glanced around and then in a quiet voice, preposterously, thanked him.

At the far end of the table, Paul Collier was watching this with an expression of strangled horror. He hopped, in a spasm, to his feet.

Thank God Jeannie was on top of things. She slipped around the table to stand behind Nat, putting one hand on each of her shoulders. Nat's clavicle jumped, and Jeannie petted her gently as she smiled at the other guests, her oversized, bundled finger pointing obscenely at the opposite wall. "Everyone," she said in her most genteel voice, "we have two choices for dessert."

The guests' eyes turned to her; they chortled, patted their engorged bellies, geared up for another round. Nat, under Jeannie's palms, sat silently and Paul Collier eased back down into his seat.

"We have angel food cake with blueberry filling, and key lime pie. Of course," and she smiled down into Mitch's sleepy eyes, "you can always have both."

NAT

IT WAS NEARLY ELEVEN WHEN THE COLLIERS GOT HOME FROM the Richardses' party, having walked the three blocks back in the brisk night air. Sam piggybacked on Paul's shoulders while Nat carried Liddie against her chest. She watched Paul; his silence made her anxious.

What a strange party that had been. The home, the setting, and the people (well, most of them) had been so attractive, but between Mitch and Jeannie, Nat felt she should have brought a small club to defend herself with, and the whole event seemed to have jammed all Paul's inner workings and left him speechless.

The girls, on the other hand, were elated. Sam couldn't stop babbling about the other children at the party, the nanny Martha, and the endless supply of Cracker Jack, which had left them blissfully wired and twitching. They clutched handfuls of flimsy plastic prizes: a chicken, an army soldier, a pistol, a ring.

When they reached the walkway in front of their house—which led pleasantly across a small lawn to three concrete steps and the front door—Nat's anxiety gave way for a moment to the coziness of recognition. They had come from someone else's place—unfamiliar, its objects and furnishings containing no memories—back to their own, and though this house was new it still felt more theirs than the one they'd just been in. So that was a start. But as Paul switched on the light and they found themselves standing in the entryway, her heart sank again. Their small living room was filled with the hulking shadows of cardboard boxes, here and there like grazing animals. Otherwise the house was mostly empty, the walls bare and showing off their occasional dents, paint scratches, light sockets, and mysterious dark streaks. They'd been in town a month and had still hardly unpacked. The whole place smacked of unsettled, continual limbo.

Nat knew she should have gotten the place in order by now, but it seemed impossible with the girls. She'd tackled a box the other day and, in her absorption, lost track of Liddie for only a minute; Liddie had pushed open the back door, toppled down a step, chipped a tooth, and cut her lip. How, Nat wondered, did the other housewives do it? Was she not capable of handling two things at once?

"It's very late, girls," she said, "so no stories tonight. Let's go get your nightgowns on." Her ankle wobbled for a minute as she crossed the living room, thanks to the two gin fizzes and glass of wine she'd drank over the course of the evening. She checked herself and made it without trouble to the girls' bedroom.

Sam's pupils had the eerie dilation of a late-night sugar high. She clambered up through her nightgown and out the top. "I'm not tired, Mama," she said. "I could stay up forever."

"I bet you could," said Nat, tugging Sam's arms through the sleeves, "but we need to try to sleep."

"Can we keep the light on?"

"No," Nat said. "Lie down next to Liddie."

"She took my airplane," Sam said, scowling at her sister.

"We'll sort that out in the morning. Sam, keep your tongue in your mouth."

"When will we get our *beds*?" Sam cried.

The movers had somehow lost Sam's and Liddie's beds on the way from Virginia to Idaho. Stupidly, Nat had signed the release before making sure the beds were among the dozens of brown boxes, and now they had to pay for replacements themselves. She and Paul didn't have a bed yet, either; they'd planned to buy one—probably from the Goodwill because full-size beds were expensive—but he'd been working so much in the month since they moved that they hadn't gotten around to it.

Nat patted the floor and Sam finally toppled next to her. "We'll go to the J. C. Penney's on Monday and find you something," she said. "I know you're tired of sleeping on the floor."

Of course, as soon as Nat got Sam to lay down, Liddie began wandering in the tipsy, lurching circles of an exhausted toddler. She roamed confusedly, shuffling in an increasingly tighter spiral until she tripped over her own feet and sat down crying. "Sweetheart," Nat began, but the child was up again. She wanted to enjoy a night on the town in the new house, sticking her finger into sockets, tasting a dead fly off the windowsill, scaling the bathroom sink.

"Mama, I want you *in* my blankets," Sam was saying. "In my blankets *with* me!"

Liddie finally stood still and began to hiccup. She stared at Nat with huge, accusatory eyes.

"Girls," Nat cried, fighting her exasperation.

"What's going on in here?" asked Paul from the doorway, and they all went silent. He sounded irritated. They waited to see what he would say. But he sighed, and came in and settled next to Sam, tucking Liddie's pink crocheted blanket around her body and rubbing her small, hiccupping back. The carpet, pressed to Nat's nose, had a comfortingly new, mildly chemical smell. She closed her eyes as Paul patted their daughters' backs and hummed "Home on the Range" until they all dozed off to sleep.

-

IT WAS STILL DARK when Nat awoke. A piece of carpet fuzz tickled her mouth. She sat up, her eyes adjusting, and tried to judge the depth of the girls' sleep by their soft, mouthy breaths.

She wandered into the living room, taking small steps to avoid stumbling into boxes. Not finding Paul, she backtracked to look for him in their bedroom. Blankets were spread on the floor but he wasn't there. She had no idea what time it was. Outside, the toads trilled in cascades, each note strung like an identical pearl on the wave of sound.

She followed their song to the backyard where she spied Paul sitting on the small square of moonlit patio. He sat with his ankles crossed, looking into the distance.

The patio ended abruptly at his feet and the yard turned to dark grass, just enough to cross in three or four strides before they reached their neighbors' backyards. Waist-high brown picket fences ran between. All the neighbors' windows were dark, and as her eyes settled she could see between the houses into a far-off blank area unmarred by billboard or streetlight. Only the sloping forms of mountains were visible, darkness against darkness, a shadow of a dream.

Idaho Falls was no San Diego, but it wasn't the worst place, either. Just remote was all, a little outpost with an attention-getting namesake: the man-made waterfall that marked the entrance to town on the banks of the Snake River. Nat thought of the first day they'd driven into town, a few weeks earlier. Like the town itself, the falls were clean and tidy and gave no trouble. They zigzagged the river at well-planned right angles and spilled about twenty feet down to the rocks, the water pouring so neatly that it barely frothed—it seemed to be made of silk. Even the misty boulders at the bottom appeared to have been hand-arranged by fastidious town fathers.

Above the falls stood the Mormon temple, tiered up to the top in rectangular layers like a masculine interpretation of a wedding cake. A single golden archangel posed on top, holding a thin instrument to his lips as if he were blowing glass. The falls and the temple: You could hardly picture one without the other. They were so pristine, so lushly manufactured in contrast to the quiet, two-dog town and endless desert beyond, that they were almost startling to come upon.

Past the falls and the temple there was a tiny downtown, a strip of Main Street with a barbershop, a candy store, a diner, and a brand-spanking-new J. C. Penney. After that, a few tire rotations' worth of neighborhoods, and then the landscape went briefly back to fields again—Mormon farmland, mostly potatoes—and finally the endless-looking desert, as brown and rough as sandpaper. Fifty miles west of town, over more blank desert, was the National Reactor Testing Station where Paul worked.

She wondered how he liked his new job. When she asked him how it was going, he usually said "fine" or, occasionally, "decent." He was not a complainer, which other wives had told her she should be grateful for, but she wouldn't have minded a few more details.

Watching him, apprehension hung in her chest like a swallowed chip of ice. The past month had been one trial after another. There was the dumb little number she'd pulled at the lake just before they reached Idaho Falls, diving into the water even though he had asked her not to. That seemed like ages ago. Before that argument had resolved itself he was off to his new job, and when he was at home he was either lost in the sleep of the dead or rummaging among their vaguely marked boxes in a futile, exhausting search for one item or another. *"Paul, where is the hand mixer? Have you seen the box with the spare linens? You didn't happen across my Dutch oven, did you?"* They had gone whole days without really looking one another in the eye, shouldering past each other in the kitchen, handing the girls back and forth like sandbags.

Then there was the day he'd come home eight hours late from work—eight hours!—claiming the bus had broken down. The more she thought about it the stranger that seemed, but the testing station *was* out there in the boondocks, fifty miles from home; it was possible they'd had no other transportation. He'd drunk more than a few beers that night and gone straight to bed, and Nat decided she was best off not prodding him about it.

Part of her was frustrated with him, with his passive stoicism even though he must have felt the distance between them, too. But she knew that he was tired, that he worried she and the girls wouldn't like Idaho. His care took subtle forms: A week ago, she'd taken her early rising daughters to the park so he could sleep in, and when they tiptoed back into the house she'd expected to find him still asleep. Instead he was sitting at the kitchen table, in his undershirt and slacks, making a button stringer for the girls to play with. Nat watched in surprise as he looped a string over either palm and pulled it tight, a large button from her sewing kit—which she'd brought on the drive to Idaho, as two little girls were liable to tear a hole in anything—spinning rapidly in the center. When he yanked the string with one hand, the button leaped, still turning. Nat couldn't help but watch, captivated; it seemed a trick from another place and time. The girls were delighted. They'd scampered out into the backyard with it and he watched them go, his face skimmed by a brief and satisfied smile.

"Hi," she whispered now, stepping out onto the patio behind him.

He cleared his throat. "The girls asleep?"

"Yes, finally." She settled onto the cool concrete, stretching her legs in front of her. She wanted to take his hand and feel its heaviness in her lap, but if he were angry with her she might be rebuffed. So she waited. She smoothed her cotton dress over her knees, idly wondering how women like Jeannie Richards kept up the curlers and high heels with children scampering around. A housewife could be a virtual shut-in, peering out through the blinds in fear of the milkman, but she still needed a good dress that nipped in at the waist and a nice pair of heels to lengthen her calf line.

She tried to follow his gaze: power lines, mountains. His face was unreadable, his hands folded in his lap. He looked like a statue of the young Abraham Lincoln.

"Well, we survived dinner at the Richardses'," she said.

"I guess so."

"Did you have a good time?"

He turned to look at her. "Did *you*?" His mouth was set in a straight line, and she felt her heart start to clatter a bit.

"It was all right," she said. "Their house was beautiful. Mrs. Richards has a knack for decorating." She smiled. "That is, they *have* furniture, anyway."

"We have furniture," he said. "We just have to find it all."

"I know. I know that." She couldn't seem to stop talking about the darn furniture.

He nodded, and she saw his mind working with some unspoken thought. "My boss seems to like you," he finally said.

"Oh, him." Nat waved the notion away. "He had too much to drink."

"Maybe *I* should have drunk more," Paul muttered.

Nat paused, watching him. She could still make light of this if she were careful. She tried to imitate Richards in a mocking baritone. "'I only drink old-fashioneds,' he said. 'Can I make you a Moscow mule?' he said. 'You have to drink it out of a tin cup. Have you seen my car, it's a new Cadillac Coupe de Ville? Look at my shoes, they're alligator Norwegians by Stetson.' Whatever that means!" She smiled at him.

"It was embarrassing," Paul said, as if to press on past the threat of Nat's peace offering, "to see him pawing all over you—"

"He wasn't pawing all over me."

"As if I weren't even there."

"I wouldn't let him 'paw' all over me whether you were there or not."

"He looked at you the whole night."

"He was *drunk,*" she said.

"Fine," Paul said, nodding. "Fine, he was drunk. But you could have put space between the two of you. You could have come over and sat by me."

"I just sat where my name card was. It said, 'Mrs. Collier.' He came and sat beside *me*."

"Is the name card some kind of higher authority?"

"I couldn't offend Mrs. Richards; she put it there. And if he sat down and I instantly got up and moved away, transplanting someone else's name card—that would have caused a scene."

Paul looked away. "You two caused a scene as it was," he said.

She could feel the wall he was trying to build up; it was her job to knock it down while it was still in progress. She threw caution to the wind, took his hand in two of her own, kneading it. Laced her fingers through his larger, knobby knuckles and tried to get him to look her in the eye. "Listen," she said. "I'm sorry. I didn't know he was going to get that . . . sloppy. I didn't want to be anywhere near him."

"And why did you say that thing about the *little, tiny CR-1*? You made it sound like I come home and tell you how small and meaningless it is."

He in fact had done this, the first day, but Nat knew now was not the time to insist. "I'm so sorry about that. I was just trying to smooth things over after Mr. Harbaugh's outburst, and I put my foot in my mouth."

"It wasn't your job to smooth things over. Let him be a fool; keep your own composure."

"It's an impulse with women—we hate to see men embarrass themselves. I can't explain it. Please don't be mad at me."

"I'm not."

"Good," she said quietly. She lifted a hand and brushed it over the top of his head, feeling his short, bristly hair. She had never known him outside the army and had no idea what his hair was like if it weren't shaved to his head. Was it thick? Would it curl? She'd seen it only this way, dark and stiff as a currycomb.

"I think I made a mistake," he said. "Coming here. Switching jobs. Moving you and the girls to the middle of nowhere."

"It's not the middle of nowhere. There's a new J. C. Penney's."

"And nothing else for a hundred miles," he said.

She shrugged. This was true. Despite its weak aspirations toward suburban life, Idaho Falls remained mostly open space, flatness, hardened lava, and vultures that circled over the road like the last thing you might ever see.

"We'll be fine," she said. "It's a two-year tour. Then you can go someplace else if you like."

His eyes darted her way. "You mean *we* can go someplace else."

"Yes. That's what I meant."

"All right." He closed his eyes. "This whole tour just isn't turning out like I expected. I thought—I thought everything would be better than it is. The people, the reactor. I was kind of looking forward to it, and now I feel like if we can just survive this tour and make it out of here, that'll be enough."

Nat felt a squeeze of anxiety. "You don't mean what Mr. Harbaugh was saying, do you—about the reactor?"

"It's nothing for you to worry about."

"Well, was he telling the truth?"

Paul smiled grimly. "The reactor's not exactly newfangled, I'll give him that. And the leadership is not . . . attentive."

"Paul, I don't want to hear that! It makes me nervous."

"We'll make it work. We always do. Certainly won't help anything if you worry."

"Well, now I *am* going to worry."

"We can make it two years."

She nodded.

"Just help me out by keeping away from my boss, all right?" he said.

"You don't need to worry about *that*."

He studied her in that opaque way he had. Then she saw a flicker of fondness work through his eyes, the softening that meant thank God, she had officially won. No going back now; no more grudge. She had punched through the wall even as he tried to build it.

He smiled at her and said, "You're a lot of work for me, you know."

This was how *she* felt, but she didn't want to get into it. She smiled and got to her knees, kissing him. "Am I worth it?" she asked.

His kiss was a good enough answer. She slid onto his lap and he reached one hand behind her head to unclip her hair; it fell around their faces like a curtain. With a quiet whisk of fabric he pulled her cotton belt from its loops and started in on the buttons down the front, cursing happily because there were quite a few. The cloak of her hair gave a blindlike illusion of shelter but of course they were on the patio in their flat backyard, which looked innocently out onto the other flat backyards, where presumably neighbors did not take off all their clothes and roll around on early summer nights.

"People can see us," Paul said.

"Where?" she asked, looking around. "There's no one out here. Everyone's asleep."

"Let's hope so," he said. He stared at her a moment and then laughed. She leaned back, her arms around his neck, drinking it in. She loved when Paul was happy. She hadn't truly realized, until they were married and living together, what a sealed-up person he was. He could spend hours in a silent house without turning on the radio or asking a question. But his reserve had always made her feel as if he were her hidden treasure, strange and rare: the secret sign, the cracked geode. Whatever strange majesty was in him was known to her alone.

There was a small rustle somewhere and he paused, but Nat kept him on track with a quick pop of the clasps at the back of her bra. She always undid these for him; poor soul, each time it was as if he had never encountered such a web of mystery.

It was an unforeseen thrill to be naked to the wind from the waist up, and she found herself energized, helping his shirt over his head, liberating him from his slacks. He seemed nearly dazed with trepidation and delight.

"Am I worth it?" she said again. "Say I am or I'm going to run out across that yard right now." Before he could answer she hopped to her feet, pulled her dress and panties down around her ankles, and looped them over his shoulders like a boxer's towel, yanking them in so he'd kiss her. He did. Then he gaped at her, which was exactly what she wanted. The concrete patio and then the cool, wet grass passed under her feet, and she trotted out to the picket fence, tagged it, and sauntered back. She felt lithe and lovely in the moonlight. She knew she was all he wanted to see. Her hair swayed down her back and she put a little wiggle in her step, laughing, and he was laughing, too, from where he crouched on the patio, her underpants draped jauntily over his shoulder. He seemed not to realize they were there.

"Get down here, Natalie Collier," he said, pulling her to the cement. She could feel the happiness throbbing from him and the fact that she had put it there, that she could create such fulfillment in another person, was intoxicating. Paul shushed her, gripping the back of her head, and when they were done she ran her fingers up his arm, over and over, from his elbow to the smoothness of his shoulder, where her teeth had left a small wreath. His heart beat right into her chest.

When Nat awoke, pale bars of light striped the carpet near her face. She sat up, her ribs aching from another night on the floor. Out the back window to the yard she could see the grayish morning sky, the watery efforts of the sun. It was early. Her daughters' feet shuffled just outside the bedroom door, and she knew they'd burst in any moment if she didn't get to them first.

Paul lay beside her, looking somehow both childlike and masculine in his sleep: shorn army hair and angular face, utterly peaceful expression. She leaned over and kissed him, pulled the blanket up to his shoulders, and got to her feet. Her bra sat upright on the floor as if inhabited by an invisible woman. She couldn't find last night's underpants so she fished a new pair from her dresser and stepped into them.

The girls' whispers were gaining in volume. When she opened the door they toppled into the room, looking startled for a moment and then grinning. "Oh!" Sam said with delight, as if her mother were stopping in unexpectedly for tea. "Oh, good *mor*ning!"

"Good morning," Nat whispered, smiling. Sam's hair was sleep-frayed out around her head and ratted into a firm, walnut-sized nest in the back.

After bread with peanut butter and some apple slices and a game of "I Spy" in their box-filled kitchen, it was still only seven A.M. Nat wanted to let Paul sleep in: because he had driven so far and then worked for the past few weeks, but also in a wifely indulgence she always allowed him after lovemaking, as if the strain of her seduction weakened him and he needed, like Samson, to sleep his way back into strength.

"Can we go for a walk?" Sam asked. Her cheeks glistened with peanut butter and bread crumbs; she looked like she'd been smeared with suet and set out for birds in cold weather.

"Sure," Nat said, wiping Sam's face and then Liddie's. She got the girls dressed, tried to wet Sam's hair down flat, and led them out into the cool morning air.

The neighborhood was quiet; only crows and cats were out. They made slow progress, Sam hopping ahead and Liddie toddling behind, Nat always somewhere in the middle. The soles of the girls' Mary Janes made little gritty skips on the pavement.

Theirs was a modest neighborhood, clapboard prewar houses with pointed roofs, small windows, milk-delivery boxes built into the wall near the front doors. Each house was about eight hundred square feet—smaller than her parents' home had been, but perfectly comfortable. At that moment, on the cusp of summer, with the street still fresh and the girls not arguing and her love for Paul snuggled happily in the back of her mind, she felt they could do fine in this new place.

They wandered along several blocks and she realized that they were nearing the Richardses' neighborhood. Here the houses were changing: Instead of humble little triangles they were newer, ranch style, each with a hedge and one rosebush planted just to the right of the front door. Everything felt a little cleaner, a little classier, and it occurred to Nat that she'd walked out her front door in the dress she'd slept in, looking like an unmade bed.

"Girls," she said, "maybe we'll walk to the end of this block and then turn back."

"Aw, Mama," said Sam.

Nat hadn't thought back to the previous night's party since she'd awoken and now, seeing the Richardses' well-kept white house on the corner, she found it strange that she'd been there just hours ago in this same dress, nervous, her hair up, pearls heavy on her neck, Paul nursing his fatigue and his frustrations as if they were hard candies, her holding that stupid regrettable meatloaf. She was relieved that there was a different feeling between her and Paul now, the old feeling, and she hoped it would hold. It made her care less about Master Sergeant Richards hanging boozily in her face, pawing at her collar (Paul was right; he had pawed) or whether Jeannie Richards thought she was plain and friendless.

Cars had begun to pass by on the road, here and there. A line of four boys filed into a sedan at the end of the street while their father looked on. Nat guessed it must be about eight o'clock. The day stretched endlessly before them. She was just about to turn the girls around when she heard a commotion.

"What's that, Mama?" Samantha asked.

"Sam, shh," she said.

What Nat heard were the deep, irregular shouts of a man's voice. She swiveled her head, trying to tell where it was coming from—inside one of the houses, she thought. There was something almost comical about a muffled male voice; it was like someone hollering into a folded towel and expecting to be taken seriously.

Then she heard a woman, yelling in return, words staccato with rage. After a moment, studying the white house in front of her, she recognized the voices as those of Mitch and Jeannie Richards.

"Girls, we should go," she said, but a crude curiosity rooted her to the spot. Before she could spare herself by leaving, the front door flew open and Jeannie herself stormed out.

If Jeannie Richards had looked beautiful at the party last night, then this morning she was stunning. Her red hair caught the sunlight like a shiny penny, and she wore a dress so gleaming white that she seemed to not only reflect light but also give off her own. Everything but her hair glowed white: high white heels, a small hat with half netting and a smattering of pearls, white wrist-length gloves.

Jeannie marched down the walk and Mitch, unbelievably, blundered right out the door after her. He was wearing the same collared shirt from the night before, half-untucked; rumpled dress slacks, and socks. His bedroom dishevelment on this celibate, decorous street was what alarmed Nat most.

There was nothing Nat could do now; she was ten feet from these people. To take off scuttling up the street would attract their attention; crouching behind a shrub would look ludicrous and incriminating if they did catch sight of her. So she stood, hoping there might be some way that, in the heat of this apparent argument, they missed her.

Mitch stopped in the driveway. "You," he said to Jeannie's prim, upright back, "never stop nagging me about every little thing I do."

Jeannie whirled on him. "Mitch, I don't *care* what you do. Have sex with Mamie Eisenhower. Have sex with the pope! It's all the same to me. *The only thing I care about is you keeping your job.*"

Nat's heart was pounding. Jeannie had just said "Have sex!" twice in front of her own home, on a Saturday morning.

"For God's sake, I *didn't* lose my job," said Mitch. "I'm doing fine at my job."

"If you sink us," Jeannie said, "after all I've put up with—"

"This happens to all the guys from time to time. A little slap on the wrist. It's those actors from Combustion Engineering. I'll bet they have a quota, got to make sure it looks like they're on top of things—"

"You can put down the bottle at work from time to time, you know. It's not a pacifier. It's not a, a *tit*."

"My God, Jean!" Mitch stepped back in a paroxysm of disgust. "Have you gone insane?"

Even in her anger Jeannie held herself perfectly erect, like a small pillar of marble. Her voice was low and eviscerating. "You can gamble any other way you like," she said, "but not with *that*."

"You don't know the first thing about my job—"

"I know a monkey could do it, and probably without getting into trouble like you."

"That's enough."

"Oh, how I wish I had your job," Jeannie sneered. "I would be so much better at it than you. I wouldn't stall out while other people were promoted past me, and I wouldn't get shoved off to the side like some piece of retired machinery, but if I *did* I would try to improve myself so that I could do better instead of worse! I certainly would not let myself get caught—" She checked herself and lowered her voice so that Nat could barely make out the words. "You never *improve,* Mitch."

Mitch's mouth was half-open in anger, his tongue showing on one side. He'd finally plunged through bewilderment into the realm of self-righteous rage. "You women, you're all the same. Jealous and bitter, always keeping tabs."

"Keep it down," Jeannie hissed, stepping toward him, her eyes darting nervously.

But once Mitch got started he only gathered steam. "You're a bunch of thankless harpies, skimming off men, spending our money on your fancy clothes and shoes while you're home without a thought in your head, flashing your muff to the milkman."

There was a sharp crack as Jeannie's hand flew, leaving a bright pink starfish on Mitch's cheek.

For a moment Mitch stood, staring. Then he clasped the side of his face in his hand. "Goddamn, what in the hell, woman?"

Nat thought the slap might have been a sort of defense of womankind but Jeannie, shaking out her fingers, stepped back. "I am *not* like other women," she said.

She pivoted on her heel and suddenly Nat was square in her line of sight. "Oh!" Jeannie said, with a jump. Mitch turned his head. His eyes widened. Nat felt like a searchlight had just swung to her.

"I didn't know anyone was there," Jeannie cried, for a split second losing her composure.

"Nat Collier?" Mitch said.

"I'm so sorry," Nat stammered. "We were just out on a walk, and we heard shouting, and—"

"How long have you *been* there?" He scrutinized Nat. "Did you get kicked out of your house?"

"We were on a walk. I'm so sorry. Girls, let's go." Nat reached for her daughters' hands. The girls, who if you asked them to could not stop wiggling for thirty seconds, had managed to stand motionless, riveted, during the entire exchange.

Jeannie popped open her clutch, removed a flat gold cigarette case, and delicately plucked out a cigarette, lighting it with her purse tucked under her elbow. Eyeing Mitch and then Nat, she exhaled a cloud of disdain. She held her cigarette to the side of her face. "I see you've found a favorite dress, Nat," she said.

It took Nat a moment to understand Jeannie's barb. Jeannie was insulting her for wearing the same dress she'd had on yesterday. How had she even noticed, in the heat of an argument with her husband? She was one of those women, Nat guessed, whose calculating mind was always at work on others of her sex, detecting their weaknesses like a mine-sniffing German shepherd.

It was terrible and awesome to have seen Jeannie Richards this way, like watching the wrath of a minor god. Nat's heart pounded. She couldn't help siding with her, just a little; Jeannie might be unstable but Mitch was a buffoon. The idea that Mitch was Paul's supervisor, that *he* was the one to make judgment calls, felt too disheartening to be true. *If we can just survive this tour and make it out of here,* Paul had said last night, *that'll be enough.*

She didn't realize how fast she was striding, head down, gripping poor Liddie's wrist as the child struggled to keep up, until she reached her front walk and Sam said, "Mama, look." Nat lifted her head and saw a pair of crows pecking at some pink, limp item in their front yard.

It took Nat several seconds of watching the birds—fighting over the glossy, rose-colored thing on the lawn as if it were a steak; the winner flying with it to a low branch and watching Nat with robotic jerks of its wedge-shaped head—to realize with a squeal that what they fought over were her missing underpants, which she must have left outside the night before and which now hung from the crow's beak, flapping gently in the breeze.

PAUL

SPECIALIST FRANKS LOVED THE MIDDAY GAME SHOWS. WHEN their three-man crew worked days, they spent lunch hours with *Tic-Tac-Dough*. Today's episode pitted a friendly looking banker against a heavy-browed former army captain who capitalized on his clout by wearing his full uniform and ribbons on the set.

"Go army!" said Franks through a mouthful of food.

"I don't know," said Webb. "I don't like his looks."

"That's 'cause you don't have any respect."

"I do!" Webb said.

Paul didn't mind the game shows in general, but he disliked the thirty-second spells of watching men think, set to ominously tinkling music. There they stood, mere inches from one another behind their podiums, all their involuntary tics and mannerisms writ large for America to see: the clenched jaw, surrendering eye roll, squirming, shifting, laughing inexplicably at one's hands, the swallowing of anxious and plentiful saliva.

"Pick the Bible," urged Franks. "Pick Bible, or baseball." They all watched the screen; there was no way not to, with Franks constantly urging it on, chastising it, sometimes smacking the tabletop and cursing it out. He leaned forward and bumped the table with his closed fist. "Oh for Pete's sake, not literature."

"Author of 1925 novel in stream of consciousness," Webb said, brow furrowed, repeating the announcer, Bill Wendell.

"What's stream of consciousness?" Paul asked, looking over the remains of his lunch. Nat had packed him a turkey sandwich, three cookies, and a fruit cup. Franks ate some kind of leftover beef concoction, cold, and the bachelor Webb munched from a large bag of pretzels.

"It sounds like a place in Idaho to me," said Webb, washing his pretzels down with Coke. He clinked the bottle onto the table and grinned, his face so thin you could see the muscles tugging it into a smile. "Like the Lost Desert, near the Stream of Consciousness."

Paul laughed.

"That's enough from the peanut gallery, thank you," said Franks. "Come on, sports or entertainment."

"Maybe imaginary geography, for Webb here," said Paul.

"Secret category," said Franks. "If he wins one more game, he gets a new car. He's won four now."

"Four *cars*?" cried Webb.

"Four games," said Franks.

"What kind of car?" asked Webb.

"A King Midget," said Paul, and they all laughed. The King Midget was a car you built yourself from a kit, powered by any motor you could get your hands on.

Franks glanced at his watch. "Rats," he said, stifling a burp, "we've gotta get back to work."

"Aw, just one more round," said Webb. Paul folded up his lunch bag and returned it to his locker, pausing to look at the picture of Nat he kept inside the door. It was from their dating days back in San Diego, taken in a booth on the boardwalk. She had been nineteen, Paul twenty. She looked beautiful and happy, with her grin that went up just a tiny bit more on one side than the other, her eyes smiling. Normally the picture filled him up with contentment, but today it pushed a small hollow into his stomach. They'd had an argument that morning, and he couldn't shake it. Things had been going great between them, and now there was a shift again.

He could still hear the tug in her voice: *I don't understand why you're being so stingy*. She had wanted to take Sam and Liddie to the Palisades Reservoir for a "beach day." He'd seen her in this kind of mood before—she'd had about all she could take of sitting around the house with the girls and was desperate for a small adventure. For this she needed the car, which Paul normally drove to the bus stop downtown and left there during the day so he could drive it home again.

So she and the girls had given him a lift to the bus stop that morning, then taken the car for their beach adventure. He didn't love the idea of them going so far—it was two hours each way to the reservoir—or of Nat having to drive home, tired, probably on some twisty road; four hours of driving for an equal amount of simulated beach time seemed a little silly to him, not to mention a waste of gas. But—all right, Nat. Take the car.

But there was more: On the drive to the bus stop she'd also asked if she, instead of Paul, could start having the Fireflite during the day. "It doesn't make *sense* that it just sits downtown at the bus stop all day," she'd said, picking at her skirt in the way he knew meant she was asking for something she'd thought about more than once. "You could leave the car with me and get a ride to work with a friend."

"What friend?" he'd asked.

"I don't know, one of your coworkers." She shrugged. "I'd *love* to have the car during the day."

"Really?" Paul asked, genuinely surprised. "Why would you need the car all day?" It had never occurred to him that she might want such a thing.

"It would make shopping so much easier," Nat said. "And entertaining the girls. It would make going to the pool easier . . . going to the . . ." She faltered, her face clouding as if she could feel herself losing ground with that one setback.

"There's a playground a few blocks from our house."

"I know," said Nat quickly, her cheeks flushed. "We go there all the time. Having the car would just give us more freedom."

"Huh," Paul said. "I don't like the idea of you and the girls driving all over creation."

"I'm a good driver," Nat protested, though they both knew this wasn't true. When she was alone she drove much too fast. She seemed to almost compulsively test fate and couldn't drive a straightaway without going twenty over the limit. She had once run over a cat, a horror that still made her cry if it were brought up. Paul let a silence hang in the air, generously, rather than contradict her.

"I don't know," he said. "I can't risk being late to work. If I'm not here when the bus arrives, I'm out of luck. What if my ride is late? What if he had car trouble?" He didn't want to have to depend on somebody else, a coworker who could be late for any number of reasons. Webb was too frequently tardy himself, and Franks had four kids or five, Paul didn't remember; in any case, too many variables. Richards lived closest to him but Paul would never beg rides from his boss, and after the party the other night he could barely stand to be around the man.

"I don't understand why you're being so *stingy,*" Nat burst out. She sounded breathless, and Paul saw, with a flop in his chest, that her eyes were teary.

"I'm sorry."

"But you're not," she said simply, and turned to talk to Sam in a too-bright voice that bounced off the windows as if they were made of tin.

Paul had pulled up near his bus stop where a dozen or so guys waited, cigarette smoke rising just above their bodies. Franks was there, leaning against the side of the shoe store with his ankles crossed, turning the pages of his newspaper. Webb sat on the curb, his wrists on his knees, hands dangling loosely. He took a puff of his cigarette and squinted up as Paul's car idled, seemed to think of raising a hand in greeting, then saw Paul with his family and looked away again. "You have a pretty damn perfect family," he had remarked later, when they were all at work. "A man could almost be jealous of you, Collier."

"Almost," Franks had joked.

When Paul climbed out of the car Nat was simmering with hurt feelings; he could almost see them in the air around her, as if the molecules bunched together into armor. She'd driven off without looking back, her stiff, pretty head upright in the rearview mirror. Paul felt like a jerk and also pathetically defiant: He *did* have his reasons for wanting to keep the car. It was true that he feared being late to work, and it was true that Nat drove too fast and that he liked knowing where she was during the day, instead of thinking that she and the girls were out God knew where.

But it also insulted him to consider what her request implied: that she was bored at home. He wanted to think of her as completely fulfilled. She had the house now, two daughters, a backyard like she'd wanted, an allowance every month out of his paycheck to buy clothes or cooking supplies or things she had her eye on; sure, his pay wasn't lavish, but what more could he do? He thought of his own mother, of her forest-walled life and uncaring husband and no outside stimulation whatsoever and then, in contrast, of his wife, who had all this love, all these wonderful things. Why was she asking him for even more?

But it was just the car. He tried to keep that in mind. She had not asked, say, for the car *and* an additional two-week vacation without him in the mountains. God, it was difficult to be fair to her sometimes. He wanted nothing more than her happiness, but somehow he still screwed things up. He made her angry or hurt her feelings and never gained anything from those stupid disruptions. And now here he was, standing by his locker like a chump and feeling uneasy, feeling unsettled because she was off driving around somewhere being mad at him or maybe enjoying her freedom and not thinking of him at all.

His brooding was interrupted by the aggressive crinkle of a waxed paper bag next to his ear. He jumped. "What the hell, Webb?"

Webb took on the soft-eyed expression of a dame in a movie. "Where do you go, Collier?" he whispered. "Where do you go, when you leave me?"

"Shut up," Paul chuckled. But he felt grateful to be pulled back out of himself, to the people and task at hand.

"The reactor's burning hot, gentlemen," Franks said through his last mouthful of food. "We're gonna have to lower the rods again." He wiped his mouth on a napkin, wandered over to the sink to rinse out his Tupperware. From behind, in those baggy overalls, he looked a bit like a giant baby.

"Why's the thing so hot?" Webb groaned. They had already lowered the rods first thing in the morning.

"I dunno," said Franks. "It's just hot. Guess we didn't lower enough the first time. Willie *Mays*!" he exclaimed, and Paul looked up, thinking this some kind of alternative to cursing, but the shift leader had paused in front of the television. "Good grief," he said, "who *misses* a question like that?" and he turned the knob, shrinking the game show contestants into a tiny square of black. He picked up his clipboard. "Let's go," he said. "This time we're lowering half an inch. I don't want to have to do it again today."

They ascended the thin steel staircase that wound up the side of the reactor silo, their boots echoing one after the other on the narrow, slatted stairs.

The tall, narrow silo served mostly as a big container for the core, which was nestled about halfway down beneath layers of shielding and gravel. Five long metal control rods traveled from the core up to the reactor head on the top floor of the silo. The rods projected about a foot above the reactor head and were lifted or lowered manually in small increments to adjust the speed of the reaction in the core. Raising the rods allowed more neutrons into the core and created more energy; lowering the rods dampened the reaction and cooled the core. The operators were constantly calibrating, checking the speed of the reaction and fiddling with the rods; sometimes Paul felt it was the main thing he did.

Each rod weighed eighty-four pounds. Most reactors used remote-control arms to move their rods, but the CR-1—like the army in general, Paul thought—was old-school and hands-on. Their crew simply leaned over the rods, unclamped the tops, scooched a rod up a little, and clamped it again. "Who needs a remote control?" Franks had said. "We can do the same thing, just with a little more elbow grease."

"Elbow grease and a pain in the ass," Webb had muttered.

The five rods were named by odd numbers—the one, the three, the five, the seven, and the most powerful rod of all, the nine. The number nine rod was what set the CR-1 apart from other, similar reactors; Franks called it their "trademark." It had been designed as a sort of emergency brake for the CR-1: If the reaction were to "run away" and become uncontrollably hot, the operators could shut down the entire machine by dropping the number nine to the bottom of the core. In a bad situation it might save the day.

The glitch, the design flaw that would be improved upon in later reactors based on this one, was that while the number nine was the emergency brake for the whole reactor, there was no emergency brake for the number nine. If a crew dropped it to the bottom when they hadn't meant to (which would be a real idiot move, and Paul hoped that never happened on his watch), it would shut down, or scram, the entire machine and they'd have to restart the goddamn thing. That would be an inconvenience, but something they'd live to complain about later. *Raising* the number nine too high, however, would have the opposite effect, flooding the core with energy, and that would be very bad. It could make the reactor go supercritical, reaching two thousand degrees in less than a second.

This had never happened in the CR-1, of course, but they had some idea of how serious a supercritical core could be. The core contained enriched uranium, hundreds of years' worth of energy in those tiny invisible atoms, but if it went supercritical all that energy would be released in a fraction of a second. This might melt the interior of the reactor or it might blow the whole thing like a volcano; they couldn't be sure until they tried it, which, of course, no one ever would.

So army brass had come up with a simple solution, repeated over and over like they were telling kids not to look at the sun: *Do not ever, under any circumstances, raise a rod more than four inches.*

The crew took great care with their increments, one man lifting or lowering the control rod while another crouched to watch it. So far, this had worked. *And if it doesn't,* one of the instructors in reactor school had grimly joked, *you'll know.*

Some guys boasted that if the reactor ever came under attack—Paul could not imagine the Russians suddenly appearing in Idaho, but stranger things had happened—they planned to pull up the nine to keep the technology out of Soviet hands. These were always bachelors—swaggering types who enjoyed the drama of a potentially suicidal scenario with themselves at the center. Their lust for heroism seemed somehow childish to Paul; once you had a family you didn't glamorize such things, unless you were bored.

Now his mind darted back to his own family: Nat, angry with him. He hated the thought of it. He stood a moment, chewing the inside of his cheek.

"Collier," Franks barked, "pay attention."

"Sorry." Paul joined Webb in loosening the clamps above the rods. Franks stood to the side jotting notes on his clipboard.

The first four rods slid into place as they were supposed to: numbers one and three first, then five and seven. When each rod hit its mark, Webb leaned forward and clamped it.

He reached the nine and Paul felt his own concentration sharpen. He squatted to keep an eye on it; Webb loosened the clamp and gripped the rod.

"Half an inch," Franks reminded him.

"Okay," said Webb, "here goes."

Several seconds went by. Paul glanced up. Exertion was written on Webb's thin face, but nothing was happening.

"Lower the rod now, son," Franks called.

"You okay, Webbsy?" said Paul.

For a moment Webb said nothing. Then he exhaled and said, "It's stuck."

Franks glanced up sharply.

"I'm sorry, it won't move—"

"Let me try." Franks waved Webb off; the young kid sagged out of the way. Franks tried the rod as Webb had, sweat droplets popping up on his forehead, then cursed and motioned to Paul.

"Collier, you try it."

The control rod was warm from Franks's grip. Paul wiped it down with the rag he kept in his front pocket, grasped the rod, and pushed down with all his might. It was as if the rod were still clamped: It didn't move no matter how he strained. His elbows, tucked at first, rose toward his shoulders; his whole body shook. With a groan he released it, stepping back.

"What did we do last time?" Webb asked.

"Last time?" echoed Paul, catching his breath.

"Should we call Richards?" said Webb.

"With all his superhuman strength," Franks muttered.

"No, I meant, just because he's in charge—"

Franks cut him off. "Collier, get that pipe wrench."

Paul stepped off the top of the core, grabbed a heavy monkey wrench from the shelf along the wall, and was back in three strides. He screwed the wrench's broached teeth against the thick metal rod at an angle, took a deep breath, and pulled the wrench upward for leverage. It was still stuck fast. His heart pounded; he could feel the blood rushing in his ears. His shift mates' eyes were trained on him, and he could see that they were nervous, too.

He regripped the wrench and strained until his neck corded and his arms shook. His brain bulged against his skull; he saw stars. "Shit," he cried, letting go.

"You're close," said Franks. "Try again."

Paul stepped back, squeezed his palms, and started over. Franks was on tiptoes near his shoulder, Webb peering from the other side. "Give him some space," Franks suddenly barked, and the two of them stepped back. Paul pulled harder. The rod gave a small grind downward, then another. Paul strained until his eyes danced with light. For a split second he felt his consciousness suspended in air.

"You got it, Collier, you got it."

The rod moved a fraction of an inch and no more. Paul's hands dropped to his knees, his arms shaking.

"Good job. Bravo," said Franks, slapping Paul on the back with a meaty palm.

"Yeah," said Webb. "Hoo!" He let out a high, dopey laugh of relief.

Paul tried to slow his breathing. His sternum cramped; his lungs flared wide open and shut as if straining their confines on either end. When he could finally inhale without gasping he examined his work and was disappointed. "The rod didn't lower as far as we wanted."

"I don't give a care, that's as good as we'll get for now," said Franks. "I'll tell the evening crew and they can give it a shot later. Let's clamp that thing."

"It ain't gonna slide loose on its own," muttered Webb, picking up the C-clamp.

Paul watched Webb and Franks bracket the rod into place. Their sense of triumph seemed to fade with each second. Suddenly they were all quiet, sober with relief, and Paul knew he wasn't the only one thinking *Well, shit, for a moment there we really had a problem on our hands.*

"THAT'S HAPPENED BEFORE? A control rod sticking?" Paul asked, a few minutes later, as they all shuffled back to the control room.

"It's happened before," Franks said. "But that was the first time with the nine."

"They've all started sticking," said Webb.

"Richards isn't going to like it." Franks held the door for them, shaking his head. "I'm going to have to put that one in the log. He isn't going to want me to, but I can't . . ." he trailed off.

"Has he told the engineers?" Paul asked. "What about Deke Harbaugh?"

"I don't really know *what* he tells them."

"I couldn't have pushed that thing any harder," Paul said. "What do we do if it sticks again and none of us can get it to move?"

Webb looked at him uncertainly and Franks made a sound of irritation: "We'll cross that bridge when we come to it."

The control room was gray walled and plain, with rows of circular gauges, a roll of paper tape that ground slowly beneath its glass case, a console, and swivel chairs. At the top of one wall was an electric sign that read HIGH RADIATION, but it sat dark. In case of a threat it would illuminate and blink, but of course it never had.

Paul had known coming in that the CR-1 was more volatile than similar reactors, mainly because it was the only one he knew of that had been built with an all-powerful nine rod. But there were other complicating factors, too. It was a boiling water–type reactor, which meant it made its own steam inside the core rather than in a separate, nonradioactive coil; the CR-1's steam, and every part of the machine the steam came into contact with, were radioactive, too.

The CR-1 had also been built without containment; instead of having a familiar round dome like most reactors, its ceiling was flat, walls straight-sided and thin. It had been built as a prototype for very remote reactors in the Arctic, where no containment was necessary because there was virtually no population. But the CR-1 was not nearly as remote as its descendants would be. They were only fifty miles from town, on a desert plain where the wind often gusted thirty miles an hour. If there was fallout from an accident, it would travel fast.

He still felt shaky; could still see Webb's startled, anxious face; hear him say *It's stuck* in a voice thinned by fright. Rods were never supposed to stick. Control was everything; measurement and precision were everything. You could never let the reactor get ahead of you. And yet it had.

If they'd been *raising* the nine rod instead of lowering it, and it stuck that badly, it would not have been hard to pull it above the proscribed four inches. Four inches seemed like nothing but they'd been warned it could spell disaster. And while no one had ever actually exploded a reactor by overlifting just one rod, they suspected that, in a machine like the CR-1, raising the number nine would have the same effect as raising them all.

Paul glanced at Franks, who was scanning the paper tape. He opened his mouth to say something but Franks seemed absorbed. Paul wondered if Franks, too, had imagined what it might look like if the CR-1 went supercritical while men were working, the core hitting two thousand degrees in an instant. If it erupted, shooting water and steam and debris everywhere, anyone standing on the reactor floor as Paul and his crew had been minutes before . . . well, he didn't even want to think about it.

But his mind kept tugging that way, seeing it. The explosion, and then, almost as frightening, the fallout: drifting wherever the breeze took it, as brainless and indiscriminating as a jellyfish. Couple hours—less even—and the cloud could be right over their families in Idaho Falls.

And where would Paul be, at that point? Thrown out to the gravel parking lot, shot full of steel punchings and metal bolts, like a clove-studded orange?

Christ, he was being morbid.

He cleared his throat almost without realizing it and Franks looked up, snapping a tense *"What?"* In the instant that elapsed, locked in by Franks's scowl, Paul lost his urge to argue. It was over now, wasn't it? They'd budged the damn rod. Franks didn't want to talk about it. But the shift leader was watching him, waiting for him to speak.

"I was just thinking," said Paul, "you know, that if the number nine sticks, we're not really in control—"

"Were we ever?" Franks said.

Paul hesitated.

Franks pointed his pencil toward the wall, its rows of gently quivering needles. Murmured, "Let's see if this thing cools down now. It's looking better already."

NAT

The Palisades Reservoir danced in Nat's rearview mirror, a dwindling circle of blue and gold. She was sorry to see it go. She'd had such a wonderful day with the girls that she felt a pang when the lake winked out of sight behind pine trees.

"Mama," Sam called from the backseat. "We're sliding." The path down the mountain was a long Jacob's ladder of switchbacks and the girls grappled for purchase on the slick leather seat.

"Sorry," said Nat. "Hang on, it'll straighten out soon."

She tried to drive smoothly—which, though it slowed her down, was, indeed, more comfortable—and the girls settled into their seats, looking out the window. Sam's fingers gripped the leather ridge where the window met the door, and shadows of the tall trees flickered over her face like a long reel of silent film. Nat sighed. What a day it had been. Her girls had run in and out of the water as if inspired, sloshing buckets up the beach, pouring the water into a big muddy sand castle that they mosaicked with pebbles. The water was getting cold this late in the summer but Nat swam with them anyway, her daughters' squeals and gasps echoing in the thin high-altitude air.

The trip had been the perfect remedy after the morning's argument with Paul—even if it was also one of the reasons for the fight—and Nat wasn't ready to go home. She didn't want to give up this sunny, carefree feeling for the quiet house, Paul's stiff shoulders, his stoic conviction that he'd been right. He was always so damn certain. She'd dropped him off at the bus stop that morning and made it just around the corner before pulling over and giving the steering wheel three smacks with her palm, her face crumpling. It was humiliating to have to beg for the car, to hear Paul fret and waffle about being late for work, as if she were a child with no proper sense of limits. Did he think she *wanted* him to be late for work? Why was he so difficult? When she could soften him up he was wonderful, he was the best man in the world, but other times he was a citadel, and it was exhausting.

So it seemed a reprieve when, reaching the bottom of the mountain, she came to a little town called Kirby that had a local diner. "Girls, should we stop for milkshakes?" she asked.

Their sun-weakened cheers convinced her that they should.

"Good," she said, pulling into the dirt parking lot and climbing out. "A little sugar will perk you right up." The girls were dazed from sun and light; they lolled against their opposite doors, shoulders lobster pink, limbs loose with fatigue. Sam came out scowling, rubbing her eyes, her dress bunched up behind her legs. Nat reached for Liddie: There was sand crusted between the toddler's small fingers. Her nails were black crescents. Mica sparkled on the bridge of her nose beneath a line of dark-brown bangs.

It was two in the afternoon and the diner was mostly quiet. As soon as they set foot inside Nat felt out of place. She'd expected something brighter and cleaner but there was a dinginess to the place, grime in every crevice, a sense of not quite caring. In the far corner stood a jukebox that wasn't playing, and there was a small dance floor where no one danced. A black-haired waitress with oily, pitted skin picked at her fingernails, a young cowboy read a newspaper near the back, and a bearded man munched absently on a hamburger while two long-haired women looked out the window.

Well, they were already inside and the girls had expectations, so Nat ordered three milkshakes. When these arrived she sighed in relief. They stood like towers of promise with sky-high whipped cream, and cherries that left pink impressions in the clouds. Within minutes the sugar brought forth its promised energy and the girls were bouncing on the rubbery seats. Nat took them to look at the jukebox.

"We get five songs for a dollar," she read, flipping through the lists. "Oh, 'Charlie Brown' by the Coasters!" she said. "You'll like that one, it's funny. One of the guys says in this low voice, *'Why's everybody always pickin' on me?'*"

Liddie giggled, but Sam looked troubled. "Why are they?" she asked. "Why *are* they picking on him?"

The machine whirred, the opening guitar of "Charlie Brown" strummed in, and the girls grabbed their skirts and hopped up and down on the small dance floor. Their shoes clapped and their pinkish legs bounced, and they spun and teetered, laughing. Nat didn't want them to get too loud but she didn't want to rein them all the way in, either, because this was their day. They were out in the world and it was warm and sunny and she was not in the mood to be the grown-up.

When the song finished Liddie stood on tiptoe and said "Kiss, Mama," and Nat burst out laughing. At that moment, her daughters' happiness seemed so simple, so easily earned and free of adult corruption, she didn't even want to go home. *We could wander the West, we three. Nothing would tie us down!* Then the thought chilled her: What a terrible notion, selfish and sinful. Of course she wanted to go home.

And she was punished for having that thought at all, because Sam, spinning vigorously though the music had stopped, toppled sideways and knocked a glass sugar holder to the floor where it shattered. Nat and the girls stared at the sparkling, shard-pierced mound on the black-and-white tile.

"My *gosh*!" cried the waitress, roused from her stupor. She flung her hands in the air. "Would you watch what you're doing?"

"I'm so sorry." Nat grabbed a napkin, squatted, and pushed the sugar into a jagged pyramid. "She didn't mean to. Sam, apologize."

Sam stared at the expectant waitress and, in a fit of defiant self-loathing, stuck out her tongue.

The waitress and Nat both gasped. The spill was easily forgivable on its own but now, with Sam's awful little flourish, it seemed to have been almost intentional.

"Sam!" Nat shouted, standing up. The little girl, gripped by contrition, whirled and buried her face in Nat's skirt.

"Don't touch that," the waitress said to Nat, meaning the glass. "You'll cut yourself. I'll get the broom." She stalked into the kitchen. Nat stood flushed, her heart racing, patting Sam's shoulders. Her one consolation was that Paul was not there. He would have been mortified. She could imagine the silent car ride home while he stewed over how he'd raised such an ill-mannered child. She could almost hear his brain turning itself inside out on such occasions, the way he'd strain to make meaning out of what she'd insist was just some small thing.

The waitress returned with a broom. "Y'all were acting just crazy, flailing around like that. Of course something's gonna get broken."

"We weren't *flailing,*" Nat said. "She was just dancing."

"People *allow* their children to be rude these days. It's backwards. Adults are wrong and kids are right." She swept the sugar into the dustpan with short jabs.

Nat's face burned. Normally she would have remained silent, but she'd been having such a good day, and she did not want this crabby woman to brush away all the hours she'd just spent building something happy. "I'm sorry you have such an ax to grind," she began, "but it's only taken you a minute to sweep that up, and we *said* we were sorry."

The waitress opened her mouth to retort—*I cannot believe this,* Nat thought, *I cannot believe I am about to get into an argument with a waitress, I should stop myself, I should just leave*—when she heard a footfall behind her and turned. It was the young cowboy from the back of the diner. He had sandy hair and blue eyes and was no taller than Nat, and he wore a faded flannel shirt and dull boots. For a moment Nat feared he had come over to upbraid her, too, that she was about to be ganged up on by affronted townies, but his eyes were kind, and instead of speaking to the women he squatted near Sam. "You want to know what I did one time?" he quietly asked her. "I knocked over a whole crate of eggs." He leaned with his elbows on his knees, watching Sam for her reaction, as if he took her distress seriously and was not cutesily performing for adults.

Sam peeked one eye out from Nat's skirt. Nat, realizing her daughter was not going to respond, spoke up in the candy-coated voice of someone talking on behalf of a child. "How did you knock over a crate of eggs?"

"I was working at a friend's ranch a few years back," he said, to Sam, as if she and Nat were a ventriloquist act. "I wasn't old enough to drive, but I got bored and hopped into the truck, backed right into a pallet of eggs stacked against the wall. Can you imagine? Eggs and shells and goo everywhere, and the farmer came out and yelled at me and hit me with his hat."

Sam listened intently, her eyebrows lifted in friendly, quizzical half moons. "Did it hurt to get hit with a hat?"

"Not really. Just my pride."

"What's your pride?"

"Pride? It means your feelings. Not wanting to be embarrassed."

"Oh." Sam seemed to ponder this. "Does it go away?"

He chuckled. "Hopefully not. The pride part is a good thing. It's the getting embarrassed that's not so nice."

The waitress stood, holding her dustpan full of sugar-coated glass as if she were about to toss it in Nat's face. "Pride keeps people from acting stupid," she said, into the middle distance.

"How about kindness?" Nat snapped.

The cowboy soldiered on, ignoring them. "I'm twenty-five now," he was telling Sam, "which probably seems old to you, but I *still* do things that make me embarrassed. It's a bad feeling, but it always goes away."

Sam nodded. She smiled quickly, then jammed her head above Nat's knees again.

The cowboy got to his feet, his eyes darting between Nat and the waitress and finally settling on the waitress. "A mistake's a mistake. No use punishing people for them."

Nat beamed at him. How good of this chivalrous man to come over and side with them against that surly woman. She felt vindicated.

But the waitress watched him with a knowing expression in her dark eyes. "Too bad we can't all have someone like Esrom to come to our rescue," she said.

Nat's face grew hot: So they knew each other. She did not know why this embarrassed her, or maybe it just made her feel like more of an outsider.

He said, "You don't need anyone to come to your rescue, Corrie."

The waitress leaned on her broom for a moment and watched him. Her eyes changed from flinty to almost sad; deep lines framed the sides of her mouth. How old was she, Nat wondered—thirty? And why did Nat feel that she had somehow stepped into a situation of greater significance, that she had done something worse to this woman than spill sugar on her floor? The quietness of the diner resounded in her ears; its perch at the base of this remote mountain made her feel like she was at the edge of the world. She'd stopped so glibly, so trustingly in this little town, forgetting that it was a gritty place, like all such places that clung to survival; it did not exist to make her day happier. She had a tiny glimmer of insight into why, whenever she set out anywhere, Paul reminded her to be careful. He was used to people and places like these. She was not.

Corrie, now plainly avoiding Nat's gaze, turned and headed for the kitchen. "See you later, Ez," she said.

"Yep," he said, stepping back to allow a few people to pass: the bearded man and the two long-haired women who squeezed by without speaking, the bells on the door jingling behind them. Now the place was deserted. There was no sound other than the electrical hum of appliances, and no people but themselves. The cowboy headed to the kitchen—for a minute Nat thought he was following Corrie—and came back with a mop, which he swirled once over the sugary spot. It left a shiny circle on the scuffed floor.

"Thank you," Nat said. "I can't believe that was such a big deal."

He shrugged. "Wasn't a big deal. I expected Corrie would get testy. People are worked hard around here. This job is just the tip of the iceberg for her."

"Well, I certainly didn't mean to make things harder. It was really just a little sugar," and then, feeling her defiance flare up again and remembering it was probably Sam's rude gesture that had been the real problem, she stopped herself. *Let it go, Ms. Righteous Indignation.*

"So, y'all aren't from around here?" he asked.

"No, no. We're from Idaho Falls."

He smiled at her sincere reply, as if there were any chance he actually thought she was from there. "Well, hey, me, too. Just out here for the day fishing with some buddies. How long you lived in Idaho Falls?"

"Since June."

"Let me guess—military."

"Exactly! My husband works at the reactor testing station."

"One of those fancy scientists?"

"No, an operator." Nat bent to scoop up Liddie, whose head sagged instantly to her shoulder. "It's the opposite of fancy, I think."

He chuckled. "There were jobs less fancy before you-all got there."

"How *was* that, the town growing so big all of a sudden? It must've been strange."

"People have different opinions. But I think it was the best thing could have happened to Idaho Falls. You know what we had before you military folks got here? Steer and potatoes."

Nat wondered what he meant about people having different opinions. She thought of the bearded man and the two women who'd walked out, one of them staring at Nat with her mouth half-open. They did not seem like people enamored of change. She asked Esrom, "What do you do, in Idaho Falls?"

"Ranch work, mostly, but I'm trying to switch over to more stuff in town. I've been working at my uncle's auto body shop. I do snow removal in winter. That kind of thing."

"Mama, can we have another song?" Sam asked.

"Oh, honey, we've got to be getting home."

Sam, recovering, smiled up at Esrom. "I like your boots."

He knelt instantly. "You do? Can you believe they were once a snake?"

Her nose wrinkled. "What do you mean?"

"Well, they were a lot of snakes, I guess. These are their skins, all shined up and made into boots. Just like your shoes were once a cow."

Sam looked horrified.

To Nat he said, "I think I scared her." He turned back to Sam: "You know how you eat a roast beef sandwich, or a pot roast? That's the inside of the cow. The outside, you can make into all kinds of things—couches or shoes. That way we don't waste things."

"Oh," she said, tilting her Mary Janes this way and that. "What are Liddie's made of?"

Esrom squinted at Liddie's identical pair of shoes. He gave one a pinch. "Giraffe," he said.

"Really?" Sam said.

Nat smiled at him. The girls were captivated; their eyes darted after his every move. They were used to Paul, to gathering around him like baby birds pecking the words out of him; he adored them, but affection seemed always to take something out of him, and they all knew he'd be quiet five minutes down the road. Words and humor seemed to come to Esrom easily, as if he plucked them from the air at no personal cost.

"I'm sorry, girls, but it's time to go home," Nat said. She leaned in toward Esrom. "We'd better get out of here before they start asking you where babies come from." Then she laughed, a little alarmed by the saltiness of her own joke. Why did she do this, put her foot in her mouth whenever she met someone new?

The door opened and two men Esrom's age tumbled in. They raised their hand to the waitress, who was fiddling with the register now, and pulled up slightly when they saw Nat. "Hey, Ez," the shorter one called. "Ma'am," he added, a little questioningly, to Nat.

"Hello!" cheered Sam.

"I was just talking to your friend here," Nat said. "I found out we both live in Idaho Falls."

"Oh," the young man said. "Well, did you give her our card, Ez?"

Esrom started. "No, I didn't. Here," and he flipped his wallet from his back pocket. It was such soft, worn leather that it fell open in his hand. He passed Nat a business card: "Idaho Falls Auto Body" was written across the middle in skipped ballpoint ink. Nat had never seen a handwritten business card before, but she didn't feel it would be considerate to comment on it.

"You ever need car repairs, ma'am," Esrom's friend said, "we're the best there is."

"Or an all-right choice in Idaho Falls, anyway," added Esrom. "My uncle owns the shop, actually. Russ and I just work there."

"Well, thank you," Nat said. "It was very nice talking to you, and learning about boots."

Esrom squatted once more to shake Sam's hand. "See you later, friend."

Sam grinned. "See you later."

They headed for the door. Corrie, the waitress, was putting a nickel in the jukebox. Now that Esrom had befriended her, Nat felt generous: "I'm sorry about all that trouble," she said.

Corrie shrugged, nodded. She leaned her elbows against the machine as Johnny Cash warbled into the room, a song Nat recognized about a pretty local girl and the man who pined for her. "Ballad of a Teenage Queen," that was it. Nat tried to smile at her over their shared taste in music, but the waitress wouldn't look Nat's way.

Nat was not going to get anything out of the waitress, she supposed. She forced a smile anyway and herded the girls across the parking lot, into the car, arranging their tired bodies on the seats. She noticed the bearded man from the diner sitting in a car across from them, the two women in the backseat, none of them talking. What strange people. She realized she'd forgotten her purse and darted back inside, where Esrom was coming her way, holding the purse out to her.

"Silly me," she said. "Thank you." He smiled. Then, feeling bold and too curious to let it pass, she pointed at the car outside. "What's that man doing? Do you know him?"

Esrom followed her gaze. "Yeah, I know him." He looked momentarily concerned. "Why? Did he say something to you?"

"No. I just thought it was odd that he's sitting there."

Esrom's friends were watching them, so he started her toward the door. In a low voice he said, "That's Corrie's uncle. He waits for her to get off her shift and drives her home."

"Oh," Nat said, wondering why Corrie couldn't drive herself, feeling that there was more to this story, but not knowing him well enough to ask.

"You know," said Esrom, "next time you go to the Palisades, I wouldn't stop in Kirby."

"They don't like outsiders?"

"No."

"But are you really an insider? You don't seem like them."

He looked at her almost gratefully. "I'm a little of both, I guess," he said. "I'm an outsider who wants to be in, and an insider who wants the heck out." He laughed to lighten this and walked her into the parking lot. "It was nice to meet you—"

"Nat," she said, holding out her hand.

"Nat. I'm Esrom."

"I know. I mean, I heard."

"Take care, now."

"You, too," she said, opening the car door. "Maybe we'll see you in Idaho Falls."

"I'd like that," he said.

He walked back into the restaurant; Corrie looked up and spoke to him, and he leaned against the counter, chatting. What did they talk about? Nat imagined they'd known each other forever, were familiar in a way she, now a military wife, would never get to be with anyone other than Paul. Whatever Corrie's story was, Esrom carried a part of it, guarded it, and this made Nat feel strangely left out—as if, having met him minutes before, she was entitled to anything more than politeness.

She sang a little as the mountains flattened toward Idaho Falls, realizing as she did so that it was the Johnny Cash song Corrie had played on the jukebox. Now that she said the words her face flushed hot. *She had everything, it seems / Not a care, this teenage queen.*

PAUL

When his bad workday finally ended—having begun with his and Nat's argument, followed by the stuck rod that put everybody in a foul mood, then a couple more hours of barked orders from Franks while they ran late on everything—Paul clocked out with a sense of relief and stepped outside for a smoke. Late-afternoon sun glinted off the steel reactor and the chain-link fence. It was just after four; the bus would be there any minute.

Franks came out to join him. He lit a cigar; Paul raised his eyebrows.

"Neighbor had a baby," Franks said.

"Nice," said Paul. The cigar's smell was pungent, a cross between a spice chest and a barnyard. It sent Paul's mind on a five-second trip back to his youth, to the smell of tobacco in small rooms, mingling with all the kinds of mustiness the cabins of his childhood contained: deerskin, flannel, moss, mud, yeast, seeping dampness, body odor, stiff and drying boots, cedar, and pine. An uneasiness pinged in his chest and he thought yet again of Nat, angry with him that morning; he wanted to get home, smooth things over. She was probably driving back from the reservoir now. He hoped she was driving carefully and then recalled that she probably wouldn't appreciate the sentiment. *I'm a good driver,* she'd said. And, *I don't understand why you're being so stingy*. The way she'd bristled with hurt as she drove away, not turning her head to smile or wave—Christ, he'd apologize first if he had to; he'd do anything.

Franks interrupted his thoughts: "They're stopping the inspections, you know."

Paul looked at him. All afternoon, Franks had seemed unwilling to talk about what had happened. Now he wanted to chat Paul up about it? Paul was almost enjoying the pain of brooding over Nat. It made him feel linked to her, if nothing else, and his mind wanted to linger there, not in this gravel parking lot with Franks.

"I wanted to talk to you earlier," Franks said, "but I was too pissed. I needed to cool down. Besides, I didn't want the kid to hear." Franks always called Webb "the kid," as if he were six years old.

"Okay," Paul said. He waited for Franks to continue.

"This past May, just before you got here, we failed two inspections in a row."

"Two?" Paul had suspected they'd failed one, given certain signs of disrepair he'd seen around, but two was a bigger deal.

"The supervisors noticed all this boron falling off the rods when we lifted them to the top of the core for the inspections." Franks gestured with his cigar, to the top of an imaginary control rod and down again. "So Harbaugh and Richards called the inspections off."

"I've seen the boron peeling," Paul said. "I thought that was strange." Boron was used in most reactors; it absorbed uranium neutrons, slowing the speed of the reaction, but usually it was built into the core itself.

"When they were building this reactor," Franks explained, "the engineers forgot to put the boron inside the core, so they just tack-welded it on afterwards. Thought it would work as well, but it doesn't. Yeah, the engineers, our best and brightest." He rolled his eyes. "Lifting the rods all the way to the top for inspections made even more boron fall off. So to keep the reactor from running too hot all the time, Harbaugh and Richards decided there wouldn't be any more inspections until we get a new core."

"They can just decide that?"

"They explained it to the engineers, I guess, and the engineers agreed."

"Why?"

"*You* know why. Because those eggheads are ashamed of the terrible job they did on this thing in the first place."

Paul shook his head, but he understood. If he'd done a shit-for-brains job on something, he wouldn't want other people examining it, either. But the news about the boron was startling. If boron was piling up at the bottom of the reactor, the rods could be higher than they thought—closer to the four inches they'd been warned never to go past. How could Richards not take this seriously?

"Sergeants are supposed to look after their men," Paul said.

Franks chuckled almost bitterly, working a piece of grit forward on his tongue and pinching it off. "Our Sarge, the hero," he said. "You think he wants to botch next year's chance to promote by screwing with this rinky-dink reactor? People will think, *He can't handle the CR-1; he can't handle much of anything*. You can get discharged over stuff like this, especially if they're maybe looking for a reason to not promote you anyway. Which, in his case, we know they are."

"He's throwing us under the bus."

"It's too late for him to do any different. What's he gonna say now: 'Whoops, forgot to mention that shit's been hitting the fan over here for half a year'?"

"But Harbaugh, too? I thought he might have more integrity."

Franks gave him a dubious look. "You've seen the man. He's dying. Would you want to fight this fight if you had half a year left to go? That poor fellow just wants to go home and water his begonias and sleep. His wife will be well set up; maybe they'll name the Admin building after him. He's not going to mess with all that."

Paul gave a bleak laugh—there sat the Admin building, left over from WWII. He wouldn't want his initials scraped into a board there, let alone his name engraved on a plaque to claim the place. But he saw that Franks was not joking.

He began to understand why Richards had flattered him about being "quiet" and "studious." What a fool he'd been to take it for praise. It had nothing to do with "study" and everything to do with being passive and stupid, too cowed to raise a ruckus. They knew straight off he'd keep his head down and go about his business; he remembered they'd complimented Franks, too. "Have *you* ever thought of taking this higher than Harbaugh?" Paul asked.

Franks looked slightly shocked. "I've never even talked to anyone higher than Harbaugh. Don't know if I could place them in a lineup." He tilted his cigar toward himself and studied it for a moment before looking up. "I'd stay with the program," he offered, his eyes sincere. "There's no need to stick your neck out. We're all in this together. We *can* fix things on our own; it's just a little more work. None of the supes wants to hear about a bunch of little dumbfuck problems we could solve ourselves." He glanced back toward the reactor. "I'm not saying we should do this, that, or the other thing. I just wanted to keep you in the loop."

"But what happens if things get worse?"

"We don't know that they'll get worse."

"They won't get *better*."

"We just have to keep the machine running till we get a new core."

"When will that be?"

"Maybe this winter. Soon's I hear, I'll let you know. Try not to worry too much."

Paul grunted. He understood discretion and self-reliance, and Franks had been at this longer than he had; maybe he knew when to worry and when not to.

"You know how humiliating it would be," Franks said, as if reading Paul's mind, "if this reactor's problems were all laid out for everybody to see, all the navy brass out here, all the air force? We can't lose our honor."

"I know."

"If we keep exercising the rods daily, and we don't take 'em out for the inspections, they should last a long time. This core's lasted four years already; we can get another one out of it. We'll just be extra careful."

"That's true," Paul said. "We'll be careful."

They had fallen into a soothing sort of call-and-response, as if the troubles plaguing the reactor were bad thoughts or demon spirits.

"Hey," Franks said, standing quickly, "there's the bus." Paul got to his feet also, holding his tin lunch pail, and Webb came jogging out with a bright hello. Poor, clueless kid. Screw this junky place—Paul just wanted to get home to his family. He toed his cigarette butt into the dirt and waited next to his shift mates without speaking, nearly overwhelmed by his longing to get away from the reactor, to feel the bus pull up on cozy Main Street with its barbershop and bustling pigeons, to look along the curb and spy the yellow Fireflite parked up ahead where, whether she wanted to or not, Nat would be waiting for him.

II

THE MAN OF THE HOUR

PAUL

Winter 1959–60

INDIAN SUMMER STUCK AROUND IDAHO FALLS FOR A FEW MORE weeks. Paul feared they were all getting just a little too comfortable, forgetting that winter had a debt to extract.

Still, he was grateful for the reprieve. He was worried about Nat and the girls, housebound during a harsh winter when they were unaccustomed to cold in the first place. Nat had spent every year of her life in San Diego, with the exception of their one winter in Virginia while Paul was in reactor school. Even there, they'd had only a few dustings of snow that usually melted before Paul scraped off the car.

Idaho was another story. The weather finally did change, and it happened in the span of one late October day. Hard flecks of snow blew out in front of a rolling wind, leaving wet spatters on the windows. The sky settled into a low steel gray. It was as if they lived in an entirely different place from the gentle, honey-gold one they'd enjoyed the day before.

Nat hadn't brought up the car again since their argument, so Paul didn't, either. He was relieved that she let it go. Even mentioning the car might bring back the tight, queasy feel of the argument, and he didn't want to let that mood back into their house. Besides, once snow began to fall she wouldn't want to drive. She'd said that herself—that driving in snow would make her nervous.

Meanwhile, the cold camped out for the long haul. Temperatures fell into the forties, the thirties, and then the teens for a couple of blistering, miserable weeks. So *this* was the Idaho winter people had warned them about. The days felt like a narrow tunnel of time, all dim early morning and shadowy evening with a handful of icy, rayless hours in between. They wore coats that went down to their ankles and shuffled to and from the house when they had to. Snow gathered on the front lawn and never melted. Paul's bus ride to work was downright freezing. The men hunched into their jackets and tucked their heads, shouldering against the thin bus windows, their knuckles bluing as they gripped the lapels of their coats.

As for Nat and the girls, they were good sports. Nat filled vases around the house with bright, gaudy silk flowers. She and the girls made construction paper hearts and stars in pink and yellow and red. The living room began, in fact, to look like a preschool classroom. Dried glue formed hard spots on the carpet; scissor clippings drifted across the floor. Paul never knew quite what he'd find when he came home from work. He didn't mind, so long as everyone was happy, but then one afternoon he walked up the short shoveled walk, arches of snow on either side, and stepped through the front door to find the girls alone in the living room, banging on pots and pans, and Nat in bed, fully clothed with the lights off at the back of the house. She wasn't sick; she just felt a little blah, she said.

The next day after work, he stopped by the electronics shop downtown and came home with a seventeen-inch black-and-white RCA Victor television. It was built into a fat cabinet with splayed wooden legs and it looked like a pig on ice skates. He had never cared for TV—its jarring flashes of gray light, the canned laughter like a hiccup in your brain—but when Nat saw him elbow through the door with it, she grabbed his face and kissed him. He'd feared she might say it was too small, or wish aloud that he'd splurged for color, but she seemed truly happy with the thing, and for the rest of the winter it was a staple of her and the girls' days. Now when Paul came home from work Sam and Liddie were lying on the living room floor, nicely dressed and watching *Lassie,* while Nat made chicken à la king a few feet away in the kitchen.

When the snow finally began to melt and tips of green peeked out from the mud, Paul gathered his courage enough to bring up the car again. The TV purchase had made him slightly addicted to keeping Nat happy. So he waited until she'd had a very good day with the girls—a nice conversation with another mom buying groceries at the PX, a dinner that turned out particularly well—and when they settled into bed he asked Nat if she'd like to start taking the Fireflite one day a week. She'd said yes, she would like that very much, and kissed him. He was so pleased with her response that he whispered in her ear, asking if she remembered that night out in the backyard, last June, with the crickets singing all around them. She smiled when he said this, looked at him for a long moment, and slid her nightgown off over her head. He was surprised by how pale she'd grown indoors all winter. It was the same start he'd felt catching his own reflection sidelong in a mirror after basic, his beard shaved off for the first time in years: as if something were missing, or more vulnerable. She'd been pared to a sort of quiet mystery, and he was intrigued by the change.

So on Fridays when he worked the day or mid shift, Nat kept the car and he got a ride to the bus stop with Franks. The arrangement worked out fine; in fact, Paul felt embarrassed by his earlier reluctance. Though he didn't love the extra proximity to his shift leader's corny jokes and halitosis, he began to find Franks slightly endearing. As soon as Paul climbed into the car Franks would say, "This is from Brownie," cradling over a muffin or square of coffee cake that still steamed as Paul unwrapped it. Paul always ate one half and saved the other for Webb, who, as a bachelor, had no one to bake for him.

As for the reactor, it continued to trouble the operators, resisting their best fixes and efforts. No new core arrived. From time to time the men would ask one another when it was coming, had they heard anything, had any of the engineers been poking around? But there was no word, and when they questioned Sergeant Richards he just said, "I'm as eager as anybody else, boys." The rods still stuck, the reactor still ran hot, but they always managed to pull things together at the last minute. "Good old army ingenuity," said Franks, who was developing a twitch in his right eye.

Soon enough, the tour would be over and Paul could get out of there. He was starting to fantasize about it, the relief of driving away from the Idaho line in any direction, knowing he'd never have to work another nerve-racking shift on the CR-1, never have to tell a prodding Nat that things were fine and she shouldn't worry. He realized that he was lying to her daily. It was in her own best interest but he still felt guilty. He could feel the lies stacking up against him like a wall built one pebble at a time, and it made him tense.

Just wait it out, he told himself. *Just hang in there and be patient.* In the meantime, work was work, and if he could get through those hours there was the brief miracle of freedom on the other side. So Paul worked the day shift, the mid shift, the night shift, coming home while the girls were eating breakfast, or sometimes just before dinner, or sometimes in the middle of the night when the entire house was asleep and he cozied up to Nat in their drafty back bedroom, hearing her murmur hello and drape her warm arm over him, thinking it nearly amazing that he could be out in that dark, nothingness world and return to this little pointy-roofed house where all the life that mattered to him lay.

NAT

Spring 1960

When spring finally came, the world was feverish with it. Birds called well before light, shaking the big tree in the front yard. Nat let the girls puddle-stomp up the sidewalk until gray water ran down their shins. She opened the windows even before it was quite warm enough, and made a canned peach cobbler as if it were already high summer.

Paul's birthday came around on June 4 and he said he didn't want a fuss, but that was just too bad: Nat loved birthdays. She spent the night before trying to dream up some gift she and the girls could give, but because Paul never asked for anything she finally decided to just surprise him. She and the girls would bring him balloons and pick him up from work, sparing him the bus ride home.

They'd never showed up unannounced before; she hoped he would like it and not be ruffled by their sudden appearance. Well, it was too late now. She pulled up at the chain-link fence outside the CR-1 and was greeted by the day security man, who passed her into the gravel lot with instructions to stay by her car. On her lap fluttered a sheet of paper with the directions she'd jotted down, dictated by Brownie Franks, whom she had phoned that morning and finally pried the necessary information out of after listening to a recap of a recent book Brownie had read and begging out of an invitation to a Tupperware party.

In the backseat, each girl clutched a balloon: Liddie's red, Sam's yellow. Sam's muffled voice pressed through hers. "Is he coming? Do you see him?"

"Not yet," said Nat, craning. She felt nearly as excited as her daughters. The girls squeezed their faces against the thin-stretched rubber, stifling giggles. When Nat glanced back she saw Liddie's nose spread wide, her face tinted red as if she'd blown a giant bubble of gum that was about to burst.

"How old is Daddy going to be again?" Sam asked.

"Twenty-six," said Nat. She glanced at her watch: It was ten to four. The day shift was almost over. When the door of the building opened she nearly jumped with excitement, but it wasn't Paul; it was Master Sergeant Richards.

Of course he saw them right away, the only other car in the parking lot and with balloons in the back, no less. He loped toward them, hands in his pockets, dimpled smile. Nat slid from the car with a little wave, clicking the door shut. She did not really wish to talk to him, and had mostly avoided doing so (they passed each other in the neighborhood on occasion, and they'd had to make brief small talk at a work party one winter evening, though Paul circled her around the room and kept her mostly out of Richards's orbit). Still, he was Paul's boss and, as she had no real choice in the matter, it was important to be polite. She prayed he wouldn't bring up their odd encounter a year before, that bizarre argument she'd witnessed in his driveway. Even thinking about it made her nervous: Richards clutching his face, shouting "What in the hell, woman?" Jeannie's sneer: *"I see you've found a new favorite dress, Nat."*

Richards reached Nat and stood, smiling. The car tilted and bumped as the girls rollicked in the backseat. Nat pretended not to notice. "Hello, Master Sergeant," she said.

"So, what's this? Have I won a new car?" Richards asked.

"It's Paul's birthday," Nat said. "We thought we'd surprise him at work." She loved the day each week that she got the Fireflite, even though all she usually did was the grocery shopping.

"Collier's birthday!" said Richards. "I don't suppose he'd have told us. What do you have in there, a caged tiger?"

"It's us!" said Sam, faintly, from inside.

"Well, hello." Richards bent and waved in the window. Sam looked at her mother hopefully but Nat made no move to open the door. Still, Richards's joking manner with the girls made her feel a bit more at ease.

"He's thirty-six!" shouted Sam, nearly splatting against the car window. "I have a balloon for him!"

"Me, too," said Liddie.

"He's not thirty-six," said Nat. Then she thought maybe this sounded too emphatic, as if thirty-six were impossibly old when Richards must be somewhere not far from that, so she repeated, "I mean, he's just not," which, it turned out, neither helped nor clarified.

Richards leaned his back against the car. He pulled out a pack of cigarettes and tapped out two. "Wind's picking up," he said. He lit hers and then his own.

"I noticed that. Thank you," she said, for the cigarette, though the smell alone made her queasy. That very morning she'd gotten the phone call from the doctor's office: "The rabbit died," the receptionist said. Nat would be having another baby sometime in early December.

She could hardly believe it: It was a surprising, overwhelming gift. She and Paul hadn't been trying *not* to have a baby, really, but their intimacy hadn't been consistent, either. Paul was under stress at work. He often came home quiet, chomping on his beer by the front window like a horse with a bit in its mouth. When Nat asked him what was wrong he muttered this and that: personalities on the job, sore back from too much lifting, his incompetent boss.

Other days he was lighter, smiling, catching her eye across the dinner table when the girls did something goofy. And he surprised her on occasion: bringing home the television set, offering to share the car. It must have been one of those days that the baby happened, and Nat liked the thought. She hoped the news would make him happy—that he'd focus on the sweetness of a newborn rather than the practicality of another mouth to feed. (A thought that frightened her a little, too—another child crying in the bassinet, clamoring for her attention, growing bigger by the day—but what could she do but be happy, and welcome the new little soul into their family, forever and ever?)

She decided she'd tell Paul after the girls went to sleep, a private time when they could relax and drink in the news together. They'd lie on the bed and speculate if this would be another girl, or their first boy; dark eyes like the rest of them, or blue like Nat's genetically underrepresented mother.

But for now, it was time to celebrate Paul's birthday. Time to inoculate him against gloom, to sow the seeds for her happy announcement later in the evening.

Being forced to mingle with Master Sergeant Richards before seeing Paul was a small glitch in her plan. Richards leaned against her car, smoking contentedly, his body blocking her view of the girls in the backseat. Sam's face must have been right behind his backside, but he didn't seem to mind covering her up. Nat thought she would have felt awkward pressing her bottom right over the face of someone's child who peered through a window.

"What about you?" he asked. Nat waited politely. He appeared to forget his question and then suddenly recall it. "When's your birthday?"

She hesitated. "Summer."

"You're a summer baby."

She forced a quick smile. "Yes."

The car tipped from the girls' careening; she spied flashes of their clothes and the bright balloons. They were clambering into the front seat now. She turned her head to peer at the reactor building. "Will the men be out soon?"

"Hm?" Richards swung toward her, and then she had an inkling: He was tipsy. She smelled it on his breath, saw it in the too-wide swivel his head made. His delayed, walleyed joshing. She stepped back, her eyes darting to the girls in the front seat.

He leaned in, smiling. Then, to her horror, he began to recite: "Shall I compare thee to a summer's day? Thou are more lovely and more tempting."

She froze.

"Rough winds do shake the darling buds of May," he murmured, with a distracted, self-regarding air.

"That's lovely," she said finally. "That's—is that Shakespeare?"

"Yes, Shakespeare," he said. "You're smart." He blew a smoke ring, or tried to, with a steady *pop pop pop* of his lips, his neck retracting like a seal's. Coupled with his sudden poetry she felt as if he were having some quiet, almost dignified seizure.

"I don't meet many women who know poetry, who know Shakespeare," he said in a burdened way.

"It was a lucky guess." She held her cigarette and averted her eyes, not sure what to say. "Do you read a lot of poetry?" she asked. "Other than Shakespeare?"

"Not really, no."

She nodded, looking toward the building and its closed door.

Then, to her immense surprise, he reached out and took a strand of her hair in two fingers, tucking it behind her ear. It was a gentle movement, not exactly lecherous, and she did not know how to extricate herself without insulting him. His cupped palm lingered at the back of her neck. He smiled at her as if the mere sight of her brought back a long-ago memory of a summer they had shared together, a beach house, tumultuous love. Where on earth was Paul?

A movement caught her eye and she quickly turned her head, but it was not Paul. It was a very thin silhouette, a stick figure almost, a man who headed first for the shallow dugout patch that marked the bus stop. He spied Nat and Sergeant Richards, however, and after a moment's hesitation started toward them.

"Hello, Master Sergeant," said the young man, smiling stiffly, and Nat recognized him as the one they called "the kid," Specialist Webb. He looked at her as if embarrassed for them all and said, "Hello, Mrs. Collier." Then he noticed the balloons and the ecstatic bouncing of the girls in the front seat, and gestured to them with a quizzical smile.

"Oh. It's Paul's birthday," Nat said, tucking her hair behind her ear over and over, the way Richards had done. "We're here to surprise him."

Webb's face lit up in a wide, unselfconscious smile. "He has no idea!"

he said. Then he stood, keeping his place between Nat and Sergeant Richards, and seemed unsure of what to do next. Nat noticed that he had a small tic, a pull on the edge of his smile. Here, there, again.

"Well," Richards said, "I guess I'll be moving on. Webb, Nat."

"Have a good day, Master Sergeant," Webb said. Nat nodded but said nothing. For several seconds, however, Richards simply stood. Webb watched him with a sheepish but steadfast expression, and Nat realized that he had surmised Richards's state and was looking out for her. She felt a swell of gratitude.

"I guess I'll be going," Richards said again.

"All right then, Master Sergeant."

"Don't you forget, we're all going out tonight. Tell Collier," he said, pointing to Nat.

"Right," Webb said. "We'll meet at the Calico."

"Oh," said Nat, her heart sinking, "tonight?"

Webb nodded. "Slocum made shift supervisor so we're all going out. Franks is giving me and your husband a ride. This was just planned spur of the moment," he added, as if wanting to make sure Paul didn't get an earful from her later.

"I see," Nat said, trying to cover her disappointment. Today of all days—on his birthday, and with her news. The operators did not socialize outside work often, and if Richards were organizing this, Paul couldn't really say no.

"So what's the Calico?" she asked, forcing cheer into her voice.

Webb and Richards exchanged a glance. "It's just a bar," Richards said. "We'll be having a few beers together, give Slocum a hard time."

"Oh. All right." She supposed this was all the answer she'd get. She let herself feel one good strong wash of self-pity—so pure it was almost pleasurable—and tried to let it go. She could tell Paul later. They'd give him his balloons now, and when he got home she'd deliver the news.

Richards winked at her. "Your Paul might make shift supervisor someday, too."

Nat stared at him, suddenly bristling and not even sure what made her angriest: his smug, simpering tone; the "Your Paul" as if he were talking about an infant son; "might" dropped coyly into the mix like a turd in a punch bowl. Of *course* he would make shift supervisor; every man did, in turn. You'd have to be incompetent not to. She twisted sideways, looking off at the wind sock in the distance.

And with that, the sergeant took his wobbling leave, drifting to his creamsicle car. He stood by it for a moment, climbed inside and sat unmoving, and finally started it up and glided away. Nat slitted her eyes after him. When it reached the main road the car let out a loud grunt, a flatulent grinding of tires; it chewed gravel and lurched for the highway.

There was a muffled commotion from Nat's car. She turned to see Sam near the windshield calling out to Webb, "Excuse me! Is our daddy coming out yet?"

She opened the door. The girls clambered up over the folded passenger seat and slid to the ground, their balloons bobbing into everything on the way out. The wind shot the balloons to the end of their strings, lifted the girls' skirts, pulled their dark hair sideways. They grinned shyly at Webb, glad to have another participant in this birthday surprise.

"Hold tight to those balloons," Nat said. "Don't let go. You'll be so disappointed if you lose them."

"There he is!" Sam shouted, and she and Liddie ran. Nat looked up and saw Paul stride from the building, his businesslike walk, head down. When he saw the girls he stopped in surprise, held open his arms, and laughed.

"I guess I'll be going then," said Webb, starting off toward Franks's car. "Good afternoon, Mrs. Collier."

"Nice talking with you," she called. She smoothed her skirt and patted her heated cheeks. So Richards had been a bother; so she wouldn't get to spend the evening with Paul, or even drive him home after coming all this way. It was all right.

Paul knelt by the girls now as they talked his ear off, hopping up and down. She was relieved to see that he didn't mind their ignoring the bus rule, which of course she knew about but just felt like breaking this one time, this celebratory day. She had paid for it by enduring Richards and hoped now to be rewarded, too—and she was, as Paul came toward her grinning with a girl under each arm, the delight of seeing them written plain on his face, even as Liddie's red balloon slipped loose and they all said *Oh!* as it whipped like a kite on the brisk wind, smaller and smaller into the sky.

PAUL

THE BOYS FROM THE CR-1 WERE OUT ON THE TOWN, AND EVEN if the town were the size of a postage stamp they weren't about to care.

They'd all hauled over to the Calico Saloon after the day shift, leaving behind three cheerless shift mates who couldn't partake in the fun (no way around it; three were always sacrificed for the greater good). Nat had driven off with the girls, and Paul wished he could have just gone home with them; it had been such a surprise to see them there, bright spots of color and *life* in that dull gravel parking lot. The girls' enthusiasm shone from their little bodies, and Nat seemed somehow prettier than ever with what looked like a dozen emotions working their way across her face. The shy way she hung back from the girls, tucked her hair behind her ear, and kissed him. And maybe he was just imagining it (it was entirely possible that he was imagining it) but her hug seemed to have something extra in it—her breasts were somehow involved; he'd felt them against his chest with more prominence than usual, so what was going on there? Was this some new, bedroom kind of hug she was trotting out to make him a little crazy before he had to climb into yet closer proximity with, dear God, his dull, stinky, large-footed shift mates, all elbows and Adam's apples and collared shirts as they piled into Franks's car to meet the other guys out in the red-light district on the outskirts of town?

There had always been a small red-light district at the edge of Idaho

Falls, as with any town founded on religious absolutism, but with the recent influx of military the area had boomed. The guys from the CR-1 favored the Calico, which seemed to have been there before time began. Dank, cinereal, with red-and-green tile floors, heavily knotted pine walls smoke-darkened over the years like a chamber in an underground mine, it whispered of gold rush days, high jinks, maybe a man or two cut down mid-celebration with gold nuggets in his hand. Now it did a steady, subdued business, a real drinker's place darkened by shadows, the slow clink of glasses, Tennessee Ernie Ford on the jukebox as Paul and his shift mates walked in.

Some people say a man is made outta mud / A poor man's made outta muscle and blood.

They were joining Richards, Kinney, and Slocum, who were already seated, sharing a pitcher. Slocum and Kinney had been off work that day; they looked refreshed, showered, and combed like little boys. Richards had worked the day shift—Paul had seen his car in the lot—but he hadn't glimpsed his boss till now.

Paul took a seat between Franks and Webb at the long table; what a trio they made, inseparable, like girlfriends. From the walls gazed the sorrowful faces of a dozen mounted animals. Pickled eggs blobbed in glass jars on the bar counter; the wood tabletop was soft and oily beneath his hand. Big Gitte, the bartender's stern and half-deaf wife, slapped a bowl of peanuts and a tiny napkin in front of him.

"What's with this fuckin' wind?" Richards asked, grinning around at them. His early coarseness absolved them all in advance: This was a man's night out, no ladies in sight (Big Gitte did not count), so they could talk like men and act like men and be as bawdy and crass as they pleased.

Franks spoke with authority. "It comes down out of the mountains," he said.

"What does?" asked Webb, practically bouncing in his chair, then realizing he didn't care and dropping the subject. "Isn't this a great place?" He was so happy to be out of both the reactor and his bachelor apartment that he grinned and bobbed, his foot jiggling the lower rung. "I come here a couple times a week. I can't believe this is your first time out here." He pointed at Paul's head and called to the men at the other end of the table, "This is Collier's first time out here!"

"That's because I'm married, Webb," Paul said. "Married men don't come here."

"But you *are* here," said Richards with a smirk.

"Guess that's true," said Paul. He avoided Richards's eyes and smiled at Webb's enthusiasm instead. He liked Webb, as flaky and dumb as he could sometimes be. He was just young, "young as a fresh shit" as Franks liked to say. Other than four weeks of boot camp followed by reactor school, this was Webb's first tour anywhere, ever, the first time he wasn't being constantly tested or hollered at or made to crawl through mud. No wonder he seemed so nonsensically happy.

Gitte returned to the table and Webb beamed as if she were his own grandma. She stared him down with no apparent trace of recognition but brought him a Miller High Life. He smiled from ear to ear, saying, "See? She knows exactly what I get."

"The champagne of beers," Kinney said.

"A toast," said Richards, raising a glass. "To Slocum, you son of a bitch, for making shift supervisor. It's about goddamn time."

"Hear, hear," said Webb.

Slocum, now officially a son of a bitch, grinned and tossed back a long draught. He was one of the older guys, midthirties, heavyset and equally heavy eyed, his thick skin punched with divots. He'd always seemed a little dull to Paul, not friendly or unfriendly, just a sort of bulk lurking on the edge of their group.

"And to Collier," said Webb. When everyone looked at Webb he said, "It's his birthday."

"Oh, right!" said Franks. "To Collier—" he paused, apparently trying to think of a toast. His face twitched and reddened with the effort, like one of the *Tic-Tac-Dough* contestants.

"I've got it," said Webb. "Here's to you, here's to me—"

"Oh, God," Franks said.

"And here's to the girls who lick us where we pee."

"Thank you for that," said Paul.

"You're a regular Keats," Franks observed. He turned to Paul. "Happy birthday," he said, patting Paul's shoulder with sudden sincerity.

Slocum started in on some long, impossibly macho tale, so Paul studied the row of frozen ungulates staring down at him from the wall: moose, elk, white-tailed deer.

"I can get you a date with one of those if you like, Collier," Richards called. "You look pretty interested."

Paul chuckled in spite of himself.

"That caribou-looking thing is hot for you," said Kinney. He slurped his beer, glanced at Richards for approval.

"Collier," Richards said with sudden brusqueness, "we're all tired of this quiet superiority thing you've got going on."

"I'm not superior to anybody," Paul said, surprised.

"He isn't. I can vouch for that," said Franks. Everyone laughed, including Paul, glad to turn the conversation from wherever Richards was trying to take it.

"I want you all to come to my wedding," Webb said.

"You're getting married?" asked Kinney, dubiously.

"Hoping to. Her name's Vanna, met her here in town, and she's the best."

"What's so great about her?" Richards wanted to know.

"Everything."

"Is she legal?"

"Of course," said Webb. "She graduates next year. She's not Mormon, even."

"Well," said Richards, raising his glass again, "congratulations." He stood halfway from his seat.

"Here we go," said Franks.

"Here's to gunpowder and pussy!" Richards said. "Live by one, die by the other, and learn to love the smell of both." Franks whistled and Kinney commenced a quiet, effete clap, as if he were watching golf. *What a suck-up,* Paul thought.

They talked and drank until the windows grew dark, and Paul was relieved to feel his head start to swim. This was more pleasant; it made everything easier.

"Where'd Sloke go?" he heard Richards ask.

Paul glanced around. He hadn't noticed Slocum leave but now registered his empty pint glass pooling on the waxy counter.

"Beats me," said Webb.

"Little boys' room," offered Franks.

"Here he comes. Here's the man of the hour!" said Richards.

Slocum reappeared across the smoky bar, a tall dark-haired woman on his arm. The men quieted and turned to look. From a distance she seemed a showstopper; as she neared, Paul could see that she wasn't quite. Still, she was a woman in a roomful of men, and Slocum strutted in as if he'd bagged a string of partridges one-handed while they all sat on their asses slurping pints.

"Well, hello there," said Richards, his manner instantly smoothing over. The woman didn't reply. She perched on Slocum's knee, smoking. Paul noticed the elegant lines of her arm, her long fingers, her impossibly soft-looking skin like browned butter. Her facial features were sharp, and the oiliness of fading makeup gave them a blurred quality; her eyes, small and close set, darted around the room unsmiling. She wore fitted blue pants, cowboy boots, and a red western shirt with fringe all the way around her upper arms and to the buttons, which were open enough to prompt Paul to avert his eyes at the last second. It was obvious that, in spite of her pointy face, her figure was a sight to behold.

"Well," said Franks, turning to his beer, "don't he look like the cat who ate the canary."

"No one's looking at him," said Richards. "What's your name, sweetheart?"

"This is Ree," Slocum announced, his wide face glistening. "I met her out in the parking lot."

"Where you from, Ree?"

She paused as if waiting to see whether Slocum would answer for her again. "Blackfoot," she said, in a slightly dry voice. She dangled her cigarette over her shoulder to Slocum's lips. He sucked like a delighted greedy baby, and Paul's stomach turned.

Richards ordered everyone shots. "What do you like to do, Ree?" he asked, apparently unable to think about anything else.

"This," she said, without looking at him.

"Do you have any friends?"

Slocum's hand roved across the fringe of her shirt. She swatted it away. "Me and Rose charge ten bucks," she said. "That's nonnegotiable."

"Ten bucks!" cried Webb.

Richards asked, "Where's Rose?"

"I'll call her." Ree's feet touched the floor when she sat on Slocum's lap, and she stood in one movement, nearly as tall as any of them. Sloke scampered after her. "We're going to my place," he called back to them, "we'll meet up there."

Richards downed his shot. "This party's not over," he said. He stood and shoved his keys into Paul's hand. "You drive."

"Me?" said Paul. "Webb and I came with Franks." He felt a dull, gathering repugnance and wanted to be home.

"I don't feel like driving," Richards said. "I need to save myself."

"For *what*?"

"She's an Injun," Franks blurted, leaning in. "You all know that, right?" He raised his hands. "No thanks, I don't play with Injuns." He said this as if he had a long and turbulent personal history with them.

Paul stood. His head swam; his legs felt strangely light. "Drop me off at home, will you, Franks?"

"Nope," said Richards. "You got my keys, you're driving. Gents, let's go."

Paul cursed, turning away. He walked out into the parking lot, struck by the wind and the grassy, wet smell of fresh rain and mud. He didn't want to be Richards's personal babysitter. Ree made him uncomfortable; she looked like a taller version of Nat, gone native, and he was hopelessly transfixed by her breasts. No good could come of any of this. But there were the keys in his hand, the satiny Coupe de Ville just feet ahead of him. Richards wandered out of the Calico, leaning on Webb's shoulders; Slocum and Ree got into Sloke's car, Kinney in the backseat. Paul rubbed his eyes. He could not stay here with Big Gitte, that was for sure.

The leather seat was welcoming, kidskin-soft. The Coupe started up gently, and Paul couldn't help but appreciate it. He'd never driven a car like this. Next to him in the passenger seat, Richards gave a soft snore.

APPARENTLY, THE TEN DOLLARS *was* negotiable. By the time they got to Sloke's apartment, Ree had been talked down to two. She and Sloke headed into the bedroom while Webb, Kinney, Paul, and the newly restored Richards passed a church key and dived into a six-pack. Paul tried not to be sore; Slocum's dust-spewing couch and greasy, water-filled sink—inverted bowls rising out of it like small, sad islands—gave him a morbid cheer, so pathetic was the life of a bachelor.

"I wonder when Rose will get here," said Richards. "Do you think Rose could be prettier than Ree? She can't be taller. That's a tall woman, Ree."

The men considered this. There seemed to be nothing more to say about it. Idly Kinney said, "I wonder how the night shift's going."

"Don't talk about *work,*" Richards said.

"It's probably going shitty," said Webb, with the sort of brazen, plastered honesty Paul could not help but admire.

Richards bristled. "What do you mean?"

"We can hardly go an hour without some false fire alarm being triggered, and then the whole goddamn fire department has to traipse out and inspect things." Webb looked to Paul, who didn't feel like getting into it, but didn't want to leave his friend hanging, either.

"The fire chief's about ready to kill us," he admitted.

"What *is* it with your shift?" Richards gestured to Webb and Paul with his beer. "Why are you the only ones complaining?" They looked to Kinney.

"It's happening on every shift," Paul said. Kinney remained silent.

"We've got to raise and lower those goddamn rods every night," Webb blazed on, undaunted. "I can't believe Combustion Engineering hasn't shut the thing down." He slurped a wash of beer past his thin cheeks, swallowed loudly, and wiped his mouth with the back of his hand. "What are we hanging on for, anyway? We were a prototype. They know how to make a reactor like ours now. We don't even *power* anything except our own damn Admin building."

"You're depressing us," said Kinney, and Webb punctuated his thoughts with a dismal, "Fuck."

Richards opened his mouth to speak, but luckily for them all there was a crunch of tires outside. A car door opened and closed, and then the car drove away. "That must be Rose!" Kinney said, and after a moment of desperate suspense, there was a knock on the door and it opened. As predicted, Rose was shorter than Ree; her face was softer and wider, her black hair curled shoulder length.

"I see I have the right place," she said. Her voice was sweet with a country twang. Richards forgot instantly about the reactor, and within a few minutes Rose was curled under his arm on the couch, patting his leg over and over as if someone had just said something mean about it.

"I'm going outside," Paul said. He stood quickly and plunged onto the apartment's small deck, grateful for the bracing air. But the spring scent soon got to his head, its rutting earthy smell, and he felt restless. He allowed himself to think about Nat, and his thoughts soon got away from him: Nat on top of him with her dress around her waist; Nat with her head back, shoulders against the wall, a favorite fantasy though it had never actually happened.

And then the sliding glass door opened and Ree appeared beside him in blue pants and a shiny bra. Paul's head swiveled twice, he was so surprised. She leaned against the railing and smoked with riveting exhalations, her ribs sliding up and down beneath chamois skin, hands dangling from the rail by their wrists. She had smooth, pale fingernails the color of opal. There was nothing on earth that Paul could think of to say. Watching Ree was, in itself, a distinct and guilty pleasure.

Then there was a commotion below them. A door slammed; there was laughter and a small shriek, a scuffle. Paul craned to look. In the dusty light of the apartment complex he saw Richards holding Rose by the arm and Webb beside them, pointing back toward the open door.

"You'll pay for being so naughty," Richards said. "You'll pay for that little trick."

Ree snapped to attention, watching them.

"I couldn't help it," Rose cried. Her laugh came in a tinkle, but it sounded forced. "I can't help the milk, that just happens."

"Now, let's cool it," Webb said. "Let's go back inside and work this out."

"I should have known better," Richards muttered. He lurched to his car and swung open the trunk, rifling around. A moment later he emerged with a coil of bungee cord. "This will be fun," he said. He patted the top of the car and gestured to Rose. "Climb up."

"What's the idea?" she asked.

"Go on!"

Paul heard the stutter of Rose's laugh as she climbed up onto the car, Richards boosting her from behind. She was wearing something that looked like a bathing suit and she was barefoot. Richards guided her onto her back and she lay stiffly, her occasional high-pitched twitter reaching them on the second-floor deck, while he looped the cord over her and through the car's doors. Kinney and Slocum had stepped outside and were staring at the scene.

"You thought Christmas was over?" Richards asked. "Here's our Christmas tree! You want to get up there, too, Webb?"

Webb swayed uncertainly in the circle of lamplight.

"Climb on up, Webbsy! Give us a show. Make up for being an asshole back in the apartment." He patted Rose's stomach. "Ready to fly, honey? We can call you Squawnik."

Paul heard the turn of shoes beside him and saw Ree duck back inside, an entire cigarette left unstubbed where she'd been.

"You're not really going to drive, are you?" Rose asked, her voice tightening. No one, Paul realized, had thought Richards would actually do it.

"I think this has gone too far," said Webb.

Paul spied a movement from the corner of his eye and heard the light, retreating slap of shoes on asphalt. He could just make out Ree's shadow bolting away from them down the highway. She ran in terror, her long legs flying. The other men down below did not seem to see her. Paul thought he should go after her but paused. She was better off away from them. On the edge of his vision a blurred light shone from one of the bars or bordellos. She must have been headed there, and he let her go.

He turned back to the scene below with a thickening dread. It had taken him a moment to deduce what was happening, and he certainly hadn't, until now, thought the sergeant would go through with it.

He put his hands on the railing and hopped down, but just as he landed the Coupe lurched into motion, spitting muddy gravel.

"Oh, shit," said Webb. "Jesus Christ."

Over the car's engine they heard Rose's long, thin scream trailing away.

Webb turned to Paul, frantic. "What do we do? Call the cops?"

"We're here with these whores," Kinney said. "We go out for a drink with the guys and get arrested for being with *Indian whores*?" He sounded nearly hysterical.

In the dark, the car turned and headed back toward them. "Get in the road," Paul said, grasping Kinney and Sloke, who were nearest him, but they jerked free. "Come on, wave your arms! Block the road." He could hear Rose's ragged, repetitive shrieks over the car's engine. "Stop, you asshole!" he shouted. "Stop the car!" To Webb he said, "Don't move unless you have to."

"Oh, shit," said Webb, "he's going to run us down. He'll run us over—"

At the last minute, Richards hit the brakes. The car wove twice and gravel shot out like shrapnel. Rose had gone frighteningly silent. Paul scrambled out of the way, Webb beside him. As it stopped, the car throbbed forward and back, and Rose slid out from the ropes like a pile of laundry and dropped to the ground on the other side.

Webb dashed around the front of the car. Paul came around the car after him, trying to tell himself the car had slowed, she must be all right.

Rose was crouched on the asphalt as if trying to touch her forehead to her feet. "Are you hurt?" Webb asked. He hovered over her shoulder but did not touch it.

She was motionless for a few horrible seconds and then lurched up, cradling one arm in the opposite hand, her face streaked with tears. "Screw you," she sobbed. "You're crazy. Get me out of here."

Richards came around the front of the car. "Now, now, Squawnik. I didn't mean for you to fall off like that. There's no need to be sore. Here," and he reached into his wallet and thrust a wad of bills at her. "For the extra fun." She glared at him so he reached out and stuffed them into the mud-spattered dip of her cleavage. One breast rode higher than the other in its stiffly boned lingerie. She turned and limped down the road.

Webb glanced at Paul. "Where do you live?" he asked Rose, following her. "Let us drive you home."

"I would never tell any of you," she said.

His head bent in her direction, Webb strode alongside her, but Paul could not hear what he was saying. He could see Webb's hands gesturing gently as he talked, the movements growing fainter as they got farther away. For a moment he thought of following them but realized it might seem like ganging up, and decided to leave it to Webb.

"Well," Kinney said, "I'm going to need a ride home."

"Where's Ree?" Slocum asked. His eyes fell on Paul, who gave a bitter shrug. The other men looked around. "She left?" Slocum cried. "She just left?" as if they'd had something special.

"Sloke, you should get to bed," said Richards, slapping him on the shoulder. "First day as shift supervisor tomorrow."

Paul's hatred for Richards was suddenly unbearable. "You're a bastard," he said. Richards and Kinney turned to him, surprised. Paul clenched his fists at his sides and felt his arms shake. "We're lucky that woman wasn't killed on the spot. I'd like to punch you in the face and leave you here."

Richards looked at him with small, drunkenly wet eyes, his mouth half-slack and cheeks flushed with liquor and excitement. "Oh, shut up," he said. Then he tossed his keys to Paul; they bounced off his shoulder and fell in the mud. "Collier's driving," he said.

Paul wished he could lay the man flat. It took all his self-control to scoop the keys from the ground and climb into the car. He was relieved when Webb escorted Rose back a few minutes later. She picked her way in with Webb's coat over her shoulders, not looking at anyone. "We're giving her a ride home," Webb said. "She lives up the highway about five miles."

"All right," said Paul, starting the car.

They were silent on the drive north. Rose leaned her head on the window, a small breath circle marking her lips.

"Goddamn, it's chilly for June," said Richards. No one answered; he fumbled for a cigarette. He looked anxious but not sorry, and Paul was filled with fresh revulsion.

Rose's apartment huddled with a few other buildings near a lumberyard just off the highway. It was a three-level building that looked more like a motel, or maybe once had been, with a railed concrete deck on each level. Spooky forms of wood and machinery made odd shadows across the flat yard; a dog on a chain barked with pathetic loneliness. A short distance away stood a tiny unmanned train depot. Its lone lightbulb and a few apartment windows gave the only light around for what seemed like miles. Paul wondered who watched Rose's baby while she worked.

Wordlessly Rose slid from the car. She'd taken the spray of bills from her brassiere and tucked them somewhere. Turning, she handed Webb a piece of paper, and then she stalked up the concrete steps to her apartment.

"What, did you get her number?" Kinney asked.

"It's some kind of pamphlet." Webb squinted at the paper, lit his Zippo. " 'Which church is the right one?' " he read. "Oh, it's a Mormon thing."

"Jesus," Richards said, and chuckled. They all glanced up as her apartment door opened and closed on the deck above them, and the cold platform went dark.

Webb flipped the paper back and forth a few times as Paul pulled back onto the highway. Suddenly he glanced up. "Oh, no," he said. "Vanna's teddy bear. It was in my jacket."

Richards guffawed. "Vanna's what?"

"I carry an old teddy bear of Vanna's," Webb said miserably, sinking back in the seat. Richards gave him a pitying grimace.

"Your flashlight, too," said Kinney. "It was in there, remember? I borrowed it when I had to take a piss on the way to Sloke's."

"I'm sure he cherishes the memory," Richards said.

"Do you want to go back?" Paul asked.

Webb hesitated. "No," he said. "Forget it." He took a last look at the paper and slid it out through the cracked window, where it whipped away behind the car in one small white flap.

WHEN PAUL GOT HOME, the house was dark except for a single light Nat had left on over the table. The kitchen held the faint carbon smell of burnt sugar. He dropped his jacket over the back of a chair and sat down to read her note: "Made some cookies. Hope you had fun. N."

He was still wired from what felt like a narrow escape. They might have spent the night beside the cooling body of a woman on the highway. A sick feeling stirred inside of him, the gut-cold confirmation of his lifelong worldview: that this darkness was really what life was. Anything else you made for yourself was a temporary and tentative fiction.

It was almost a relief to think this way; if nothing else, it felt familiar. It was as old as time itself. It was Old Testament and myth and legend and childhood. It was his father staggering drunk around the cabin while Paul hid under the bed; it was his mother brought home from a bar with her face bashed in. It was the reactor's steadfast tendency toward malfunction, it was the part of Paul that wanted to fuck a woman tied to a car at the same time he wanted to rescue her.

His own mind was too awful tonight, so he got up and shuffled to the refrigerator. He took a bottle of whiskey from the small cabinet above it—warmed by the humming fridge, dust bunnies blowing every which way when he moved the cabinet door—and poured himself a few fingers' worth. He settled back into the chair, sipping. His thoughts did not calm down, they just came a little slower.

When he looked around his placid kitchen—the pot holders hanging by the stove, Nat's yellow dishwashing gloves draped across the sink—he knew he didn't deserve what went on here. He wasn't any better than Richards himself. He'd brought his family to Idaho Falls where they lived next to a reactor that might blow up. He hadn't stopped Richards from tying a woman to the roof of his car and driving forty miles an hour down the road.

This line of thought was its own narcissism; he could tell because it almost felt good. It was easy to revel in murk. Fighting it was the much harder thing, an act of will, like a drunkard resisting the drink. He always tried and perhaps overcompensated. Nat teased him for his stiffness, the order he liked to create around him. She didn't know how easy it was to slip. She couldn't comprehend how effortless her own life was, and how fragile, but he knew.

NAT

NAT HAD WAITED UP SEVERAL HOURS FOR PAUL'S RETURN. SHE didn't resent him for cutting loose with the boys—she liked to see him relaxed and carefree—but when he wasn't home by midnight she finally decided to turn in. The day seemed to have been incredibly long, what with the morning's exciting news, the disappointment of driving out to the reactor and back empty-handed, the stupid late urge to bake cookies, and the disproportionate penance of cleanup.

Just before turning out the lights she remembered she hadn't made Paul's lunch, so she set aside some Tupperware from dinner: meatloaf on Wonder bread, cold macaroni and cheese, mandarin oranges. It was oddly pleasurable to pack his lunch, to think of him opening it at noon like a little hello from her while she and the girls ate the same thing here at the table. Plus, it was a balanced meal.

As she finished up she had an idea: Here was a clever way to surprise him with the baby news. She took a napkin from its holder and over the thin, floral-pricked paper wrote, "Have a great day, father of THREE! Love, N." The "H" from "THREE!" ripped through, so she tossed that one and tried again with a lighter hand. Grinning, feeling mischievous, she slid the note into the bag, crinkled down the top, and set the bag on the top shelf by the OJ so he wouldn't miss it.

Sometime very late, she heard Paul come in the front door. His shoes made soft twin thuds in the entryway; water ran and redoubled into a cup. There was the quiet clink of glasses and a few glugs of poured liquor. That surprised her because Paul was only a beer drinker; they kept some whiskey on hand but it had been the same bottle for years, moved with them in the moving truck. There was a long period where she didn't hear anything at all and she dozed off again.

Eventually she blinked awake to a thin vertical glare of light through the doorway, and he came in. He shut the door on the hall light and moved around the room in darkness.

"Paul?" she said.

"It's okay," he said. "It's me."

"I know," she said, trying to follow his movements. "Did you have a good time?"

"It was fine," he said. His voice was gruff and smoky, almost sore. She could smell the alcohol and cigarettes even across the room. She heard him shuffle to the dresser and toss his clothes onto it: the quiet, intimately familiar jingle of his dog tags as they shook free of his neck and head to land almost soundlessly on the fabric.

The bed shifted and Nat put her arm around him, pleased to find him in his white undershirt and briefs. She'd told him he reminded her of James Dean this way, which he said was silly; he had none of Dean's upsweep of hair and besides, Dean was a draft dodger. Nat had rolled her eyes at him. It was the *shirt,* she said. The *general impression*. And he'd laughed: *All right, Nat. Whatever you say*.

For a few minutes she lay there, her arm over his chest, her nose hitting the edge of his sleeve so that her breath ruffled fabric and her lips touched skin. She thought he had fallen asleep, an instant descent into the brain-pull of liquor and fatigue. But all at once he pushed up on one elbow, slid his hand behind her head, and was kissing her with such urgency that she squirmed to catch her breath.

"Geez," she laughed, "what's gotten into you?"

He reached under her and flipped her up onto her knees, and she smiled back at him. Then, wordlessly, he gripped her hair. There followed a breakneck minute of startled discomfort, her hair pulled so tight that she looked up at the ceiling, swallowing with vertebral effort; a few nonrhythmic internal thumps, more like a creature ramming its head against a wall than anything else. It wasn't quite violent, it wasn't kind, and there was no love in it. It was more like a brief possession, a transfer of some dark thing she didn't want. Now, whatever it was, she held it.

He let out a hoarse, bleak groan and loosened her hair. She waited, feeling like an odd piece of equipment, until he slumped onto his side of the bed.

"Okay," she whispered, mostly to herself, and patted her way to the nightstand for the box of tissues. She handed some to him and he cleaned up robotically, tossing them to the floor beside the bed.

For some reason this bothered Nat as much as anything else. "The girls will see that in the morning," she cried, getting out and fetching the wastebasket to gather them up. She bumped back around the bed and returned the bin to the bathroom, catching a shadowy glimpse of herself in the mirror: wild hair, hormonally swollen breasts, stomach she liked to remember as smooth but which in reality was doodled with faint lavender parentheses. She'd kept up her good cheer but now it was time to admit that the entire day had been a terrible disappointment. This was the final blow, her quick stint as a pommel horse for Paul's drunken frustrations. His huffing breath in her ear, her neck craned up, the way he released her as if he already regretted the whole thing. She looked down at the wastebasket of stiff tissues and her eyes welled over.

When she climbed into bed she kept herself at her far edge, arms crossed. She pinched her nose and tried to take a deep breath.

"Nat," he murmured, "I'm sorry."

"Oh, it's just fine," she snapped.

"I meant for something different."

"Like *what*?"

"Come on." He shifted closer to her, touched her elbow, imploring. Everything about him seemed oddly heavy: the way he moved, the way his body pushed down the bed.

"I'm fine," she said. "I just had a bad day. Please go to sleep."

He repeated her name in a choked way and she turned, startled, to see that he was nearly crying.

"What in the world?" she said. Here they were, in bed, both crying;

it was a comedy of errors. She did not want to comfort him. She did not have a single ounce of human energy left, and yet the sight of him undone was terrible, turned a deep pity in her that was almost, on its own merits, a kind of love. "Jesus, Paul," she said, "next time you drink like that, sleep on the couch."

He rolled her all the way toward him and stared at her, his dark eyes apologetic. He had been like this before, but not often. She had the irritated, practical thought that it was going to be very hard for him to get up for work in the morning. He mumbled about how much he loved her, his hand loosely cupping her neck; he lay his thumb in the divot between her collar bones, a gentle pressure that her pulse bumped against, again and again. She didn't know if she should push him away, laugh grimly, or weep with sadness.

"Okay," she said, putting his arm back around her waist. "Go to sleep now."

He finally slept. Listening to his tranquilized breath she had the odd sensation that he was someone she had known too well and too long, a selfish brother, and not the person she wanted sharing her bed. The feeling passed in a heartbeat, shuddered away.

PAUL

PAUL AND WEBB WERE QUIET THE NEXT DAY AT WORK. WHEN THEY found themselves side by side at the lockers they didn't say anything at all. Later, in the lunchroom, Franks ribbed them through a mouthful of turkey sandwich. "So, you two went back to Sloke's place last night for a little intellectual conversation?"

"It wasn't anything special," said Paul.

"You both look like shit."

"I know," Paul said. Webb was still too gray faced to speak. Paul could see Franks revving up for more, but since he couldn't stand around all day protecting Webb from having to talk, he took his cigarette outside. Richards's car wasn't in the lot; he hadn't showed.

Paul sleepwalked through the hours. He tried to focus, but his thoughts kept pulling back to the previous night as if attached to a lead sinker. Rose strapped to the car and the awful moment he'd realized it was not a joke. Nat telling him to go to sleep, his gurbled damp apologies; how she'd patted his shoulder in a motherly way while her eyes wandered to the ceiling. At one point he had the panicky insight that perhaps no woman on this earth truly loved a man; how could anyone expect them to? Then his thoughts manned up, came in and grabbed these neuroses and chucked them aside, saying, *Get ahold of yourself; you support your family, you put a roof over their heads, your wife seems happy with you 99 percent of the time. Don't lose your mind here. Everything is fine.*

"Are you with us, Collier?" Franks shouted. "Shape up! You don't pay attention, one of us is going to get hurt."

"Sorry," Paul said. He finished his task, then dragged himself into the bathroom where he sat staring at the wall, feeling hangdog.

Not long before the end of the shift, Franks told them the rods needed to be raised again. Paul pointed out that the mid shift would be there, fresh and rested, in less than an hour.

Franks gave him a disappointed look. "We notice it, we fix it," he said. "Since when do I work with a pair of pussies?"

When Webb went to lift the nine rod, it stuck the worst that Paul had ever seen. He immediately went to fetch the pipe wrench. It didn't work. Each man tried it; as the seconds ticked by they took on an odor of anxiety and exertion.

"Get another wrench," Franks said. Paul gritted his teeth and strained to force the wrench. The rod jerked upward, several inches.

"Oh shit," said Webb.

Franks cursed. "Get it down," he barked, and he and Paul pushed in the other direction. Veins bulged in Franks's forehead. Paul slid slowly backward; he let out something between a groan and a yell. The rod inched down.

For a moment they had to catch their breath and could not speak. They gasped for air, pacing, hands on their hips. Finally Paul said, "We should call Richards at home."

"And tell him his day crew is so hungover and useless they can't even get through the chore list? You can go call him if you want."

"It wasn't our fault the thing stuck," said Webb.

Franks ignored him. "You had better be worth something when you get here tomorrow, Collier."

"Are you going to write this up?" Paul asked. He jabbed his finger toward the logbook on the shelf, its blue leather binding and roughed-up pages.

Franks bristled. "'Course I will," he said.

"You carry that damn thing all around like a diary but only record half the things that go wrong."

"I've been writing things down."

"Not all the time. Sometimes you record an incident, sometimes you skip it. I can't figure out your rhyme or reason."

"Well, I'm writing it now." Franks strode over and snatched up the book. "Mind your own damn business."

"We're all tired," said Webb. "Let's go easy on each other." He appealed to Paul: "See? He's writing it down."

"Yeah," Paul said. He watched the shift leader's meticulous cursive swirl across the page and wanted to smack the short pencil right out of Franks's thick hand. His precious, useless logbook—what good it did them! But the shift leader looked so sincere, flipping to another page on his clipboard, sweat droplets chasing one another down his cheeks, as if writing down the stuck rod was going to solve their problem, as if the message would get past Richards and Harbaugh anyway. Webb gazed off to the side, chewing a thumbnail and jittering his foot. Paul felt a sudden stab of pity for them all. They could *die* for this nothingness, this shit hole. It was their life, this lifting and sweating and shuffling and dodging, this penning of warnings that no one would read, this making of endless excuses. It was a service no one would love them for, and they were veterans of nothing more than their own blank, tenuous days.

Paul had not been to Sergeant Richards's home since the night of the dinner party, so it was odd to see the house again, quiet and in daylight. It looked plain and demure, as if it were asleep and Paul would somehow startle it by walking to the door.

He parked on the street and strode up the drive past Richards's car. It was hard to believe that he'd been driving it the previous night—that Rose had been strapped to the top. It seemed an ugly, ridiculous dream.

Mrs. Richards answered, her eyes widening in surprise when she saw Paul. "Oh, Mr. Collier," she cried. "Hello. What brings you here?"

She was as perfectly coiffed and manicured as ever. Her eyebrows were drawn onto her forehead in delicate red arches, her lipsticked mouth dainty and impeccable in its *O* of surprise, as if she were about to blow out one birthday candle.

"Is the master sergeant home?" Paul asked.

"He is," said Mrs. Richards, looking cautious. "He had a headache today and didn't go in. I'm sure you knew that." She opened the door fully and stepped back to let him in. "Please, have a seat."

Paul heard her pad down the hallway, followed by whispering. He stood next to the couch, as if sitting would have been some kind of concession.

After a few moments Richards came in, wearing the masculine version of his wife's surprise. "Collier!" he said guardedly. "I wasn't expecting you. Sit down, have a drink."

"No, thank you, Master Sergeant." He could not bring himself to ask about the man's convenient headache. Richards fixed himself a drink and wandered over with a mellow ambivalence that set Paul's teeth on edge.

"So what's this about?" Richards settled onto the couch, stretched out his legs.

Paul cleared his throat. "We had a serious issue with the nine rod today. I thought you should know right away."

"Well, all right, thank you. I'll get the specs from Franks next time I see him."

"It's more urgent than that. I'm concerned that the reactor is failing."

Richards, eyeing Paul, took a sip of his drink. He placed it on the table and sat back, one leg crossed on the opposite knee.

"We know that boron is crumbling into the core of the machine," Paul said. "The rods are sticking, and we have to try to force them around every four hours. Between the false alarms and exercising the rods all the time, all we do is busywork. We're running around like chickens with our heads cut off. Today the nine stuck worse than I've ever seen. When we jerked it loose it shot up three inches."

He was gratified to see that this drained some color from Richards's face.

"We can't go above four," Paul said, though of course Richards knew this; it was like telling an adult not to stick something in a light socket. Every operator had been told the four-inches rule until it was second nature. Never, ever, unless you are a goddamn death-craving lunatic, raise a reactor rod above four inches.

"Well, I have something to tell you." Richards gathered himself, leaned forward, and opened and closed his hands as if this were big news. "The men don't know this yet, but we have a new core ordered for this winter."

Paul blinked. "That's half a year away. And I did know that; Franks told me."

"Oh." Richards frowned. "He wasn't supposed to say anything."

"I don't know if we can continue another six months like this," Paul said.

"You can. Have some faith."

"Some faith?" Paul cried. "It's not a matter of faith. We need to be honest here, Master Sergeant."

Richards's false joviality was gone. "You remember what happened to Oppenheimer, don't you?" he said.

"I do," Paul said after a moment, feeling his blood cool. J. Robert Oppenheimer had been one of the preeminent physicists on the Manhattan Project. Then, six years ago, he'd been stripped of his security clearance. Paul had still been in petroleum supply back then but he heard talk of the trial from time to time, the theories people had for the scientist's harsh punishment: political distaste, Communist affiliation, personality clashes. He didn't know the ins and outs of it all; he was, however, steeply aware that to lose one's security clearance was a humiliating insult. Even Paul, a rookie operator, now had a higher clearance than Oppenheimer did.

So he knew what Richards was getting at but didn't want to take the bait. "Luckily," he muttered, looking away, "I'm no Oppenheimer."

"But you could be," Richards said, and it was not stardom he spoke of. He took a sip of his drink. "Try to just live your life," he said, suddenly a pal. "Don't worry so much. Live your life!"

"Like you do?" Paul said, his heart speeding up. "Live like you do, not giving a shit about anybody else?"

Richards drew back, affronted. "What are you talking about?"

"You know what I'm talking about."

There was a pause. Paul heard Mrs. Richards fumbling with something in a nearby room. Richards said in a low voice, "This is inappropriate."

" 'Live your life.' I saw what you did last night," Paul hissed. "You could have killed the woman. Now I feel like we're all just strapped to the roof of your car."

"Aren't you a . . . *poet,*" Richards said, and his face fairly rippled. "The things a man does, the things men do, are not to be spoken of afterwards."

"I'm tired of seeing the things you do. You've got men in harm's way every day to keep that reactor limping along, just so you'll look good—"

"The reactor is perfectly safe—"

"How can you say that? We keep patching it up like it's, I don't know, an old couch. It's a *nuclear reactor*. If something goes wrong, people die. And what about our families—what about your family? Do you want them fifty miles from a failing reactor? Wind can travel fifty miles in no time."

Richards gave a hostile, incredulous laugh. "You're a hysterical woman. I wish you could hear yourself."

Paul was pulled up short by the name-calling; he groped for a new tactic. "Maybe we could go to Harbaugh and whoever else and tell them that if something doesn't change soon—"

"Go for it," Richards said, spreading his arms wide. "You go on and tell Harbaugh. I'm sure he'd love to hear all about it. The man's *dying* and he's got a job that provides life insurance for his family, so I'm sure he'd just love to start a big ruckus at work in his twilight moments."

"Don't you see? It's time we started talking about what's going on—"

"Oh, good idea! Once we start talking, who knows where we'll stop? I can think of so many people who'd love to hear about all kinds of things. Your wife, for instance! She'd love to hear about the party you were at last night, and all that time you spent alone on an apartment building deck with a—" he stopped and shrugged, letting the silence hang.

Paul's stomach turned. "I was only there to drive *you,* you pig. I tried to go home."

"That's a moving story."

Paul struggled to control himself. "I need to know that you'll do something about the reactor."

"I know exactly what I'll do about the reactor!" Richards cried, his voice quavering with righteous offense. "I'm going to take your wife and I'm going to fuck her on top of it, that's what I'm going to do! That's what I call living my life—"

Without thinking, Paul pulled back his right elbow and let his fist fly at Richards's jaw.

He was in a red haze and knew, even as his arm swung out, that it was an unforgivable offense, but for a split second he felt elated, thrilled. Then his fingers crunched, and shock waves rang through his arm. It hurt more than he'd expected; he hollered with the pain.

Richards went over sideways, comically, his drink arcing through the air. For a minute he lay sprawled on the carpet. Then he sat up on one elbow and held the side of his face, cursing, cords of pinkish slobber dangling through his fingers.

There was a shriek from Mrs. Richards, who ran into the room. From the rear of the house their child began to cry.

"I'm sorry, ma'am," said Paul, backing toward the door.

Richards staggered to his feet. A bright red daisy imprinted his cheek. "You're a coward," he marveled, the words rounded and hung together, his mouth stiff, unclosing. "You're a miserable, sad, poor coward." His slow, honking laughs stacked up like an engine that couldn't get going.

Jeannie dabbed at the spilled drink on the carpet with her apron. When her husband glanced at her, she stopped. There was nothing Paul could think of to say. He strode, shaking, out the door and down the driveway.

"Don't touch my car!" Richards's thick voice called after him.

The Coupe was bathed in sunset and looked as if it had been sculpted entirely from orange sherbet. Paul hocked back a wad and spat right on the driver's side door. Saliva splatted against the creamy paint and oozed down like bird shit. Richards went apoplectic in the doorway. Paul got into his own car and, balancing his right wrist atop the wheel and steering with his left, drove away.

WHEN PAUL REACHED his own house he sat for a minute, staring at his right hand. It was puffed up, speckled like a strawberry. He could raise his fingers, but stiffly; the fattened skin strained.

He could hear Sam and Liddie squealing in the backyard, playing with the hose most likely. Nat had let them turn half the lawn into a mud pit where they filled buckets with swampy concoctions of leaves, grass, and water. Even in chilly weather they played out there in undershirts and underpants, and Nat hosed them down outside before letting them in. Paul had tried to tell her that they were the only ones on the street, so far as he could tell, who let their children do this, but she claimed it was good for them: being outside, concentrating on their bizarre little projects. *Let them have fun; they're only girls for so long.* All Paul knew was that when he got home from work it appeared his people had taken to hog farming.

He was glad he could slip in the front door without the girls seeing him, but Nat was lying on the couch and opened her eyes.

"Hi," he said. "Don't get up. I didn't mean to wake you."

"I wasn't sleeping," she said. "I was listening to the girls."

"Okay," he said, heading for the back bedroom.

He was struggling to unbutton his uniform when she came in. She watched him for a moment. He felt self-conscious and ashamed about the previous night, the tail end of which he wished he couldn't remember at all but, goddamnit, he did; he was definitely and unavoidably aware that he had clambered onto his wife's back and relieved himself like a bucking, drugged-out horse. But now even that fine display was overshadowed by the fact that his hand was the size and shape of a boxing glove and he might have cost himself a career in the army, and if that happened he would look like such an ass before his family and the world that he might as well just go somewhere and quietly kill himself.

"Did you get the note in your lunch?" Nat asked.

This was the last thing he'd expected her to say. "Oh," Paul said. "I never even opened my lunch bag today. We were behind, so we just worked through the break. I guess it's still in the fridge." He was babbling, feeling he'd been granted a reprieve but also that somehow, inexplicably, he was getting himself into more trouble.

"Well, that's just lousy," Nat said, with a vehemence that made no sense. Her eyes narrowed. "What happened to your hand?"

For a brief second he considered saying he'd injured it at work. "I got in a fight," he said.

"What?" she cried. "With who?"

"Master Sergeant Richards."

Her face drained of color. Quietly she repeated, "You got in a fight at work with Master Sergeant Richards?"

"At his house."

"Why were you at his house?"

"I drove there and got into a fight with him."

"Paul. Why would you *do* that?" She sounded scared.

He fumbled uselessly with a button and gave up. He hadn't thought what his answer would be, but now his brain scrambled with the bind he was in. He couldn't tell her about the previous night at Slocum's apartment, and he didn't want her to know how bad things at the reactor had gotten; she'd never let it go.

"He's a jerk," Paul blurted. "He's rude to the guys at work and he's just a real asshole."

"If he's 'rude' to the guys at work, why can't *they* fight him?" She pressed a hand to the side of her face, and then a look of recognition crossed her face. "Did Webb say something about yesterday?"

Paul paused. "What about yesterday?"

"Never mind." She shook her head. "What's going to happen to you? What happens when someone does this?"

"I don't know," Paul said. He started to chuckle, thinking of the absurdity of it. He had punched his sergeant in the face. "Hell," he said. "Maybe this is a blessing in disguise. You know, they're starting to build power plants all over the country. I bet civilian operators make twice what we do. We could move somewhere better than this, make more money. Maybe they'll build one in San Diego."

"Have you lost your mind?" Nat said. "This is a good thing because *maybe* someone will build a power plant in San Diego?"

"Fuck the army," Paul said, quietly delirious. "What, do we love the army all of a sudden? Remember when I was at Fort Irwin and had to drive every weekend to see you? Remember reactor school? Yeah, those were the days."

"Paul, come on," she said, looking troubled. "You're more loyal than that."

"It would be a relief to leave that reactor behind."

"I'm having another baby," Nat said.

All Paul's loony hilarity suctioned from the room in a second. He felt he'd been standing there bundled in farce, and now he was left ant-sized in his underpants.

"Oh, no," he said.

"Thanks," Nat said tearfully, "that's just the reaction I was hoping for." She stood with one arm across her waist, the other gesturing bitterly. "I found out yesterday morning. I was waiting for a nice time to tell you. But since I didn't get to yesterday afternoon, or last night"—her eyes flashed—"I decided I'd leave a note in your lunch today. I didn't think there was any rush. I didn't think, 'I'd better tell my husband I'm having a baby right away so he doesn't go punch out his boss and lose his job.'"

"Maybe it's not so bad," Paul said, feeling short of breath. "There have been fights at work before. No one's been discharged over them. They could dock me some pay, maybe." He began to wander the room as if the answer were on top of the dresser or headboard.

Nat turned and left, and he assumed she was too disgusted to speak to him. He sank onto the bed, his hand throbbing as if something were trying to emerge from it. His knuckles were indistinct, a fat slab with a scalloped edge. Nat returned with a frozen TV dinner. Part of him thought she might sit beside him and hold it to his hand, but he wasn't surprised when she just passed it to him.

"Thanks," he said, pressing the cold aluminum box to his skin. She stood in front of him, looking away. "I'm sorry, Nat," he said, but she turned and headed out to the backyard where the girls were. He could hear them greeting her with happy yelps—"Mama, look at this!"—and he regretted his reaction to her news; of course he was happy to have another baby. He loved their children.

The full stupidity of his actions dawned on him. What a fool he had been to approach his boss in the spirit of rational discussion, only to blow the whole thing so fabulously that he'd come to this, sitting in a dark room shunned by his wife, his hand blown up like a balloon. Who would ever take him seriously now? Richards would have the last laugh, and the reactor was no safer than it had been the day before. He couldn't have done any worse if he'd tried.

IN RETROSPECT, THE PHONE CALL didn't surprise him. Franks hollered across the room "Collier, Department of the Army on line two." Paul froze, his heart thudding, and forced himself to pick up the receiver. He heard a familiar southern accent—Sergeant MacKinnon, whom he'd talked to before coming to Idaho—a voice silkened and vaguely hostile from a lifetime of delivering unwelcome news. "This isn't necessarily typical, Specialist Collier," MacKinnon said, "but a six-month billet has opened up at Camp Century, and it's been decided that you'll do a tour there."

"Camp Century." Paul couldn't believe what he was hearing. "That's the Arctic Circle."

"They're building a new reactor out there, the PM-2A. It's based on the CR-1, so you'll be perfectly suited to take her on her maiden voyage."

Paul's mind spun; should he be relieved, or more worried than before? He wasn't out of the army after all—an initial consolation—but instead he was being sent away. Nat and the girls were the ones who'd be stuck near the reactor, and he would be long gone. This might actually be the worst scenario he could have come up with; he'd exchanged their safety for his own, which he would never have willingly done. This deployment seemed almost custom designed to torment him: Richards knew he was worried about the reactor, so what a cruel twist it was that Paul's family would stay right in town while he was sent thousands of miles away, oblivious, a blindfolded idiot in exile.

"Did Richards ask to put my name in? Did he push to have me sent?"

"No, no. It's never anything personal, always a joint decision. Your name just came up."

Paul wondered if this could be true. No, he wasn't that stupid. Of course Richards had had some say in this. Probably brought it up all on his own.

"So, Collier, here's the deal: We have you leaving June seventh."

"You mean July seventh?"

"No, June seventh. The day after tomorrow."

A moment of disbelief; wind whistled through his body.

"The good news is you'll get back a couple days before Christmas."

"My wife's having a baby the first part of December."

"Oh! Well, congratulations."

A long pause.

"So I'll give you your flight numbers and the names of a couple of guys to get in touch with when you reach camp."

Paul sweated, armpits cold, crunching his toes in his boots till they ached.

"All right. Go ahead."

When he told Nat, she barely said a word. She sat across from him at the kitchen table with an aghast expression. Then she got up and strode into the back bedroom, closing the door behind her. Even when Paul called her name she didn't come out, and he ended up taking the girls to a diner downtown. He ordered a milkshake and let them share the leftovers in the tin cup; Liddie squirmed and panted through a brain freeze, and Sam seized upon her sister's weakness to suck the rest of the cup dry. Nat was asleep when they got back, and Paul spent the night on the couch.

He felt he was going through his own useless, panicky brain freeze, never reaching any conclusions. The thought of leaving his family for six months horrified him. *You can't leave Nat and the girls* his brain would chant, until he wanted to reach inside his head and strangle it; a minute later he'd be verbally slapping himself to buck up and be a man and do his job, stop being such a goddamn softie. Then he'd imagine something going wrong with the reactor while he dabbled away in ignorance on his distant ice floe, and his mind would run through the cycle again.

He worked one last, good-for-nothing day at the reactor. There was a false fire alarm and a sticky third rod—disconcerting, but by now commonplace. At quitting time he rode the bus back into town and, at the curb, said good-bye to his two shift mates. Franks slapped him on the shoulder; Webb stood to the side looking oddly stricken. He was like a gawky kid brother and Paul realized, as dumb as it sounded, that Webb might miss him nearly as much as anyone else. Webb smiled lopsidedly as Paul stammered out some weak farewell—"Hang in there, Webbsy; hope to see you married when I get back"—got into his car, and drove away.

That night, Paul packed his duffel bag. It somehow took him a couple of hours even though all he really needed were uniforms, a toothbrush, socks, and aspirin. He'd be given all the formidable outer- and underwear he needed; a corporal who'd called earlier that day assured him of that. "Plus, you'll never get sick out there," the man had said. "Viruses can't survive in the Arctic."

"I don't *care* about getting sick," Paul had snapped, and the man wished him good luck and hung up.

Nat climbed into bed right after the girls went down and left Paul in the living room for the second night in a row. She'd cracked the bedroom door but he couldn't bring himself to face the razor-sharp wall of her shoulders, so he poured himself some whiskey and plopped on the couch, staring at his duffel.

Outside, the street was quiet, without light. He lay awake, feeling the throb and almost-hum of a house full of sleeping people. He pictured the tiny baby turning in Nat's belly like a sweet unblinking shrimp. He thought of this baby growing, growing in his absence, and it didn't seem possible that Nat would swell and bloom and then have that baby all by the time he got back. It made him feel entirely useless, peripheral to the major workings of the world.

He wandered to the back window and remembered their night outside nearly a year ago, after the dinner party at the Richardses'. Nat walking to the fence and tapping it, her sashay back like something Paul would have dreamed of when he was sixteen. His life felt like an alternating cycle of blind luck and kicks in the ass.

He eventually climbed into bed and could tell at once that she was awake. "Hey," he said, leaning up on one elbow. "Hey, will you at least talk to me?"

She whispered, "What is there to talk about?"

"I don't know," he stammered.

She turned to look at him. "You are in *charge* of us. You brought us here and said it was a good thing, no deployment, we'd all be together. And then you go and act like a, a fool, and get yourself sent away from us. What are we supposed to do out here by ourselves for half a year? Do you know how long that is? You won't even be here for the birth of the baby!"

"I know," he said, feeling sick.

"I can't talk right now." She buried her face in the pillow. "I just don't want to talk about it. I'm sorry."

"Nat!" he cried, nearly thrashing with frustration. "I leave at eight tomorrow morning! I'll be gone for six months!"

He threw himself out of bed and stalked into the living room. He spent the night drinking himself into a fabulous headache, mentally arguing with his father over which of them was more of an asshole (his father, definitely, hands down), and writing his daughters a sloping, left-handed note for Nat to read them sometime in the middle of his deployment. He set the note on the counter, collapsed onto the couch, and dozed. When daybreak came he wandered back into the kitchen to make coffee and it caught his eye; he'd forgotten about it already. Now the writing looked like something from a horror movie, or the deranged scrawl from above a prison urinal. He imagined reading it in a slurred, lisping voice—"DEAR GIRLZZZ"—winced, and threw it away.

Around six A.M. he heard a noise from the back bathroom and went down the hall to listen.

"Nat?" he said, stepping around the door.

Oh, his poor Nat. She was hunched over the toilet in her nightgown. The seat was up and she held her hair back with one hand, staring into the water with wet, animalistic focus. A ribbon of saliva twirled from her mouth, heavied, plopped in.

Paul knelt beside her and put his hand on her back. "It's okay," he said, which was only a somewhat helpful thing to say if you were the onlooker and not actually doing the vomiting. Beneath his palm her shoulder blades jumped. "My poor baby," he said. She sat back, panting, and he reached for a towel.

"Thank you," she said, taking it and leaning against the wall. "Ugh," she said after a moment. "I hate that." Her voice was quietly husky. She wiped her mouth and looked up at the ceiling, her chest rising and falling. A greenish sheen glistened on her forehead.

"Are you all right?"

She nodded. "I feel a little better now."

"Is it from the baby?"

"I guess so. Or just . . . nerves. It'll pass."

They sat for several minutes in silence. Then Paul heard thumps and squeaks from down the hall. No looking back: The girls were up.

"I have to be at the airport in an hour," he said. He glanced at her, wondering what he'd see in her eyes. Sadness? Relief? Mostly she just looked tired.

"I know," she said.

"I can take a cab if you want. You can stay here with the girls—"

"No," she said. "We'll bring you. I'll get dressed in a minute." She wiped her forehead on the towel and wobbled up; he jumped to his feet and helped her. All her skin seemed to recoil from him, even the tendons of her forearm as his fingers closed gently around it, as if her body had decided on its own that he was not welcome. She bumped past him and into the bedroom.

BY SEVEN A.M., AGAINST ALL ODDS, they were dressed and waiting at the airport. Nat had the girls in their Sunday best. Paul knew they had no other plans for the day; they'd be home by eight, bouncing off the walls in their pretty dresses. But he wasn't about to argue with Nat's vision.

She still felt awful. He could see it. She swayed next to him in her blue cardigan, her arms around her waist. There were dark bags under her eyes and her face was pinched and colorless. No stranger would have taken her for pregnant, but now that he knew, Paul could see the gentle puff of her belly. It gave him a bleak sort of pride, a heart-twisting happiness that somehow just felt like pain.

The small group of passengers—some alone, some with families—gathered in the corrugated metal hangar watching the plane lower its stairs just outside the door. Paul tried to think of something encouraging and memorable to say, something wise and useful enough that it would heal the whole situation in one swoop, but Sam was hopping up and down and trying to get into his arms while prattling excitedly about a woman at the far end of the building who was very fat.

Nat tapped her shoulder. "Hush, Sam, that isn't polite."

Paul tried to hold Sam gently still, left-handed, by the top of her bobbing head. A bubble of desperation filled his stomach: He'd been waiting for an eleventh-hour conversion, a sudden lifting of Nat's blockade, but it might not come. He might actually get on that plane and fly off to the end of the world with her still upset with him, which meant, really, that she would be angry for six months. The last time they'd been together, his stupid drunken misstep two nights before, would sit between them like a placeholder. It carried extra weight and gravitas now, as if it represented the way they always were even though it had been an aberration, and half a year would pass before he could prove it wrong—make any kind of amends.

Liddie, standing at Nat's knees, watched the other people in the airport with her dark, curious eyes. The thought of not seeing his girls for such a long time was a punishment. They were still young enough to change by the month. When he got back, they'd have thinner limbs and narrower faces. They'd talk differently.

"I can't wait to see the baby," Paul tried, and this seemed such an impotent and ineffectual sentiment, so little in the face of what would transpire, that he wished he hadn't said anything. Nat's eyes glinted at him and then away.

The radio sputtered into a voice: It was time to board. The other passengers shuffled forward with the quiet, anxious determination of any people in an airport. Paul knelt to hug Sam and kissed Liddie's soft cheeks. He reached for Nat. Goddamnit, he needed to hug her or *something*. He was just about to lose his mind.

"I smell awful," she said, stepping back. "I smell like throw-up."

"That's fine," he said, "it'll keep the other guys away." He tried to smile.

"*What* other guys?"

"Exactly."

She turned from him, wiped her eyes with the back of her hand.

"I'm sorry," he said, finally getting his arms around her. He squeezed her barbed shoulders, beginning to panic. "Forgive me. I didn't mean for this to happen. I did a stupid thing and now we're all being punished for it. But it was a mistake."

"I know it was," she finally said.

"I'm so happy about the baby."

"Really?"

"I am. I'm really happy, Nat."

"Okay," she said, finally looking at him. "Then me, too." She was a forgiving person. That was what he could count on; every day was a new dawn with her. She never fell into a black hole of resentment or bitterness. It seemed the finest quality a human being could have.

He pressed his forehead to hers, smelling the overfresh detergent of her sweater and a faint, acrid tang on her breath, and whispered a few moments of embarrassing, spineless sweet nothings that were thankfully drowned out by the blare of the intercom: "Final boarding for Flight 23 to Andrews Air Force Base, Maryland." The announcement sent them into a second round of panic and suddenly they were plastered to each other like high schoolers, Nat gripping his shoulders, petting his face, as if she were somehow trying to climb up into his arms, and for his part he was kissing her like a madman, completely ignoring the people around them and his own children stepping on his boots. He was so dizzied with simultaneous relief and dread that he nearly cried, himself; hugged her, held her hair, buried his face in her neck and felt the lovely swallow of her throat.

"Last call, Flight 23 to Andrews Air Force Base. The doors are closing."

He straightened up and his eyes moved over his family—pale, squeamish Nat, doe-eyed Liddie, Sam wriggling like a crayfish—trying to memorize his little tribe, these three people that he loved so incautiously, past all reason and beyond his wildest predictions.

"Be careful," he blurted, holding Nat by the shoulders.

She looked at him, startled.

"If anything goes wrong, just get out of town. All right? Just drive till you get somewhere safe."

She laughed nervously. "What in the world would go wrong?"

"I don't know." He fidgeted, feeling half-sunk with dread, anxious enough to pop out of his skin. "At the testing station. With one of the reactors. Or, I don't know, a natural disaster, anything. I don't know! Just promise me you'll get out of town."

"Of course. Whatever you say."

"All right."

"We love you," she said. "I love you."

"Love you, too. Write to me," he said.

"We will!" Sam cried.

"I mean it, Nat," Paul said. "You're all I've got."

She smiled at him quizzically. "Okay."

"You think I'm joking," he said. He swung his densely packed duffel bag up onto his shoulder, so long and heavy that he felt as if he were lugging another man by the arm; kissed his wife and daughters each one more time, and walked out through the beautiful spring air to his waiting plane.

III

NOW THAT YOU'VE GONE

PAUL

CAMP TUTO, GREENLAND

It was the wind that woke Paul up. It blew endlessly across the ice cap, sometimes in a whistle like a teakettle, sometimes in a scream like the engines of distant jets coming in for landing.

Paul could not see the other men in the Quonset hut, as they were all sleeping in the dark, but they were there on bunks all around him. The hut smelled of musty wool and a sharp, pickle-relish body odor. He worked his arms free from the thin standard-issue blankets he'd burrowed under the night before. They were scratchy and familiar, still in circulation from Korea and probably the Second World War. Beneath the blankets he was wearing three pairs of long underwear. Each layer shifted in a slightly different direction so that the seams crossed his body like longitude and latitude lines, running weirdly under his armpits and over his swaddled crotch.

He'd been having a bad dream, and it lingered with him, queasing his stomach and flitting across his back. He squeezed his shoulder blades, trying to shake it off. The last image had awoken him with its creepiness: Nat, reaching into the oven to pull out a tray and then retracting with a shriek, her arms burned to the elbows, hands pink and shiny as skinned animals. But it was just a nightmare; none of it was real.

He reminded himself that everything back at home was fine. First thing each morning at breakfast he'd ask Rodgers, the signals officer, if he'd heard any big news from the States, and for a moment his heart would clench until Rodgers said, "Not really, no," or mentioned a grim account that had occurred someplace other than Idaho Falls. Then Paul would feel himself settle a little, breathe a small sigh of relief, for a moment escaping the knowledge that if something happened in Idaho Falls it wouldn't matter whether he knew anyway, because he'd be of no help. He'd left his family in one remote corner of the world while he was stuck in another, and if they needed him he would not be there.

When Paul first arrived in Greenland the reactor at Camp Century was not fully assembled, so he and fifteen other men were being held for a few weeks at Camp TUTO, about a hundred miles south. Everything he could see was white and brown like some sort of visual trick: dirt, and snow, and dirty snow, and snowy dirt, and snowy air, and sometimes blowing dirt. The men had kept themselves busy by shoveling snow (mixed with dirt); cleaning out the "honey buckets" (urinals); and pouring sixty-gallon cans of beef stew out onto the ice in the hopes of taming an Arctic fox and keeping it for a pet. They'd just been told that the reactor at Camp Century was now finished and about to go on line, so whenever the weather let up they would be headed north.

Someone's alarm went off in the dark, and Paul clambered out of bed to pull the chain on the ceiling that lit their one bare bulb. Ten men sat around on their double-stacked bunks, scratching their heads and rubbing their eyes.

"Do you hear that wind?" Specialist Benson marveled.

"I think it's died down since yesterday," said Specialist Mayberry, already lighting a cigarette. Mayberry was a tall man with roosterish black hair, and he was neither a construction worker nor a nuclear operator, but a geologist on his fourth tour in Greenland. He worked mostly in a cave, he said, built below Camp Century and filled with long core samples that had been drilled out of the ice and stored in what looked like poster tubes. He said Camp Century was a dream compared to his old Greenland station, which was called Fistclench.

There was a hum of either agreement or disagreement and some wild speculation about future weather. They had just finished lacing up their boots when Mayberry paused and asked, "Do you hear that?"

They all froze. Off in the distance, incredibly, they could hear a faint chutting sound, a motor. "It's the mail plane!" Benson shouted, and everyone scrambled. The light outside was blinding; the cold seized their chests. But there was the plane, tilting from side to side in the wind as it descended toward the camp's short airstrip. Everyone cheered and a few men waved their arms slowly back and forth over their heads, as if this were a search party that might have no idea where they were.

Paul's heart lifted. Mail! He hadn't yet received a letter from Nat. He didn't know for sure that she'd written to him—after all, it had been less than a month—but it seemed that a letter should be arriving soon. And as the seconds ticked by, watching the plane waver and struggle, the more convinced he became that there was something on it for him. Surely she'd have dashed off a note shortly after he'd left. Surely she missed him.

The plane came in over the runway; they could even see the pilot wave. But strong wind buffeted the craft, and it tipped in wild diagonals for a moment before revving and ascending again. Paul stood with his hands in his pockets, flicking his thumbnail, too superstitious to say anything.

"We don't want the pilot to kill himself," someone pointed out, graciously.

"Can't he just drop the mail?" Benson asked.

"No, they don't do that here."

"He's coming in again," said someone else. "He's almost got it."

This time, the soldiers waited in silence as the plane's wings tilted up and down, faster and faster. It bucked like a paper airplane in front of a fan. The engine strained. But at the last moment it whipped up yet again, its engine whirring, and this time it headed away from them without turning back, in the direction of the sea.

Paul felt his shoulders droop. *It's nothing, it's nothing.*

"There he goes, back to the States. He'll try again next week, probably." Mayberry tossed his arm over the devastated Benson's shoulders and said cheerfully, "Do we need to call for the chaplain, gents? Or are we all going to be okay?"

They shuffled back down the walkway toward the mess hall, another small hut where they would crouch elbow to elbow and eat. "Mayberry," one of the soldiers asked, "how do you stay in such a good mood all the time?"

"I work in an underground ice cave," Mayberry said. "This is like summer camp for me. This is my social hour."

"You poor bastard," the soldier said, holding the door open.

Paul took one glance back at Baffin Bay, where the cargo plane, with Nat's words to him on it or not, was now just a speck in the sky.

THEIR PLATES WERE FORKED CLEAN on the cafeteria-style table and the soldiers sat smoking, trying to relax before heading off to whatever chores were in store for them. Every task at Camp Century had to do with fighting a climate hell-bent on discouraging them. They scraped ice off vehicles, whacked it with brooms from the wooden overhangs, clanged chunks of it out from underneath the boxcars that giant tractors towed on skis from one base to another. The ice crept up on them as if it had been plotting ages for just this, the opportunity to seal them over.

The other common task was latrine duty, which Paul knew he'd be up for soon, and which involved pulling buckets out from beneath holes in the floor and emptying them a quarter mile away. "Just wait till you get latrine duty at Camp Century," Mayberry chuckled in perverse delight: Because there was no dirt on the ice cap, they dumped all the waste onto a section of ice they called "the Shitberg." He claimed that in one hundred years or so the Shitberg would detach from its glacier and land in Scandinavia like a grotesque tall ship from the days of the explorers.

Mayberry passed around sections of a few *Washington Post*s that a pilot from Andrews AFB had left them. These were more valuable than cigarettes or chocolate, and the men examined them until they were tattered, poring over every word as if they were documents from a fascinating and faraway time. Paul, thumbing through the car section, held up an ad for a 1937 Horch in outstanding condition. "Fellas, look at this," he said.

"Sorry," said Mayberry without glancing up, "but this ad for a box of used silk ties is distracting me right now."

Paul chuckled. He leaned over Mayberry's shoulder to read Miscellaneous. "Hey," he said, joining the game, "a gray ottoman, good condition. Original chair not included."

"A wedding dress," countered Mayberry. "Never been worn. Includes garter!"

"Complete set of dental instruments," said Specialist Benson from behind his own paper.

"A whelping box."

"Here's a woman scaling back her 'extensive wig collection,'" Mayberry said.

They all read awhile, growing lazy since their sergeant had not yet come along and told them to get moving.

"Say, there's something I've been meaning to ask you," Paul said to Mayberry.

Mayberry flapped his paper and looked at Paul. "Yes?"

"What's the deal with Camp Century? Couple guys just back from there said now that the work crews have finished the reactor, they're just digging off in another direction, making more tunnels."

His friend smirked. "Yeah?"

"Camp Century is a research institution," spoke up Benson in a newsman's clipped, formal diction. He adjusted pretend glasses on his nose. "Please note the lack of any visible weapons. We have only one rifle for fending off the occasional polar bear."

Mayberry chuckled.

"I've heard all these theories—" Paul said.

"We are studying the polar ice sheet," Benson continued. "The army is fascinated by the ice sheet. It's in love with the goddamn ice sheet."

"While studying the ice sheet *is* the noblest work of mankind," said Mayberry, the geologist, "it's not the reason they built Camp Century."

"Well, why then?" Paul asked. "I've heard they have plans for a lot more bases up here, not just Century. And a guy back at CR-1 told me about some test tracks he'd seen up at Camp Century, like railroad tracks beneath the ice, but with nothing on them yet."

"All right." Mayberry lowered his voice, though Paul did not know if this were in a joking fashion, or out of real prudence. Mayberry held his hands a short distance apart, slightly cupped, as if explaining a tricky football play. "They say that Century is only the first of a whole line of bases across the Arctic, like you said. These bases will all be built under the ice like Century, connected by underground ice tunnels. The tunnels'll have train tracks in 'em so that we can transport weapons—missiles, nuclear warheads—back and forth under the ice, to whichever base they're needed. If we get intel that the Soviets are attacking from above, we can move into position quickly and counterattack. Just sailing along under the ice. No one would ever see us."

"Sounds like the DEW Line on steroids," Benson said. Everyone groaned at the mention of one of the Army's greatest debacles, the "Distant Early Warning Line" of radar stations across Alaska, Canada, and Greenland that had cost a billion dollars and boosted American military confidence for only nine weeks in 1957, from the time of its celebrated completion until the Russians launched *Sputnik* and in one moment rendered the new technology obsolete.

"It would take forever to build such a thing," said Paul.

"Maybe not. Century was built in only seventy-odd days."

"It would take a ton of weapons."

"We have weapons. What do you think we're doing with all that shit from the war?" Mayberry asked cheerfully.

Paul shook his head. "How do you know so much, anyway?" he asked Mayberry.

Mayberry smiled. "Being the camp geologist is kind of like being the chaplain. You get this, this aura of virtue," he said, waving his hand, "like you're somehow outside of the real world. Everybody talks to the chaplain. Everybody talks to the geologist."

A FEW DAYS LATER the wind died down and they were allowed to head north to Camp Century. The three-hundred-mile trip took a week. They inched across the ice in a long line of heavy vehicles, swathed in plumes of exhaust. The transport crew was a man short, so Paul filled in on a giant tractor called a Polecat, driving six hours on and six off while towing a fuel canister behind him. He spent the entire time fretfully smoking and praying that he would not go up in a spectacular ball of flame.

They couldn't turn off their vehicles for fear of them not restarting, and eventually Paul's body became so used to the endless vibration he could hardly remember what it was like to be still.

He had never seen anything like the polar ice cap. It was a vast, glittering, lifeless world. The ground and sky were entirely white and blue, as if they were trapped in a Wedgwood plate. They were told to be on constant lookout for deep crevasses that angled through the snow, high-walled and plunging. The threat was frightening at first; numbing as time went on.

They didn't see Camp Century until they were almost on top of it. Its sloping entry ramp ran thirty feet down into the ice. Below them, they knew, were the mysterious tunnels, the barracks, and the nuclear reactor.

One vehicle after another turned off, down the line. They all climbed down. "Shit," the man next to Paul said. Otherwise they quietly stared. They'd stay here, underground, for the next 150 days.

NAT

NAT WAS FIVE MILES OUTSIDE TOWN, AT ONE IN THE MORNING, when the tire blew.

Paul had been gone a month, and she had taken to late-night drives: two or three times a week, nothing excessive, just enough to clear her head. She was too tired and queasy to take the girls many places during the day, but at night, when they slept like angels, the walls hemmed her in. So a week after Paul left—after putting the girls to bed, sacking out on the couch, and then waking uselessly at eleven P.M., twitchy and restless—she'd had a moment of inspiration. She snuck into the girls' room and carried them one at a time, wrapped in their comforters, out to the car and laid them each across the backseat.

Liddie awoke for a moment and then, as soon as the car started, snuggled back down; Sam crawled up by the window and looked out, groggily amazed. Just having them outside the house—at this unexpected hour, on a little adventure—filled Nat with a swell of maternal fondness. Her girls were charming in their nightgowns, sleepy and pleasantly confused; they were such good sports.

She rolled down the driver's side window and the Fireflite rumbled quietly out of town, past the gleaming moonlit falls to the highway that stretched like an open book, straight and limitless. It was this immeasurable space all around her that called her outside. It was like the ocean: It begged people to come and gaze.

Her new routine was to drive thirty or so miles one way, just to get it out of her system, before turning back around. Four weeks in a row the drives couldn't have gone better; the girls even fell back to sleep as soon as she returned them to their beds. The relief of having cut loose, plus her cold, wind-stiffened skin, put Nat right out once she got home, too, and helped her through a few more days of sitting placidly, watching the girls play, tidying their messes and humming responses to their queries and requests.

And then, her little joyride went to hell. The highway was dark around her and her window was down and she could feel the smile playing on her face, captain of her little ship, until a sudden *thwack* rocked the car and it yanked across the road to the left, where it struck something—a large rock?—on the side of the road. The jolt felt huge and Nat clutched the wheel in terror, pulling the car back toward the center. A few shaky seconds later she realized that, thank God, she had corrected, and they were upright and not spinning and they hadn't tumbled off the road into the yawning blackness. But the car ground against the asphalt with a horrible racket.

"Mama!" Sam cried.

"Sam, you okay?"

"Yeah."

"You, too, Lid?" Nat called.

"She's still asleep!"

"How is that possible?" Nat almost laughed, but she was too wound up. She felt as if waves of ice water were coursing from her limbs. That jerk and wallop, forceful and totally unexpected, had shaken her. And now the front of the car seemed to be dragging against the road like a chastised beast. It made an awful metallic clatter, but there was nothing she could do, given the time of night and the isolation, but keep driving. A bitter, burning smell came up from somewhere inside the car.

They did make it home, the last half mile at a junky crawl. Nat thunked the Fireflite up near the curb and got out, her hands on her forehead.

The right rear tire was shredded away with steel showing through, and she knew this was bad, very bad, and probably very expensive. She was a stupid woman. What had ever compelled her to adopt this bizarre habit? They could have been killed.

Sam climbed out of the car and stood beside her and said, "Daddy is not going to be happy about this." Then she reached for Nat's hand and held it a moment, like a wise, straight-talking little priest, and Nat bent to kiss her in gratitude. She gathered Liddie and—feeling chastened, knowing she had deserved this for her folly—took the girls back into the house.

NAT'S NEIGHBOR CHRISSIE KNOCKED on the door the next morning at six-thirty, curlers in her hair, her tiny white dog standing beside her on the stoop as if it, too, demanded the answers to its questions: What had happened to Nat's car, and when on earth *had* it happened, because Chrissie was sure it was not like that when she went to bed, and goodness were Nat and the girls *all right*? Nat stumbled out replies—*We're fine; I'd just gone for a couple groceries when the tire blew*—while Chrissie jiggled her head in horror or sympathy and the tiny dog squatted to pee, its eyes fixed on Nat the whole time.

Nat sent Chrissie on her way, assuring her that she would be fine taking the bus until she could get the car fixed. An hour later another neighbor, Edna from down the street, came by, angling for new or different information. Nat figured she should be grateful for anybody visiting her at all, but she wished people would make social calls for reasons other than to interrogate her about her mistakes.

She started two or three letters to Paul over the next couple of days, planning to tell him about the car, but abandoned all of them. To write to him without mentioning it would be a sin of omission, so she found herself unable to write at all.

The girls' nearly constant requests and non sequiturs intensified when they were just stuck around the house. One afternoon Nat found herself glancing at the round wall clock so obsessively that she thought she might actually scream. And then she did. She let out one frayed, bizarre shriek and the girls, hopping around the living room, froze. Nat got up, fetched a dishcloth from the kitchen, and draped it over the clock face.

That night after she put Sam and Liddie to bed, she slumped onto the couch feeling the odd mix of wired and exhausted that she'd come to expect most evenings, and wondered what in the world to do with herself. Each night she was physically and mentally worn out but spiritually ready for some kind of part two, an aspect of the day that never came. For a short while the drives had almost filled that need. Music sometimes worked. But nothing worked quite enough.

Paul's deployment stretched before her like a test from the Bible. Why had he brought this upon them? She could still startle herself, thinking of him coming home with his puffed-up hand. *Punching his boss*—it was mortifying. She'd never worried that Paul had anything but their best interests at heart; if anything he was too responsible, too careful. Then he'd lost all self-control at the worst possible time. She didn't pity herself for the deployment (she was an army wife, if a newish one, and it was her job to bear up) but for the fact that it had been so avoidable. And on two days' notice! At least if she'd had advance warning, she might have forced herself to make some friends.

She *was* cultivating one acquaintance, another young army wife named Patrice whom she'd met at the playground. They were not, however, good enough friends that Nat could call her just to say, "Hello, I'm bored." Perhaps she could couch a phone call in practical terms: "What would you do if your car had a blown-out tire?" or, maybe, "How long is it acceptable to keep from your husband that your car needs major repairs and it was your fault because you were, say, taking your daughters for drives in the desert at night, which were the only thing helping you not feel like a madwoman?"

She'd forgiven Paul, in spite of everything; she couldn't make herself feel angry anymore, not with all this space between them. She longed for the daily relief of his homecoming, how the girls' high beams of attention would swing from her to him for that brief and blessed time. She missed his short, unexpected laugh when the girls did something funny, or when one of her anecdotes struck home. She missed the warmth of him in bed, falling asleep with his hand on her back. He was the only one in Idaho who knew her at all, the only person on earth who did, maybe, and now he was gone, and his absence was like a suction in her chest.

She pushed herself off the couch and wandered into the kitchen, opened the junk drawer, and navigated its paper clips, pen caps, a bottle of clear nail polish. Her fingertips found a small rectangular scrap that had worked its way to the back: the business card from the young cowboy she'd met near the Palisades Reservoir. She trapped it and pulled it out, looking over the slanted handwriting with its skipping ballpoint ink. She'd been downtown many times over the intervening year but never on the back street where his repair shop was, on an auto row that trailed toward the train tracks and where she never had any business.

She wondered if Esrom still worked there, if he'd remember her. Maybe he would cut her a deal on car repairs. Even if he didn't, it might be nice to see him again.

Then again, maybe he wouldn't remember her at all, and she'd be embarrassed. This gave her pause. She examined the pale blue letters as if they might suddenly move and form a new instruction specific to her.

She walked over to the wall clock, lifting its absurd veil of towel to discover that it was only eight P.M. There was a chance one of the men was still in the shop; she was aimless enough to try. She paused for a moment with the receiver against her neck and dialed the number.

The phone rang five times and she nearly hung up, but then a young man's voice answered, slightly breathless. "Car shop," he said.

Nat paused at this bare-bones greeting. "Hi!" she said. "I have, I need"—oh, for crying out loud—"There's a car here that needs repair."

"All right," the man said. "You can drive it on down any time and we'll take a look. Except on Sundays, we're closed. Otherwise, nine to five."

"It doesn't drive," Nat said.

"You need a tow? Sure. Let me take down your address."

Nat recited it and then asked, before she could stop herself, "Is this by any chance Esrom?"

There was a brief, curious pause. "It is."

"I think we met once, about this time last year. You gave me your card at a diner in Kirby, out near the Palisades Reservoir."

After a moment, he laughed. "Well, I'm glad you called."

This was a tremendous relief, and Nat could feel herself smiling. "Your friend said your shop was the best there is in Idaho Falls."

"My friend says a lot of things. It's Nat, right?"

"It is! Gosh, you have a good memory."

"I'll come out myself tomorrow morning. Aim for ten?"

"That'd be great. Thanks so much." She hung up, still smiling, and felt the heaviness in her chest lift away. Now she had something on the calendar for the next day, *and* a solution to the problem with the car. It was almost silly how much this helped.

THE NEXT MORNING DAWNED hot and bright, and Nat awoke early. She felt a twinge of anxiety, a mysterious motivation to get herself pulled together, and then she remembered the previous night's phone conversation. Esrom was coming over.

She hustled into the bathroom, splashed cold water on her face, put on makeup. In her closet she rummaged until she found a halfway decent dress that still fit over her small hill of belly. (She *felt* noticeably pregnant, but no one had commented yet, not even her nosy neighbors, so she mustn't have been showing as much as she felt.) Buoyed, she went into the kitchen, boiled some eggs to devil, and baked a coffee cake.

"What is going on today?" Sam asked when she pattered in, rumpled and blinking. "Are we having a party?" Her eyes lit up. "Is Daddy coming home?"

"No, no," Nat said, her face reddening. "Nothing special. Just a normal day."

"Oh," Sam said, looking disappointed.

"Well," Nat said, "we have someone coming to look at the car today. That's one small thing that is happening."

Sam's face lit up with joy: Any announcement filled her with extravagant expectations. "It's really nothing," Nat said and, seeing that Sam could not be convinced, poured a bowl of Pep cereal to distract her.

The morning passed slowly. Nat got the girls dressed, and they played several rounds of Candy Land. The sole thing Candy Land had to recommend it was that each round moved mercifully fast, so after half an hour Nat felt rather accomplished. It was midmorning by the time she heard an unfamiliar truck's rattle in the street, and a minute later there was a knock at the door.

When she opened it, Esrom was standing there, holding his hat and keeping to the back edge of the step. "Hello again, ma'am."

"Hello!" she said.

"I remember you!" Sam squealed, appearing from behind Nat.

Nat restrained her gently. "Thank you so much for coming."

"It was no trouble," Esrom said, "but I'm sorry to see what happened to your car there."

"It's terrible, isn't it?"

"It's pretty bad. You're lucky you all weren't hurt."

"We were out in the middle of the *night,*" Sam said.

Esrom looked at Nat.

"Well," Nat said, " 'middle of the night' is a bit of an exaggeration."

"No!" Sam's voice was squeaky, her eyebrows energetic. "It really was in the middle of the night. Mama pulled me out of my bed and everyfing."

Esrom laughed. "Well, all right," he said.

Nat felt her face flush. "We went for a drive," she said. "Just for some fresh air. It was late, yes. That's why I had to drive all the way home on that tire."

"You should keep a spare, ma'am. If you don't mind my saying."

"The spare is *on* the car. We had to use it when we were driving out here from Virginia. We never replaced it."

"Well, if it's in use," he said kindly, "it's not the spare anymore."

Nat nodded. She wanted to tell him that she understood, that she was not typically a stupid person, but she was too sheepish to say anything.

"I saw some fluid under the car," he said, "when I peeked under it. Think it might be transmission fluid. Did you hit something while you were out there?"

"I did. I hit a rock."

"Okay." He frowned, as if genuinely aggrieved on her behalf. "Well, I don't like the look of the fluid. It's all burnt. Let's hope that's the start of a puddle and not the tail end of all the fluid you had."

Nat didn't know what to say to this mostly incomprehensible possibility.

Sam, wriggling a little closer to Esrom, could contain herself no longer. "Do you remember me from the milkshake place?"

"'Course I do," Esrom said. "It's Sam, right?"

"Yes! That's right!"

Nat was touched that he remembered Sam's name. "And Liddie," she added, tapping her younger girl's head.

"Well, I couldn't forget Liddie." Esrom shook her small hand.

"How are your friends?" Nat asked. "How's business at the auto shop?"

"Oh, fine, thanks. Growing bit by bit." He gestured toward the car. "I'm going to need to get under the hood to see what all has gone wrong. Can I borrow your keys—see if I can start it?"

"Certainly," Nat said, and ducked back into the house, then brought them to him.

"All right. I'll let you know when I'm done."

Nat thanked him and ushered the girls back inside. Sam and Liddie perched in the window. They hooked their fingers over the windowsill, staring as if Esrom were the first man they had seen in years. The oscillating fan flapped the lace edge on their socks, lifting and dropping their skirts as it aimed. Nat puttered into the kitchen, sprinkled a fine rust of paprika over the deviled eggs, and sliced up the coffee cake. Then, inspired, she brought out canned peaches, which she nestled into little iceberg lettuce beds so they wouldn't dribble onto the cake, and went outside to invite Esrom in.

Her heart dipped when she saw the Fireflite hooked up to his truck in a sad diagonal. "Oh, no," she said, startling him out of his cowboy reverie.

He turned and took a few steps toward her. "Yeah, it doesn't look good. It won't even start up. I suspect that rock you hit made a hole in your transmission pan, and that the fluid leaked out while you were driving so far on that tire. You might've burnt up your transmission."

"Is that a big fix?"

"Yeah, it's big, I'm afraid."

"*Darn* it." Nat felt the hot rise of anxiety, how disappointed Paul would be over the waste of money, her poor judgment, the whole thing. She pressed her fingers to her forehead. After a moment she could feel the cowboy's eyes on her so she straightened up, smiled, and said, "Would you like to come in? We have lunch on the table."

"Oh," he said. "Thank you, but I should be getting back to the shop."

"You don't have time for lunch?" She felt even more foolish, now, for going to the trouble to make the eggs and coffee cake; she was transparent in her pathetic desire for any kind of a friend. The day in the diner came snapping back to her: the waitress's harsh eyes, her sense of being left out. One embarrassment always called up another in quick succession. Her eyes stung with tears and she hoped he didn't notice, but his sudden change of heart and soothing, solicitous tone, as if she were an unhappy horse who might kick him, made her suspect that he did.

"I'm sorry," he said. "Of course I have time for lunch. That's real nice of you." His eyes held crinkles at the edges from time spent in the sun, and his smile was warm, although his teeth had obviously never been worked on, crossing one another here and there like a fence that needed mending.

When he pried off his boots in the entryway, stepped inside, and saw the table laden with food and three kinds of silverware (dear God, she'd put out cloth napkins, what had she been thinking?), his eyes widened. Nat felt exposed by her ridiculous effort: the gently crumbling coffee cake, fussy perfection of deviled eggs lined up like oysters on the half shell, satiny peaches that glistened in their own syrup.

"We have food," Sam was singing, "we have special food today-ay."

"Holy smokes," Esrom said, "this is like Easter."

"Oh, no," Nat said, "we eat this way all the time."

"No, we don't," Sam muttered.

Nat and the girls sat in a semicircle, all tilted slightly toward Esrom while he ate. He reddened and squirmed under their attention, but enjoyed his food with such gusto that soon Nat felt more at ease.

Sam prattled endlessly, sputtering deviled egg in Esrom's direction as she regaled him with the bright wanderings of her consciousness ("I once ate a coffee cake with a *real* coffee bean on top, but the bean was like a dis-gus-ting rock"; "I can play Go Fish and I always win"; "I seed a vulture eating a dead turtle on the side of the road and Daddy said, 'That's ashes to ashes, dust to dust'"). Liddie nodded vigorously at Sam's statements so they could be partially claimed as her own. Liddie's little voice was still soft and slurred, so most of what she said was hard to understand. It was Sam who could always translate—"She says she has a doll that sleeps, and when you give it milk it pees"—and they could see from the satisfaction on Liddie's face that this was correct. Liddie hated to be misunderstood; it was one of the few things that enraged her.

They dug into the coffee cake, and Nat poured milk around the table.

"Ah, cold milk," Esrom said. "I don't get that every day. At my place we usually drink warm milk."

For some reason this nearly embarrassed Nat, and Sam blurted, "Why?"

"We got cows."

"Do you eat 'em?" Sam asked. "Do you make 'em into boots?"

Esrom laughed. "That's right, the boots," he said. "No, we don't eat our cows. Else where would we get our milk from? Our neighbors, Lind is their name, we trade them for beef once a year."

"Oh," said Sam. "Then you're not a real cowboy."

"Sam," Nat said, disapprovingly.

Esrom waved his hand to show her he didn't mind. "By your high standards, maybe I'm not. But I do ride a horse most every day. Does that count?"

"Yeah," said Sam, generously. She thought for a moment. "Why are all your neighbors named Lind?"

Esrom helped himself to another square of cake. "I like you," he said. "Say," he added, "I found something this morning you girls might like." He reached into his front shirt pocket and produced a strip of shed snake skin, half a foot long. It was transparent, thinner than tissue, and lined with pale marks that made it look somehow ancient and valuable, like a scroll. The girls leaned closer.

"It's a snake skin," he told them. "I found it this morning. It's only part of it."

"Where's the other part?" Sam asked.

"I don't know. Maybe blew away."

"Is it a rattler? Did it die when it lost its skin?"

"Well, I can't say for sure if it's a rattler," Esrom said, "'cause this is only the head end. If you find the tail of a rattler, you can see the little bumps where the skin shed right over the rattle. See here?" He pointed carefully. "The skin peeled over its eyeballs. And no, shedding its skin doesn't kill it. Snakes just do that from time to time."

Even Nat found herself leaning closer, and then remembered that she was an adult and set about gathering the empty plates.

"Have *you* ever seen a rattler?" Sam asked Esrom.

"Oh, sure. They're all around."

"You ever kill one?"

"Well, I have," said Esrom, "if I find them too close to the house, or in the barn. Otherwise I leave 'em alone."

"Good grief, Sam," Nat sighed. "Girls, wash your hands. They're sticky."

"Here," said Esrom, "you girls can keep the snake skin."

Sam and Liddie gasped and hopped up and down, then instantly began fighting over it. Nat told them it would stay on the windowsill until they could control themselves. Esrom stretched out his legs and took the cup of steaming coffee Nat offered him, while the girls washed their hands at record speed and ran back, dripping water all the way. From the window Nat could see her neighbor Chrissie walking her little white dog down the street, stopping to gape at Nat's dangling car. Chrissie peered into Esrom's truck as she passed and then, not seeing anyone inside, looked around the street and up at Nat in the window. Nat felt a twinge of uneasiness and turned her back. She didn't want to rush Esrom away.

Not that she could have, anyhow. "We have a lot of toys we can show you," Sam was saying, and she and Liddie got to work. They galloped from their bedroom into the living room over and over, showing Esrom their plastic toy telephone, a Dennis the Menace doll, a Betsy Wetsy with missing eyelashes and fluttering, clouded eyes.

"Sorry about them," Nat said. "We don't have company over much."

"They're great," said Esrom. "I never been so finely treated while collecting someone's car."

"Are you getting work in town these days, like you wanted?"

"Oh, yeah." He wiped his mouth with a napkin, nodding. He seemed a little surprised that Nat had remembered so much about him. "Lots of auto work."

"I was surprised that anyone answered last night, when I called."

"I was the only one left, catching up. I like fiddling with the old cars." He looked almost sheepish and changed the subject. "Say, I never asked, where'd *you* grow up?"

"California. San Diego."

"Whoa," he said. "That must have been nice."

"It was. Growing up on the beach and all."

He laughed out loud, as if the very idea of doing such a thing were preposterous. "Sometimes the lava flats remind me of an ocean," he said. "Is that stupid? Would somebody only say that if they'd never seen the ocean?"

"It's not stupid," Nat said. "It reminds me of the ocean, too. That's why I was going for night drives. I just like being out there. It's another world. You get to escape yourself." She blushed and swiped crumbs into her palm.

"So what'd your husband say?" Esrom asked. "When he saw that busted tire? He must've been surprised."

Sam was trotting toward him with a wooden camera and she cried, "Oh, our daddy's not here at all! He's in Antarctica for a year!"

"Oh," Esrom said.

"Not quite," Nat said. She turned on her serious voice: "Sam, do you remember what we talked about?" She meant the conversation where she'd asked her children not to advertise that the head of their household was thousands of miles away. "My husband's deployed to a base in Greenland," she explained.

"When's he due back?" Esrom asked, and Nat felt a tiny trigger of alarm. He raised his hand. "I'm sorry. I didn't mean to be personal."

"No, it's fine. He's due back in December. I'm hoping this baby can hold out for his return, but that doesn't seem likely."

Esrom glanced around, as if "this baby" might be hiding beneath the table or asleep somewhere nearby. Then he met her eyes and laughed with the realization: "You're having a baby?"

It seemed so obvious to her, but here was another person who hadn't noticed. "Yes," she said, "in early December."

"How about that," said Esrom. "Well, congratulations."

"Thank you."

He smiled for a moment as if thinking of something, and then jerked himself into motion. He stood and rubbed his palms on the front of his jeans. "I should be getting back to the shop now," he said. "But I can't thank you enough for lunch. I'll be braggin' to the guys all afternoon about it."

Nat wished she had enough food left over to wrap up for them, to make it seem less like all her ministrations were directed at Esrom. "It was no trouble."

"I'll call you when I know more about your car."

"Yes. Thank you."

"In the meantime, how do you plan to get around?"

"The bus, I guess."

"That's a lot of work."

"Maybe it'll finally teach me a lesson."

"You don't need a lesson," he said, with more emphasis than she'd expected. "Sometimes things just happen."

"Oh. Well, all right."

"And, ma'am—"

"Nat."

"Ma'am, Nat, I hope you don't mind if I check in every once in a while. To see if you need anything. I'd want someone to do it for my own wife."

Nat's eyes darted to his ring finger, bare. He caught this and said, "I mean, if I had a wife. My own wife, or mother—I wouldn't want them to be alone."

"That's fine," Nat said. "That's incredibly kind."

"I can't help it," he said in a self-deprecating tone, "I'm a Mormon."

But of course, Nat thought, and wondered why this had not occurred to her. Most of the locals here were. This new knowledge gave Nat the usual pull of suspicion, but also made him seem more trustworthy, somehow.

When Esrom opened the door Sam and Liddie gathered at his heels, looking bereft. He noticed their expressions and squatted down. "Miss Liddie, next time I see you I'd like to know all the troublemaking that Dennis the Menace doll has been up to. And Miss Sam, you'll have to tell me what you've been taking pictures of with your wooden camera. Can you do that?"

"Yes," the girls chorused, throbbing with eagerness.

"All right, then. I'll see you all soon," he said, and waved, ambling down the grassy slope to his truck.

PAUL

"Ah, home sweet home," Specialist Mayberry said, throwing his duffel onto the floor and flopping onto a bunk across from Paul, who was reclined on his own with a newspaper. "How's tricks, Collier? Aren't you working today?"

Paul glanced at his watch. "In an hour," he said.

"Yet again, our schedules keep us apart," Mayberry said. "How's your precious reactor?"

"She's a gem," Paul said, and it was true. The PM-2A never got too hot, never set off a false alarm, and never, ever, threw them a stuck rod. While she did her beautiful work Paul obsessively compared every belabored move the CR-1 would make in the same situation, his mind bothered with visions of stuck rods, radioactive steam, inextinguishable uranium-fed fires. He was beginning to think he was imagining things, that the scene at home couldn't possibly have been as bad as he remembered. He'd even confided his fears to the chaplain. "I have bad dreams about it," he'd said. "I feel . . . worked up." The chaplain gave him three aspirin and a glass of water.

Specialist Benson poked his head into the room and said, "We're gonna play pinochle in the lounge, if anybody wants to join us."

"Sure," said Mayberry.

"Not me, thanks," said Paul, deciding he had enough time before work to drop Nat a line. He found his pen and notebook, opened the cover to peer at the photo of her he kept inside.

Benson stepped to Paul's shoulder. "Ooh, is that your wife, the famous Nat?"

Reflexively, Paul flipped it over.

"Yeah, it's her," Mayberry answered for him.

"Let us see."

"She's a looker," bragged Mayberry. "She'll make your wife look like the cleaning lady."

Benson tried to lean over Paul, mouth half-open, the gap between his teeth showing; something about his expression, the rowdy anticipation, bothered Paul in a gut-pronged way.

"He keeps it in his little book," Mayberry teased, as if Paul were mute. "He won't show you."

"How'd you see it, then?" Benson asked.

"I fished it out one time, naturally."

"To do what with it?"

Mayberry didn't answer. Paul was not looking at him, so for all he knew his friend had simply not thought of a response yet. But in Paul's mind, Mayberry or Benson did something lewd, and before he could stop himself Paul ducked out of the bunk and stood. "Will the two of you *shut up*?" he snapped.

"We were just being appreciative," Benson said. "We didn't mean to rattle your cage."

Paul squatted, his back to them. He zipped open his duffel and slid the photo between two layers of folded clothing. The silence was thick, and their eyes were on him. He felt like an ass.

"All right, I'm heading out," said Mayberry after a minute, and Benson followed.

Paul sat back down on his bunk. The only sound in the room was the heater's weak rattle, never quite keeping the room at fifty degrees. By now he was too flustered to think of anything to write to Nat, anyway. "Be careful. I love you" was really all he wanted to say, but she was going to stop taking the message seriously if he sent it again, the same way people said "Drive safely!" to one another and then immediately disregarded it because they were just making a ten-minute trip to the convenience store.

After a few minutes, realizing the guys weren't returning, he opened the duffel bag and took out the photo again. There she was, nineteen-year-old Nat, smiling in front of the pleated curtain at the back of the booth. Her smile was almost shy; her eyes looked not into the camera but past it, at Paul, as if asking him why he'd wanted her to pose for this silly thing. He'd wanted a picture to take back to Fort Irwin with him.

He'd always loved Nat's tilted smile, the small dimple on the right where her mouth went up higher. Though the picture cut off just below her shoulders, he could see the straps of her swimsuit tied behind her neck. He remembered that purple swimsuit, its salt-and-coconut smell, and the way it sat right on top of her collarbone and tied at the nape of her neck. He wished, even now, that he could untie it. The thought of those straps sliding down over her shoulders, from this distance in space and time, was decadent and riveting.

He wondered when she'd gotten rid of that swimsuit and wished he'd asked her to keep it. But that was six years ago—so much had happened since then.

He'd met Nat on a liberty weekend while he was stationed at Fort Irwin. He and a couple of army buddies had made the drive out to San Diego, craving the ocean, craving mountains and color and being among people who weren't wearing tan uniforms. They felt nearly insane with joy as they approached that seaside town, where bright pink bougainvillea seemed to curve up every trellis and the ocean glinted an unbelievable, darker-than-sky blue.

Paul had seen the ocean before, but it still amazed him. It made the world seem vast. The guys around him were laughing, joking, hamming around, and showing their muscles. Paul sat, smoking, and listened to the ocean's thump and rush as it bashed the world clean. It was so opposite the quiet world of forest and pond he'd grown up in, where leaves sank and rotted into the water, butterflies sucked mud in silent groups, toads spun jelly tapes of spawn like rolls of film. The ocean turned over whole, tiny lives in an instant, without a care.

"That farmer's tan, Collier," said one of the soldiers. "It's killing me."

Paul flipped him off with a grin. This gesture did not come naturally to him, but he'd learned that it was a somehow satisfying response when someone made fun of you and you didn't feel like talking back. People always laughed and seemed pleased, which was strange.

There were eight or nine girls in a group near them, and a satellite pack of guys who seemed to know the girls and had set up their towels close to them. "Those chimps have moved in," one of the soldiers said, eyeing the young men, who were batting a volleyball back and forth among themselves. "It's like they pissed a ring around that whole section of beach."

"I think the girls have sighted us."

Another soldier sprang up, suddenly vigorous. "I'm going in!" he said. "I'm going in that goddamn water." And he ran for the ocean's edge like his pants were on fire.

Paul waded in a minute later, pointed his arms above his head, and made a shallow, bellyish dive. Everything was tinted green from below, the sun shining through turbulence, waves tossing gold dust everywhere. He bobbed out almost to his buddies, hoping they did not notice that he stayed where his toes could touch bottom.

"Well, I'll be. Look who's coming in," one of them grinned. Paul followed his gaze. The group of girls moved from the beach down toward the water. They dithered a bit at the shore, dabbling their feet in the foam, sneaking glances at the young soldiers when they could.

It was a great feeling to be noticed, as Paul knew they would be. What they had was a fleeting thing. They were young, and on leave, and riveting in their carefree maleness. This was not wartime anymore, so there was no longer that urgency that had once melted women; it was more of a game now, with a less certain winner, and that made it more fun. The girls could toy with them a little.

And then the sun glinted off the back of something, some huge shiny gray thing, and Paul's heart stopped. Had he imagined it?

"Hey," he said. Something in his voice made everyone look up.

He'd been sure it was a shark. Things could have gone very differently: He might have panicked, gone thrashing onto the beach screeching like a schoolgirl. He was spared by one of the young women who pointed and called, "Look, dolphins!"

"Dolphins," Paul laughed with relief, as if he had known. And there were dozens of them, maybe twenty feet away, arcing in and out of the water like swiftly drawn commas. They were very fast. A few came close enough that Paul could see their squinty eyes, their blowholes like little cranial belly buttons, water coursing down sleek sides. Paul even forgot the girls for a moment, though they had drifted closer, watching. Within a couple of minutes, all the dolphins were past.

The spell was broken. Laughter and shouts could again be heard from shore. Paul turned back and saw all the bright pea-sized people lounging on the beach, unaware of what had just taken place. They would be no worse off for not knowing, but Paul felt privileged, enriched, somehow.

When he looked back to the people in the water with him he noticed that, just on the other side of his friends, a dark-haired girl had swum up. His eyes skipped over the guys and lingered on her. Before he could force himself to look away she had turned and smiled at him, a full smile, delighted at what they had seen. It dawned on Paul that she had skipped over the people in between them, too.

As evening fell, the large group of young men near them built a bonfire, and a huge, beefy blond fellow shouted, "Hey! You guys army?" When they hollered back yes, he invited them over. Paul spotted the dark-haired girl sitting across the fire from him, holding a beer and chatting with a friend. She did not appear to be attached to any fellow in particular, which cheered him.

He felt tongue-tied and out of place with these civilian kids. His graphed and gridded army life, with all its specifics and regulations and endless acronyms and isolated bases, seemed a world away. He was twenty years old. He was scuffed around the edges. Most of these kids were just a year or two younger than him but they seemed shiny and unmarred by life, new pennies found on a sidewalk.

Around the bonfire silhouettes lounged and reclined. Paul set his sights on the dark-haired girl, hesitated, and then walked over, perhaps too briskly. He sat beside her and pushed his feet into the sand. One of his small toes was weirdly shaped from childhood frostbite and he didn't particularly want her to see it.

"Hi," she said, smiling, not seeming surprised by his arrival. She was sitting with a towel over her shoulders, her fingers laced around her knees. Her face and feet were shadowed then sparked with light, over and over.

"I'm Paul," he said and held out his hand.

"Natalie," she said, shaking it.

"That's a nice name."

"Everyone calls me Nat, actually."

"Nat is a nice name, too," Paul said. A beat passed and his mind churned for something to say. "That was amazing, seeing those dolphins."

"Wasn't it? They're beautiful. They come up and down this coast all the time."

"I've never seen anything like that before," Paul said, a little disappointed to hear that the event wasn't as rare as he'd thought.

"A couple years ago," Nat said, "this huge pod of dolphins went by while I was out swimming. There must have been at least two hundred, jumping out of the water as far as you could see in either direction."

"I wish I could have seen that." He meant he wished he had been there with her to see it, realized she might have divined his meaning, and then felt mortified.

"I think they call it a dolphin stampede. Where are you from?" she asked. "The Midwest?"

"No. Maine."

"I've heard it's beautiful there, with all the lighthouses and cliffs," she said.

"Yeah," said Paul, though he had never seen either of those things.

She'd grown up just a few miles away, she said, and had two brothers, much older. They had both moved out of the house, had children of their own, and she was the only one left with her parents. Her father owned a medical supply business, and her mother was a secretary.

The wind shifted direction, and she waved smoke out of her face with a small cough. "My parents think I'm spoiled. They grew up in Dayton, Ohio." She shook her head, frowned. "They think I have no direction because I'm so much younger than my brothers and they've kind of let me run wild."

"Oh. What does that mean?" Paul asked.

She chewed her thumbnail, thinking, and didn't seem to hear the question. "See, my mom wants me to have *some* direction, as she calls it, but not too much. Just enough to become a stenographer and get married. But I hate typing! I can't even type."

"Typing is hard," Paul said. God, he sounded like a dolt.

"I'm boring you," Nat said.

"No! No, no." Now Paul wondered if he seemed a little too wild-eyed and emphatic. He felt as if he had just stood up and bellowed, *"Your talk of typing could never bore me!"*

The night felt late now. Everyone was sprawled about dreamily, and across from Paul someone had pulled out a guitar. Three or four embers at a time rose from the fire and spun in the wind, then blinked silently out. Paul liked that last spiral they made, the whirl of energy before they were nothing.

"Want to go for a swim?" Nat asked.

Surprised, he said, "Sure."

She let the towel around her shoulders drop and stood, picking her way around a couple of loungers to head down to the water. She smiled back at Paul over her shoulder and chatted about night swimming, how it was something she had done for years, how it never made her afraid and how there was no better feeling than having the moon right above you.

The ocean felt slightly warmer now because the night air was cool. The ocean seemed made of hammered tin. They walked in up to their waists and Nat rubbed her arms, laughing. "You can't think about it," she said, "or you'll never go in!"

Paul grinned at her and prepared himself to dive. He paused to look back at the bonfire. There was some small worm of doubt wriggling in his mind. What was it? Then he realized: He felt that one of Nat's friends should have volunteered to come with them. Though she was only with *him,* and he was honorable, he thought she should be chaperoned, or that she should ask to be. None of her friends knew him from Adam. He was thrilled to be alone with her, and yet he couldn't help but wonder if she did this often, went down the beach with guys she did not know. None of her friends had glanced up when they left.

He decided to assume that it was only his own charm and appeal that brought her out of her shell. *Don't ruin things for yourself, Paul.* Anyway, she had already dived and come up some distance away, treading in a rippled circle. "What are you waiting for?" she called, laughing. In the dark at that distance she looked small, and could have been anything: a buoy; a sleek and lovely seal.

Paul plunged into the froth of a low wave and pulled himself through the dark, shallow water. Moonlight shone through the surface, but he could not see much of anything, which was exhilarating and unnerving at the same time. He popped up once for air, saw that she was still several feet away, and dipped back down until he could come up beside her. When he surfaced, sputtering, treading water with ten times the exertion of her occasional kicks, she laughed. "You made it," she said.

For a moment he thought he could pull this off. He'd passed the army swim test years before, after all. But the expression on her face changed as she watched him, and he soon realized that after a minute or two of treading water he was not going to be able to keep it up.

"I can't," he coughed, his arms and legs churning, "I'm not really good at this," and for an instant he saw himself the way she must see him: wide-eyed, thrashing, his limbs uselessly slicing water. He felt as if the truth about him was suddenly knowable in every humiliating detail, that he'd grown up so poor he'd never gone swimming, that he knew nothing of this world of youthful leisure. He was failing, completely, before her very eyes. But she scooped one of his arms under hers and bobbed them both just a few feet closer to shore, where they could touch ground again.

He hacked miserably; the more he tried to control it the worse it seemed to get. "Just relax," Nat said, and she was right. A moment later he caught his breath. But he knew with a sense of despair that the night was over for him. He would go back to the beach by himself and get smashingly drunk, and in the morning hopefully forget how he'd blown his one chance with this kind, beautiful girl.

"Are you all right?" she said. "Wait, are you going back?" She touched his arm. "Don't be silly. We can stay right here; we don't have to go out deeper."

He looked at her. A wave washed over his chin and he rubbed a hand down his face and back up again.

She laughed. "Did you think I wasn't going to be interested in you anymore, just because you can't swim?"

Was she interested in him? What exactly did that mean? He tried to ignore the next wave that sloshed over his face.

"I don't care at all whether or not you can swim," she said.

He found his voice again. "I wouldn't have blamed you."

"Oh, you're silly. The fun part is being out here." And amazingly, though he still cringed in anticipation of his own doom, she started talking again. As if he hadn't just looked like the world's biggest fool, she chatted away, animated, smiling, her hands gesturing: There were islands off the coast of San Diego, she said, *just over there, out that way,* where she'd taken a boat ride once. She pointed in another direction and said she'd gone abalone diving with friends near Bird Rock, that the abalone were bigger than softballs and her mother would pound them and fry them in butter. *They're everywhere! Sometimes all you have to do is turn over a rock, and there they are.*

Paul did not know what the hell an abalone was, and he was so washed over with relief that he leaned in and kissed her. Then he pulled back, shocked by his own daring. For a moment he feared she might turn and swim back to shore, or—though he sincerely hoped this would not be the case—slap him, or cry. He had never kissed a girl before; he had no idea what to expect from one when he did so.

But she smiled. She gave him one soft, small kiss of her own in return, which surprised him even more. His stomach seemed to temporarily whisk off somewhere else and then come back. He put his arm around her, feeling her breath and wet hair on his shoulder, and turned with her to look back at the shore, where they could not tell their beach fire from the others that dotted the long, dark strand.

NAT

Things, Nat decided, were looking up. She had managed to grow her budding friendship with Patrice, the army wife she'd met at the park down the street, and they got together a few mornings a week to let their girls play. Patrice had an angelic blond four-year-old named Carol Ann who made Nat's girls look like poorly behaved beasts, but Nat was willing to weather an occasional humbling in exchange for companionship.

Because Patrice's husband, Bud, was not deployed, she was kept busy with the usual tight schedule of shopping, cooking, and cleaning that Nat had almost entirely let go. After an hour at the park they would go their separate ways, and Nat felt as if Patrice were being sucked out onto some briskly moving highway, having dabbled in Nat's drowsy life and enjoyed the break, but there was a real world of responsibility and human interaction to get back to.

Nat's car was still in the shop; she and the girls took the ten-minute bus ride downtown when they needed to but spent most of their time at home. She drifted through the days, maybe doing laundry, maybe not, maybe cleaning the kitchen, maybe letting it go, maybe chatting with the mailman one day or maybe not talking to another adult for forty-eight hours. It didn't matter as much as it might have, though, because she also had Esrom's visits.

He kept his word, dropping by to check on her and the girls every couple of days. It turned out that the Fireflite's transmission was completely wrecked and would have to be replaced. Esrom said he'd repair it with no charge for labor if he could work on it in his spare time, but his uncle was charging over a hundred dollars for the part alone, a sum that nearly made Nat grow faint. She began to tuck five dollars here and there from Paul's paychecks, wanting to settle the bill without him knowing, but between Esrom's leisurely pace and her own slow accrual she realized that she would not be getting the car back soon. It didn't much matter; riding the bus was not as bad as she'd feared, and the girls even found it to be a bit of an adventure. Besides, it meant that Esrom continued to drop by.

She found him the same way each time, holding his hat and standing at the back edge of the top step. He always knocked rather than ring the bell, as if he mistrusted that simple technology. And he brought some nature-made trinket for the girls—a hollow wasp's nest, smooth as a gourd; a chipped arrowhead carved from obsidian—that they exclaimed over and then lined up on their bedroom windowsill, like a parade of harmless fetishes.

He said that a couple of weeks ago, while on horseback inspecting his neighbor's fence, he had seen an unusual silhouette at the edge of his vision and ridden over to inspect it. As he got closer he realized that it was two bucks locked at the antlers, big males who, during a fight, had become entangled and were now forced to live eyeball to eyeball, confused and hating each other as they starved.

"If they were humans, they would've figured out a way to take turns eating," Esrom told the girls, whose little faces were scrunched, trying to picture such a thing. "But being animals, they weren't able to figure it out, and they were starving to death. One would try to pull his head down to eat, and the other would startle and yank them both up. Or they'd pull their necks down in different directions, getting nowhere. Lord knows how long they'd been stuck like that. I didn't get much meat out of those fellas, but I did get two nice racks of antlers."

He told them about a litter of coyote pups he'd seen on his ranch land, so fluffy and trusting that they stumbled right up to him until the mom flashed into sight and bossed them back underground. "Back when we'd had sheep, I'd have had to shoot them," he said. "But I was glad not to. They were just like dogs."

"Oh, I want one!" Sam cried. "I want a coyote pup."

"Coyotes don't make good pets," Nat began, but Esrom said, "I know. I want one too."

At naptime, Nat ushered her girls to the back of the house. She assumed Esrom would take his leave, but when she returned to the kitchen she saw a pair of boots just outside the window at eye level. "Oh, for Pete," she said with a laugh and walked outside, where Esrom waved distractedly from his ladder. He was grabbing fat, sloppy armfuls of leaves and seedlings from the gutters and chucking them to the ground below.

"Stand back," he called as another mound of rotting maple pods rained down.

"Stop that," Nat said. "Don't you have a coyote pup to train or something?"

"Coyotes don't make good pets," he said. "I thought you knew that."

Nat crossed her arms. "You've got my little girls dreaming about getting one for Christmas."

The street was quiet. A few kids played at the far end, but most of the mothers were inside, children napping. She felt she should keep Esrom company when he did these sorts of chores; it didn't seem right that he should be slaving away of his own goodwill while she was inside, resting. She hoped her endless chatter didn't annoy him.

"You can go in," Esrom called, as if reading her thoughts. "I mean, you don't have to stay right here."

"I'll sit for a minute," Nat said. "It's nice out." And it was, the sky crayon blue, dragged with wisps of clouds.

"I won't be able to come by again till late next week," Esrom said, climbing down from the ladder and scooting it further around the side of the house. "My neighbor's moving his cattle and I usually help him."

"Okay," said Nat. "You don't have to feel responsible for us, you know. Moving his cattle where?"

"Just to another pasture."

"Do you like that kind of work?" Nat asked.

Esrom tossed another wad of compost to the grass. "I don't know. I never thought about it. Actually, I'm trying to get onto the fire department out at the reactor testing station."

"Oh," Nat said.

"Yep. Just got an apartment in town with some friends."

"Really?" she said, surprised. She associated him only with his mythical ranch; she liked the idea of him there.

"Can't live on my parents' farm forever, right?"

"I guess not."

"I'm close enough, I can still help out. But it was getting tight over there, all my brothers and sisters growing up. And my dad's a little, I don't know."

"What?" Nat prodded.

Esrom's mouth pulled to the side. "We butt heads sometimes. Things can just feel small around home."

"Oh," said Nat, not knowing exactly what he meant, and feeling she should not press further. "I admire Mormon people," she said stupidly. "The close families and everything."

Esrom looked suddenly tired. "Thank you," he said.

"Have you been fishing out at the reservoir lately?"

"No, not this year. Workin' too much."

"That's too bad."

"No, it's a good thing. I need to be working. I was having a slow spell there for a while, back when we ran into you in that diner." He paused and looked down at Nat as if studying her, hesitated, and said, "I've been wondering, what were you doing at the reservoir that day last summer? You ladies driving that far from home, all by yourselves?"

The way he was looking at her, her heart sped up.

"Oh, we were just on a day trip," she said. "It's not *that* far away."

"It's a good long drive just for swimmin'."

"Sometimes I just need to get out. I wish I could be content like other people, you know, just happy to stay in one place. But I've never been like that. I mean, I can stay in one area, but I need to move around *in* it. I want to see things. Sometimes," and her face burned because she could tell she was taking her own reply too seriously and talking too much, "I feel like a piece in a china cabinet, you know? Like I just sit still, waiting for something. Like I haven't taken a deep breath in years."

Esrom watched her.

"I'm so sorry, that was too much of an answer," Nat said.

"No," he said. "No, it wasn't."

"You must think I'm a lunatic. I don't mean to sound discontented. I have a very good life."

"I know you do," he said. "Anyone can see that. You for sure don't sound like a lunatic."

"Paul and I had gotten into an argument," Nat said. Why stop now? "I wanted to use the car more. He was worried about being late for work. We fought about it a little. I was upset."

"Oh," Esrom said. "That makes sense. You seemed—like there was an edge to you."

Nat rolled her eyes at herself and laughed. "Goodness, I'm obvious. Guess I won't take up poker."

"So now you have the car all to yourself when your husband's away, but then you go and bust it?" A smile pulled the corners of his mouth.

"Well, when you put it that way, I feel stupid."

"It wasn't your best move, maybe."

"How's your friend?" Nat asked. "The waitress—Corrie? The one who hated me."

"Don't worry about her; she hates everybody."

"She doesn't hate *you*." This came out sounding a little too familiar, and Nat wished she had restrained herself.

"Well, no," he said, not seeming to notice. "Her life is hard. Her and her sisters—they're way out there in the middle of nowhere." Nat waited for him to elaborate, strangely hungry to hear more about their relationship, more about these sisters who had popped into the conversation just to absurdly bother her, but Esrom glanced toward the street and twisted on the ladder to see behind him. "I think someone's trying to get your attention," he said.

Nat turned. Jeannie Richards, of all people, had pulled the cream-colored Coupe up to the curb and rolled down the window. Nat hopped to her feet in alarm. She had not spoken with Jeannie since Paul had punched her husband in their own home. She'd passed Jeannie in the neighborhood once or twice, but one or both of them had always been in a car, a level of distance for which Nat was grateful. She was utterly ashamed by what Paul had done. And now here was Jeannie—what for? Had she been gathering up her anger these past weeks, now ready to unleash it upon Nat?

But Jeannie waved, as if the two of them were old pals.

"One second," Nat said to Esrom, and hurried down to the car window.

"Hello!" Jeannie beamed. "I was just coming by to see how you were." Her toddler, Angela, was asleep across the backseat.

"Oh," said Nat, "that's very nice."

"I'm the new Liaison Office wife," Jeannie explained. "It's my job now. To check on all my little chickadees and make sure they're doing well."

"How admirable."

"I've always liked to volunteer," Jeannie said, a little primly. "So, how *are* you? Your husband's deployed?"

"He is," Nat said. "We're doing fine. Look," she twisted her fingers together, feeling queasy, "I need to apologize for what Paul did to your husband. I'm just—I don't know what to say. I don't know what came over him. He has never done anything like that before."

"Really?" Jeannie arched her eyebrows. "He seems to have a bit of a temper."

"I've never known him to *punch* anybody," Nat said. "Please don't think he's like that. I really can't explain it. But I want you to know how sorry we both are."

Jeannie let out a low chuckle. "Well, perhaps my husband doesn't bring out the best in everyone."

Nat laughed, tentatively, surprised. The argument outside Jeannie's home a year ago floated up suddenly between them—Nat could *feel* it hovering there—but she thought that to mention it would be a mistake.

"Your husband's all right, then?" she said. "He's . . . recovered?"

"Goodness, yes." Jeannie brushed off Nat's concern with a wave of her hand. "He's a veteran of the Second World War, he can handle a skirmish in his own living room."

Nat groaned inwardly, ashamed that Paul had treated a WWII veteran so disrespectfully.

"Men are never blameless, are they?" Jeannie plucked a cigarette from her gold case and pressed it between her lips, offering one to Nat, who took it to be sociable, though she was wondering at the back of her mind how long Jeannie planned to chat. "Men have secrets. If we knew all the things they did, we'd go live on our own island of women." Her eyes glittered with some dark knowledge Nat couldn't fathom; she felt that Paul was being included in this in an obvious and deliberate way, but she wasn't sure exactly how. Jeannie glanced up at Esrom on the ladder. "That one, though. That man might actually *be* blameless. He looks like a cherub."

Nat would never have described Esrom this way, but she turned back to him now, considering.

"Who is he?" Jeannie asked. Her brow crumpled prettily. "A cousin? A brother? I've been seeing his truck around here."

Adrenaline pricked Nat's spine. "No, he's not related to me."

"Is he a friend of your husband's?" Jeannie pressed.

"No."

"Well, who is he then?"

"The gutters were clogged," Nat said.

"Oh!" Jeannie smiled kindly, as if pleased that they'd breached Nat's resistance to arrive at an actual answer. "So *Housing* sent him out. Fabulous! I was wondering when they'd have people take care of the gutters; ours are awful. What's his name?"

"I don't know," Nat said, ashamed at her own quick disloyalty.

"Would he do mine, do you think?"

"Your what?"

"My gutters," Jeannie laughed.

"I'm not sure," Nat said. "He seems kind of busy. Running around from one job to the next."

They both watched Esrom take a slop of leaves and rain them down onto the lawn. He wiped a hand on the thinning cotton of his shirt, yawned, went back in for more.

When Nat turned back to Jeannie, she saw the woman staring at her midsection with slightly narrowed eyes. This went on for several seconds until Jeannie forcibly dragged her eyes back to Nat's face with a curious smile. Nat waited for her to speak her mind, but she didn't, so finally Nat said, "I think you may have noticed—I'm having another baby."

"You caught me looking. I *thought* so. I thought, Nat Collier wouldn't have just ballooned for no reason. How far along are you?"

"Almost six months now. Can you believe it?"

Jeannie nodded, sucking on her cigarette. After her initial surprise—which seemed, oddly, like a confirmation of unpleasant news she'd been dreading—her reaction seemed strangely robotic, chilled. She could not seem to meet Nat's eyes. She tapped ash out the window. "Congratulations."

"Thank you."

"Children are a blessing," Jeannie said, and sighed. She tossed her cigarette to the dirt and waved in Esrom's direction. "Hello! Hello! You, yes! Can you come here for a minute?"

It took a few tries before Esrom understood that Jeannie meant him. He squinted at her for a moment and descended the ladder in his clunky boots. His hands and arms glistened with gutter slime; he wiped them on his jeans with an apologetic smile. "Hello, ma'am?" he said, his head tilted to the side, wondering.

"Hello! Is Housing sending men around to do the gutters?"

Esrom glanced at Nat, then back to Jeannie. "I'm not sure, ma'am."

"Well, could you do my house next? I know I should call the office, but since you're already out I'm sure they won't mind. I'm at 413 White Pine. If you could come by this afternoon, that would be fabulous."

"I, ah—"

Nat's innards seemed to drop to her feet. She pushed one hand to her cheek. She wanted to blurt that Esrom was not some hired help, but her friend; yet she knew that this would sound strange or maybe even suspicious, and would she be too bold to call him her friend? Maybe he wasn't her friend. Maybe it was only his Mormon sense of duty that brought him to Nat's house to help her. After all, most people did not clean their friends' gutters.

"He might be busy," Nat tried weakly.

"Well, he gets *paid,* you know," Jeannie laughed, as if Esrom were not there.

Esrom looked openly to Nat. He was asking her for some kind of sign, she knew; this conversation confused him, and he couldn't quite figure out, coming into it late, why Jeannie was ordering him about and Nat made no move to correct the misunderstanding. There she was, basically selling him down the river, asking him to perform unpaid labor for this bossy neighbor lady.

"All right," he said to Jeannie. "I can help you. I'm almost done here."

"Terrific. Nat, you take care. Call if you need anything. Remember, I'm here to look out for you." She glanced at Esrom. "I mean, if you're ever without *other* help."

"Thank you," Nat said, her face hot.

Jeannie waggled her fingers, first at Nat, then Esrom, and drove away. He was already moving back up the ladder to finish the last few feet of gutter. He scooped out the muck with his hands in that easy, natural way men had of dealing with physical exertion and unsavory tasks. His face was impassive, his movements calm and measured; he did not seem angry. But when he climbed down from the ladder and set about gathering the seeping brown piles into a large paper bag, he did not speak to her. She bent once to help him—her hands pink and clean, fingernails with thin white lines at the tips—but catching sight of her awkward, pregnant leg straddle he said, "It's all right. I got it." So she stood back, looking uselessly at the street until he had finished. Her heart still pounded. Military wives looking out for each other, her foot.

"Can I get you anything to drink before you leave?" she asked Esrom. "Something to eat?"

"No, thanks." He rolled down the top of the bag and pressed the air out with one short puff. He walked down the grassy decline to his truck, tossed the bag in back, and climbed into the cab.

Nat trotted after him foolishly: "Would you like to come in and wash up? Can't I wrap some food for you to take?" The sting of his rejection, after Jeannie's pointed observations, was almost too much.

"I'm fine. No point in washing up, really." He seemed to think that this sounded petulant because he forced himself to meet her eyes and he said, "See you later, ma'am."

The "ma'am" was a rebuff. It stung even though Nat knew she'd acted like an inconsiderate snob, sending him off to work for her neighbor as if she owned his time, and yet she also could not appear to overly care that this bothered him. He was a man who sometimes helped her around the house. He was not her *friend*.

His old pickup rattled down the street, dusty, rust-eaten at the haunches. Nat stood and watched her own yard for a minute as if something might happen. The baby in her belly gave a sideways flop like a frog off a rock. She rubbed her forehead, sighed, and went back inside to see if the girls were stirring.

JEANNIE

JEANNIE WAS SILENTLY GRATEFUL THAT NAT COLLIER DID NOT attend the Frankses' dinner party that evening. She was in no mood to witness Nat's glow as she paraded her small round belly; hear people's exclamations over her news and her chirpy, saccharine replies: "I feel very lucky, yes," or "It *is* more work with Paul gone, but we'll manage."

"I know you don't work for the Housing Office," Jeannie had told the young cowboy that afternoon as he dutifully enacted his part of the charade, scooping rotting leaves from the gutter in her backyard. "You don't have a badge, or a marked truck, and you didn't hand me a form to sign."

"You need an official form to clean someone's gutters?"

"Cute. This is the army, doll. There's a form for everything."

Jeannie standing by the base of the ladder with her iced tea, which like its predecessors was a Long Island, thank you very much: "Be careful, sweetheart. I've seen deployment widows like Nat Collier a hundred times over. She's so sweet and needy"—here, startled eyes from the cowboy—"but the second her husband comes home she'll be fawning all over him like he's the leader of the free world."

"With all due respect, ma'am, I think you have the wrong idea."

"No, hon. I think you do."

"Ma'am—"

"You know what? Forget it. Just leave the gutters. Why should I care, if Mitch doesn't? Here, take a five—"

"That's too much, ma'am—"

"You people around here could use it. Almost makes me cry to look at you all."

SHE WISHED PEOPLE WOULD acknowledge that her life wasn't easy. Funny she should want them to notice, when her every act was orchestrated to obscure effort; but every now and then, just for an instant, she wanted them to see how hard she tried.

Not all things come easily to other people like they do to you, she imagined herself saying; gave herself a fantasy moment in which she gripped a satisfying hunk of Nat's hair and gave her a shake. *We don't all have adoring, faithful husbands and get pregnant the moment he looks us in the eye. Not all of us glide through life trusting that our husbands will wake up in the morning and do what's best for us. Some of us have to be vigilant. And being vigilant will make you tired.*

She was becoming so silently inflamed, reliving her conversation with that dumb young cowboy and conducting this imaginary sneak attack on Nat Collier in her head, that she finally had to go into the bathroom and run cold water over her wrists. She placed one against her forehead, feeling the simultaneous pulse. Then she returned to the Frankses' party, as calm and pleasant as could be.

NO MATTER HER SHORTCOMINGS, Jeannie was excellent at parties. She believed that when she stood before Saint Peter's gate, he'd make a list of her transgressions—moodiness, a penchant for alcohol—but compare these to the way she had planned and conducted herself at social gatherings, and give her a pass.

She was standing patiently next to Mitch, who as usual was spinning some tall tale about his time in Nanumea—"So Grady and I go thrashing into the jungle with this crazy man right behind us, hollering, and we hear gunshots! He's got guns! He's shooting guns at us for having crept underneath his daughter's window!"—when her eyes wandered the room and latched on to a person she had never expected to see again in her lifetime.

Between the sight of this person, the drone of Mitch's multichapter tale, and the restrictive bind of her undergarments, Jeannie thought she might pass out. She could feel her face draining color as if a hole had just been shot in her jaw.

After one stunned moment she managed a smile that she hoped was both distant and friendly, the way someone's face might look if they were studying a postcard from a past vacation before throwing it away. "Eddie," she said as a young man and his female companion approached.

"Jeannie!" Eddie smiled broadly, without that same distance, and then corrected himself. "Mrs. Richards. It's been a while."

"It certainly has. Since Belvoir," Jeannie said. She felt the yellow-brown décor of the Frankses' living room press in around her and thought she might be crushed by the oily, diarrheal painting just behind her.

Eddie grinned, handsome and dark. He was a charmer, like Jeannie, and he knew it. His eyebrows were expressive, his facial features symmetrical and strong without Mitch's Cro-Magnon undertones. Jeannie was not surprised to see that he was now attached. She was, however, caught off-guard by the fact that his attractive companion was Negro.

"This is my wife, Estelle," Eddie said, briefly setting his arm across the woman's shoulders.

"Wife?" cried Jeannie, with an unnecessary tinkle. "How darling."

Estelle smiled at him and then back at Jeannie. She fairly glowed with affection for her husband and looked like someone who had received a good amount of love in return, a glossy pet.

The Enzingers were doing their best to extricate themselves from Mitch's storytelling. Jeannie tapped his arm with her free hand. "Mitch, you remember Specialist Hollister, from Belvoir?" With looks of relief, Len and Kath scuttled off.

"Oh, yes!" Mitch boomed, with a forced transfer of attention. "Yes. Hello. But of course." All this bluster meant that he did not, of course, recall Specialist Hollister at all, which was quite all right by Jeannie. "You're stationed here now? How long have you been in Idaho?"

"Four days," said Eddie. "Just moved in. I start up on Monday."

"You're at the CR-1?" Jeannie asked.

He winked. "Yes, ma'am." His southern drawl was always held back behind his words. It was, Jeannie admitted, the nicest southern accent she had ever heard, not sprawling all over his conversation but just kept sensibly in check, adding a sort of gentility to anything he said—not that he was an especially genteel person in any other respect.

"Well, welcome aboard!" said Mitch.

"And how did you two meet?" Jeannie asked, posing the question mainly to Estelle in case the men wanted to talk man things among themselves. They should always be left that option.

"I was a secretary at Belvoir," Estelle said, rather shyly, "and I saw Eddie every day. I couldn't help but notice him!"

"Of course not," Jeannie said warmly.

"You know, I think I remember seeing you there, too."

Jeannie clamped her lips shut and nodded.

"Mrs. Richards was always bringing in treats for the rookies," Eddie said. "She's got the most giving heart. She'd bake us brownies, or, what were they—blondies? All the time, just because. We managed to convince her we were studying real hard."

"I took pity on you," Jeannie stammered, then added quickly, "for all that schoolwork you had to do."

"You did have her fooled, then," Mitch boomed. He enjoyed talk of Belvoir. It *had* been a lot of work, endless studying, and sometimes Jeannie thought the men liked to pretend that they'd made more time for fun than they really had. Of course, hard work had to be rewarded with some hard play.

Jeannie gave Estelle what she hoped was an apologetic smile. She knew that she should try her best to make small talk: Where were they living, did Estelle like her apartment, did she want to hear Jeannie's recommendations for reasonably priced décor? But she felt suddenly tongue-tied, an unusual ailment. She opened her clutch and removed the flat, filigreed gold case that held her Virginia Slims, offered one to Estelle, and took one for herself. Lighting it, she felt somewhat calmer, although she noticed with dismay that her fingers shook.

"Did you ever think you'd end up in Idaho?" she finally managed.

"Well, Eddie's talked about places we might be stationed ever since we were going steady," Estelle said, and Jeannie looked at her more closely: How old was this girl? She might have been anywhere between seventeen and twenty.

Jeannie snorted lightly. "*I* certainly never expected to live here. Then again, Mitch and I got married a long time ago now. No one was talking about Idaho then. It was during the war."

"Korea?"

"No," Jeannie said, slightly miffed, "World War Two."

"World War Two?!" Estelle shrieked, as if Jeannie had just let slip some reminiscence from antiquity.

"We were very young."

"I hope Eddie and I will last, like you two have." Estelle's eyes radiated a genuine warmth that Jeannie found off-putting. "I hope we will stand the test of time."

It was one thing for Jeannie to poke a little fun at her own age, but another to see how seriously Estelle seemed to believe Jeannie was a million years old. The appropriate response would have been to express shock at the fact that Jeannie was even a day older than herself. Apparently, Estelle did not know the code.

Jeannie looked the young woman over: her broad, youthful face, curled lashes, chemically relaxed jet-black hair. "And where were you two married?" she asked, exhaling cigarette smoke. "Surely it wasn't Virginia."

Estelle seemed to deflate slightly. Her face reddened. "We went to Ohio."

"I see," Jeannie said.

Estelle glanced around, chewing her lower lip.

"Dear." Jeannie tapped Mitch's arm. "It's getting very late." And it was: past midnight. Who would have expected a party at the Frankses' to go so long?

"Aw, Jean," Mitch said. "The nanny's staying over anyway."

"I'm just getting awfully tired, and a woman needs her beauty rest."

"*That* you certainly do not need, ma'am," said Eddie, reaching out and, dear God, pressing her hand. Jeannie wished there were some way to dull that mischievous twinkle in his eye. "Nice to see you again, Mr. and Mrs. Richards," he said, and took Estelle's arm as they drifted in the opposite direction.

"What a fantastic man!" Mitch observed. "A good conversationalist."

"He didn't say a word, dear," Jeannie muttered. "That was yourself you heard talking."

"What?" Mitch asked, leaning toward her, but she waved him off sweetly with a smile.

"Let's fetch our coats."

Sliding on her luscious sable (which she feared she'd someday end up having to pawn, if Mitch didn't get his act together at work), she felt shaken. When she'd first taken up with Eddie she'd thought: Of all the places in the world that a young soldier could be sent, all the cities and towns and remote bases, what were the chances that they'd end up in the same spot? She hadn't known the nuclear world as well then, or what she would be in for: an endless revisiting of the same few places and people, all revolving through their small, specialized little universe. Whether you liked them or not, there they would be, four months down the road, five, six.

They were almost at the door when they heard a knock and it swung open.

"Goodness," said Jeannie, "who could it be at this hour?"

Kinney and Slocum piled in, still in their khaki uniforms. They pulled their covers from their heads and held them at their waists like schoolboys.

"Kinney, Sloke!" said Mitch. "We were wondering if you'd make it."

Brownie Franks scuttled up the hallway. "Well, I'll be!" she said. "Coming in at the last minute! I'm afraid we've eaten most of the food. Can I throw some spaghetti on the stove?"

Jeannie felt her heart speed up. An impromptu round of after-midnight spaghetti and booze was not on her agenda, thank you. She thanked Brownie for the nice evening and herded Mitch toward the door.

"Jean, we can't leave now," Mitch whined. "The boys just arrived."

"Or scrambled eggs?" Brownie was saying. "I could whip up some eggs." It was terrible to watch her squirm this way, perspiration beading on her upper lip. There should always be an abundance of food, even when one's guests were leaving at one A.M. Why didn't she hire help for these events if they took so much out of her? Brownie glanced at the faces around her desperately, her pupils dilating and shrinking with the effort to make contact with someone, *anyone* who would tell her whether spaghetti or eggs were required.

Kinney tipped toward Mitch, all twitchy fawning, desperate to speak before Slocum could. "Master Sergeant, did you hear? Deke Harbaugh's passed."

"Oh, no!" Brownie cried.

"Good God," said Mitch.

"Just this evening," added Slocum. "His wife called."

"It was the lungs?" Brownie said. "The lungs thing?"

"Yes," said Kinney. "He went into the hospital yesterday. Didn't want anybody to know."

Jeannie felt a twinge of guilt; she was the Liaison Office wife, she should have known. Someone had probably called her house that evening, but of course she'd been out. Now she'd have to make it up to poor, grieving Minnie Harbaugh. From the corner of her eye, she saw Eddie advancing; everyone wanted to know what the fuss was.

"This changes things," Slocum said, looking directly at Mitch. There was an intensity to this statement, like a coded message, and the three operators looked at one another.

"Shit," said Mitch.

Brownie blinked at him, wet-eyed. "Poor Minnie," said Brownie. "Can you even imagine? Your husband *dying*?"

"Maybe I can," said Jeannie darkly. Everyone's surprised glances told her she'd gone too far, so she patted Mitch's arm, laughed in a strained manner, and said, "Of course I'm kidding. I'm sorry. This is all horrid."

"You're in shock," Brownie said, stroking her arm. "We'll have to organize something for Minnie straightaway."

Jeannie nearly jumped at the thought. "Well, it's certainly too late tonight," she said. A long night's vigil at the widow's bedside, all the light of Jesus radiating from her shiny face: This was just what Brownie Franks would see herself doing. Not Jeannie. Nope. Rest in peace, Deke Harbaugh, but Jeannie was going home to her bed.

"Someone needs to sit with her," Brownie fretted. "I'll go tonight. Jeannie, will you come tomorrow?"

Jeannie's heart sank. There was no way out of it.

Brownie was glancing toward the kitchen. "I'd bring her a plate but we're mostly out—"

"Well, you can't bring scrambled eggs," Jeannie said, then tried to soften this: "I'll bake a casserole."

"Oh, good. Yes, perfect. Lasagna?"

"I don't know," Jeannie said irritably. "Whatever I have on hand."

When Franks and Len got to them the whole thing started again, and it seemed to take twenty minutes for Jeannie to get Mitch out to the car. By now she truly *was* tired, but Mitch couldn't stop talking.

"Deke Harbaugh," he said. "I don't believe it. So suddenly. He looked all right last week. Didn't you think?"

"I hadn't seen him in months," Jeannie said.

"His color was poor, but then again it always was. His eyes were bright. He came in on Wednesday, or maybe it was Thursday, and I thought: He looks like a satisfied man today. His eyes are bright and cheerful."

Jeannie sighed. Was Mitch his personal doctor? And where was the shock in this news, really? She'd been relieved whenever Harbaugh made it through an evening's dinner. She'd liked him: his slightly crusty personality, his directness. But anyone could see he walked around with one foot in the grave.

"We worked well together," Mitch went on. "We . . . cooperated. See here's the thing, Jean. We get someone new in, and they aren't going to know the drill. They won't know our method."

"I'm sure they'll pick it up quickly."

"I don't think you understand."

"Change is difficult for everyone."

"You don't *understand,*" Mitch said again, and it would turn out that Jeannie didn't.

Jeannie's morning coffee was cooling beside her on the kitchen table, her hair still in rollers and her feet in their slippers, when the phone rang. She stood, surprised, wondering who would call on a Monday morning at seven just as the schoolchildren down the street climbed aboard the bulky, hyperventilating yellow bus. School had started a week ago, and the morning air already felt different, a little cooler, as if summer had finally been packed away.

"Hello?" she said. She leaned against a cabinet, unwinding a curler from her hair and setting it on the counter. Her hair sprang back against her head in one red loop, a firm rose.

"Jeannie?" said a male voice.

Her fingers paused on the next curler. "Yes."

"This is Specialist Hollister. Eddie."

"Eddie," Jeannie said. She froze for a moment, then took a deep breath and unrolled the next curler. "How are you?"

"I'm fine. Can you talk for a minute?"

Mitch had left for work just moments before. The space in the driveway still held some faint notion of him, as if he might instantly reappear.

"I can talk," she said.

"It was nice to see you at the party," he said.

"It was certainly a surprise to see you."

Eddie chuckled. "A good surprise or a bad surprise?" he asked, in that light, teasing drawl.

"Well, a little of both, I suppose."

"How's your friend's wife?"

"Who?" Jeannie asked.

"The man who died at the party."

"Deke Harbaugh? He didn't die *at* the party."

"You know what I mean."

Jeannie sighed. What a polite and depressing line of conversation. "Minnie's making do," she said. It had been two consecutive nights of sitting vigil, good God, Jeannie holding one of Minnie's hands and Brownie the other, until Minnie's family finally made it into town from out of state and they could hand her off like a weepy, stubborn, oversized child. *I can't fall asleep if you don't rub my back. Deke always rubbed my back. Can you make me a gin and tonic? Every night Deke made me a gin and tonic.* Either this were a fantasy lived out postmortem or Deke, lead man at work, had at home suffered in oppressed servility to his plain, frowning, liquor-and-touch-demanding wife. And how did he manage it with all the coughing? Frankly, by night two, Jeannie didn't give a care. She passed Minnie's hand to the sister from South Carolina, and down the street she flew.

Eddie cleared his throat. "So you have a baby girl now."

"I do." This perked Jeannie right up and she recalled, through the weird and risky rush of adrenaline Eddie's voice made her feel, that the pleasant chatter from the back room was his child's.

"She's a sweet girl? Smart?"

"Yes, of course."

"Aw," said Eddie. He hesitated. "Does Mitch know?"

"Absolutely not," Jeannie said, with a sudden coldness in her abdomen, and she put a hand there in reflex. "He never will, either," she added. She hadn't even meant to tell Eddie about Angela's parentage, really, except that soon after she got pregnant back in Belvoir, Eddie had taken up with this ridiculous little daffodil in bobby socks and, in a blaze of jealousy, Jeannie staked out his house for an afternoon and confronted him after the girl left. He was delighted by the news, moved; he knew he and Jeannie were special together. He also had quite a banner day for lovemaking. To his credit, he ditched the teenager and treated Jeannie like a lady up until her departure for Idaho Falls.

"I'd like to drop by," he said.

"That's out of the question."

"Just for a few minutes."

Jeannie shook her head, though of course he couldn't see this.

"Come on, Jeannie. Please?" The "please" came out very southern, with two syllables.

"It's not a good idea."

"Aw, Jeannie. I need to see my little beauty."

And this was where Jeannie's vanity got in the way, because despite what they'd been speaking of immediately prior, she assumed that he meant her.

"You can't charm me, sir," she said, the corner of her mouth pulling up into a smile, which she covered with her hand, as if he could see. When he waited her out she sighed and said briskly, "Fine. Ten o'clock. No sooner."

"Thank you, ma'am," said Eddie, and he hung up.

By the time ten o'clock came around, Jeannie had vacuumed, wiped down the front bathroom mirror and sink, fed Angela breakfast and cleaned her up, taken a shower and shaved her legs, applied her makeup, and finished styling her hair. Angela watched her solemnly from the living room as if she could somehow read the motives behind all this hustle and bustle and knew it was no good. Luckily, it was Martha's morning to watch Angela. Jeannie packed nanny and child off to the library with instructions to eat lunch in the park afterward. When they left, she paused for a moment, holding her uneasy stomach. Then she sprang into motion again.

She scooped up the small pile of toys that had appeared in the space where Angela had been. Then she paced up the hallway for a few minutes, aggrieved to notice that her pale blue pumps left marks in the freshly groomed carpet. These seemed suddenly, incredibly obvious, like tracks left in snow by some desperate, lunatic squirrel. So she vacuumed that strip again, shoeless, and then sat at the kitchen table, smoking her third cigarette, as ten rolled by and then ten-fifteen and then ten-twenty.

At ten-thirty, Jeannie heard footsteps and then a knock. She took one last drag on her cigarette, stubbed it out, and went to answer the door.

"Good morning," said Eddie, freshly showered and combed like a little boy before church.

"Come in," Jeannie said.

He stepped over the threshold, and Jeannie cringed for a moment as if some alarm might begin to ring all up and down the street. The street remained silent. Jeannie took a deep breath and led him toward the kitchen table, but he took a seat on the couch, so she turned quickly, circled the couch, and perched opposite him.

"This is a nice neighborhood," Eddie noted. "They have us in a tiny duplex on Alvarado."

"How awful," Jeannie said, sincerely. "Can I get you anything? Coffee? Cigarette?"

"I don't smoke Virginia Slims," Eddie smiled.

"Well, I have Chesterfields, of course. And Lucky Strikes."

"Maybe later." Eddie held up a hand, as if he were a model of restraint. "Thank you."

Jeannie smiled and lit herself one.

Eddie looked around the room. "So, where is she?"

Jeannie blinked. "Who?"

"The baby. The baby girl."

"Oh," Jeannie said. "Why, she's out with the nanny."

"Really?"

"Yes. They went to the library and the park."

"She's old enough to go to the library and the park?"

"She's almost two years old."

Eddie shook his head in wonder. "Well, I'll be. I guess I still pictured this little baby. What do two-year-olds do? Is she walking? Talking?"

"Walking, yes. Talking, a little. She has dark hair and long, long eyelashes. She looks nothing like me," Jeannie said.

This brought a smile to Eddie's face.

Jeannie stood and walked to the wet bar. "What can I get you to drink?" she asked.

"It's ten-thirty in the morning," Eddie laughed.

Jeannie shrugged, poured them each a gin and tonic without waiting for his preference, and handed it to him with her most brilliant smile.

"Ha. That's good. You're right, it's always five o'clock somewhere." Eddie slurped without further reservation. Jeannie sat beside him on the couch, at an angle, their knees almost touching: his broad and rounded in their khaki slacks, hers slender and shimmering under panty hose. She reached out and touched his knee, lightly.

"You were always lots of fun," she said.

"I don't know how much longer I'll be fun for," said Eddie.

Jeannie cocked her head to the side, as if this statement deserved all the sympathy and care in the world. "Why do you say that?"

"Aw, you know. It's time for me to grow up a little. Me and Estelle, we're both from big families. She has six brothers and sisters. We want at least that many kids."

"Oh," Jeannie said.

"And we're partway there," Eddie grinned. "We got one coming in April."

Jeannie felt, irrationally, as if she had been slapped in the face. Her stomach gathered into a fist of frustration; hot tears appeared behind her eyes. She felt like some angry little girl about to throw over a board game she had just lost.

"Congratulations," she said, clearing her throat.

He raised his glass in a toast to himself and drained it.

What did she want from Eddie? Her first impulse, upon seeing him at the Frankses' party, had been to run; but now that he was here in front of her, she felt a desperate pull of attraction. It was not a casual interest but a sudden, deep-seated need. Did she want longer, more admiring glances from him, some clearer sign that she was irresistible? Sure, he smiled at her; he was flirtatious, but not entranced. He was married now, to some brainless little filly who would give him six kids. That shouldn't have mattered. Jeannie had pulled out all the stops. She was powdered and curled and perfumed and high-heeled and caressed by elaborate support garments.

"What do you remember most from Belvoir?" she asked, handing him his refill, and he launched into a stroll down memory lane that was startlingly Mitch-like. He had a wealth of enjoyable memories, it turned out, though none of those stated involved Jeannie. Still, his cheerful yarns carried him through several more drinks until their knees, finally, did brush together, and they were laughing freely. They were having a good time now! He began to tell her about his childhood in Tennessee, being chased by a cow across a field.

"You mean a bull?" Jeannie asked.

"No, a cow."

"You were chased by a cow?"

"Cows can be mean," Eddie said. "Cows can get angry."

Jeannie covered her mouth, giggling. She had lost track of whether this mirth were genuine or slightly manufactured. It had started out genuine, she thought. Maybe she was just helping it along.

"Don't be snooty," he sniffed. "Obviously you don't know cows."

"I don't," Jeannie confessed. "Oh, Eddie. Don't get sore. You tell a good story."

He smiled. "Do I?"

She was close enough now to smooth the collar of his shirt. "The best." She brushed her fingertips over his shoulder. "Do you miss Belvoir?"

"Not the work. But . . . other parts of it."

"Me, too."

He drained his drink again.

"You're kind of an old man now, aren't you, Eddie?" she asked fondly. "I'd thought of you as this young kid, just a kid who smiled shyly at me when I'd bring in brownies."

"I'm twenty-four," he said, a little startled.

"You were so young when we were together. I thought you were fresh out of high school! All the wives giggled over you. They thought you were so handsome."

"I know," Eddie said.

Jeannie stood and refilled their tumblers, then sat back down. She had slid off her pumps and they sat to the side, pale blue and satiny, like overgrown Barbie shoes.

"Of course, I won't pretend that I didn't get a lot of attention from the fellows," Jeannie said.

"There was some talk," said Eddie.

"All of it respectful, I presume."

"Oh, of course."

"Everyone was a little bad back then. Was it something in the air?"

"No one was as bad as we were," Eddie said, and this goofy cliché was exactly what Jeannie had hoped to hear. She knew, instantly, that victory was hers, and her confidence soared.

Eddie set his drink on the coffee table, and Jeannie used all of her willpower not to slide it onto the coaster. Outside, far across the street, two mothers walked past with prams. Jeannie's face felt very hot. Eddie put his hand on her knee and she giggled. He seemed to find this encouraging because the hand moved up her thigh, under her skirt, and found the edge of her garter, which he unclipped while he kissed her.

"You seem familiar with those," Jeannie remarked when she came up for air. Her head was swimming.

"You could say." He leaned in to kiss her again, but she heard a noise just outside the door and pulled back.

"Geez! The mailman! Come here." Awkwardly she slid over the back of the couch. Eddie vaulted after her with a surprised, "Oh, shit!"

They crouched for a few minutes, listening to the light crunch of the mailman's shoes on the top step, and then the flutter of mail to the floor.

Jeannie laughed in relief, leaning into the back of the couch. "Oh my word," she said. "This is bad." And predictable Eddie, who nearly salivated like a Pavlov's dog each time he heard "bad," was on her in an instant, his body covering hers. It felt divine, to lie there beneath him while he unbuttoned her dress and unhooked her bra and slid away her nylons and panties, though Jeannie found herself suddenly obsessed with whether or not his large feet stuck out on the other side of the couch. "Your feet, your feet," she kept whispering, but Eddie did not seem to think this was reason enough for caution, or maybe he assumed she had some kind of absurd fetish, or maybe he just didn't understand what she was saying.

By the time Martha and Angela returned, Eddie was gone, the empty tumblers had been washed and dried, and Jeannie felt a bit like she had made love to a truck. "Mama!" Angela cried as soon as she burst through the door, but Jeannie patted her head and steered her back toward the nanny. "I'm sorry," she said, "I'm terribly sorry, but I've come down with a migraine again."

"Oh, no," said Martha, wringing her hands.

"Can you please stay for the day? I don't think I can keep my eyes open with this jackhammer in my head."

"Oh, my. Yes. Certainly, ma'am."

"Thank you, Martha. There are baked beans in the pantry." This was one of Angela's favorite meals, baked beans and a slice of white bread.

Jeannie drifted back toward the bedroom, where she had already lowered the shades. The room became remarkably, blissfully dark, even during the day. She sank into her bed, still feeling the heavenly weight of Eddie's body, the slight rawness of her rarely kissed lips, the numb, happy seasickness of alcohol. She heard Martha turn on a television program in the living room. It was almost like a lullaby, the perfect muffled and constant noise, and Jeannie finally didn't have a troublesome thought in her head as she drifted off to sleep.

NAT

Two letters had come from Paul since he'd left. One he'd written on the cargo plane to Greenland. He said that he missed Nat, that he could see the ocean from a tiny window on the plane, that he hoped she was eating well and getting lots of rest. "Remember, pay attention to what's going on and always be careful," he added, which he probably intended in a loving way but which seemed paranoid to her. She wished he'd told her more about the airplane; she'd never ridden one and couldn't imagine any time in the future when she would.

When she spied the second letter a week later it made her heart jump, but this note was brief as well. He was not at Camp Century yet, he said, but waiting for the weather to clear up north so they could head there. He reported that there was not much to do other than play cards and eat; that it was very cold; that he could see the polar ice cap on the edge of miles of brown dirt; and that there was an Arctic fox that skirted the edges of camp looking for handouts. The fox must have been the most compelling observation he had because he wrote three full sentences about it (it was not pure white but slightly brown; it had small ears like a cat; and so forth) and he asked her twice not to forget to mention it to the girls. So she didn't forget. She mentioned it several times, in fact, until Sam finally blurted, "Mama! You *told* us about the fox!"

When a third letter from Paul arrived weeks later, it was six sentences long and written in a stymied, bewildering manner.

"Dear Nat," it said. "I hope you are well. I miss you and the girls. Sometimes I feel almost like you are a dream that I won't be allowed to come back to. Nat, you are my angel. Always be careful. I love you. Paul."

Nat read the letter over and over at the small, round kitchen table. She hated this letter. It was like a telegram from some incomprehensible place. She had it memorized within minutes. Each flat, pithy sentence turned a different key in her, as if her heart were a series of separate but connected gears.

She was warmed by the thought that he missed her and the girls, but the line about being a dream made her feel sad and almost indignant. Of course he would come back to her. She was doing nothing but waiting right there, and she could not fathom nor tolerate any doubt about his return. Besides, it was melodramatic. She was not a dream; she was flesh and blood.

She was both flattered and embarrassed when he called her his angel. She knew she was *supposed* to be his angel, because men were inherently unstable and needed a woman's love the way a pilot needed a compass. Men were the providers and the doers and the protectors of everything—finances, morals, property—and yet there was something off about them, everybody knew it, something that needed to be sheltered from certain realities, such as childbirth or the sight of a woman without support garments. It had always puzzled Nat, this way she was supposed to treat men, because it didn't seem to fit Paul and it felt foreign to her. And yet they were becoming it, as if it were inevitable. Distance was making them proper, and making her his angel.

She had lost track of time when she finally looked up from the letter. It was dusk; kids called and ran around at the end of the street. She hadn't written to Paul since he left. If she wrote, she'd have to tell him about the car, but then she'd feel like a ditzy little girl. She'd begged for that thing, fought with him over it even, and to admit that she'd gone out and wrecked the tire so soon after he left would undermine whatever argument she'd built up in the first place. He'd think she was the worst kind of fool. "I'm a good driver," she'd said, that morning in the car. "I'll be careful." And he hadn't responded, because he'd known better.

She picked up a pen and a thin sheet of lined paper and wrote a note that felt neither satisfying nor honest. "How are you? The girls and I are doing well. We walk to the neighborhood playground a lot." That was true. "The girls loved hearing about the fox." True, also.

When she'd sealed the envelope she set down her pen and stared at her dull, dodgy letter. It seemed meager. What was happening to her and Paul? What was he thinking, what was he doing, a million miles away? Who was he with, what did he eat; did he dream about Nat, wake up antsy for her the way she did for him? She should be with Paul. She should be with him. The idea was obsessive and impossible. She leaned her forehead into her hands and stayed that way until the room around her grew dark. She let herself inhabit that muffled grief: for her own useless self-pity and for the inscrutable man in an ice tunnel, writing letters she did not understand to his faraway angel.

THERE WAS A LONG quiet spell when she did not receive anything from him at all. These weeks were the worst of the deployment. She occasionally saw her new friend Patrice when they took their girls to the neighborhood park, but other than that she was alone nearly all the time. She missed Esrom more than she liked to admit; it horrified her to think how she'd humiliated him in front of Jeannie Richards, how he might never drop by again. She kicked herself for it. His visits had punctuated her days, and now each sunrise to sunset stretched on twice as long as before.

WHEN A DARK GREEN CAR pulled up along the curb outside her house one morning, Nat assumed it was someone who had the wrong address and would soon discover their mistake, turn around, and drive away. She watched the car from the kitchen where she sat with her coffee, waiting to see what it would do. The driver's profile looked familiar, and she realized that it was Esrom.

She couldn't help it; his reappearance thrilled and flustered her. She wished she had washed her hair.

Esrom waved and started up the slope of grass. "Hello," he said when he reached her.

"You came back!" she said. "I thought you might never—well, I'm glad to see you."

"Don't be silly," he said, reddening. He was one of those people who flushed instantly, a distinct visual *whoosh* like a semaphore of emotion.

She laughed from relief and happiness. "Where's your truck?" she asked.

"Well," he said, smiling, "I thought you could use this."

She looked around. "Use what?"

"The car." When Nat stared at him wide-eyed, he explained, "It was my buddy Jacob's. It's a Dodge Wayfarer, 1949. The thing had been rode hard and put away wet, as they say, but we fixed it up. It'll last you ages now. The landlord said our carport was starting to look like a used car lot, and some of 'em had to go."

"You brought me a car?"

"Yes," he said.

"Oh, no. Oh, that's wonderful of you, but I can't take a car."

"Why not? It was just sitting unused at my place."

"Because it's . . . I don't know."

"You've been without a car for weeks now," Esrom pointed out.

Nat nodded, fiddling with a loose thread in her pocket. "I haven't even told Paul about it yet."

"Well then, take this one in the meantime."

Nat looked anxiously at the green car.

"Listen," said Esrom, "I hope you don't mind my asking, but what are you going to do when you have this baby? You can't take the bus to the hospital. Or if one of the girls gets sick?"

"I was planning to get a ride with a neighbor when I have the baby," Nat said. "Other than that, we've been riding the bus and it's just fine. Nice, even. It's less than ten minutes to downtown."

"It's good to be able to rely on yourself, though."

Nat couldn't deny that, although whether she'd be relying on herself or on him she couldn't tell.

"And now if you need to, you know, get out on a little day trip or whatever you like," he added, "you'll have the option."

Nat felt her own smile tug at the corners of her mouth. She looked Esrom in the eye; he wasn't wearing his hat, and he looked younger without it, plain, sandy haired, blue eyed. He really wanted her to take the car. He was proud of his work, she could see. She felt nervous accepting such a gift, but could she refuse it on any sensible grounds? The thought of driving anywhere she needed to go was too tempting to pass up.

"Thank you," she said. "This means a lot to me." She didn't want to make too big a deal about it, though, so she asked, "Can I make you some food? Would you like to come inside?"

"I gotta get back. Got some training today."

"Training?"

"The testing station fire department."

"Congratulations!" Nat said.

He smiled shyly. "Thanks. Well, I'm not in yet. Just training."

"That's wonderful," she said. The car, his news about the fire department—this was the happiest day of Nat's summer yet. "Here, let me give you a ride home," she said. "I'll test-drive the car."

He raised his hand to protest—"I can take the bus"—but Nat trotted up the walk, opened the front door, and called, "Girls! Mr. Esrom is here. We need to give him a ride home."

The girls came springing out of their room, elation written on their faces. "Mr. Esrom, Mr. Esrom!" they cried, scrambling to the entryway and dancing around him. They were dirtying their nice white socks.

"Hello," he said, laughing.

Sam flung herself around his leg. "Are you coming in? Did you bring us anything? Can we make you cookies?" She sounded like a giddy, unfiltered version of Nat.

"We're just driving Mr. Esrom home. He's letting us borrow a car for a while," Nat said.

"A car?!" the girls cried, and Sam sprinted down to inspect it, Liddie hurrying behind. In two seconds they were in the backseat of the car, sliding back and forth across the gray broadcloth and beaming out the window.

Nat opened the door to the passenger seat, but Esrom pointed at the driver's side. "I thought you wanted to drive."

She paused. "Sure, if that's all right with you." She slid into the driver's seat and burst out laughing, running her hands over the large steering wheel, opening and shutting the ashtray. It made a satisfying click. "I love it," she said. "It'll break my heart to give this thing back to you."

"I don't want it back. But you hang on and see. Heck, maybe you'll test-drive it and it won't even be up to snuff." He raised his eyebrows, grinning, and now looked absolutely like a little kid. "Go on! Drive it."

She eased out into the street and headed toward downtown, wanting to bounce in the seat like her girls.

"Mama," Sam called, "there's that lady from the party, the party wiff the Cracker Jack and the toys."

Nat saw the familiar swirl of red hair and refined, high-heeled walk: Jeannie Richards striding along on the sidewalk, pushing a large pram. She should have expected to see Jeannie: This was the hour of her daily walk, and she was like clockwork in the neighborhood, her fine legs pumping forward as she clicked along with a strangely placid look on her face, as if the movement sent her into some trance. But it was not trance enough: Jeannie's head swiveled, Esrom raised his hand politely, and Nat, against her better manners, accelerated through the neighborhood, her heart pounding. The girls whooped and Esrom said, "Whoa there, Nellie."

"Sorry," Nat said. For a moment her happiness was dampened. Jeannie's expression had been critical and all-seeing.

"You okay?"

"That was rude of me," she fretted. "Why didn't I just slow down and say hi?"

"I thought you two were friends."

"It's a long story." Nat hesitated. "I'm sorry you had to go do work for her, that day. She's my husband's boss's wife. I let her push you around.

Now I've offended *both* of you. Boy, I'm a piece of work, aren't I?" She shook her head. "How was it, when you went to her house? Was she nice to you? Please tell me she paid you."

He hesitated. "Yes, she paid me."

"Did you have to talk to her?"

"Um." He squirmed. "She talked a little."

"She scares me half out of my mind," Nat confessed. "Especially since Paul punched her husband in the face."

"What?"

"It was terrible. I'm not even sure why he did it. He's not *like* that! He could have lost his job. He still might, really; I don't know what's going to happen in his next promotion cycle." She felt herself chewing her thumbnail and lowered her hand back to the steering wheel.

"Anyway, I think that's the main reason Paul got sent to Camp Century. He got himself into a fine fix."

"That's terrible," Esrom said.

Signs flapped on telephone poles they passed; Nat glimpsed the word MISSING and the blurry black-and-white image of a smiling, braided young woman. She pointed: "That Zeigler girl's still missing," she said. Sixteen-year-old Marnie Zeigler had disappeared three weeks before from the tiny town of Arco to the west. Signs covered every telephone pole and tree trunk, flapped wordlessly from shop windows, occasionally came loose and tumbled down the street as if to haunt the locals.

"We raised the Zeigler barn," Esrom said, "about a decade back."

Nat felt she was having an eerie brush with celebrity. "You *knew* the Zeigler girl?"

"A little bit, yeah. Went to church with them for a few years. That was back when my dad associated with other families."

"Huh," Nat said. She peeked at Esrom's face and noticed his tense posture and shaded expression. "Can I ask what the story is with your own family? I don't mean to pry, but you seem sad when you talk about them."

"Oh." He shifted uncomfortably. "You know, me and my dad just have some trouble. There's eleven of us, you know." Nat felt her eyes widen—she hadn't known. "I'm the oldest. He wants all of us to stay on the ranch forever and help him, which maybe we would if he weren't such a damn a-hole all the time." He said this last part in a hushed, gritted voice because of the girls. "We don't see eye to eye on religion matters. We used to, when I was young, but then I just lost my heart for it. It wasn't calling to me. Some of the things just fell away from my heart, is the only way I can explain it."

"I understand," Nat said. "The same kind of thing happened to me."

"Really?" he said, looking at her. Then he shook his head: "He's a jerk to us boys and he's a monster with the girls. Won't let them go to school outside the house anymore; makes my ma teach them. Caught my sister Abra with a lipstick in her pocket and locked her in the bedroom two days. She's fifteen. I understand not wanting her to be worldly and all, but I don't see punishing a fifteen-year-old girl for wanting to try on some lipstick." He grimaced. "It was light pink. She wore it once."

Nat nodded, thinking how she allowed Sam and Liddie to smear their faces with her cosmetics, their tiny eyelids heavied with blue shadow, their lips ringed like circus clowns'.

"I don't want to talk too much about it. Works me up. Plus, your girls." He gave a nod toward the backseat, cleared his throat, and sat up straighter. "So I got my own place. I go back home every couple days to check on things, but I don't stay long anymore. My pa's worse with the other kids if I rile him up."

"I feel awful now," Nat said. "I mean, life must be so much harder for your sisters, and here I'm this pampered thing—"

"No," he said firmly. "There's no point in comparing yourself. Whatever good you have in life, you deserve it."

He pointed a right turn ahead, and she saw that they had reached a part of town untouched by the recent boom. Her car (her car!) bumped over the train tracks and down a slope, past a house where some young men sat outside at midday, a ditch freckled with litter, a stray dog who looked at them with depressed shoulders and yellow eyes. They reached a brick apartment building and Esrom pointed. "Right here."

"Okay," said Nat, trying to keep her voice bright, but the condition of the place bothered her. The yard was a patch of weeds and dirt. Esrom didn't climb out of the car immediately—Sam had him from behind by the ears, tilting his head this way and that, making him laugh, while Liddie bounced around the backseat in delight—and Nat felt another, more acute bother: the recurrent misgiving that she should not be taking this car. God, she was an emotional basket case. In her mind she saw Jeannie Richards's face again, the accusing expression she'd worn as they passed her on the street.

"Samantha," she said, "please cut it out!"

Both Sam and Esrom looked surprised. Sam released Esrom's ears and slid back to her seat, eyes brimming. "We were just playing," she said.

"Is something wrong?" Esrom asked.

"No. I don't know," Nat said. And here he'd just recovered from talking about his family. She blurted, "Do you think this is all right?"

"Is what all right?"

"This. You giving me this car."

"Well, it's all right with me," he said, smiling. But he must have noticed her discomfort because his face changed a little.

Nat pressed the rim of the steering wheel—it was so clean, he must have shined it, polished every inch, before he brought the car over—and tried to think of what to say. What she wanted to express was how grateful she was for his help, and how much she enjoyed his company, and how relieved she was that he'd come back even though she'd been so rude to him in front of Jeannie Richards.

Jeannie Richards: She had seen Esrom and Nat together on several occasions now. This sent Nat into a little spiral of anxiety. Of course, they had done nothing wrong. But if Jeannie, who lived three blocks away, had seen them, then her neighbors must have noticed Esrom's truck at her house at different times, too, and she didn't mean to be snide, but these women were busybodies; their hawk eyes scanned the neighborhood for anything out of place, for any change, for any event that was, by other people's standards, not an event at all. Someone's garbage can lid laying to the side and not securely clamped on the can: That was an event. The lone beep of a car horn at two P.M.: That would be considered an event, and a mystery.

But she glanced over at him and thought the bright hot incriminating thought *If I have to stop seeing him I will never make it through this terrible summer*. So she forced a smile and said, "Never mind. It's nothing."

"Someone's coming," Sam called.

A short, stocky man in cowboy boots waved nervously as he walked up to the car. Nat recognized him as one of Esrom's friends from the diner, though he looked like he had aged in the interim.

"Oh," said Esrom, glancing up, "it's Russ. Excuse me." He opened his door partway.

"Hey, Ez. Where you been? I'm locked out," Russ said.

"Locked out?" Esrom said. "All right. I'll let you in."

"I lost my key," Russ said.

"Oh, my," said Nat. "What happened to his face?" There was a large square of gauze taped to Russ's cheek, something shiny seeping through it.

"He rides rodeo," said Esrom quickly. "Hey, friend," he said again, as if Russ had not heard his first greeting. "You lost your key again?"

"I lost my key," Russ repeated. Nat wondered if they were just going to call out the same things to each other, over and over. She thought that something was not quite right with Russ; something seemed heavy, or dull. He tried to smile at her, but his eyes bounced away at the last second. "I was locked out," he was saying to Esrom, "and I was worried those guys was gonna come back."

"Well, they ain't here, are they?" said Esrom, in a way that was somehow soothing. "Look, you go back around. I'll be right there."

"Who's your friend?" Russ asked, grinning again in Nat's direction; his eyes roved over the top of the car. "You all make a nice family."

Esrom rolled his eyes and pivoted Russ around. "I'll be right there." He turned and smiled at Nat, then slid his hat onto his head and tipped it to the girls with a wink. His face looked strained. "Thanks for the ride," he said.

She cleared her throat. "Well, thanks for the car!"

"No trouble." Esrom gestured to a couple of cars on blocks at the end of the lot. "It's raining cars around here, as you can see."

As he turned to walk away, she suddenly felt the senseless, overwhelming urge to call him back. It would likely be no more than a couple of days before she saw him again, but even this seemed too long, which made no sense because she'd just been telling herself they'd been seen together too much. *Stay in your seat, Nat Collier,* she thought—this was ridiculous, this outpouring of confused feeling, and she feared that she was about to embarrass herself—but her unwise heart won out, and she turned off the ignition, slid from the car, and hurried around the front. The two men swiveled in surprise.

Now, standing before them, Nat had no idea what to do with herself. She hopped awkwardly forward and folded Esrom into a quick hug. Her heart pounded from this silly boldness, but he returned the hug, gingerly. "You've been very kind," she said, stepping back and gently gripping his shirtsleeve. "I'm so grateful."

He nodded, looking self-conscious and pleased. "All right," he said.

She was still holding his sleeve.

"I need to get in the house," Russ keened. "You wasn't home, or Jacob. I was just sittin' out here."

"You're fine," said Esrom, and added quietly, "Take care, Nat." She took her hand back, and scratched behind her ear for something to do.

Esrom gave Russ a gentle shove and the two men moved around to the back of the building, Russ with a tilting shuffle that Esrom had to shorten his stride to accommodate.

Nat walked back around to the driver's seat and slid inside. She watched Esrom and his friend for a moment, feeling curious and sad.

"I miss Mr. Esrom already," Sam said.

"Me, too," said Liddie.

The men were behind the building now. Nat glanced up and saw another man out on his very small balcony, looking down at them with a sort of insolent curiosity. She started the car and backed it up, moving out toward the road. A coyote slipped out of the grassy field to their left and trotted across the dirt in front of them. "Girls, look," Nat cried, and they clambered up onto their seats to watch the animal as it made its way down a street lined with collapsing decks and abandoned Victorian era houses.

"This isn't like our neighborhood," Sam observed.

The man on his balcony threw down a wad of trash; it tumbled through the dry grass and came to rest in a little pile, with rusty tin cans and paper bags that had long ago begun to fray and melt into the dirt. He was fumbling with the top of his pants and Nat had the sudden, certain fear that he was going to urinate off the balcony. She put the car in gear and thunked out onto the road, the girls sliding in their seats behind her.

"Mr. Esrom will be fine," she said when they were at a distance, then realized this hadn't responded, really, to anything anyone had said.

PAUL

PAUL PULLED HIS FACE INTO THE COLLAR OF HIS JACKET AND CLENCHED his fists in his pockets. His reactor was at the farthest end of Camp Century's center tunnel, called "Main Street," and the walk felt long in the still, subzero air. He strode quickly into the breath cloud that his nostrils made, listening to the crunch and echo of his boots against the packed ice floor.

Ahead, clanks and clatters. A group of soldiers scraped the walls with long-handled shovels, cutting seventy-pound blocks of ice and dragging them to the surface on sleds. Mayberry had told Paul, with a sort of perverse delight, that the ice was moving over an inch a day, filling in the tunnels the Army had made.

One of the guys on scraping duty raised his hand to Paul. "Collier," he called, "we've got an extra shovel."

"And I suppose it's got my name on it."

"Say hi to your nuke friends for us. Don't forget your lead underwear."

"It's nice of you to care about my underwear."

"He must be getting desperate!"

"See you," Paul said, passing them. Though it was a favorite myth about the nuclear operators, they did not, in fact, wear lead underwear. There were other tales about them, such as the one about their bodies becoming hairless the longer they worked the reactors, or that they only fathered girls (this last one, at least for Paul, had come true). But the job seemed so lacking in mystery and intrigue to Paul by this point that the rumors only made him laugh. You could get used to anything if you did it every day.

Halfway down the tunnel he heard someone call, "Hey, Collier," and looked up to see Mayberry striding toward him, juggling an armful of papers. He hadn't ever mentioned the incident with Nat's photo, for which Paul was grateful. It humbled him every time he realized how much more forgiving other people were than he.

"Hey, yourself," Paul said. "How's the ice cave?"

"Brilliant. Got some great samples in there." He shook his head as if describing a gorgeous woman or a classic car. "Say, did you hear we're getting some guests from out your way?"

"Really? More guests?" A week prior they'd had to freshen up and look nice for some senators from the East Coast and an obscure member of the Danish royal family. Mayberry had had to cut his hair and trim his beard; he was still a little miffed about it.

"Not till mid-September, actually." It was late August now. "Just when I get my beard grown out again, they'll make me trim it. Now where did I . . . ah. See?" He riffled through his armful of papers and plucked one from the middle. "There's a supe from your other reactor coming. The Idaho place, the CR-1, right? Yep, here he is: one Master Sergeant Mitchell Richards. Do you know him?"

Paul felt as if all his internal organs had just grown tiny hairs and bristled.

"You know the guy?"

"I do."

"You tensed up there, kind of." Mayberry eyed him. "What's he like? One of those controlling master sergeants or a lazy, drunk one?"

"Well, both," Paul said. "Listen, there's some bad blood between me and him."

"What's the story?"

Paul hesitated.

"Come *on*," Mayberry said.

So Paul talked, though he didn't enjoy telling any of it: started with Richards ditching him at their first, awkward meeting; skipped over his boss's drunken overtures to Nat and the ugly business at the Calico Saloon, but briefly mentioned the mounting problems at the reactor and wrapped it all up with hitting Richards in the jaw. At that finale Mayberry whooped, lifted one leg off the ground, and hopped in a circle, all his papers flapping.

"You need to get out of that cave more," Paul said.

"Paul Collier, man of action! You going to teach him another lesson? It'll be the Showdown on Ice!" Mayberry shuffled his papers back together, chuckling. "This is the most exciting thing to happen to us in five months."

"Wish I could be as jazzed as you."

"We don't get a fight? Really?"

"I sure hope not."

Mayberry sighed. "All right, I get it. Just try to avoid him, maybe. Steer clear."

Paul gave him a look.

"You'll get through it." His friend clapped him on the shoulder and started in the opposite direction, still grinning. "See you back at the boudoir."

Paul shook his head, reaching for a cigarette as he made his way down the tunnel, then giving up because his thumb was too cold to flick the lighter. Goddamn that Richards—it was ridiculous, perverse even, for him to show up here. Amazing how you'd be kept from the folks you loved, and the last damn person you wanted to see just popped up in front of you like a paper silhouette at a shooting range.

NAT

WEEKENDS WERE QUIET AND LONELY FOR NAT SINCE PAUL had gone. Weekdays, the world was full of women out running their errands, bobbing babies on their hips, smiling and shushing and scolding, eager for adult conversation. Come Saturday, however, these women were solidly booked up. Their husbands were home and it was as if they didn't even see Nat on the street, or if they did, they gave her a quick hello with a slightly pitying glance. Men had the amazing ability to keep women busy, to fill up their minds and thoughts. One man in the house crowded out everyone else.

As they hit the halfway point, then passed it, Nat made a long paper chain to hang across the inside of the front window, as the army wife deployment pamphlet had suggested. They would tear off one ring of paper a day until Paul returned. Each torn oval was a relief, a wafery rip of satisfaction, its flutter into the wastebasket like a banished butterfly; *we won't be needing* you *anymore*. But some part of Nat also held back, knowing that when Paul got home everything would change, for good and bad. She did not feel that she was wronging Paul by having Esrom for a friend, yet she knew full well he wouldn't like it, either. Then again, there was always something Paul didn't like. It didn't matter anyway; she wasn't going to stop. When Esrom came to the door she felt her heart swell with happiness; when he left she moped like a child.

NAT'S FRIEND PATRICE CAME over for coffee once or twice a week—their friendship having graduated from mere playdates at the park—with her four-year-old daughter, Carol Ann. Other than Esrom's visits, these were the highlight of Nat's days. Female companionship was exhilarating, like tapping into a world she had been divorced from for ages.

"So, tell me about your charmed life," she said one morning, pouring Patrice a cup of coffee. "Does your husband come home every afternoon at three? Does he do the dishes for you while you put your feet up?"

Patrice chuckled, stirring sugar into her cup with small, delicate tinks. "Oh, of course," she said. "He comes home bringin' flowers. He makes the dinner, too."

"Really! What's his specialty?"

"Pheasant under glass, oysters Rockefeller, and crème brûlée for dessert." Her Georgia accent pulled each word in delightful, unexpected ways.

"He's amazing!" Nat said.

Patrice, with her thick inch-long eyelashes and frozen swoop of ice-blond hair, didn't look like she'd have much of a sense of humor, but she was somehow both refined *and* funny. Her eyes twinkled as she sipped from her cup.

In army wife fashion, theirs was a fast-moving friendship. Nat was learning the hard way that if you wanted friends in the military, there was no time to waste. Years' worth of closeness and trust and shared jokes were accelerated into weeks. Patrice had already told Nat of the time when, newly arrived at a duty station and with Bud away on duty, she'd had a life-threatening miscarriage. She'd had to call upon a neighbor woman—whom she'd had coffee with on exactly two occasions—to watch Carol Ann for a week until she was out of the hospital. "A week!" Nat had cried, marveling over this. But what else could Patrice have done? This was when Patrice confided that she was unable to have any more children, her eyes welling with tears. And there you had it: the deep, almost instant, and precious military friendship. "When we moved to Belvoir," Patrice confided, "and I left my best friend Louise back in Georgia, I almost thought I'd rather trade Bud being deployed again." She'd looked uncomfortable even admitting this. "Don't ever repeat that," she said. "I love Bud." And Nat had said, "Of course, of course."

Now Sam and Liddie were playing with Carol Ann in their room, and with Patrice all to herself in the kitchen, hot coffee and poppy seed muffins on the table, chilly wind rattling the panes, Nat felt cozy and content, happier than she'd been in some months. Suddenly her life felt like it was full of good things: healthy daughters, the regular kindness of Esrom, girl talk with Patrice. And Paul, of course: She'd nearly forgotten to be thankful for Paul. She gave quick, silent thanks for his safety.

"That girl is still missing," Patrice said, "the Zeigler girl," and Nat's head snapped up.

"I know," Nat cried. "I can't stop reading about her. Sometimes I wake up at night wondering where she is."

"Really?"

"I just can't help it."

Patrice seemed to make a conscious decision to glide over this particular quirk. "*I* think she ran away. Say," she said, switching topics, "whose car is parked in front of your house? The green car?"

"Oh." Nat twitched inwardly, looking at Esrom's green car. She was in the mood for confidences, not white lies.

"Didn't you used to have a yellow car?"

"I did, yes. That's our—our new car."

"Where's your yellow one?"

"I didn't tell you? It's in the shop. I drove home on a blown tire. I'm saving up to pay for repairs, but a friend let me borrow this one in the meantime."

"What friend has an extra car lying around? Is she on vacation or something?"

Nat hesitated. "Yes."

Patrice shrugged. "Well, just get your yellow car fixed before Paul comes home, and he'll never even think to ask. He'll be so thrilled to see you again and meet the new baby, he won't care about a few dollars spent on the car. He'll let anything slide."

"You're right," Nat said. "Thanks." And she held out the plate of muffins for Patrice, biting into one herself. She did not like to lie, but there was no way to explain the car's origins without making Patrice suspicious. The car was hers, and the person who'd given it to her was hers also, if she kept quiet about him and made sure no one scared him away.

THE NEXT DAY THE ZEIGLER GIRL was found. To everyone's relief and amazement she was located alive in the home of a forty-six-year-old widower who'd been hired by her father to castrate sheep the previous spring. The man was in custody; Marnie Zeigler was back with her parents, occasionally trotted out in a plaid jumper to make quick, chipper comments about how fine she was and how the whole thing had just been a terrible misunderstanding.

That night Nat called her mother. She was fidgety and bored, agitated by the news of the Zeigler girl, and the practical issue of needing help around the baby's arrival was as good an excuse as any to call, though their conversations were never easy. She'd been hoping her mother would volunteer to come up to Idaho, but Doris never mentioned it. This bothered Nat, because Doris Radek volunteered for nearly everything else on earth.

Everything was fine back in San Diego, Doris said, their family's small medical supply business chugging along, Nat's brothers' kids growing and doing the requisite things (baseball, Boy Scouts). Doris babysat the grandchildren and played canasta with her daughter-in-law Marva. Nat's father was busy with his role as Esteemed Loyal Knight of the Benevolent and Protective Order of Elks, and her brother George had joined up, too, as, Nat supposed, just a regular Elk.

As the conversation was drawing to a close, Nat blurted, "We had some strange news around here. A sixteen-year-old girl went missing for a month and then they found her in this middle-aged man's house."

"Goodness, Nat," cried Doris, "could you be more morbid?"

"They found her alive," Nat clarified. "But it's so strange. When you see the father on TV, you can't tell if he's grieving or complicit."

"Why," said Doris, "are you bringing this up?"

"I don't know." Nat was talking quickly, her heart pounding. She'd known her mother wouldn't want to hear about this but couldn't stop herself from talking. "It's all just so strange and because it's a local story, you can't escape it. You know how people get with a story like that."

"It's sick," Doris said.

"Yes, maybe so," said Nat.

"Well. I'll see you in December." There was a pause, staticky with distance, and Doris said, "Take care of yourself, and be good, Nat."

Be good, Nat, her mother's sign-off since time immemorial. Nat had always thought she was good—or good enough, anyway; she remembered a hazy time when everyone thought she was good, when she was a pampered and beloved small child, tossed in the air by her father, sitting patiently beneath the warm, steamy clicks of her mother's curling iron. Her brothers, twelve and thirteen years older than her, were dashing, all sun-glowing skin and right angles, calling her Princess and asking for kisses in front of their girlfriends, as if Nat's early pre-feminine affections deemed them worthy of a lifetime of later womanly devotion.

But when Nat reached eleven or twelve, she felt a shift in her parents' attitudes, and they seemed to regard her with suspicion. Had this guardedness always been there, just hidden within them, or did they really look upon her as a new person, the untrustworthy substitute for the innocent little girl who'd mysteriously disappeared?

By the time she got to high school, her family was mostly out of the house. Her brothers had moved out and were now married; her mother was involved in countless time-consuming charities and clubs; her father fully invested in the medical business, the Benevolent Elks, and their church (Saint Ignatius, or "Iggie's" as its parishioners nicknamed it, light and whimsical as an ice cream parlor).

Just before the start of Nat's junior year, her neighbor Meredith Petterson held a pool party at her house. The Pettersons were a well-to-do family who also went to Iggie's, and Meredith was a neighborhood jewel, with shoulder-length blond hair and bobby socks and fitted cardigan sweaters that were somehow modestly tantalizing. Their house stood at the steep of the hill with a turquoise pool nestled among oaks, tiki torches flickering, and a catered buffet (nothing casual about the Pettersons) of cold shrimp and cocktail sauce and lightly sweating petit fours on a wide oval plate. Being perfect parents, the Pettersons had funded and set up all of this, then drifted discreetly back to the house.

Nat swam with her friends Heidi and Ed, twins she'd known since childhood; she lounged in the cooling air and ate a lot of shrimp. At one point she looked across the pool and noted, at a table beneath the sparking torches, the youth minister, Pastor Tim. He was laughing, shirtless, in the center of a group of high schoolers. Other than the shirtless part, this was not unusual; Pastor Tim was only in his midtwenties, a guitar-playing missionary who sang hymns in a sort of over-emotive, preening falsetto and who also had, it was now revealed to everyone, pectorals crafted by the very hand of God.

Nat had seen these firsthand herself, a few weeks prior, a fact she was still trying to reconcile: She felt almost as if that had been not her but another person. It was widely understood that Pastor Tim was cruising among the young female parishioners in pursuit of a Mrs. Pastor Tim. ("He has a good job with the church," Doris had whispered once in the pew, as if writing an ad, "and you know as a minister he's exempt from the draft.") All the parents looked on, not disapprovingly, but with a sort of hopeful discretion: Many wanted their daughters to be his final choice, but they did not want to hear about his other test runs.

Nat had been an early contender; flattered and nervous, she had gone with him to a roller rink, an Italian restaurant, and a drive-in movie. He held her hand on all three dates, his own palm damp and squishy, his knuckles as hairless as a baby's. After the movie he'd taken her to a beach overlook, claiming to be familiar with constellations; he pointed out the Big Dipper and Orion and then removed his shirt. "I want to see *your* constellations," he said. Nat had paused, wondering, in a stupid panic, if he meant her nipples like she suspected, but self-consciously thinking he might be referring to her moles. The whole thing was done in five minutes. Nat went along with it—was a participant, even; she could not claim otherwise. For a moment she had been excited, and then realized that it was mortifying. She had the odd thought that she was being a good soldier, that her mother would be strangely proud; the thought of rejecting and offending him seemed too horrible; even as it happened she didn't rule out the fact that she might become Mrs. Pastor Tim. Then it was over and she felt so nauseated that she knew she could not look at him again. She pulled off her socks and used one to line her underpants, stuffing the other in her clutch. The sides of the clutch bulged with it and she spent the drive home fiddling with the clasp. After that she did not return Tim's calls. Her mother fretted over this at first, but it only took him a week or two to move on to Meredith Petterson.

And there they were now, Meredith and Pastor Tim, walking over. Pastor Tim's swim trunks were covered with gigantic red hibiscus flowers. Meredith wore a terry cloth cover-up that made her look downright matronly. They seemed to think themselves the First Couple of Iggie's all of a sudden.

Forget them, Nat thought, her stomach giving one good turn. Pastor Tim caught her eye and she turned her head away. She didn't feel betrayed by him, because the whole event had been too stupid and embarrassing for a word like that. Instead she felt she had been given some kind of clairvoyance that allowed her to see people for what they really were. All of these folks would continue going to church and letting Pastor Tim lead them and give them advice, as if he were wise; but she was untouchable, she'd been inoculated against him.

"Pastor Tim's got reds," Heidi said.

Nat turned to her. This sounded like nonsense. "What are reds?" she asked, thinking Heidi must be joking about the flowers on his stupid shorts.

"They're—pills," Heidi whispered. Her nose wrinkled as if she were trying to reconcile Pastor Tim's mild, still-morally-upright creepiness with this bold, illicit move.

Nat tossed her wet hair behind her shoulder and slid one leg over the other. She was aware that this crossed leg was very bare, tan, and long, and she saw Pastor Tim glance at it. It made him seem so vapid that she stretched it and pointed her toe lazily for a moment just to bother him.

Pastor Tim leaned forward, smelling of Aqua Velva. His blue eyes looked widely excited and the front of his blond hair had been styled into a Kewpie doll point. "Seconal," he said, opening his palm. "These babies will get us all so high you won't ever want to come down."

Meredith gave a nervous laugh. "He says they're all kinds of fun."

"Who's up for it?" Tim asked, looking around, his mouth slightly open. Nat's stomach rolled. "Anyone?"

"I guess I'll try one," said Ed, but Tim seemed not to hear him. His eyes hopped from Heidi to Meredith to Nat.

Nat wasn't sure quite what possessed her. Maybe it was her impatience with everyone standing around, captivated by the power of the stupid pills; maybe it was her newfound superiority to Pastor Tim; maybe she just couldn't stand Meredith's anxious giggle and womanly waffling. "I'll go first," she said.

"Just one," said Pastor Tim. "These are very strong," so Nat, looking him right in the eye, took two. "Wow," he laughed, "way to go," and passed her a beer.

Soon everybody had tried one, and Nat began to feel very loose. Pastor Tim put his hand on her knee and miraculously she didn't care, just leaned over into his shoulder. Then his laugh was a sudden turnoff and Nat wandered away, tiptoeing around the edge of the pool like a tightrope walker. Above her head the diving board pronged against the black sky. She made her way to the ladder and climbed up.

At the top she wavered. The tiki torches lifted and simmered, licked the pool, the sky; someone said, "Go, Nat!"

She paused. She slowly bobbed. Then, before she could think about it, she hurled herself backward into an arch.

There was the plummet, and should have been a revolution; instead she got only partway around and hit the surface, face-chest-thighs *slam* like a ton of bricks had been shot into her abdomen.

For several stunned seconds she sank. The total-body slap reverberated through her and she was immobilized, a bird who'd hit a window. Her lungs began to strain. Her head felt placidly dopey, unconcerned with all this lack of motion, the upward striving that should have been.

She took a breath and then the true shock came, water sucking in like a siphon, lungs shrieking *No, no, no*. Her whole body clanged. And thank God it did, that scream of self-preservation breaking through the surface, propelling her to the stairs, where she staggered up, stars exploding around her eyes, and vomited into the shrubbery.

No one had noticed the length of time she'd been under, the thirty or so seconds before it occurred to her to surface. She'd never felt so lonely.

She stayed at the party only a few minutes more. She forgot her bike at the Pettersons' and walked home, going back for it, a little embarrassed, the next day. But by then no one cared, because the news was breaking that Meredith Petterson and Pastor Tim had gone missing.

There was instantaneous panic, but it was short-lived: Within twenty-four hours they were found, sleeping blissfully and naked as babes, in an abandoned shed up the hill. Meredith had been painted from head to toe with the contents of an ancient, stinking can of petroleum jelly. As the story went Mr. Petterson found them snoring while a four-foot king snake studied them from the corner of the room. The details were precise and lurid. Nat found them conflating in her mind with the day's newspaper coverage of the Zeigler girl; she had trouble for a moment remembering which one had been found naked in the shed, Meredith Petterson or Marnie Zeigler (of course it was Meredith); the fact that she was obsessed with this at all suddenly steeled her resolve to roll the *Post-Register* into a tube and shove it in the wastebasket.

She would have hardly given Pastor Tim a second thought if he hadn't continued to plague her family. As soon as his activities with Meredith came to light, half the congregation, led by the priest, moved for his immediate dismissal. Some of them must have suspected early on that his interactions with the girls had gone beyond damp, prayerful hand-holding, and apparently it hadn't bothered them so long as he kept it discreet, but to be discovered the way he had was unforgivable. And the drugs involved—it was too much.

The other half of the congregation—including, to Nat's horror, her parents and brothers—sided with the disgraced pastor. This faction actually left the venerated stone chapel for a small former record store across town, where they crowded among leftover shelving to hold their own disorganized, poorly lit services and drink sugary wine out of Dixie cups. Pastor Tim led this spin-off, called the Improved Saint Ignatius Church, and Nat's father and brother George served as lay ministry.

"We've known Tim since he was yea high," her mother had explained, holding her hand to her knee, when Nat had finally confronted her about their family's absurd loyalty. "He's a good kid, and the Cloones are a good family. Mike Cloone's an Elk, and his wife's a pediatric nurse."

"But *they* don't even go to his church!" Nat had cried. "I saw him, Mom. I saw him giving the girls at the party pills."

"We don't know what was in them. They could have been sugar pills."

Nat sputtered. "Mom! He was *not* walking around handing out placebos!"

"Fine. I'm just saying what I heard."

"From whom?"

"He and Meredith have split, you know."

Nat stared at her. "I'm not interested," she said.

Her mother, who seemed suddenly to have an elderly heart in a middle-aged body, adjusted her hands on her lap. "Good people sin and should be forgiven. Evil people seek only rebellion. That's Proverbs."

"I'm not trying to rebel," Nat said. She really wasn't. But she had been pushed into it.

She graduated high school, spent a year taking typing courses and then skipping out on them, going on dates here and there. She wasn't chaste. The big reveal with Pastor Tim had shown her that all the buildup, the mystery and fanfare, were for nothing. It was so simple! You did this, and this, and this, and it could be much more fun than it had been with Pastor Tim, and the world did not blow up in a ball of hellfire. You were not consumed instantly while demons chanted your name. It was a relief and a letdown all at once, but it seemed, for the first time, honest. Nat realized that she was attractive to men in an unexpected, athletic way, that she could influence them through simple actions: a wave, a smile. They were as malleable as children and as eager as dogs. It all made for a good time, but when it was over she felt lonely: None of them stayed around for long.

Her parents wouldn't give her the money for college—they believed everyone should earn his or her own way, as they had—and while Nat considered this fair, she also wasn't motivated enough to put together all that money. This was spoiled of her; it wasn't admirable. How could she recoil from her parents at every occasion while still living off them in her childhood bedroom?

It was Paul who'd gotten her out of her teenage stagnation. Just when she'd thought, with a somewhat overblown teenager's perception, that her life might be defined by the Improved Saint Ignatius Church and her parents' disapproval, that she was destined for nothing but occasional casual relationships and nothing real to show for them, Paul had dropped into her life wholly unexpectedly. He was a wonder—different than anyone she'd known: quiet and dark, formally chivalrous, so unlike the goofy, ponyish surfer boys she knew. He was still and thoughtful and serious. He listened closely to everything she said; whereas she'd barely seemed to register with Pastor Tim and the boys who followed, she meant everything to Paul. He was like an emissary from some other place, time out of mind, a land where people had meticulous, tender depths, where they behaved more carefully than modern men.

She'd wanted to elope, wanted to get the heck out of Dodge as fast as she could, thought marrying an army guy (and one she really did love) would whisk her away quick and easy; but it turned out army life was a little more complicated than all that, and until Paul got accepted to reactor school at Fort Belvoir she found herself with two little girls and somehow living at home, *still,* where her mother treated her like a child with children.

She kept a vestige of the faith she'd been raised with, a quiet view of God as someone who could occasionally be appealed to and wanted the best for people, but who did not often meddle in daily affairs or sports or politics. And indeed, despite the mixed things she'd done, her life had turned out well. She had her own home, or a rented one anyway. She had a yard with three tomato plants and a big muddy pit where the girls played. She had the exhausting luxury of being home with her children; she had a husband who provided for her. But sometimes, in dark and quiet moments, she wondered if she had married Paul too fast. It had all happened like lightning: courtship—marriage—baby—baby, and now a third on the way. Hadn't she just been nineteen? Wasn't it just yesterday she was standing at the top of the Sunset Cliffs, gripping rock with bare brown toes? For years she'd been convinced that Paul had saved her from something, from that sad, complacent quality she'd seen in people the night of Meredith's party, the part of them that was easy to take advantage of. But in gloomy moments she wondered if what she'd thought was brief clairvoyance hadn't actually been a combination of youth, defiance, and beer. Maybe she hadn't given herself a chance. Maybe she had seen a problem but jumped toward the wrong solution.

But no, she loved the girls, adored her family, cared for Paul in a way that was beyond love, beyond this life, that shocking intimacy of marriage and creation. How did anyone withstand it? It was like weaving your entrails together; it was beautiful and awful; of course it would bring up these startling feelings from time to time. Depressive thoughts, she reminded herself, weren't any more real than happy ones just because they were harder to have. But she couldn't help feeling a tiny bit sorry for herself, feeling antsy and sad, feeling that her parents had been trying to get rid of her, and Paul had helped them do it, and now he was thousands of miles away and she was alone, summer nearly over, the dishcloth-covered clock on the wall ticking quiet, desperate seconds.

She couldn't picture what Paul was doing, what his world was like, but he knew everything of hers: He had made it. This didn't seem fair. But she reminded herself he had made it out of love, and softened again.

Her mind wandered to Esrom. What was he doing this warm, breezy night? Maybe working on a car outside his new apartment by the beam of a big chrome light, maybe playing cards at the fire station in his undershirt. All right, so she didn't really need the part about the undershirt. Playing cards, then. Details were easy to come by. She was happy with this little train of thought but then had the sudden, baseless notion—rising up from who knew where—that his kindness, his friendly drop-ins, extended to other lonely wives like herself, and she came to her senses five minutes later wringing her skirt murderously in her hands.

She listened to the radio as she tidied up the kitchen: The Everly Brothers, the Five Satins with their heartbreaking *doo-wop, doo-wah*: *In the still of the night / I held you, held you tight,* the pauses in the last line that reached into her chest and wrung her breath out: *In the still . . . of . . . the . . . night.* Why did music need to be so soft and so sad? She swiped crumbs from the kitchen table, let them fall into her hand, tossed them into the trash. Circled a rag over the countertop and sang with Toni Fisher: *Watching that clock till you return / Lighting that torch and watching it burn.*

The curtains flapped above her bed as she climbed in, alone, alone. She was, by her best guess, twenty-seven weeks pregnant. Paul would be home in fifteen weeks. These were the numbers she recited to herself at night, little hash marks in her brain.

When she was almost asleep, her mind, tired of numbers, fritzed to another plane, one that was already wholly extant and pre-supplied with story line. She was in a small bare room, sounds of rustling grass and birds outside, smell of oaks and flicker of distant light. Truck tires curved up the drive and parked just beside the wall; a figure got out and stood by the window. He peeked in, just to check on Nat, to make sure she was peacefully sleeping. This was very thoughtful, but Nat had known to expect him, and she'd left the window open, curtains flapping in the breeze. She loved this dusky dream, which was why she'd called it up night after night when her limbs felt too hot in the sheets, too overcome to be embarrassed by her quickened breathing, her hands brushing the tight hill of her belly, the space below it like a slice of peach; the five final seconds of sensation strong enough to drug her into thinking the hands, the breath, hadn't just been her own.

AT THE END OF AUGUST, the Summer Olympics were held in Rome, and to Nat and the girls' amazement these were actually shown on TV. This had never been done before and everyone was abuzz with it, grocery shopping at the PX, riding the bus: *Did you see the opening ceremony? Did you see those shots of the Colosseum?* The events were recorded during the day and flown to the CBS studio in New York each night, and every morning Nat and her daughters awoke and headed straight to their magical box to watch real footage of the athletes. Heck, with entertainment like that, they might not have needed a car at all.

Nat was captivated by the women's swimming, and Australian Dawn Fraser in particular. Dawn Fraser was like Superwoman. In plain clothes—collared shirtdresses and pumps and everyday polyester pants, posing for photographs—she could have been any other freckly young woman, cheerful, square-chinned, perhaps with slightly rounder shoulders than most girls; but in the water she was a rocket, a jet, something propelled by science or magic and not mere human muscle and effort. Fraser had won all golds and silvers in the 1956 games four years prior, and big things were expected of her.

Esrom came by one afternoon just as the TV announcer was working up to the women's 100-meter freestyle. He stood gabbing at the door in his usual easy manner, and for a moment Nat, embarrassed by the private thoughts she'd had about him and trying to comfort herself with the fact that he could not know them, had trouble looking him in the eye. Then she realized she was going to miss the race if she didn't get back inside, so she grabbed his arm and dragged him into the house.

"What, what?" he laughed. "Was someone sneaking up behind me out there?"

"I'm sorry," she said, "but I don't have time for your *Cow gave birth last night* and *Boy is there a big melon on the vine* today."

"I wasn't going to say either of those things," he protested.

The girls came hopping over with *Mr. Esrom, Mr. Esrom* piping every which way.

"Is this pajama day?" he asked. "Where're all the pretty dresses?"

Nat looked around and realized that things had gotten a bit out of hand: There were dishes in the sink, the girls were still in their nightgowns, hair back-combed by sleep and never fixed, teeth a bit scummy from eating licorice whips and watching the world's finest athletes for half the day.

"Haven't you been watching the Olympics?" she asked.

"We don't have a TV."

"At the apartment, or on the ranch?"

"Either."

"Do you like sports?"

"Sure." He shrugged. "What's this, a swimming race?" He sat on the floor, Nat beside him on the couch, the girls clambering knees-elbows-hair against his face and neck, and Nat didn't even tell them to settle down.

"It's the women's swimming," she said. "That's Dawn Fraser from Australia."

"It's hard to tell them apart what with the caps and the swimsuits—"

"Lane four. She's favored to win."

"Shouldn't we root for the American?"

"You can if you like," Nat said. She grinned at him. "It might be fun to root against you, actually."

"Well, all right," he said. And when the gun went off Nat cheered for Dawn Fraser, and Esrom and the girls, not even knowing which lane they were supposed to focus on, shouted, "Go America! Go America!" at the tops of their lungs.

It was silly—really, it was ridiculous—but watching Dawn Fraser swim, Nat wanted her to win with a nonsensical fervor, as if Fraser's success had some kind of bearing on her own, placid life. She clenched her fists, she felt short of breath as Fraser and Chris von Saltza pulled neck and neck, fighting for the pool wall with all they had, their arms spinning circular froths of water. A dozen men in suits, holding stopwatches, stood poised above their heads. The world had paused to watch these women swim.

Fraser and von Saltza touched the wall at what looked like the same moment, and, as one, the men bolted from the poolside to confer. The whole thing had lasted only one minute and one second. Nat grabbed her own hair, awaiting the verdict. Esrom reached up and touched her arm and said, "You okay there?"

A minute later the newscaster's head and shoulders appeared and in his cultivated voice announced that Dawn Fraser had, for the second Olympics in a row, won the women's 100-meter freestyle, and Nat stood, yelling with joy.

Instantly, Sam and Liddie took on Nat's happiness as their own. It was mayhem for a few minutes until the three of them quieted down. The girls were bouncing all over the couch, so Nat eased beside Esrom onto the floor, despite his protestations that it was too hard and so forth.

"Goodness, I'm not a princess," she said. She pointed at the TV, where assistants were wreathing the podium for the medals. "Did you see her? Did you see how amazing she was?"

"I did."

"It's so *hard* to swim like that."

"I actually thought they were going to swim maybe six or eight more laps."

Nat looked at him to see if he was joking. "No," she said, "it's a two-lap race. But they swim all-out the whole way. It must feel like sprinting a mile." She suddenly felt almost teary over what had been accomplished, over how great it must have felt to swim that way, to get into the water and move all your muscles at once and breathe fast and ragged till you thought you might die. And with everyone cheering like crazy on top of it, studying you through binoculars from the stand, breathing along with you because they wanted so badly for you to win.

"You know, I had an idea," Esrom said. "When the baby's a little older, you could lifeguard at the pool."

She turned to him with a delayed reaction, trying to put together what he'd said. "I could be a lifeguard?"

He started to stammer as if fearing she found this laughable, as if it contained some fault he hadn't anticipated. "Well, you know, they always need lifeguards. The lifeguards get to swim for free when they get off work."

"*Thank* you," Nat said, wanting, for a delirious and stupid second, to lean over and kiss him. She was still embarrassingly choked up from the joy of Dawn Fraser's win, from her mild case of lonesome self-pity, from the end-of-summer blowing through the air and leaves gathering on the windowsills and doorstep.

He studied her. "Are you all right, darlin'?" he asked. His voice was unbearably fond and kind, and she couldn't stop herself from sliding beneath his arm, resting her head on his shoulder, and taking his far hand in her own. He froze; she felt his heart speed up beneath his shirt and he kept his arm somewhat stiffly in the air, as if he were being held at gunpoint. Then he settled his arm onto her shoulders, loosely, and this sent such a charge of closeness and contentment through her that she shifted position just a hair every minute or so to be against a different part of him, cheek on shoulder, chin on clavicle, eyebrow against the warmth of him through his shirt. It was a muted ecstasy of affection. Even in its restraint it made her heart pound because it was so wanted and so new, but also nothing, of course; so they watched that way as Dawn Fraser and Chris von Saltza and Natalie Steward climbed in bathrobes onto their podiums, and the stodgy, brassy Australian national anthem, which neither of them had ever heard before, cackled through the speakers of the television set.

JEANNIE

Jeannie was partial to her house when her husband was not in it. She hadn't been disappointed to hear that he was going on a weeklong trip to Greenland to visit that god-awful army base; the week of his departure sat ahead of her on the calendar like a pretty little vacation. Certain simple things had come to feel like a luxury at this point in her life: taking a couple of days off from vacuuming; eating canned tomato soup for dinner a few nights in a row, by herself, after Angela had been put to bed; watching TV in a quiet house until the programming ended at midnight and the screen went black, just because she could.

Whenever he was away, however, Mitch felt the need to call home. Jeannie found this irritating and odd, considering that he could live in the same house with her and not feel the need to speak for weeks. He was a sporadically sentimental man, and being away was about the only thing that made him appreciate his family. Or perhaps he liked other soldiers to witness him making a phone call to his wife; it made him seem upstanding and responsible. She didn't know, and she didn't particularly care.

As expected, he called on Friday, around dinnertime.

"Mitch," she said, trying to infuse her voice with warmth, although she was peeved that the phone cord did not reach far enough to get her to the wet bar for another drink to pass the time.

"Hello, milady!" said Mitch in a jolly voice. "How's life on the mainland?"

"Everything's good, dear. We're just finishing dinner."

"What did you have?" Mitch asked.

Jeannie sighed. He acted as if he were a prison inmate, desperate to know what people were eating on the outside. He was away for one week, for God's sake, in a place where people cooked nice meals for him.

"Tomato soup," she said, though only Angela had eaten, and she'd actually had white bread and baked beans. But that took too many words to say. Jeannie glanced at her child, who was silently pushing the last of her baked beans to the edge of her plate and then boosting them over one at a time, like lemmings. "Angela," she sighed, "if you are done eating, then you may be excused."

"What?" Mitch nearly hollered.

"How's Greenland?" Jeannie asked.

"Cold as a witch's tit!" Mitch marveled. "We're living beneath the ice. In tunnels."

"Is it pretty?" Jeannie asked, without interest. "I'd imagine that Greenland would be pretty."

"Hell, no," Mitch said. "Is an ice cube pretty?"

"Maybe," Jeannie said.

"Well, this place isn't. And the men are stir-crazy and weird. There's not a woman in sight for two hundred miles."

"That's probably good for everyone involved."

"Hey, I ran into an old friend of ours."

Jeannie perked up. "How is that horrid Collier?"

"As enchanting as ever." There was a pause; Mitch was trying to be clever, and he wanted Jeannie to appreciate it. She let out one stingy giggle to satisfy him. This seemed to be the encouragement he needed because he kept going. "That man walks around this place like he sat down hard on a broomstick. His clothes never even know they got taken off the hanger."

Jeannie laughed, genuinely. "Mitch!"

"This is the perfect place for that man. I can't think of any landscape to which he'd be better suited."

Mitch was actually being funny. Jeannie was impressed. "Well," she said, "at least you only have a few days there. Then you won't have to see that sorry fellow again for a while."

"It's a shame," he plowed on, covering Jeannie's last couple of words, "that he's got that nice wife waiting for him at home. What could she see in him? You know? What *is* there?"

"It's a mystery to me," Jeannie said, feeling less generous toward her husband now. She looked at her fingernails, then out the window. The street was quiet; everyone went inside like clockwork at dinnertime. "She doesn't seem to miss him much."

"What do you mean?"

"Oh, nothing." Jeannie snapped her head irritably toward the hallway. "Angela! What are you doing in there?"

Angela let out a string of muffled, unintelligible words, but Jeannie figured that if she could speak, everything was all right.

"What do you mean, she doesn't seem to miss him much?" Mitch pressed.

"I just meant, how *could* she miss him much?"

"I never understand," Mitch said, "how men like him win women like that."

Jeannie felt annoyance ripple under the entire surface of her skin like an electrical impulse. "Mitch, it's unseemly to talk about another woman from four thousand miles away. Are there people around you?" She sighed, and decided to give him what he wanted. "I hardly think he's 'won' her," she said, "because she's been out gallivanting all over town the entire time he's been away."

"Really?"

"Yes. She's been seeing some townie cowboy. He's at her house every time I drive by. He bought her a *car*."

"That's fascinating!" Mitch said. "She's been running out on that sour-faced Collier?"

"Let's talk about something else."

"I wouldn't expect that of her," Mitch said. "I just really wouldn't have expected that."

Jeannie guffawed. "You don't know her in the least," she said. "How would you know what to expect and what not to?"

"I just never would have—"

"I need to put Angela to bed," Jeannie said. "Would you like to say hello to her first?"

"Why, sure."

"Angela!" Jeannie called. The little girl scurried in as though she feared she might be in trouble for something.

"Say hello to your father," Jeannie snapped. "He's in Greenland." Of course that could mean nothing to Angela, who took the phone cautiously from her mother.

Jeannie could hear Mitch's blustery voice on his end, starting and stopping in long strands of conversation. Angela listened patiently, concentrating, with her mouth open. Mitch must have tried for a reply because Jeannie could hear several short, insistent questions in a row before she gently pried the phone from Angela's grip and said, "She's a little tired; it's almost her bedtime. Isn't it late for you out there, Mitch?"

"Was she really on the phone?" he asked. "I couldn't hear her."

"She was. You should have seen her smile when she heard your voice," Jeannie lied.

"Oh, good. Well, I'll be home Monday morning. Flying all day Sunday."

"All right."

"They say there's a little nightlife here on Saturdays. Can you imagine?"

"Well, have fun."

"Mm." There was a long silence, so, to fill it, Jeannie quipped, "Give my love to Collier." She was immediately annoyed with herself. She hated playing into Mitch's weakness. He obviously grew a little excited each time Nat Collier was mentioned.

"I still can't believe what you said about his wife," Mitch said. "I wouldn't have taken her for that kind of girl."

Jeannie felt a stab of unease, coupled with distaste for her husband. "It's certainly something we should keep quiet," she said, suddenly pious. "It really isn't any of our business."

"Oh, I know. I guess I'm just amazed. I guess I thought—"

"Mitch, I need to put Angela to bed. Have a good night. We'll see you Monday."

"Can you believe it's fall already?" Mitch said. "Hell, before we know it, it'll be Christmas." Christmas always made him happy.

"All right, Mitch," Jeannie said, and she set down the phone with a gentle click. It was not until a few hours later, when she sat bolt upright in bed and felt a wash of anxious self-doubt, that she realized what she might have set in motion.

NAT

"IF THERE'S ANY TRINKET YOU'VE HAD YOUR EYE ON, YOU SHOULD ask for it as soon as Paul gets home," Patrice said, sipping coffee in Nat's kitchen as the occasional hard flake of snow spiraled past the window. "New shoes, a purse?"

"I don't need anything."

"Oh, Nat, have some fun! What would you ask him for?" Patrice's blue eyes twinkled.

Nat paused. A few months ago she would have thought a car. Now, she didn't really need anything. She felt surprisingly content: But, of course, when Paul came back, everything would truly be in place.

"Oh, never mind. I give up on you. I can tell you what *I'd* ask for: a Chanel handbag, one of those quilted ones with the little chain straps." She pointed: "Ha! I saw your baby kick."

"I felt it," Nat said. Her belly was huge now and still growing, the button flipped inside out so that it poked from her rotunda like an impertinent tongue.

"This will be your boy," Patrice said, lighting a cigarette. "I just know it. He'll be sweet as can be and adore his mama. Just like my husband," she added, rolling her eyes. Patrice's mother-in-law lived with them for half the year.

"I never met my in-laws," Nat said. "They passed away. Isn't that strange?"

"Why? How did they pass away?"

"No, I mean it's strange that I never met them. Hasn't everyone met at least one of their in-laws?"

"Consider yourself lucky," Patrice said. "You could have a mother-in-law who lives with you. She could fill your refrigerator with prune juice and leave her teeth on your bathroom sink and feed your children hard candies twenty-four hours a day." She turned toward the hallway. "What are you doing, girls?"

"Dressing up Liddie," Sam hollered back.

Patrice turned back to Nat. "Did your mother decide when she's coming out to visit?"

Nat nodded, feeling a scrunch of anxiety in her chest. "Right after Thanksgiving," she said. "She'll stay till the baby arrives."

"Why doesn't she just come out for Thanksgiving?"

"She always celebrates at George and Marva's. No changing it."

"Oh. *Hm.*" Patrice raised her eyebrows.

Nat smiled and rolled her eyes, grateful for this quiet, discreet taking of sides. She got up to refill Patrice's coffee. As she turned back to the kitchen table, she spied the pickup truck parked along the curb and Esrom ambling toward the house. Her heart leapt: She loved catching sight of him, but this was poor timing. He removed his hat as he neared the door.

"One moment," she said to Patrice, setting down the filled coffee cup. "Help yourself to a Danish."

"I will. After all, I brought them," Patrice said. She turned in her chair to see where Nat was going.

"Esrom, hi," Nat said, opening the door before he could knock.

"Just thought I'd drop by." He peered back toward the kitchen. "Why are you whispering? You got a fugitive back there?"

"No, I just have a friend over." She studied his face, enjoying it, and looked away.

"Hey!" Esrom said. "That's great."

Nat was slightly embarrassed—why did she always feel like everybody's favorite village idiot? *Look, hooray, Nat Collier has a friend!* But she knew he was genuinely pleased for her.

"Mommy, is that Mr. Esrom?" Sam asked.

How did she even hear us? Nat wondered. It was uncanny.

Mary-Janed footsteps thundered down the hall, and all three little girls appeared. Esrom knelt to greet Sam and Liddie. They squealed his name and sprang into his arms. He hugged them both at the same time and then, seeing Patrice's curious face peeking around the corner, released them and stood. Carol Ann darted for her mother's hand.

"We have Danish! Come in and have a Danish," Sam said. "Miss Patrice brought them."

"Oh, hello. This must be Miss Patrice," Esrom said, lifting his hat from waist level and setting it back again. Patrice gave him a close-lipped, cautious smile, still holding her coffee cup.

"Come on in!" Sam said again.

"Well, I wouldn't want to interrupt."

"You won't," she insisted. "I'm not having *that* much fun with Carol Ann."

"Sam," cried Nat. "Yes, you are. Look at how you dressed up Liddie."

They all turned to Liddie, who was suffering a swimsuit over a poofy dress that squeezed from the swimsuit's leg openings in tulle cascades, as if her little hips were twin waterfalls.

"Is Liddie having fun?" Esrom asked. His eyes caught Patrice staring. "I was just checking on Nat here. That car still working all right for you?" he asked, his voice a little stiff and self-conscious.

"Yes, it's been a godsend. Thank you."

"Great." He smiled shyly and bent to address the girls. "I'm sorry I interrupted your dress-up party." He winked at Liddie, who beamed.

"Awww—" said Sam, looking almost teary.

"Hush, dear," said Nat. "Thank you, Esrom. Take care now."

He gave her belly, with its newly protuberant navel, the smallest glance. She caught it and laughed, placing her hands against it. "I know, I got bigger overnight!" she said. "And my belly button's sticking out now. Sam tries to ding it like a doorbell." She knew she was being too loud, and a little rustic, but with Patrice and Esrom in the same place she couldn't quite seem to normalize.

Esrom blushed on her behalf. "You take care, too."

Nat shut the door and motioned the girls back down the hall. She busied herself rearranging the Danish on the plate at the kitchen table. Patrice leaned against the doorframe, watching her.

"Please don't tell me *that's* the friend who gave you the car," Patrice finally said.

Nat stayed silent.

"Oh, Nat, what were you thinking?"

"He's a very nice person," Nat said. "When the car broke down he came out to fix it."

"And he still has it?"

"Well, yes. I was saving up the money to pay it off, and he's been fixing it in his spare time." She pressed past Patrice's raised eyebrows. "He and the girls hit it off, so he checks in from time to time to see how they're doing."

"He checks in to see how your daughters are doing."

"Yes."

"I don't think that's it."

"It is."

Patrice crossed her arms. "First of all, you let a grown man play with your daughters, and you didn't even know him? He could have been a creep."

"He's not a creep."

"Well, you're lucky for that. And he knew your husband was away!"

"He's good-hearted," Nat said. She plucked a dish towel from where she'd draped it on a chair and dabbed it absently on the table.

"I'll say!" Patrice cried. "That's a beautiful car. What, he just gave it to you? No strings attached? And please don't just repeat that he's a nice person. Do you know how this looks?"

Nat froze.

Patrice's mouth pulled to the side and she shook her head. "It doesn't look good."

"Patrice, I swear, there is nothing inappropriate going on." Nat said this but she felt the clench of guilt in her heart and she could see her errors in stark relief, every one of them. The extra dash of makeup when she knew he was coming by. The dream, not just that once, but all the times she brought it back on purpose afterward.

"How often does he come to your house?"

"Maybe a couple of times a week."

"And he comes inside the house."

"Yes."

"And he gave you a car."

Nat nodded, squeezing the towel.

"He's been fixing your other car for, what, a couple of months? Nat, he *likes* that you're driving his car."

This was both accusatory and insightful and Nat had to catch her breath. "You make that sound terrible—"

"How long does he stay when he comes by?"

Nat paused. "I don't know. An hour or two."

"Have any of the neighbors seen him coming or going?"

Her throat burned and it was difficult to answer. "Probably."

"And what do you think they're saying?" Patrice cried. "Do you mean to tell me it's never occurred to you that this might look bad, for people to see that man over here all the time in this tiny neighborhood?"

"It . . . occurred to me," Nat said.

"But you didn't stop him from coming over."

"No. I knew people might gossip, because they always do. But having him over seemed more . . . more important to me than what they might say about it."

"And was that fair to Paul?"

It took Nat a moment to answer. "I don't know why it wouldn't be," she said, though she was being willfully obtuse. When Patrice continued to look at her she cried, "Patrice! It's nothing like that. I would never cheat on Paul. I just wanted a friend."

"You *are* cheating on Paul," Patrice said.

Nat stared at her, horrified.

"Listen. I understand that you were lonely after Paul left. It's hard to make friends. It's hard to be changing duty stations all the time and moving all the time and being a stranger everywhere you go."

Nat nodded, her eyes welling with tears, grateful for someone who understood.

"But you have me now, you have a friend. So you shouldn't need him anymore, right?"

"I guess so," Nat said quietly.

"So?"

Nat looked toward the window. The green car sat at the curb. She remembered how spotless it had been when Esrom brought it over, imagined him burnishing every inch of it with a cloth, the incredible thoughtfulness of that.

"So?" Patrice said again. "Is there something you are getting from your friendship with him that you can't get from your friendship with me? Because if there is, then I think we know you're in dangerous territory here."

Nat couldn't bring herself to say anything.

Patrice crossed her arms over her chest. "This really bothers me, Nat. It just really bothers me. I don't—I wish—I wish you well, but I don't know if I can . . ."

"Patrice, please," Nat cried.

"People will think I'm keeping your secret, and I never intended that."

"I don't *have* a secret," Nat said. "That's the whole point! I obviously haven't tried to keep anything a secret." She flapped her arms in frustration. "What is wrong with all of you people? Why do people take a good thing and try to make it bad? Good things don't take *away* from the world, they just add more good—"

Patrice stared at her. Her lovely face had gone nearly blank with anger. "What are you *talking* about?" She shook her head, speaking slowly as if Nat were dense. "I'm an army wife just like you," she said, "and we do *not* do this. This is not how we act when our husbands are deployed. You're breaking the rules."

Nat felt a flare of defiance. "Oh, screw the rules," she said.

Patrice's voice shook. "The rules are here for a reason. When you flout them, you're saying you don't care about your own husband."

"Stop talking down to me," Nat cried.

"Well," said Patrice, "maybe you deserve it!"

Nat's anger twisted into something else, a horrible, hollow feeling, and she burst into tears.

"I can't come over anymore," Patrice said quietly. "I'm sorry."

"I don't think you're sorry at all," Nat wept through her hands, "because you're being cruel."

Patrice watched her, softening for a moment from anger to sorrow. She took a deep breath, trying to meet Nat's eyes. "Why don't you stop seeing him right now?" she asked, quietly. "It would be so easy. Just don't let him in the house again. Can you do that?"

Nat looked at her. Her heart felt momentarily lighter; she was being offered a second chance.

Patrice waited.

Just say yes, Nat told herself. *Don't be so stupid!* She opened her mouth, shut it again.

"Fine," Patrice said, the word quiet with rage. She plucked her coat and scarf from the back of the chair and strode for the girls' bedroom. "Carol *Ann*!" Nat heard her say, adding, with frantic sweetness, "We need to leave, sweetheart."

"You hafta go so soon?" Sam asked.

"No *back*talk, Sam!" Nat cried. A moment later Sam's perplexed face peered around the corner. Patrice wove past her, tugging Carol Ann by the hand. In an instant they were through the kitchen and the living room, a swirl of chilly air marking their exit as the front door opened and slammed.

Liddie shuffled around the corner, still dressed in layers of absurd clothing, crying now. "Why they go, Mama?" she asked.

Nat bolted to the television as if it were some lifesaving device and turned the power knob, and it worked its instant magic; the girls drifted toward it, their tears drying up, mouths slightly open. Then she fled into the back room so she could cry in peace. She sprawled on her side on the bed, pinched off fingerfuls of snot, pounded the pillow, while in her tight-stretched belly the baby rolled and turned, pushing in all directions, as if it had a dozen fists.

THE EVENING SEEMED INTERMINABLE, but somehow she got the girls fed and bathed and into bed with a story. The round clock on the wall made one tiny click after another, magnifying her loneliness. Finally she yanked it down entirely, pulled out the batteries, and buried it in a back closet between a stack of old blankets, pressing a quilt over its blank unmoving face. For a moment she felt better, but when she returned to the dark living room, her heart sank again.

Eventually she dozed on the couch, on her back with her round island of belly rising up. She felt too sad to sleep in the bedroom at the back of the house; on the couch she felt somehow more connected to the world, as if she weren't so alone.

Sometime after midnight she heard the quiet drag of tires in the street. Groggily, she sat up. An engine rattled softly just outside. She got to her feet, pulled her afghan around her shoulders, and peeked out the front window. A few hard, tiny snowflakes whirled from the sky, not enough to collect anywhere, yet.

Her heart jumped when she saw Esrom's truck, dim in the moonlight, start to pull away.

What was he doing here? She kicked her feet into her slippers and stepped outside, waving her arm over her head. The wind whistled right through the blanket and she shivered, hurrying down the walk. He looked back at her, hesitated, and then put the truck in reverse until it was in front of the house.

"Hi," she whispered, her eyes darting to nearby dark windows. If people saw them now, who knew what they'd think? "What is it? Are you all right?"

He could hardly meet her eyes. "I'm fine," he said. "It's freezing. You should go back inside."

"What in the world are you doing out here?"

"I'm sorry," he said.

"Why?"

He was staring down at his hands. His cheeks looked cold, his nostrils slightly glistening; the tiny, thin lines at the corners of his eyes seemed as if they had been drawn there by the tip of a needle. "I was just driving home from the station," he said. "I have this thing—"

"You have what thing?" Nat said gently, confused and flattered.

"Well, I just have this thing where when I come home from the late shift, I circle around by your place and make sure everything looks okay, and then I head home."

"Oh," Nat said. Her house was not even remotely on the way to his apartment from the testing station; it was significantly out of the way. But he was so flustered that she wanted to be careful with his feelings.

"It's all right," she said, "it's really fine." And the truth was she liked it more than fine, she liked it quite well. Now she couldn't squelch the thrill that was running through her: It was as if she had called this habit of his into being through her own little dreams, and she felt excited and cared for and somehow powerful. "How long have you been doing this?" she asked.

"A couple weeks. I'm really sorry. It's a strange thing to do. I didn't mean any harm by it."

"I know that. I know. I just . . . I'll admit it. It makes me feel special, actually."

He tried to smile but it came and went quickly.

"So!" she said briskly, realizing there was no way to make this chat seem normal. "How was work tonight?"

"Fine. Couple false alarms at one of the reactors." His eyes darted to her and she wondered if, by his hesitation, he meant Paul's reactor but didn't want to mention her husband by name. In any case, there were more than two dozen reactors out at the testing station; surely some of the others were equally troublesome. So she didn't need to ask, which was a relief because some part of her, though she hated to admit it, didn't want to mention Paul, either.

"So, I thought of something," she said. "I know this will sound silly, and it's not even necessary, it's nothing at all—"

He nodded.

"Do you think when you come over from now on, you could maybe ride the bus?"

"Oh," he said. He thought for a moment. "Oh, so my truck won't always—"

"Yeah."

"Does it, is there something—"

"No. Not at all. But it just sits out there. You know, for a long time."

"Right."

"And people are really silly about stuff like that."

"Okay."

"People are ridiculous." Nat felt her face flush; she thought of Patrice's stone-cold judgment, Jeannie's snide, probing questions, and her stomach squeezed. She felt angry that such unpleasant thoughts were intruding on her happiness. And the flip side of that was that this happiness should not exist, which was becoming clearer by the second even though she was acting like they could just tiptoe around it.

"Are you all right?" he asked.

"Yes."

"Did something come up? Did this—did I cause you trouble?"

"No," she lied.

His face narrowed with concern. "People are dumb if they think that. What? They wouldn't want someone looking after their own wife, or their sister?"

Nat blanched, thinking maybe there really was nothing more to this than his brotherly concern, which should have been reassuring but was somehow galling. It mortified her to think she might be more invested in his visits than he was.

But no, no. Here he was at midnight. His truck idling by her house. At midnight, goddamnit, and Nat was being a good person, she was not doing anything wrong, but damn that Patrice and damn Jeannie Richards and damn all of them if they came poking around at something that was making her feel happy. If they didn't have anything special, if their relationships were all so staid and normal and taped down along the lines . . .

"Nat, are you okay?"

"Esrom," she blurted, "be honest. You really think of me just like family, a sister?"

Instantly, she realized she should not have asked. She was about to end everything, because once their relationship was called out by name, it would have to stop. What did she expect him to say? What did she want him to?

His hands, loose in his lap, flattened on his jeans; his shoulders stiffened. He was so visibly squirming, so obviously afflicted, that she felt sorry for having said it out loud.

"I don't know how to answer that," he finally managed.

"Oh, it's okay," she said quickly. "Don't worry about it—"

"I like being around you," he said. "I like that . . ." He faltered, took a breath, started up again. "Well, you know, most of the time I think people are just shitty to each other. But with us, it's like we can just be as nice to each other as we want, and we take care of each other, and yeah, I think you're beautiful, and it's almost like, I don't know, a fairy tale." His face had gone white and he said, "I sound like a fuckin' idiot."

Nat had never heard him curse that strongly before and she let out a small sympathetic laugh, though she thought she might cry. "You don't sound like an idiot," she said.

She stared at him, at his handsome-in-its-own-way face, and realized the depth of her affection for him. She tried to give herself a breakneck version of her spiel about *things just adding more good to the world*. It wasn't working. It hadn't convinced Patrice and it wasn't convincing her. She had asked the question, and now he'd answered it, and now she had ruined everything. There was no way to take it back.

"Esrom, I think you're a wonderful person," she started, hating herself.

As soon as she said it his head snapped back a little. "Don't worry," he said. "I'll go now."

"No, I didn't mean—"

"I know what you're gonna say, and you're right. I should never have come over so much. I should never have started driving by. It was selfish of me. I could have brought trouble on you, much more trouble than I'd get into myself. Your"—he fumbled a little—"your husband will be coming home soon. He sure ain't going to want me loitering."

Now Nat did spot a sliver of light in Edna Geralds's window. She turned her back and hunched toward Esrom, hoping it was dark enough to obscure her for a few moments more.

"Could you tell the girls good-bye for me?" he was saying. "I don't want them to think I just forgot about them."

"Oh, the girls," she cried. "They'll miss you so much."

"I'll come by and get the car tomorrow," he went on. She could see the effort it took for him to speak, the way he took his sorrow and shoved it into this absurd, manly to-do list. "Don't you worry about it, I'll take care of it. Can you get to the shop to pick up your other one?"

She could not think of anything she cared about less at that moment. "Sure. Yeah."

"Call them first, make sure they have it ready."

She held herself around her belly, feeling bitter and lost and full of sadness, angry at Jeannie and Patrice and her neighbors, angry, unfairly, at Paul. What she wanted to do was beg Esrom not to stop driving by at night. She wanted to hear that quiet grind of tires straight from her dream, to know for a fact that someone was thinking of her. *Please,* she wanted to say, *keep doing it, at least a while longer, and then I won't be so lonely and I won't hate everyone.* But there was no way she could say this, no proper way to ask for it, because it was not a proper request. It was improper to be lonely; it was improper to be bored; it was improper, most of all, to be filled with anything like longing. And even if you were good and stayed in your house and loved your children and your husband—and, yes, she did love her husband—people could sniff out this longing in you; they had pointed fingers at Nat for as long as she could remember, hissing *That one, that one is not satisfied.* Because there was no cure for it, it was worse than any one thing you might actually do.

He said, "I can't believe you're going to have your baby and I'll never see you again."

He said, "If you need help of any kind, you know, if you're in a bind of some sort, you can still call me."

He said, "I should have been more careful, because I never thought you were my sister."

PAUL

PAUL HAD FIRST SPOTTED THE DELEGATION OF VISITORS—SOME American congressmen whom Paul didn't know, and two Danish officials—when he was sitting in the chow hall, hunkered over a bowl of split pea soup. They shuffled in behind the lieutenant colonel who was giving them a tour, each man bundled identically in parkas and gloves and hats with earflaps. Master Sergeant Richards was easy to recognize because of his height and the fact that he looked so absolutely peeved in this getup, his arms at his sides as if they had been tied there.

Of course it was only a matter of minutes until the group reached Paul's table, and he'd stood with the others to salute. The colonel gave a short talk about the visitors, then spied Paul and pointed. "Ah, here's another nuclear man," he said, pushing Richards stiffly over like someone trying to set up a reluctant couple on a date. And then Paul and Richards had been eyeball to eyeball for an uncomfortable minute.

"Hello, Master Sergeant," Paul said. From the corner of his eye he could see Mayberry bobbing up and down with excitement.

Richards's blue eyes flicked to him. "How are you, Collier?" he said flatly, and they shook hands.

"I'm just fine." *Loving it here at Camp Century.*

"I think, Sergeant Richards," the colonel piped in, "you'll be thrilled to see firsthand how much your CR-1 has contributed to the development of our beautifully functioning PM-2A."

Paul and Richards stared at the colonel. "I expect to be thrilled," Richards said, and he shuffled toward the exit with the rest of the group.

PAUL DODGED RICHARDS MOST of the next day, but encountered him again that evening walking down the main tunnel. As much as he didn't want to, it had to be done: "Master Sergeant," Paul called, and picked up his pace.

Richards turned with an expression that was either blank or disdainful. He pointed to himself. "Me?"

"I wanted to speak with you," Paul said.

Richards watched him from an arm's length away.

"I wanted to apologize for what I did back in Idaho Falls," he said, willing himself to look Richards in the eye. "The incident at your house. I was out of line. I think we should try our best to put it behind us because we'll have to work together when we get back to the CR-1—"

"We won't be working together for long," Richards said.

"Sorry?" There was an ominous sound to this; was there something Paul didn't know?

"I'll be transferring back out to Fort Belvoir in February," Richards said.

"Oh," said Paul, trying not to brighten visibly.

"I'm leading training on the simulator there."

"Congratulations." Paul wondered if this development somehow nullified his truce offering.

Richards shrugged. "It'll be easy. What can go wrong when you work the simulator?" He gave Paul an oddly vacant grin. "So we'll only have six weeks together on your precious reactor once you get back to Idaho Falls, and then I'll be out of there for the rest of my life."

"Oh. Well, good, I guess." This was more of a relief, in fact, than Paul could let on. "How *is* the reactor? I suppose you've got that new core up and running. Probably a relief to have everything working so smoothly—"

"Bah," Richards said. "The new core? Right. That's not coming until next spring."

"Oh," said Paul, his heart sinking. "I thought it would be in by now."

Richards shook his head. He almost seemed to enjoy this scandalous, disappointing news. "They'll push that back till kingdom come. We'd be *lucky* to get one in the spring. Harbaugh died, did you hear?"

"No, I didn't," Paul said, feeling genuinely sad. "I'm sorry to hear that."

"Yeah, well, we all knew it was coming."

"I guess so. His family—how are they doing?"

"I don't know," Richards said. "Think they left town."

"So the reactor," Paul tried to circle back. "Is it still getting the stuck rods, is it—"

"Collier, for Christ's sake, don't be such a nag. Are you trying to piss me off some more, or are you going to actually smooth this over like you seem to have set out to do?"

Paul swallowed. He *had* been trying to make things better, and maybe standing there prodding Richards about the reactor again, like he'd done in their worst encounter back in Idaho, was not the way to go about it.

Richards looked around. "So," he said with a sweep of his arm, "I've already toured your reactor. I've seen your weather station and your mess hall, which you all are so strangely proud of, and some tall fellow even showed me a room full of ice tubes. You've all gone insane up here, is what I think."

"Could be."

"What do you fellas do in the evenings? Cry to the chaplain?"

"There's a club we go to."

"Oh, I've heard of this club," Richards said.

"We *call* it a club, anyway."

"What do you have at this club? Dancing? You boys dance with each other?"

"It may come to that, eventually."

"It's open tonight, right?"

"Yeah, it's open," Paul said, warily. He did not have a good track record with escorting Richards to drinking establishments.

"Think the asshole who punched me in the face can buy me a beer?"

Paul did not know what to say. His heart sank at the same time he felt relieved: They weren't enemies. But they were right back where they'd started.

Richards slapped him on the shoulder. "You poor kid! You really don't know your ass from a hole in the ground, do you? Listen, if I had my way you'd be sitting out in front of the public assistance office right now, cryin' for a job. I think you owe me a beer. You owe me a few." He was actually grinning. His hand was on Paul's shoulder as if they were friends. He may as well have been dangling Paul upside down by the feet and shaking him for quarters, while telling him he'd been promoted.

"I can buy you a beer, Sergeant," Paul said.

He did not really want to have one beer with this man, let alone "a few," but there was no excuse on this earth that he could possibly make. He didn't know if his apology had gone staggeringly better than he'd expected, or if Richards was still silently loathing him, or if the man would just take a free beer from anybody. But considering that a beer at the club was only a nickel, Paul felt that this must be a primarily symbolic gesture. He and Richards walked down the ice tunnel.

"So how's the family?" Richards asked.

"They're fine," Paul said, though he didn't really want to talk about them with Sergeant Richards. "Nat's in a family way, you might have heard. She's about eight months along now."

"Another baby? You two dirty little rabbits!" Richards crowed. It was remarkable how even the mere mention of a couple of beers could make Richards act as if he'd already had them. "She must be as round as a watermelon."

"I guess so," Paul said, and managed to keep himself from adding *I haven't seen her in five months,* because it sounded accusatory.

"Did I ever tell you about the watermelons we grew on Nanumea?" Richards said. "Pure gold inside, sweetest you ever tasted. Not too huge, about the size of a football. We'd throw 'em over the water and blast 'em with our Tommy guns, and holy hell, if those things didn't explode like a pig stuffed with confetti."

This was an odd transition from talking about his wife, but Paul wasn't going to get particular. He pointed to a Quonset hut, no different from any of the others, and said, "So, here's the club."

The hut was crowded because it was the only place to be, and the moment the door closed behind them they were engulfed in stuffiness, the smell of recycled breath and long-bundled bodies, coats hanging like seal skins from the wall. Like any of the other barracks it was a windowless, nailed-board tunnel. The floor was covered with thin beige carpeting marked by seeping, concentric stains. There were a handful of couches and chairs around the room, and a wet bar tended by a Filipino steward. A stereo was playing, which everyone depended on because it was the only thing capable of adding atmosphere.

The steward, a quiet man named Palacios who must have felt his life had taken its most punishing turn, said hello and passed Paul a San Miguel. "I owe this man a beer," Paul said, pointing to Richards, who said he'd changed his mind and wanted a whiskey instead.

Paul nodded to Mayberry and to Benson, who was staring openly; Mayberry, it turned out, wasn't great at keeping secrets. Benson, grinning, fisted his hands and threw an imaginary punch behind Richards's back.

"Good evening, Master Sergeant," everyone said.

"Collier here tells me this whiskey tastes like shit," Richards said happily. "To Camp Century! My heart bleeds for you poor sons of bitches." He raised his glass, socked the whiskey down his throat, and then headed back to the bar for another.

"And the lion laid down with the lamb," Benson marveled when he had gone.

"Which one of them is the lamb?" Mayberry asked.

"Thanks for bringing the supe to our party."

"Sorry," Paul shrugged. "He just followed me home. Let him talk and he'll be fine." He pointed at Mayberry. "Behave yourself."

Richards sauntered back to them along with the two Danish officials. "Hallo," said the first, whom Richards introduced as Sorensen, a ruddy man with shiny, almost waxen skin and a flop of strawberry-blond hair. "I see you're taking part in Denmark's favorite pastime."

"Being bored, and sitting in an igloo?" Benson asked. Then he reddened and said, "With all due respect, sir."

"I am a civilian. There's no need for 'sir,'" Sorensen said. Benson moved over to give the two Danes his space on the couch.

"He meant drinking," Hansen said. "Bottoms up."

Conversation rolled along, remarkably amicable, with pauses filled by steady imbibing; most of the men had heard one another's stories. Richards launched into tales from his time in Nanumea and seemed to genuinely enjoy himself. Paul felt sleepy and oddly satisfied. Maybe when he got back to Idaho Falls, things would be different. They'd head into the new year and get a new supervisor, someone who might actually take action to improve things. And he and Richards might even go out on a good note.

Clinking glasses, the murmur of voices, radio bopping along; Paul leaned his head back and closed his eyes. He heard Roy Orbison's "Only the Lonely," with its spasms of bass drum like knocks on the door; Connie Francis's cute honk, her sweep of trilling backup singers: *There are no exceptions to the rule / Yes, everybody's somebody's fool.*

"So what's the first thing you're going to do when you get home, Collier?" Benson asked.

From where he was sitting Richards blurted, "I'm going to go skiing. The slopes are perfect right now. Snow looks like icing on a cake."

There was a pause, and when Paul felt it was respectful, he answered the question. "Well, kiss my wife and kids," he said. "Smoke a cigar."

"You smoke cigars?"

"Not usually."

"I'm going to get my boys a puppy," Benson said. "Little black cocker spaniel with a red bow."

"Get an Alsatian," Richards murmured from his armchair. Everyone ignored him.

"We could name it Sookie," said Benson, still on the subject of his fantasy puppy. "Or Sooty. Which one is better?"

"How about Blackie?" asked Richards. "Because it'll be all black."

"Or maybe Four-Legs," whispered Mayberry, "'cause it'll have four legs."

Paul stifled a laugh into his beer. The group quieted for a moment, and a thought came to him. "I'm going to get Nat a new car," he said, feeling suddenly inspired. "It'll be brand-new and all hers. She can drive it to the store, to the reservoir, wherever she likes." He couldn't help but smile. This was the best idea he'd ever had.

"To the reservoir?" asked Benson, unfamiliar with the Idaho Falls area. "Why's your wife driving to the reservoir?"

"To swim. She can drive it anywhere she likes," Paul repeated, stirred by goodwill. He thought of the thrill Nat would get when he drove home a new car just for her. She'd throw her arms around his neck; she'd smile from ear to ear. He was going to be generous with her every day, from here on out. He was going to be his best self all of the time.

"Do you really need two cars?" Mayberry asked. He was proud that his household of seven got by on one, but Paul figured that this must be because Mrs. Mayberry never set foot outside the front door.

"She already has a car," Richards said.

Paul turned to him, assuming that Richards was somehow referring to Mayberry's wife and feeling confused by this, but too sleepy and content to press further.

"I'll take the Fireflite, and she can have a *new* car," Paul went on. "That way I can get to work on my own, and she won't have to drive me to the bus stop if she wants the car for the day." Paul felt he was talking a little too much. He doubted this group of lounging men could really care about the specifics of his family's car situation.

Richards was looking at Paul with a strange, wide-eyed expression. "No," he said, "I mean your wife already has a new car."

"I'm sorry?" said Paul.

"It's a green Dodge Wayfarer."

Paul sat up and looked Richards in the eye. "*Who* has a new car?" he asked.

The Danes glanced between Paul and Richards, probably unsure as to whether they were following this conversation correctly.

"Your wife," he said pointedly, speaking loudly as if Paul were deaf or slow, "is driving a new car already. Her friend gave it to her."

"What friend?" asked Paul. He tried to think of who Nat knew: Chrissie next door, or Edna, whose daughter occasionally babysat for them; a woman named Patrice whom Nat had mentioned getting together with a few times while Paul was at work. They were all nice ladies, but Paul couldn't imagine any of them giving her a car.

"Her friend," Richards said, taking a sip of his beer. "The *cow*boy."

Everyone was looking at Paul now, and he felt his face turn deeply red. "What are you talking about?"

Richards sat forward with a bleary expression. "I'm sorry," he said.

"Sorry for what?"

"I gotta go to bed," Richards said, rubbing his eyes. "It's been nice, fellas. But it's cold and weird here."

"Sir," Paul cried, and his voice felt far-off and desperate even to his own ears, "are you talking about my wife, Nat Collier?"

"I apologize," Richards said. "It was just something Jeannie told me. There's a fellow who's been hanging around your house since you've left. A cowboy type, a local. He gave your wife a car."

"That doesn't make any sense at all."

"Now, now. I'm sure he's merely a friend. People have just noticed, is all."

Benson and Mayberry exchanged glances. One of the Danes looked on openmouthed, holding his beer below his chin.

Paul's heart sped up; he felt clammy and horrified, as if all his insides had just been drained from his body, landing in a bucket below him with a heavy slop. Everyone stared at him in pity. He said to Richards, "If you are lying, I will kill you."

"Whoa," said Mayberry, snapping to action and putting a hand on Paul's shoulder. "We've all had a bit to drink here. I really don't think the master sergeant knows what he's saying."

Richards stood, a little wobbly, and buttoned the flaps of his hat under his chin. He looked ridiculous. His expression grew solemn, almost maudlin. "I sure wish to God that I were lying, Paul," he said.

He had never before called Paul anything but his surname, and this seemed to confirm that the rumor Richards had just told was true: Richards felt sorry enough for him to call him by his first name.

Paul bolted to his feet. "You stop right there," he shouted. "Do you know what you have just said? Do you know what you have accused my wife of?"

"They are going to fight," said one of the Danish men, in quiet wonder.

"No, they're not." Mayberry scrambled to his feet behind Paul and put his hand across Paul's chest. "No one knows what they're saying here. *You* don't," he said, pointing to the retreating Richards; and then, tightening his grip on Paul, "and you sure as hell don't, either." He waited a moment until Richards had left the club, and then he nudged Paul to the door and steered him in the opposite direction down Main Street. "Good night, gentlemen," he called back through the door, before shutting it.

The empty cold surrounded Paul all at once. It was a horrible place. "Did you hear what Richards said?" he cried. "Do you think he's crazy? What in God's name is going on here?"

"Don't waste another thought on it." Mayberry led him to their barracks. "The guy talks out of his ass, you know that. Besides, he's half-drunk, and probably still pissed at you for sucker-punching him. It's a pretty low way to get back at you, making up stories like that."

"What he said seemed so specific," Paul said. "A green Dodge Wayfarer? Why would he make that up?"

"You heard all those tall tales he was inventing about Nanumea. If he could invent a, you know, seventeen-year-old island girl with a twenty-inch waist and a lust for army techs, he could invent a green Dodge Wayfarer."

"Maybe," said Paul dully. He jerked away from Mayberry. "*I'm* not drunk. You don't have to lead me everywhere like some fucking horse." Then he felt very strange and he said, "I'm going to be sick. I'm going to throw up."

"You need to go to the latrine?"

Paul paused, swallowing. "No."

"It was a load of BS," Mayberry kept saying. "He wants to get back at you, or he's just stupid. Why the hell would your wife be driving around in another man's car? Everyone would see. No woman would be that foolish. It's deployment gossip and nothing more. Get it out of your head."

They got back to the barracks, where a few guys were already sleeping. Mayberry opened the door. Paul paused for a moment, then went in. Mayberry clambered up to his bunk and tossed his boots down to the floor with two leaden thumps.

Paul slid out of his own boots and fell into his bunk in his uniform, his head spinning. He tried to close his eyes and force himself to sleep, hoping the beers he'd drank would take him there faster. But all the alcohol tossed seasick thoughts back and forth in his mind. Could it be true Nat had befriended some local asshole cowboy, driving the man's car around so that everyone could see? It sounded ludicrous, and yet Paul couldn't tell himself with certainty that it was something Nat wouldn't do. Maybe it had started innocently; maybe she didn't realize how it would look. He burned with horror to think of Nat opening the door of their house to this person, her smile welcoming but shy, the dimple in her left cheek showing: He could see it all. And every time he thought he had imagined the worst—Nat touching this guy on the arm, or sitting carelessly next to him on the couch without remembering to tug down the hem of her skirt first—he would realize that there was something even worse to imagine, until his mind seemed to be tumbling down a long corridor with dozens of tiny doors opening and closing, flashing images that tormented him.

"Go to sleep, Collier," Mayberry called down from his bunk.

"Leave me alone," Paul said.

"Both of you, shut up," someone grumbled.

Nat loved him; she loved their family. But he knew—and this knowledge had burned into an ulcer on his brain—that Nat was sometimes not careful, that she neglected to observe the rules other people followed.

She didn't safeguard her honor. Even when he'd first met her, Nat had been loose. The word jarred him, but it was the only one that fit. On that San Diego beach, she'd asked him to walk away from the bonfire. They'd strolled from the safe circle of friends who were supposed to be watchful, away from men she knew. No one in the group had seemed concerned about her honor, actually, and what Paul had hoped was a sign of their unscrupulousness might have just been evidence that Nat had little honor to lose in the first place. She had invited him to go swimming with her in that dark, wild ocean. When he kissed her, she'd kissed him back.

Richards had reached over and touched Nat's neck at that dinner party, had smoothed the napkin right onto her lap, and she hadn't flinched or told him off. A drunken buffoon had touched her in front of her husband and an entire dinner party, and she had *thanked* him.

Paul flipped in bed, kicked the cot twice, hard, as if it were a body below him. When Nat was supposed to be home taking care of their family, stepping nobly into an enhanced role in her husband's absence, what had she really been doing? Spending time with the sort of man who would move in on an absent soldier's pregnant wife? This was the kind of sordid thing Paul heard of other people involved in, the sort of thing his parents might have done, but now it was his own family, his own wife.

He didn't know how he could stand the next few weeks, doubly tortured by his exile and by not knowing what Nat was doing, what she had done, while he was away. He rolled onto his side and gritted his teeth. The room fell into sleep sounds. A bunk creaked, and, above Paul, Mayberry cleared his throat. Someone across the room was snoring.

JEANNIE

JEANNIE'S LITTLE VACATION WAS OVER AND SHE READIED HERself for Mitch's return. A paper-wrapped pork tenderloin came to room temperature on the counter; a fresh bottle of Old Smuggler stood lookout on the wet bar. In a plume of steam over the stove, she blanched pearl onions and picked away their skins. They rolled gently in a pan of oil like peeled eyeballs.

Martha took Angela for a haircut while Jeannie enjoyed a Mitchless nap. The scent of onion clung to her fingertips when she awoke. She rolled onto her side, not sure why she felt sad. It was no surprise that Mitch was coming home; Mitch was always coming home. She looked at his half of the bed, still made, and wished Eddie would materialize there. But, no: Eddie was off trotting around town with his pregnant child bride, most likely. So Jeannie got Mitch. That was the way it would always be.

The windows rattled; Jeannie shivered as she slid out of bed. For two weeks it had been bitterly cold. Up until his departure for Greenland, Mitch had been spending an awful lot of time in his "study," the private hideaway at the back of the house, where he kept a space heater. Jeannie had a love-hate relationship with Mitch's study. Despite its cultivated aura as a place of "man's work," she knew it was mostly a quiet spot where he could stare into space and politely avoid his wife and child.

Most of his work documents were classified and could not be brought out of the office on base, so how much paperwork could he have to do anyway?

Apparently he'd been bringing more home; he was spending a lot of time typing away at his desk. Each key shot rang out like a minor celebration, followed by a long pause. He was hogging the space heater back there, and Jeannie decided that at least until he returned it should be used for the benefit of the entire household.

Maybe he's compiling his memoirs, Jeannie thought drily, buttoning her cardigan. She hadn't set foot in his study in weeks; he didn't like it cleaned because, he complained, she moved his things and he could never find them again. If by this he meant that his bottle of Scotch was moved from one side of the desk to the other, well, surely he could locate it.

The study, she soon discovered, was locked. This struck her as either childish territoriality or a typical Mitch oversight. She fetched the spare key from her jewelry box and pushed open the door, which resisted against thick carpet. As soon as she had the door open, though, she began to cough. The room reeked with an acrid, bitter smell. Her eyes watered; she fanned the air in front of her face with her hand.

With a start, she saw that the window was open. A thin layer of snow dusted the sill and the carpet below was wet.

"What on earth, Mitch?" she grunted, struggling to close the half-frozen pane. It stamped into a long line of snow, throwing glittering powder onto the carpet. She knelt and swept the snow into her hands, where it instantly melted. She wiped her hands on her skirt, surveying the room, her fingers below her nose.

Mitch's typewriter was out on his desk. It was a white Sterling portable with a pebbled finish and sea-green keys, a beauty. She had bought it for him upon his last promotion, and though it hadn't seen much use, when it was out of its case it lent an air of modernity to the room's masculine blah. Looking at the typewriter Jeannie recalled a time, several months ago, when Mitch had set Angela on his lap here and let her clack the keys. Angela had been thrilled to roll out the paper and witness the marks she made. Jeannie was peeved with Mitch over something at the time, of course, and recalled wondering snidely if the marks on paper surprised and delighted him as well. And yet the memory was still mostly a good one, little Angela with Mitch hunched around her, encouraging her to whack those typewriter keys.

Perhaps it was the glimmer of this memory that kept Jeannie rooted to the spot. No matter how often she disdained him, Mitch was hers, and his business was her own. The throat-burning smell, the open window, his new and furtive typing habits: He was doing something peculiar in here, and she needed to know what it was.

Lightly she stepped back across the room, closing the door behind her. She was the only one home, but still. With quick efficiency she began to rifle through the desk drawers. Cigars, lighter, stapler, paper clips, Scripto pens. The deeper drawers were more of a challenge, filled with folders and papers, and, at the bottom, a small collection of magazines that made Jeannie's face burn. Apparently Mitch had a thing for a lady named Paula Page who looked dignified enough, even maternal, as she sat on a bed, except that she'd forgotten to button her collared shirt, and one gigantic, flattish, liver-shaped boob hung straight out the front and dangled due south.

The pictures upset Jeannie: This was not a perky USO gal blowing kisses to the troops or the good clean fun of a swimsuited twentysomething in the waves; this was raw, unfamiliar. Was this what Mitch wanted, was this what Eddie wanted? She felt suddenly absurd, like a Tiffany lamp. She was prim and pristine and light in the chest. Her bras were tiny, well-locked safes. But, no—these *pictures* were absurd, not her. She shoved them into the bottom of a drawer and piled every other book and magazine on top.

This wasn't what she was here for, anyway, to judge Mitch and his odd manly needs. But she did want to know the source of the chemical smell, the reason he kept a window cracked in the dead of winter.

Nothing within the desk had any particular odor, so Jeannie tried the closet. As soon as she opened the accordion doors she knew she was close. She knelt and dived straight for the back corner, bypassing a row of polished shoes, a box of ties, an ancient football she'd never seen him hold. Tucked in the far right corner was a glass jar of cotton balls, a small dish of what appeared to be water, and a white pharmaceutical bottle. "Spirits of Salt," the label read, and in tiny letters: "Muriatic Acid." In cursive, as if this needed to be made pretty: *"For Stomach Troubles or Industrial Cleaning."*

What was Mitch up to, then? Stomach trouble, or industrial cleaning? He'd never complained of an upset stomach. Jeannie studied the bottle and carefully unscrewed the cap. It was powerful; her mucous passages instantly shrank. She recalled, dimly, this harsh smell. Her grandfather, who'd suffered all his adult life from stomach pains, drank this stuff in tiny, diluted amounts. She recalled having seen it on his nightstand, lifting the cap once to smell it (a move she'd instantly regretted) while her grandmother made lunch. (She paused here, the bottle in her hand, as it occurred to her that she'd been a lifelong snooper.) An engineer for Boeing, her grandpa called the liquid by its more scientific name, hydrochloric acid. Eventually he'd stopped drinking it because it didn't appear to help him, and not long after that he had died.

Jeannie held the bottle at arm's length. Could Mitch have an ulcer? Was he under some unknowable stress? She felt a pang of worry and care. Mitch was not the type to suffer in silence, but maybe he had been ill, afraid to tell her.

And yet. This was Mitch. She looked back at the jar of cotton balls, the bowl of water. She picked up a cotton ball and turned it in her fingers. It was dry, but its crunchy texture implied that it had previously been wet, and it was tapered to a point. She lifted it to her eye. A smear of gray covered the point, almost like pencil, or a smudge on one's hand made by newsprint.

A hunch began to nag at her.

Jeannie set the bottle on the carpet, moved back to the desk, and stood, staring at the drawers. Had she missed something? She went over the contents of each drawer in her mind. Then a corner of paper beneath the typewriter caught her eye, and she lifted the heavy machine. A small stack of papers was being pressed, or concealed, below. She waggled them back and forth from beneath the Sterling and extracted them, frowning.

They appeared to be a series of boring forms, the usual bureaucratic nonsense Mitch dealt with every day. There were records of reactor maintenance, taken from a three-ring binder—she knew what they were because they said, at the top, "Reactor Maintenance"—and pages that had apparently been torn from a logbook, the left edge of each lightly frayed. It was these she scrutinized first. Why had these individual pages been removed? Handwritten notes from the operators, and their signatures, made a column down the far right. Mitch had been acting queerly ever since Deke Harbaugh died, she recalled. Why had that affected him so? He'd acted as if there were aspects of his job only Harbaugh could understand, which was silly; it was an army reactor. Didn't all the operators understand everything the same way?

She flipped to one of the maintenance sheets. It did not seem particularly interesting or monumental. It listed several minor-sounding procedures that had been undertaken on the reactor over three weeks during the past spring. Jeannie switched on the small desk lamp by the typewriter and held the page to the bulb. Squinting, she noticed a small difference between the look of the paper on four of the lines. The surface on those lines was slightly fuzzy, and when she studied the type it looked fresher and darker than that on the rest of the page. The entries in question recorded the control rods being moved by Specialist Collier on three separate occasions and by Specialist Webb on another.

So this was it. This was what Mitch was up to. She could imagine him sitting at his desk, dabbing a cotton ball in acid water and then running it ever so gently back and forth over the page until the printed words lifted away. Fanning them, blowing on them, and when they were dry feeding them into his beautiful typewriter—her gift to him—to disguise whatever had previously been written there.

She didn't know the ins and outs of the information he had changed, nor why he had done it, and she didn't much care. The rub of it all, which she could see so plainly and with a sinking heart, was that he hadn't done a very good job. His new entries were often a hair above or below their companions on the lines, the ribbon darker, and while the surface of the paper had been only subtly changed, when she studied them closely she could pinpoint where. Of course, the paper trail at the reactor must be vast—this made her feel slightly better—but even so, if

Mitch had sought out whatever information was here to change, wouldn't someone else, too? And wouldn't it be fairly easy to see where the documents had been altered?

Good grief, Mitch, the idiot. All she wanted was for her husband to finish out his own humdrum career. He was seventeen years in, just three more to go; one more tour and they would be done. He'd have his pension, they'd settle in St. Louis, and finally her transient life of sacrifice, her endurance of Mitch's endless quest for nubile divertissements, would be rewarded with stability. She'd always feared that something might stop them from meeting this goal, but she hadn't known what. At a party she'd struck up a conversation with an army wife whose husband died just three months shy of retirement. He'd stumbled from a cliff while hiking. In Jeannie's case, she could probably count on Mitch not to get himself killed—he was good at that—but she didn't know if she could rely on him to make good decisions, to protect his career, his name and hers. Each promotion made her superstitious; with every increase in their station she felt it more likely that they would fall. If he screwed it all up now, there would be no fixing it.

She returned the forms to their spot beneath the typewriter and then, on second thought, lifted the bulky machine again and removed just one page. The typewriter thudded back onto the desk. Jeannie's eyes flicked over the unfamiliar words; she wondered just how important all this was. Would it work? Would it really save face for Mitch? Would it incriminate someone else? Stepping back, her foot bumped the bottle on the floor, and when she turned she saw that a small, pulsating burble of acid was making its way onto the carpet.

With an almost-silent squeal she bent for the bottle, realized she couldn't touch it with bare fingers, and dashed into the hallway. There she nearly collided with Martha and Angela, and this time she did shriek. Martha, startled out of her wits, yelled also, and the two women froze.

"I'm sorry!" Jeannie cried. "I need to take care of something." She slid past Martha, grabbed a washcloth from the bathroom, and darted back into the study, closing the door behind her. She didn't have time to worry about how strange all this looked. Stooping, she used the washcloth to lift the bottle and tighten the cap. She balled up the cloth and dabbed at the carpet. To her relief she saw no hole, but when she flicked at the fibers they drifted up and away, like dandelion fluff.

"God*damnit,*" Jeannie hissed.

"Mama?" Angela called from the hallway.

"We are going to the bakery!" Martha shouted, in a panic. "We are going out!"

Jeannie set the bottle back in the closet and replaced the cotton balls beside it. The room fairly reeked now, so, feeling Mitch-like and idiotic, she reopened the window. Tucking the sheet of paper under her arm, she hurried into the hall. She had to dash to catch Martha, who was bundling Angela so thoroughly that only the child's eyes and pigtails showed.

"Martha," Jeannie panted, "there's no need to go back out."

Martha paused and slowed her scarf winding. "Are you sure?" she asked, with exaggerated deliberateness.

"Of course. It's freezing out there. Angela needs lunch. How was your haircut, dear?" Jeannie reached for the scarf and for a moment both she and Martha held it as if they might begin to have a wrapping war, Jeannie twirling it one way and Martha the other.

"Fine," Angela's muffled voice said.

"Your pigtails look nice and cleaned up."

"I hungry."

"Oh. Martha will make you some tomato soup." Jeannie had won the scarf battle and she folded it against herself, stroking it flat.

"Are you sure, ma'am?" Martha stammered. "I didn't know—I thought maybe your friend?"

The air went out of Jeannie in a rush. She stared into Martha's eyes and, gathering herself, smiled broadly. "I'm sorry?" she said. "You thought maybe what friend?"

Martha looked away. "Nothing," she twittered. "Nothing, of course. Angela, I'll get you some soup."

NAT

It had been almost two years since Nat last saw her mother, so she was not sure what to expect. She tried to prepare herself for some kind of drastic change: a sizable weight loss, or maybe gain; some mild, elegant arthritis. She was surprised when her plump, purse-lipped mother climbed easily down the steel steps of the small airplane, clutching a handbag as big as a board game. The only new thing Nat could detect was her thick coat, black-and-white houndstooth. She had rarely seen her mother in any kind of jacket. Doris Radek was of that retired generation who liked to sit in the sun and thumb through the *Ladies' Home Journal,* and she always wore sleeveless dresses.

"Do you remember your Grandma Doris?" Nat asked, her voice sugary with nerves, as she nudged her girls forward.

"Aren't you lovely," her mother said, smiling at the girls; and then to Nat, "I prefer 'Grandma Radek.' 'Doris' isn't quite appropriate."

"Oh, right," Nat said quickly. "Your Grandma Radek, then."

Nat's mother bent to kiss each of the girls in turn. They stood stoically as Nat had instructed them to do. Then Doris leaned forward to tap her cheek against Nat's. Nat was both comforted and slightly put off by her mother's smell, which was the same as it had always been: a mixture of lipstick, fading nicotine, and the baby powder she patted all over herself after every shower. Taken together these created an unsettling aroma, like that of an overgrown infant with adult habits.

"Look at you!" Doris exclaimed, in a somewhat obscure way.

"How was your Thanksgiving, Mom?" Nat asked as the two of them lugged her suitcases to the car. It was a gray day, and the sky sat low like a dull, chilly lid.

"Thanksgiving was wonderful," Doris said. "Gorgeous weather. Fall in San Diego, you can't beat it. And Marva did a fabulous job as usual. You know how she is—every last detail taken care of."

"Yes," said Nat.

"And those beautiful boys!"

"Lyle and Stephen?"

"Yes. They're twelve and ten now. You've never *seen* such well-behaved children."

"Probably not," Nat admitted.

"Stephen has given guest sermons!" Doris marveled. "At age twelve!"

These were the kinds of standards her mother's peers held. Young Stephen's guest sermons were probably an improvement, Nat thought, over Pastor Tim's at the very much Improved Saint Ignatius Church. Tim must be in his thirties by now; Nat pictured him sunburned and pigeon-chested, hairline receding (she advanced his aging out of spite), holding forth in his dimly lit record store. She heaved her mother's suitcase into the trunk, pausing to stretch the small of her back.

The car dipped as Doris squeezed into the passenger seat. It was a challenge to get the girls in after her. Nat crammed in Liddie and then Sam, who scowled but, at Nat's warning glare, accepted her cramped fate.

Nat almost expected her mother to say something about the return of the yellow car: "Oh, I see you have the Fireflite back," or some such. She realized, however, that her mother had never known it was gone, and this cheered her. It would be the same when Paul came home. She really could pull off her lie, and everything would seem exactly the same as it had when he left. That morning she'd snuck into the girls' room, bagged their trinkets from Esrom—arrowheads, small rocks printed with fossils, the now-tattered and flattened snake skin—and, though it hurt, thrown them away. Luckily these items had fallen behind a bookshelf, had been forgotten for weeks despite the girls' initial love for them—with the exception of the snake skin that Liddie liked to carry around, fondling absently, like a mildly occult pacifier—and Nat hoped they'd stay out of mind if out of sight.

"Marva is on the flower committee," Doris was saying, still on the subject of her beloved daughter-in-law. George's wife was a prim, double-chinned woman who once suggested that Paul was "lowborn" and that Nat had abandoned her family by marrying a military man and moving away. This was an interesting opinion given the fact that Marva herself had moved from Tucson to marry George, a man so boring that in his thirties he seemed almost elderly. Nat had never really known her brother, but chafed at the slavishness with which both Doris and Marva doted upon him. Marva actually cut George's food for him: She cut his food!

This is not nice, Nat told herself. *Control yourself.*

The drive home proceeded mostly without incident, except that every time Doris worked up some bit of conversation, Sam was suddenly inspired to speak from the backseat. Interruptions made Doris peevish. "Sam, hush!" Nat said, more strongly than she had intended. Then she wanted to apologize but knew her mother would find an apology to a child ridiculous.

When they reached the falls, Nat brightened. Here was something to show a visitor. Doris leaned forward in her seat, appropriately impressed. Nat slowed the car, watching the cold, rushing water. The Mormon temple was so bright white against the gray sky that it looked lit up.

"That's quite a building they have," Doris said, and Nat hoped she would hold her tongue against the Mormons. She didn't want the girls to hear any pointed remarks. Thankfully Doris didn't say anything more than "They must have deep pockets," and Nat nodded and gave a little shrug, which committed her to no particular assessment.

They were almost at their street when Nat felt the cramping start in her back and abdomen. She pulled the car up to the curb and paused, trying to pay attention to the feeling. Doris got out of the car, and Nat felt the band of pain start at her back again, working its way forward. She knew what this was, but she didn't know whether to feel dread or relief. She got the girls into the house and put them to bed, then paced up and down the hall, a heavy, gravid beast of burden.

"Just go to the hospital," her mother called from where she sat smoking at the kitchen table.

"You're probably right," Nat said.

"Got here just in time, didn't I?" Her mother exhaled a slow plume, looking around. "I guess we'll be fine here. I'll wash this floor for you."

"Okay."

"I don't know what I am going to do with those girls all week, though."

"They love to color." Nat shuffled down the hallway and back, her elbow prodding the wall again and again like a walking stick. "They can watch TV."

"What should I do when Samantha gets lippy?"

Nat ground her molars together. Then the pain subsided and she felt normal enough to be irritated by her mother. "*If* Sam misbehaves, I send her to her room."

"Do you have a yardstick on hand?"

"No," Nat lied. She walked stiffly back down the hall. "I'm going to go to the hospital now," she said.

Outside, she could see her breath. She set her bag in the passenger seat. Then she had a stab of sentimentality and decided to go back inside and kiss her girls good-bye, just in case she never returned. She lugged herself through the kitchen and past her mother, who glanced up, curious.

In their bedroom, the girls were sound asleep. She bent low over each of them in turn. Liddie was soft and breathy, with dark eyelashes spilling down her cheeks; Sam was stretched out flat on her back, wild limbs and hair tossed everywhere, as if she had fallen onto the mattress from the ceiling. Nat felt a sudden, desperate affection for them, her little big girls.

She huffed back through the kitchen past her mother. Her forehead was starting to sweat.

"Are you sure you should be driving?" Doris asked, still at the kitchen table.

"I'm fine. There's no traffic this time of night."

"Wait," her mother said as Nat reached the door. Nat turned around impatiently. To her surprise her mother came to her and patted her shoulder. Nat felt grateful for this kindness, though she had to breathe through her mouth to avoid gagging on the cigarette-and-baby-powder scent.

"Be nice to my girls," Nat pleaded, only half-joking.

"But of course. Good luck, dear." Doris leaned in to kiss Nat but missed her mark, from shyness and unfamiliarity, and pegged her wetly on the neck. The kiss sat on Nat's skin and announced itself until she shrugged it off just outside the door. Then she shuffled down the cement steps, to the dark and waiting car.

There was a light layer of new snow on the road, just enough to leave thin imprints of tire tracks. Nat drove for a couple of minutes and sat out a contraction at a stop sign where no one else showed up. When the fist released her she drove again. She tried to cover as much ground as she could before the pain's next winding ascent through her abdomen. The following contraction turned her belly from its normal pregnancy firmness into a rock-hard, bulging expansion that overtook her body from rib cage to anus. The brakes ground sharply as she pulled over, clenched the wheel, writhed in her seat. *It will be over soon it will be over soon* she chanted in her head, and then it was, lifting as suddenly as it had come. When the pain left she felt nothing of it at all; it had just floated away. She gunned another mile down the road, felt the pain build, and waited until it was unbearable before yanking the car back to the shoulder. Her body was nothing but center, nothing but hurt for one horrible minute—her limbs and head incidental, just stuck there waiting—and then she was free, driving as fast as she could, not because she thought the baby's arrival was imminent but because she simply wanted to get off the road and into the hospital. Her limbs were not yet shaking away from her; she did not have the sickening sense that her body was opening itself in a perfect circle against the car seat. She still had an hour or two to go, both a relief and a discouragement.

In front of the hospital, however, she had the sudden and senseless thought that maybe if she didn't go in, she could avoid the whole rest of it. Her body might just forget, or decide to pick this up some other time. But no, she was in its clutches, this thing that turned her into a simple animal: no negotiation, no speech, no poetry.

Once in high school she'd gone for a beach walk, during yet another bonfire night with her friends, and come upon a large flat shape ahead of her. It was a sea turtle, its lower body tucked into a smooth damp hole in the sand. Nat had knelt beside it, watched the mucousy pulse of one egg after another down the well-dug chute. The turtle stared straight ahead, unmoving, as if it were alone. One of its front flippers was carved with deep, smooth, nearly crippling scars. When Nat leaned too close it opened its tulip-shaped beak and she sat back quickly in apology. It was the first time she'd ever witnessed such a perfect and critical focus, such coarse and untaught beauty.

She grasped the door handle and pushed it open but suddenly she couldn't make herself stand. She sat half out of the seat with her arm stretched to the handle. Paul was so far away that his presence was impossible, and he'd never been allowed anywhere near her during childbirth anyway; this made room for the soothing, heartening fantasy that Esrom was beside her. His kindness would make all this bearable. She imagined that he had brought foals and calves into the world in a gentle, welcoming way, whispering words of encouragement to their huffing animal mothers, and it was only fair that he might do this for her, too. She pictured his hand on her head, his cheek by hers, talking her through each wave of pain.

At the front of the hospital an attendant in a white uniform noticed her and settled her into a wheelchair, asking if her husband was parking the car. "No," Nat said. She was taken to a white room, familiar in the way all single-function rooms are familiar: three beds in a row separated by shower curtains. A woman in the far bed shouted for her husband, or someone named "Mr. Jackson," in a parched and agonized voice. Nat heard that voice and felt an almost-paralyzing dread: It would be her own in an hour or so. She changed into the thin and useless gown, and held out her arm when the nurse asked for her pulse. Her belly grew hard again, harder than she thought flesh could get, and she felt both the desperate urge to thrash away from it and also to curl herself around it, as if it were just a very sensitive monster that would respond to comfort. But it responded to nothing, only intensified, and pinned her to the bed with its strength. When she came out of the contraction she leaned her head back against the hard mattress and imagined that if she opened her eyes Esrom would be there, telling her that she was wonderful and brave.

"There's no need to be dramatic," the nurse said. She pressed a needle of clear fluid into Nat's arm and promised her that things would grow fuzzy soon.

MR. JACKSON, THE MAN who'd been called for so many times by the woman at the end of the room, showed up the next morning with three children in tow. He hurried past Nat's bed, but the littlest child turned to peek back. The girl's dress was askew and her hair looked like it had been styled with an eggbeater. That was what happened when the mother was in the hospital.

Nat lay in her quiet bed, a shower curtain on either side and no window in sight. She listened to Mr. Jackson talk to his wife and admire the new baby, who she surmised was a boy. The daughter peeked back around at Nat, who raised her fingers in a little wave.

A neighbor had volunteered to bring Doris and the girls by for a visit the next day, but that seemed ages away. At the moment the baby was having her first bath and a bottle. She had been born at three in the morning, pulled out by the doctor in one long slippery rope. Nat could still feel the immense relief of that expulsion, the baby's hard little body sucking out into the world so that Nat's belly slumped like pie dough, the pain finally gone. For a few long seconds the baby was silent, then let out three chirps like a tiny exotic bird. And then—"It's a girl!"—while Nat, pushing away the half second of disappointment that she might never have a boy, allowed herself the joy of a healthy, beautiful baby. Scrunchy and purple fisted, her dark hair plastered to her soft, blood-flecked skull, the baby jerked at the light and was swaddled up. Nat held her, kissed the sweet creased fingers with their translucent lavender nails, ran her fingers over the dewdrop nose.

"What will you call her?" the nurse asked.

Paul and Nat had talked idly about baby names a year or so before; Nat mentioned that if they ever had another girl she liked the name Sadie, and Paul agreed—said he thought it was sweet. So Nat had banked on this early approval. "Sadie, I think," she told the nurse, who peeked over her shoulder and smiled at the baby in a rare moment of friendliness.

"She looks like a Sadie," the nurse had agreed. "Those brown, brown eyes."

"Oh, good," Nat said. And then it seemed a huge weight had been lifted from her shoulders, the baby born and named.

Now, with Sadie off getting her bath, Nat lightly dozed. When another nurse announced a visitor she almost didn't hear. "What?" she said, groggily, thrashing up in bed.

To her surprise Esrom peeked around the corner, and her heart leapt. "Oh, hi!" she cried. "What are you doing here?"

"I just wanted to check on you," he said, still behind the curtain. "Is that all right? Are you, would you rather be alone?"

"No, please come in." She clutched the sheet awkwardly to her neck; her breasts were bound under gauze to wait out the milk. She tried to smile as if this were all perfectly normal. "I had the baby," she said. "She's beautiful. Are you hiding back there?"

He stepped into the room.

"Where's your hat?" she asked. His hair went every which way without it, and she found herself giggling.

"In my truck," he said. "Are you all right?"

"I'm great. How did you know I was here?"

His eyes met hers. "Saw your car was gone last night."

"Oh," she said, and her face flushed. "How did you get *in* here?"

"I said I was your brother." This silenced them both for a moment. Nat felt a stab of terror that his visit would be uncomfortable, but suddenly he let out a chuckle as if it had fully dawned on him: "Another girl! That's incredible."

"Isn't it?" she said.

He shifted. "So you drove here *yourself*?" he asked. "To have the baby?"

"Oh, yes. I had plenty of time." She cleared her throat and gave a wave of her hand. "It was all right." It did feel all right, now that it was over.

"I wish you could've called me."

"Well," she said simply, "I couldn't."

"I felt like someone should see you," he said, looking agitated. "I remember my ma having each of my brothers and sisters. Well, we were kept at the front of the house but I could hear it going on. When it was over and they were cleaned up we could go back and see, and she would be sitting there with the new baby and her hair in a braid."

Nat nodded him on.

"I just thought someone should see what you did. Like otherwise it would be, I don't know. A wasted miracle."

Nat paused. She recalled each time Paul had come in to see newborn Sam and Liddie, the way anxiety and awe sat plain on his face as he took a baby into his arms. He'd held each one so tenderly, looking a little choked up, while she'd sat, dazed, near his elbow, smelling the cigarette smoke and fresh air in his shirtsleeves, sharp against the cloistered room she'd been in for so many hours. He'd asked her if she was okay and she'd said "yes," which had somehow been true though part of her wanted to lie in someone's arms and cry for a hundred years.

Esrom was watching her. She focused again, smiling.

"How have you been?" she asked. "The fire department?"

"Oh, fine. They let me on full. Maybe I'll still do some odd jobs on the side, I don't know."

"That's wonderful." She was smiling and smiling, loving the company, not wanting him to leave.

The nurse bustled around the corner, adjusting her hat. "Oh, Mr. Collier!" she said. "Welcome! We'll have the baby back in just a moment, after her bath."

Esrom held up his hands. "I'm not—"

"Is this your first? You'll be used to it in no time. Now, you'll need to step out for a moment. Mrs. Collier, I need to check your"—she lowered her voice to a whisper—"bleeding."

"Really?" Nat said, disappointed. "He needs to go?"

"Well," said the nurse, "I'm sure you'd be more comfortable with some privacy. Do you mind, Mr. Collier?"

Of course Esrom had to leave. Of course he couldn't just stay here. Nat remembered, vaguely, that she wasn't supposed to see him at all. But it was so wonderful to have him show up that she couldn't have sent him away. She just couldn't have.

"I'm glad to see you're all right, Nat," Esrom said. "Do you need anything? Back home?"

The nurse glanced up with a quizzical expression, but her smile seemed fixed in place no matter the circumstances.

"I'm fine. Thank you so much. It made me really happy to see you." Nat glanced at the nurse and, suddenly not caring, said, "I wish you didn't have to leave."

He looked as if he wanted to say something but, his eyes following hers toward the nurse, nodded, bade Nat good-bye, and slipped off around the corner.

She might never see him again. Until that moment, with the impending baby, this fact had been easier to ignore. But then he'd appeared, and now his absence would seem crueler. She slumped back against her pillow as the nurse lifted the sheets and nudged her knees apart.

"Healthy as a horse," she said, removing a towel from underneath her and replacing it with a clean one. Then: "Oh, dear. Everyone gets this way. It's the hormones. You'll feel better once your milk is gone."

"I'm sorry," Nat said, snuffling into her hand.

"It's fine. I'll get you something to help you sleep."

"I miss Sadie. Is she finished with her bath?"

"I'll go and check, dear. You just rest." The nurse tucked Nat in like a child and then she, too, whisked around the corner.

Nat closed her eyes. Mr. Jackson and his brood had left. The silence was deafening. It seemed to close in on her until the nurse came back with the baby in her arms, swaddled so tight she was lozenge-shaped. Nat jolted up, reaching, greedy. "Hello," she said. "Hello, darling." She wished Esrom hadn't missed this. She wished Paul were here. But it wasn't a wasted miracle because she had been there to see all of it.

Sadie squirmed, her eyes two closed lines. She let out a quick, tiny sigh. Her weight in Nat's arms was perfect: almost nothing, and yet so much something, at the same time.

IV

CIVILIZATION

PAUL

THE ARC OF MOUNTAINS CIRCLING EASTERN IDAHO LOOKED, FROM the airplane, like the toothy jaws of an untriggered trap. They were bluish white and brown, heavy with snow this time of year, sloping down into the smooth band of valley that flattened a path between them. Paul had been fortunate enough to sit at the back of the army cargo plane where there was one small window no bigger than his hand. The world below him was cold and beautiful, mostly uninhabited, with skinny roads leading to the occasional small circle of a town and then away again. It was hard to believe that he had left his family down there all these months, tiny specks in what looked like mostly wilderness.

Turbulence tossed the plane as it descended. Paul glanced around at the nine other passengers sitting quietly in the gray hollowed-out cavity. Their faces wore expressions of mild anxiety or expectation, depending upon whom they were returning to and how long they had been away.

Gradually the forms of civilization below him began to take shape, and Paul could see cars moving along the roads; yards with fences; the occasional flimsy, snow-covered metal playground. The plane made its jerking, wind-battered descent, and all at once the ground was rushing up at them, and they were coasting for a moment over dead, snowy fields. The plane's wheels hit the runway with a thump, a tipping hop, and another thump; Paul felt it decelerating against the force of the wind.

He had not heard from anyone back home in weeks, except for a brief telegram from Doris saying that Nat had given birth to a baby girl on December 7 and that both mother and baby were fine. When he received this message, his hands shaking, he realized how anxious he had been. He was plagued by nightmares in the weeks leading up to the birth. His father stalked through his dreams, enormous, throwing a shoe at him, telling him to stop his blubbering. He dreamed again of Nat reaching into the oven, turning back to him with burned hands. In one dream she came toward him and they dangled like meat, and he awoke thinking he might actually retch.

Mayberry had told him he looked like shit.

All of the soldiers on the plane hopped up, trying to squelch the inner competition they felt to be first off the aircraft, and Paul moved slowly so as not to add to this atmosphere, which embarrassed him. Nat and the girls would be inside the airport with the small gathering of other families.

Outside, the wind roared. "Oh my God," said the first man in line. Everyone hunched down the stairs and waited for their bags to land. Paul peered over his shoulder toward the airport window, but it was shiny and reflective and he could not make out the faces of the people waiting inside. His stomach was beginning to ball up. He turned back to the baggage hold, waiting to hear his name.

There was the awkward checking of each bag's name tag and the effort not to cheer when one's own bag was revealed. Paul spied his own bag as it fell—it had a heavily taped corner where a rip had started—but he allowed the man nearest it to check the tag first, then call out in disappointment, "Collier." Paul stepped forward to his bag and swung it up onto his shoulder. He strode toward the airport terminal, the wind beating at his duffel and trying to spin its heavy bulk as he walked.

"Can you believe it?" a fellow soldier shouted as they went through the door. "We got sent to the Arctic just at the start of Idaho spring, and now we're home just in time for the Idaho winter. It's the longest goddamn winter in the history of the world."

A man behind them reminded everyone to please watch their flipping language because they would be around women and children now.

Hearing those words sent a shot of adrenaline through Paul and he looked up, scanning the handful of waiting families in search of his own.

"Paul!" he heard from somewhere to his left. "Paul!" His head jerked to the side and he saw Nat, waving an arm over her head in his peripheral vision.

"Excuse me," he said, ducking through the other soldiers, who were all lost in their own reunions or lack thereof. He bumped into a man's shoulder and apologized, cleared himself of the crowd, and found himself directly in front of his family.

"Paul!" Nat beamed, and she raised her arms and hopped against his chest as if she were nineteen again. He closed his arms around her, crossed over her back; her hair pressed against his chin. She felt exactly the same in his arms as he remembered, and for a split second tears came to his eyes. Then she pulled back and smiled up at him. He wanted to kiss her, that sweet mouth he'd dreamed about all those months; cup her face in his hands, let his hands wander, in fact, the moment they were alone, because what good was a deployment if you didn't at least have that? It was your right to become a fiend for at least a week, to make all those bored and longing thoughts come true and feel the absurd and giddy power in it. But he was revisited by Richards's bizarre, treasonous revelation and found he couldn't even bring himself to kiss her. He released her, knelt quickly to see his girls.

Sam and Liddie wriggled onto his knee, wearing frothy unseasonable dresses, each of their heads topped with a large bow. He hugged and kissed them while Nat turned and fumbled for something. He realized she was taking the baby from her mother's arms; he'd completely forgotten Doris would be there. "Hello, Doris," he said, standing quickly and leaning over to give her a peck on the cheek, which she received with no visible emotion.

"Welcome home," she said.

"This is Sadie May," Nat said, pressing a small oval bundle into Paul's arms. She pulled back the edge of the blanket and there was the baby's round, sleeping face. Paul's heart leapt. "She's two weeks old today," Nat said.

"Well, hello," Paul whispered, and he could not stop the smile that spread across his face. Sadie was a pink rosebud. On top of the blanket fold her fingers twitched, shiny, wrinkled. Paul felt one between his thumb and forefinger and his eyes swam. She was peely. She was silk.

"She just fell asleep a few minutes ago," Nat said.

"Can you imagine," said Doris, "with all this noise?"

"Hello, Sadie May," said Paul. "It's nice to meet you." A man he did not recognize appeared and snapped a flashbulb picture of them, and Paul blinked at him in confusion, then looked back down at his baby girl.

"The newspaper's here," said Nat. "We chatted with the reporter while we were waiting. He said it makes good press for the testing station to show soldiers coming home." This was Nat, gabby in the face of emotion. "You're the only one with a new baby, though. One soldier's dog died while he was away. Isn't that sad?"

"Okay," said Paul, not caring. "She's perfect, Nat. She's beautiful."

"Isn't she?" Nat smiled.

"And you? How are you feeling?"

"I'm just fine."

"You're tough," Paul said, unable to contain his admiration. Then he cleared his throat. "Can we get out of here? I'd like to go home."

"Of course," Nat said, taking Sadie back from him.

"Liddie, get in your stroller," Doris said.

"I no want to," Liddie said. She and Doris stared each other down, a match that would not end well.

Nat, awakening to Liddie's disobedience, knelt and looked her in the eye. "Liddie," she whispered, "get in the stroller now."

"I no want to," Liddie repeated.

Paul reached down and lifted her onto his shoulders. "You don't need that stroller 'cause I'll carry you," he said, marveling at how much bigger and heavier she felt.

"Really?" Liddie beamed. Happiness worked across her face, eyes sparkling beneath their curtain of chestnut fringe. "All da time?"

"Well, for now, anyway."

"Who will carry *me*?" Sam asked, glowering darkly.

"You're older," said Nat. "You can walk."

Sam shuffled tearfully along behind them, Nat carried the baby, and, with a sigh, Doris pushed the empty stroller. Paul pitied Sam. Yes, she was the oldest, but she was still only four and a half. He swooped back to her and picked her up sideways under his arm. She shrieked with delight as he bounced her through the airport, parallel to the ground; he gripped Liddie's thigh with the other hand and she clung to his face, giggling.

"Paul," Nat said, "be careful!" In the corner of his eye, her face shone.

At the door, they had to get the girls bundled up. Paul thought for a moment and said, "I can fetch the car and bring it around. No sense in trucking these girls through that cold."

"Good idea," said Nat. "See, girls? This is what it's like to have a man around again."

Paul felt his smile wring sideways. He stepped toward the door and then turned back to Nat. She was smiling at him with such openness, it was hard to believe what Richards had said. "Paul, you need the keys," she said. "I'm parked to the left." The lot, like the airport, was small.

"Which car did you bring?" Paul asked.

Her smile faded, and she seemed to visibly shrink. "What?"

"Which car?"

"The Fireflite, of course."

"Just wondering," he said. He took the key from her outstretched hand, turned on his heel, and started out across the wind-battered parking lot.

THERE WAS NO GREEN Dodge Wayfarer in front of the house. Paul glanced out the corner of his eye at Nat, who was holding baby Sadie on her lap.

The sight of the baby softened Paul. She was truly beautiful, and impossibly small, and she slept as soundly as if there were nothing taking place around her, instead of the hubbub of two older sisters and their grouchy grandmother.

"The house looks good." He got out of the car and held open Nat's door.

"Oh, I'm glad!" Nat said over the wind. She hurried up the walk with the baby, calling back, "I got someone to trim the hedge. It was getting wild. Girls, hurry inside."

"Who?" Paul asked, holding the door as Doris scooted out, trying to keep her knees together.

Nat turned back, confused.

"The hedge, who trimmed it?"

"Edna's boy from down the street."

Paul strode ahead and opened the door. "The nine-year-old?"

"He's fifteen. He's just short."

"Oh," said Paul. This conversation about Edna's short fifteen-year-old seemed ridiculous, and Paul felt a sudden surge of anger against Nat, which he struggled to control. He held the door until Doris bustled in, smoothing her hair and huffing about the weather.

The house was just as Paul remembered, yellow-flowered kitchen and small, carpeted living room. He could tell that Nat and Doris had half-killed themselves cleaning for his homecoming. There was a fresh bouquet on the kitchen table and some kind of loaf cake. His slippers had been set out by the armchair as if he had just slid them off that morning to go to work. This struck him as odd, actually, the slippers waiting like mute and loyal dogs, and when he walked past he nudged them under the chair with his foot; but after he washed his hands and face in the bathroom and walked out again, he saw that they had been returned insistently to their displayed spot. Apparently it mattered to Nat that they be kept there.

The afternoon felt very long. Luckily Paul had the girls to occupy his attention. He sat on the living room floor with them while they showed him their dolls. He was not normally one to get down on his knees and play with the children, but he could see the delight in their eyes when he did so, and he had missed them. Liddie asked him to brush the long, white-blond hair of a doll that was supposed to be a baby, though Paul did not think it would be normal for such a tiny child to have hair down to its feet. Meanwhile Nat changed their real baby's diapers, mixed up a few bottles' worth of formula, and tried to make occasional chipper spurts of conversation. He could see that her happiness was dimming, that hurt was winning out over the cheerfulness she'd been trying to maintain.

She made a Swiss steak for dinner. Even in his anger, Paul wouldn't have told her how much steak he'd choked down at Camp Century, how he'd be content never to see it again. Then she gave Sam and Liddie their baths while he sat in the armchair, obediently wearing his slippers and holding baby Sadie, who slept. He couldn't remember if it was typical for a newborn to sleep this much. He studied her rosy, satiny face, the tiny white bumps across the top of her nose, and the faint blue veins at the temples, while Doris, with occasional groans, mopped the kitchen, and the girls splashed and giggled and whined in the bathtub down the hall.

There was the spiraling gurgle of water down the drain, and Sam and Liddie came careening out of the bathroom in a waft of warm air and shampoo scent, their wet hair flying, nightgowns flapping around their clean pink knees. "We want you to read our bedtime story, Daddy!" Sam cried, clambering onto his lap. Liddie looked a little less sure. She hung back around Nat for a moment; she had always been a mama's girl.

"Watch out for the baby," Paul said, holding Sadie to the side.

"Daddy will read, and you can sit on my lap," Nat offered. They went into the girls' room and Sam sat on her bed close to Paul; Liddie leaned back against Nat; the baby was laid in her bassinet in the master bedroom. Paul read them a book in which an orphaned elephant moved to London and became friends with an old lady, then returned to Africa to rule as king after the previous king ate a poisoned mushroom and died. The girls listened with rapt attention and Sam wanted to study the picture of the first elephant king turning green, his face crumpling, as the poisoned mushroom took his life. "All right, climb into bed," Paul said, but Liddie piped up, "Wait, our prayers!" and she knelt by Sam's bed with her hands folded.

"Why," grumbled Sam, "do we hafta do this just because Grandma Radek came into town?"

"Sam," Nat hissed. "Knees. Now."

Paul stood quietly off to the side as Nat knelt with them. Their three dark heads bowed in unison. Nat asked each girl what she was grateful for that day. Sam said, "Daddy coming home!" and beamed up at Paul, then pressed her face onto her hands again. Liddie said she was grateful for baby Sadie, which was unexpected because Paul had not seen her so much as look at the baby the entire day. Sam, too, found this preposterous: "You're supposed to say you're thankful for *Daddy*," she hissed, through gritted teeth.

"Sam," Nat said gently, "we can't control other people's prayers."

Sam glared at Liddie. "Mama *said* we're supposed to be thankful for Daddy coming home safe. Remember?"

Liddie's face seemed to gather some rare force of will. *"Be. . . . quiet,"* she said.

Sam, galled and stunned, burst into tears. "You always say the stupidest prayers!" she shouted.

"Girls!" Nat cried. "Your father did not travel all the way home from Greenland to hear you fighting like animals."

"How do you think God feels," interjected Doris, appearing in the doorway so suddenly that they all jumped, "when he hears selfish little girls arguing when they are supposed to be praying?"

Paul felt sorry for Nat. She must have known he'd be critical of this whole routine anyway, and probably thought he was just sitting there smirking inwardly at how awry it had gone. She couldn't win, with her mother finding the prayers inadequate and Paul thinking them unnecessary. In reality, he did not so much disapprove as pity the girls for being ganged up on at prayer time.

Nat rushed them through the Lord's Prayer, chided Sam for not participating, and shooed them into bed.

"Good night," said Paul, hugging and kissing them each in turn.

"I'm glad you're home, Daddy," said Sam.

He patted her knee one last time under the sheets. "I missed you girls."

"Now go to sleep," said Nat. "No talking. It's very late."

The living room was soundless except for the intermittent gurgle-pop of the radiator. Doris sat in the smaller armchair, her hands folded on her lap and her eyes closed. She was either praying, sleeping, or pretending to pray or sleep, which was her way of giving Paul and Nat privacy. Her hair was in curlers and her face gleamed beneath its thick nightly layer of Mercolized Wax.

"Can I get you anything?" Nat asked Paul. "Cake? Ice cream?"

"No, thank you," he said.

She nodded, still standing by the couch. Her hair fanned loose from its ponytail; her eyes were darkened by half moons. She'd given birth just two weeks ago. Beneath her skirt her stomach bulged in a small, fluid-filled hill, and Paul had glimpsed faintly rust-stained tissue paper in the bathroom waste bin, though the next time he'd walked into the bathroom it was gone.

"You should probably go to bed," he said.

"I know." She worked up a tired smile. "But I wanted to hear your stories about Greenland."

"There's not much to tell. I just went to the reactor every day. It was like the CR-1, but it worked better."

"What were your friends like?"

"They were fine. Just normal soldiers."

"Was the food awful?"

"Not really."

Nat nodded. She laid her hands over her belly as if it made her self-conscious. "Well, should we turn in then?"

Paul hesitated. "Why don't you? I might stay up and watch TV for a while."

"Really? You like TV now?"

He shrugged. "Yeah, sure."

"Well," she brightened, "I'll sit up with you."

Paul was quiet. He did not want her to sit with him on the couch. He did not want to have to watch her face, with its constant stream of quiet emotions. He did not want to force himself to return her conversation, as if he still found her trustworthy, as if they could talk the way they had before he'd left. But he was also scared to stop pretending, because if they began to talk about what had happened when he was away he didn't know where it would end up or what he would have to do about it.

Nat came around the front of the couch and slid next to him, fitting her head lightly against his shoulder. He could feel that her body was not at ease, but she was trying. It was excruciating to be so close to her after six months of lonely dreaming and torturous sensual thoughts. Every part of her held a distilled power: her arm against his, breath rising lightly in her chest, the gentle curve just above her upper lip. His desire for closeness, the sudden and indulgent opportunity for it after all this time, seemed a cruel thing coupled with his hurt and anger. He attempted to breathe slowly, as if he were undergoing some painful medical procedure or trying to avoid nausea. In through the nose, out through the mouth. His mind felt unstable. He was worried that he might stand up and start to shout at her. He did not think that he could tolerate another second with her sitting next to him.

He was saved by the baby, who began to warble from her bassinet in the bedroom. At first Nat sat listening to see if she would settle down, but her little yaps and groans increased in urgency, until she started to work up a newborn's croaky, vibrating cry.

Doris, sitting bolt upright across from them and now most certainly pretending to be asleep, opened her eyes and said in a fully awake voice, "The baby's crying."

"Thank you, Mother," Nat said, "but if *you* can hear the baby and you're sitting right across from us, don't you think we can hear her, too?"

"Don't worry," Doris said. "I'll be heading home on Tuesday, and you won't have to listen to my nagging anymore."

These two women had been alone together far too long. "It's not that," Nat said, twitching with irritation. "It's just that of course we can hear the baby—"

"I'm only trying to help."

"Of course you are," said Nat, in a smaller voice.

Doris closed her eyes again. Her face beneath its jelly reflected light like a small, placid lake.

Nat got up and went into the bedroom. A moment later Paul heard her talking to Sadie in a quiet, fond voice, and for a moment he thought his heart would break. Then he got up, turned off the living room lights, pulled a knit afghan from the back of his armchair, and yanked it to his chin.

Across from him, Doris opened one eye.

"You can have my easy chair," Paul told her. "It's more comfortable than that one."

"I would never take your special chair," Doris said, as if he were a possessive child.

"I'm asking you to."

"Aren't you going to go sleep in—"

"Good night, Doris."

She stayed where she was, that shadowy gargoyle. Paul lay still until he was almost able to forget that she was there. From where he lay he could see out the window where the stars looked impossibly high and cold. A few whorls of snow spun past that would amount to nothing. Paul tried not to do it, but his mind returned to the vision of Nat with another man, talking, laughing, letting him into this living room over and over. His mind seized on the house's front door and he saw Nat opening it, wearing a pretty dress, smiling; but not for him. She was happy to see someone whom he could not picture. It hardly mattered whether or not something had "happened." Spending time with a strange man, accepting his car, all this with your husband thousands of miles away, was wrong in and of itself. It meant that his trust in her was a fiction, and that the beauty of his life back home, the one thing he'd counted on, was a half truth, too. His jealousy turned to disgust and then to a physical illness in his stomach that almost made him writhe.

Nat came back down the hallway, froze in surprise when she saw that the lights were out, and whispered, "Paul?" She waited where she stood, repeating his name once more. Then he heard her retreat into their bedroom, shutting the door behind her with a quiet click.

After a long while, Doris's breathing turned slow and huffy. He felt relieved that she finally slept, although her repeated breaths—each one starting up with a quiet, wet gurgle, like a coffeepot—drove him nearly mad if he concentrated on them. He yanked a small pillow over his head to muffle the sound. Through a small space between the afghan and the pillow, he could see a slit of window, spidery with frost, and the sky black as ink behind it.

"WELL, WOULD YOU LOOK at who's back!" Franks boomed as Paul stepped through the lunchroom door. "It's Nanook of the North."

The scene was just as Paul had remembered, the guys sitting with their lunch pails, the television on, the smell of coffee.

"Collier," Webb said, raising a hand, and he looked genuinely happy to see Paul. Next to Webb, another young man—Paul's temporary replacement—got to his feet.

"You remember Webb," Franks began.

Paul gave him a look and crossed the room to shake Webb's hand. "How could I not remember Webb?"

"And this is Sidorski. He's from Chicago."

They shook. "So you're the one who's been holding this outfit together, then?"

"By the skin of my teeth," Sidorski said.

"Say, Webb," said Paul, "you *got* a new tooth."

Webb blushed. "I did," he said. He tapped the new front tooth with one finger; it was somewhat whiter than its mates. He looked older with the hole filled. "It's porcelain," he explained. "Turns out it wasn't as expensive as I thought it would be." Then, suddenly shy, he smiled with his mouth closed.

"It looks good," Paul said.

"Yeah, you're both beautiful," said Franks. "Collier, did you hear about the break? They're shutting down the reactor altogether over Christmas."

"Huh," said Paul. "That's strange. What's the thinking behind that?" They occasionally ran test SCRAMs on the reactor, shutting it down by dropping the nine rod to the bottom of the core, but it was always restarted within hours, never left to sit for weeks.

"The engineering guys thought it would be good to rest the control rods," said Franks. "With all the trouble they've been having."

"We all wish they'd just leave it shut down till the new core arrives," said Webb.

Franks explained, "The twenty-first is our last day before the break. Then we start up again after the New Year, January third."

"Two weeks off," Webb said with a shrug. "Not half-bad."

"Which shift gets the joy of restarting this thing?" Paul asked.

"The night shift," said Franks. "Don't worry, we'll be on days again by then. They'll do all the heavy lifting; we come in first thing in the morning and take over from there."

"It's good luck for us," Sidorski pointed out.

"I feel a little guilty," said Webb.

Franks handed Paul the restart to-do list. The chores were familiar because Paul had done the procedure before. He didn't envy the men who'd be on the overnight restart crew. *Secure feedwater valves to isolate rod drive seals from feedwater pump pressure,* the chore list said. *Disconnect inlet and outlet lines to rod drive seal assembly. Remove tie-rod studs. Remove pinion shaft extension from thimble,* and on and on it would go, into the night. If all went according to plan, by the time his shift got there on the morning of January 4, the machine would be up and humming again after its cold, silent weeks.

"The damn thing's worse than ever," said Franks. "Even Richards admits it's ridiculous. He's almost sympathetic about it, when he's not off drinking in his plywood palace."

"What if we just didn't restart?" Paul said, surprising even himself, speaking the idea as it came. "What if we all just said no, we're going to wait until that new core comes? We're not restarting with this goddamn core?"

The men stared at him. His heart pounded with his own rashness.

"We'd be AWOL," Franks said.

"They'd just kick us out and get new guys," said Sidorski after a moment. "They're finishing up a whole crop of operators at Belvoir right now."

"He's right," Webb agreed, reluctantly.

Sidorski said, "I'd like to back you, Paul, I really would—"

"I think he was joking," said Franks. He looked squarely at Paul. "You were just messing around, right?"

Paul paused. "Yes," he said. "But just—think on it. Turn the idea over in your heads."

"Absolutely not," Sidorski laughed.

"All right then," said Paul. "I understand." His face felt hot; he wished they would stop staring at him like he'd lost his marbles somewhere on the Greenland ice.

"So," said Webb, changing the subject like a pal, "we finally pieced together what happened between you and Richards." He pantomimed a hook to his own jaw.

"Oh, man alive," cried Franks. "You should have seen it. He hid in that office for about three days. When I finally stopped by, his jaw was black and blue to his ear. I didn't think you had it in you. You're a crazy bastard."

"I'm not proud of it," said Paul, meaning what he had done, and not exactly conceding that he was a crazy bastard.

"And how was your little reunion out in Greenland?" Franks asked. "Bet you loved seeing him pop up out there."

"It was a dream come true. Look," said Paul, "I've still got to work with the guy until February, so let's not fan any flames." He turned to Webb. "Say, you married yet?"

He regretted this instantly because Webb's face fell. "Naw," Webb said. "That's over with for now."

"Oh. I'm sorry."

Webb shrugged and fidgeted, looking away. "Maybe Vanna and I will get back together. I mean, maybe we'll try again. I can't say," he trailed off.

Paul was surprised by the depth of his pity. He wanted badly to say something comforting but realized he was not cut out for such things. "Give it time," he tried. "You never know what the future holds."

"Pardon me, Dear Abby," Franks said, "but we've got to move the rods now. You checking in with Richards?"

"I'm not officially back until tomorrow," Paul said.

"You aren't taking any leave?" asked Franks. "Hell, why not just stay home until the restart? Why come back for just a few days?"

Paul winced. He'd known this would come up. Soldiers usually took a period of leave at the end of a deployment, to readjust to daily life with their families. "I'm saving my leave for some other time," he said. "Summer, maybe."

"It seems like there could be no better time," said Franks. "You've been away for half a year, got a new baby at home."

"Well, sorry. You're stuck with me again, as of tomorrow."

"Okay," said Franks, uncertainly.

"I'll be seeing you fellas," said Paul, turning for the coatrack. "Hang in there."

The younger men turned back to their work, but Franks looked at him with a furrowed brow and nodded. "You, too," he said.

Paul stopped at J. C. Penney on the way home to buy a Christmas present for each of the girls, the Etch A Sketches Nat said they had been asking for. Then, feeling generous, he'd grabbed Liddie a teddy bear and Sam a Barbie.

He had almost never been in a large department store and found that, on this dark and lonesome-feeling day, he rather liked the brightness of the lights and the large interior to wander around in. A forest of white and silver trees had been set up in the store, decked with tinsel and bubble lights, and some mothers were gathered around it with their small children. Paul smiled, a little sadly, and tucked his packages under his arm. He hadn't known what to buy Nat, so he chose an elegant new apron and a whisk, because the loops in her old one were bent out of shape.

It was nearly dark by the time he pulled up in front of the house, and he saw that Nat had lit the candles in the front window. This was one of their few Christmas decorations, and something he liked so much that they continued the ritual past Christmas and through the rest of the winter. He'd liked feeling, in those weeks before Christmas, that she lit the candles not just to warm the house for the holiday, but for him as he came home in the dark from work. They had taken on a private meaning for Paul, like getting a smile from her as he spied the house from the end of the street, something that appeared to be public but was really meant only for him.

Seeing the candles lit now made him sad. He pulled up to the house and parked the car, carefully tucking the girls' gifts under a picnic blanket in the passenger seat to be brought inside at a later time.

"Daddy!" they yelled, running toward him as he came through the door.

"Hello, you two." He kissed them both.

From the back room, he could hear Sadie's squeals—not quite crying yet, but getting there.

"Where's your mother?"

"Wiff the baby," said Liddie.

"Mommy yelled at me today," Sam reported, tears in her eyes. "She was mean."

"Your mother's not mean. She's just tired," said Paul.

"I love Mommy," said Liddie loyally, with a glance at her sister.

"Where's Grandma Radek?"

"We took her to the airport today," said Sam. "She went home."

"Really?" Paul tried to conceal the relief in his voice and then felt guilty that he hadn't said good-bye. "She went home? For good?"

"Yes. Back to Old San Diego." For some reason Sam seemed to think that this was the city's full name, and there was no changing her mind.

"I'll be right back," Paul said, and slipped down the hall to stand outside the back bedroom. The door was open just a crack. There was a brief silence, and then Sadie began to quaver again. Paul pushed open the door.

"Hi," he said.

Nat looked up from the bed, where she was bouncing and shushing. "Hi," she whispered.

Paul held out his arms. "I'll take her. You lay down."

"Are you sure?"

"Yes."

"Thank you," Nat said.

Paul took the squirming baby into his arms and laid her over his shoulder. He could hear Nat slide under the sheets as he left the room.

Back in the kitchen, he could see that she had started dinner: The wet breasts of chickens lay nestled in a pan, sprinkled with a reddish spice. The oven was set at 350, but there was nothing in it, so he slid the pan of chicken inside and figured he could wake Nat in a little while. "Girls, don't touch those candles," he called as he looked up and caught Liddie hovering near one.

"Okay, Daddy," she said.

"Let's play house," said Sam, and she turned Liddie around and fastened a tiny apron around her back. It was a dress-up apron so it closed with a little latch instead of a tie. "I'll be the daddy so I am in charge."

Paul settled onto the couch with Sadie on his chest, and she squirmed, grunting. "Shh," he said, placing the afghan over them both and patting her tiny back. She was the size of a sweet potato. Her little fists rubbed on his chest. He moved her head up higher so that it was below his chin and hummed to her.

"Cook something for dinner," Sam said to Liddie. "Like this. Mix something in a bowl." Liddie mimicked her, watching.

"Good," said Sam. "I'm going to work now." She walked around the back of the couch, waited a moment, and hopped out again. "Hello!" she called. "I'm home from work!" She said this again and again, with a triumphant grin on her face. Liddie, apparently, did not know how to respond. She whisked the imaginary food in her bowl and smiled. "I'm home from *work*!" Sam repeated, until finally Liddie said, repeating something she'd heard from her older sister a dozen times, "Good for you."

NAT

THE HAPPINESS NAT'S CHILDREN SHOWED AT THE HOLIDAYS WAS almost enough, for a day or two, to make up for everything else that had gone wrong. Nat was certain now that some kind of a disease had bloomed between her and Paul, but she could not imagine what it would take to overcome it. So she watched as Sam and Liddie tore into their presents with shining eyes, bounded around the house two days straight in their plaid nightgowns, and chewed caramels till they complained that their jaws hurt. From his armchair Paul smiled distantly as if watching them experience feelings he could not remember having. Nat set out food and gathered up the empty plates and fed the baby, and from the outside, viewed through the front window, they might have seemed happy enough. And then, just like that, the holidays were over and gone.

JANUARY 4 WOULD BE PAUL'S first day back at work, the morning he and his crew would take over the reactor after the night shift restarted it. The day before, Nat was filled with both relief and dread: relief, because she'd felt chained to Paul's melancholy when he just sat around the house, and dread because she could not believe he had been home from work for two weeks and she hadn't found a way to resolve the discord between them.

Paul's return to work meant a new set of chores for Nat, which were a source of mild anxiety but also a welcome distraction. His uniforms needed to be cleaned and repinned, bag-lunch ingredients purchased, food prepared for the upcoming week. Nat bustled about, laundry humming in the dryer, a whole chicken roasting in the oven. After dinner she stepped outside to throw out the garbage and felt the full icy slap of subzero air in her face. The weather had been severe through the holidays, setting record lows. At least Nat was slightly used to it, this being her second Idaho winter. One morning about this time last year, she had been walking out to the car and nearly stepped on the front half of a tiger-striped cat frozen solid to the walkway, its entrails unwinding behind it like a kite flown by Satan. Paul had taken care of it, chipping the stiff creature loose like some remnant from the Ice Age. Coyotes, they supposed.

She pried open the half-frozen garbage can lid and tossed in the bag. When she made her way back around to the front of the house she was caught off guard by the sight of Jeannie Richards's car heading down the street.

Nat frowned and picked her way down to the street, but Jeannie was already nearly out of sight, turning the corner on her own block. It was fine by Nat if Jeannie didn't stop for small talk, and of course Jeannie might have had other business at Nat's end of the neighborhood—she *was* the Liaison Office wife, after all—but it still seemed somehow suspicious.

Maybe Nat was becoming paranoid. She'd soured irrevocably on Jeannie over the summer; the gutter incident had put her over the edge. The woman was a spy, a meddler, a witch. In a crueler time she'd be seen as a bad omen by other women, and, in fact, Nat rather felt that way now.

Nat turned back to the house and noticed that the flag on their mailbox was up. This was odd, because she hadn't placed any mail in it that morning. She stepped over to the box, flipped open the door, and saw a small white envelope inside. Pulling it out she noticed that it bore no stamp, and that the envelope was made of a heavyweight, almost linen paper. She slid her finger under the flap. Inside there was a single page that made no sense to her: a gridded pale-blue sheet that appeared to be from Paul's work, with a list of dates and notes about the reactor.

Jeannie had almost certainly placed the envelope there, but it seemed unusual for her to leave it with no note or explanation. And surely such a technical document wasn't intended for Nat—but would Jeannie Richards really leave mail for *Paul*? The very idea was strange and almost inappropriate. Perhaps it was just some errand Mitch had asked his wife to run, something Paul was expected to file; maybe he'd be back at work before Mitch was. In any case, it hardly looked urgent.

Nat shoved the page into her coat and went back inside. She meant to ask Paul about it, but when she walked past the living room she saw that he was sitting on the floor reading Sam and Liddie a picture book, and she didn't want to interrupt. Quietly she removed her coat and hung it by the door. She stood, watching her husband and daughters.

They looked so dear, Paul absorbed in his reading, with a tilted dark head on either side; Sam's finger poked between her lips, Liddie watching openmouthed, as if whatever the story contained was hard to believe. Paul was such a good father. He always had time for the girls, never spoke to them harshly, and every time he saw them seemed genuinely delighted.

Suddenly, this abundance of love between Paul and their children made her feel bereft. He'd been so in love with her once; was he still? What had happened since he'd come back from Greenland? The moment he'd gotten home, things were different. He seemed hard-pressed to look her in the eye, let alone touch her. He kept his distance as if it were Old Testament days and she were on her time of the month, eating raw pork right in front of him while airing out her skin lesions. Oh, she could joke to herself, but it hurt: She'd approached him several times and was rejected every one. Why was he avoiding her?

There was no way he could know about her friendship with Esrom. That was impossible, and even so, she had kept herself from letting it go too far. Yes, she felt guilty for having thought about Esrom more than she should, for thinking about him, frequently, still; but when it came down to it, she had been faithful, and she loved Paul yet.

Had *he* met someone while he was away; had his heart, inexplicably, changed course?

The army pamphlet had warned of reintegration pains. "What to Expect After Deployment" listed several ways a husband could act upon his return (quiet, withdrawn, irritable) and possible reasons for this (feeling like an outsider, missing his buddies, and so on). *You cannot know what his life has been like and might not understand if he described it to you anyway. Do not prod or nag,* it said. *Be prepared to listen, but do not talk endlessly about the hardships you suffered while he was away. There is nothing he can do about them anyway.*

What had made her choose Paul? Six years ago, back in San Diego, she'd had several interested boys around, but Paul had shown up on her beach and she'd picked him. The other boys were happy and glib. They were good at everything. They liked a girl for a minute or a month or even fell in love, maybe, but somehow that could happen without changing their inner lives.

She'd sat by that bonfire and talked to Paul and seen that, instantly, she'd made an impact on him. He was unusually stoic and oddly grave but also easier to affect, somehow, than anyone else she'd known. When she touched him she could almost see the fingerprints.

Tears burned her eyes and she covered her mouth with her hand, listening to him read to their girls: *If you run away, I will run after you. For you are my little bunny.* He had loved her once, but somehow it was gone. She'd taken him for granted and he could tell, and that was enough.

It must be possible, she thought, for a husband's love to just dry up, shift to something else. Didn't other wives complain? The car, his job, the kids: A man's love could come to you like a charming traveling salesman and get you hook, line, and sinker; and just when you felt certain of it, move away.

PAUL

THE NIGHT BEFORE THE RESTART, PAUL WOKE FROM A POST-dinner doze in the armchair to spy Nat bustling around between the tiny laundry room and their back bedroom. She was scrubbing and bleaching his work coveralls; she went at them with a vengeance, the stout swish of bristles scouring fabric. Next she pulled his khaki uniform from the dryer (this he wore on the bus and for meetings; the coveralls were for the reactor floor and break room), flapped them around, pressed and ground them with the iron. Then, apparently having blown off a little steam, she laid them out over the bed and calmly pinned all his badges into place, marking distance with a tape measure. He had the odd sense of having watched her fight someone without her knowing. When his uniforms were finished she emerged from the bedroom slightly sweaty and placidly smiling. She reported, sheepishly, that the kitchen sink was clogged. Paul was not surprised. Nat wasn't careful about separating out grease; she was always in a hurry while cooking. Several times a year the sink would stop up.

He tried suctioning the drain, to no avail. Then, staring at the two inches of greasy gray water, he decided to take the sink apart from underneath. He fetched a metal pan, a drain snake, and his wrench from the laundry room, pulled off his collared shirt, and slid all of Nat's cleaning products out from under the sink, setting them off to the side like an unspeaking audience. He was on his back loosening the metal slip nuts when Nat returned from putting the girls to bed.

"Oh, I'm sorry," she sighed. "I was hoping you wouldn't have to do that."

"It's nothing," he grunted.

She pulled a kitchen chair over and sat. "I'll cheer you on," she said.

"This won't take but a minute."

"Okay," Nat said. Still, she sat. Paul wiggled the P trap loose and turned his head as water and grease spilled into the pan. It wasn't clogged, so he moved on to the trap arm, squinting.

"Are you mad at me?" she finally asked.

"Well, I wish you wouldn't put grease down the sink."

"No, I mean, about something else?"

He paused. His heart gave a jitter midbeat. "No."

She leaned forward and enunciated as if her words alone could shake him. "Did I do something to make you angry?"

He ran a screwdriver along the inside of the pipe stub-out. It came out with old potato peels and a wad of coffee grounds. He stuck it back in and this time it returned several balls of fat, beaded with water. He wiped them on a rag.

"Paul?" Nat said.

"I'm trying to fix the sink here. Would you please stop nagging at me?"

There was a hurt silence. "I'm not nagging. I want to talk to you. I want to know why you've been so cold to me ever since you came home. You were away for six months and now it's like you can barely look at me."

"It's been an adjustment coming back," Paul said. "I'm tired. Everything feels different."

"Nothing is different," Nat said. "Everything is exactly the same here." She thought for a moment. "Well, there's Sadie. But she's good different. What can I do to make it easier for you? I've been cooking your favorite meals. I've tried to keep the girls occupied. I've been trying to make conversation—"

"It just takes time," Paul said.

"I feel like it's more than that, this time."

"Nope," Paul said. He didn't like feeling watched. Her pale, humiliated face just gaping at him as if he'd slapped her. He picked up the drain snake, his hands shaking not from the task but from knowing that she was forcing his hand.

He threaded the tip into the stub-out and tightened the setscrew. He cranked and pushed until the tip finally felt loose and then wound the snake back out. It emerged with a fine plug of rotten garbage, which gave him an upswing of satisfaction. "There," he said quietly, scraping the clog into the pan.

"Did you get my last letter?" Nat asked.

"I think so."

"I only got four letters from you, all those months, and none toward the end. Were you busy?"

"Sort of. You know I'm not much of a writer." He waited a moment and said, "Neither of us wrote many letters."

"You could have called on the phone. Patrice said"—she faltered slightly and recovered—"she said her husband called sometimes when he was deployed. I was so embarrassed; I didn't even know someone *could* call home from deployment."

"I don't think a phone call would be worth much, over all that distance." She looked doubtful and he sighed. "We'd have had to shout over the cackle, some bored intel guy listening in. It didn't seem worth the effort." He could tell that this wasn't what she wanted to hear, and he felt angry again: It wasn't fair for her to judge him, to pepper him with questions and demand answers, after what she had done. He squinted into the open pipe, pushing the drain snake through.

"Are you disappointed that we don't have a son?" she blurted. "That we have only girls?"

His head snapped up. "Of course not."

"Really?" Nat was chewing her thumbnail. "I just wondered, because my mother said she thought you might be—"

"That never even crossed my mind," Paul said, genuinely taken by surprise. "I love our girls."

"Oh, I'm glad. I love our girls, too." She smiled but then it dimmed. "Sometimes I feel like you love them more than you love me."

She was all over the place; it made Paul nervous.

"And I wish your family could have met them," she went on.

"What? Why?"

Her smile faltered. "Well, because . . . it would have been nice for them to know their grandchildren. I wish I could have met your parents."

Paul scoffed. "No, you don't. Anyway, my whole family's been dead for years. My mother, my father."

"I know, Paul. I'm so sorry."

"Don't be. It's really better for them that way."

"How can you say that?"

"They were miserable people."

"But no one is better off *dead*."

"Some people might be."

"You scare me sometimes, Paul. You can be very cold."

"I just told you that I love our daughters."

"About other things."

"Well," Paul shrugged, "you knew what I was like when you married me." He paused. "Did *I* know what you were like when I married *you*?"

"What do you mean?"

He screwed the slip nuts back on with a quiet grunt. "Do you think I had a good idea of what you were like when I married you?"

"Why would you ask that?"

"Ow. Christ." His hand tore slightly against the sharp edge of a metal nut. He sucked on the knuckle once, hard.

"Why don't you finish that later? It's hard to talk to you like this."

"I'm almost done." He stood, wiping his palms on a dish towel. He turned the sink on hot and watched the water go down. "Good," he said to himself.

"That's terrific!" Nat said, hopping to her feet. "You fixed it." Her persistence toward goodwill was admirable. She tried to look at his hand. "Did you hurt yourself?"

"It's a stupid scrape," he said, jerking away. "I'm fine."

She nodded, rebuffed; turned the water on and off, still trying to rally. "I wish I knew how to fix things around here like you do. Then I'd be prepared for your next deployment. Maybe you could teach me sometime."

"But then you might be lonely."

Nat's brows knit together. "What?"

"Then you might be lonely when I was deployed," he said, a little louder. "If you didn't need to call someone to come over. In fact, maybe I should just break this again right now? Then you could call someone."

"That's absurd," Nat said, staring at him.

"Then maybe you wouldn't even have to be lonely while I was at work."

"Paul, stop shouting."

"I know how you hate to be lonely," Paul said. He realized that he was repeating himself. "Everyone seems to know it, I've heard."

Nat asked, "What do you mean? *What* have you heard? Paul, listen." She reached for him and he stepped back. "Whatever you've heard is not true. People are stupid. They'll say anything."

"People just make things up? They just invent some story about you having a man over here all the time while I was away?" Paul felt sick, saying this. He stared at the countertop instead of at her.

"People see something perfectly kind and decent and they think it's scandalous—"

"I'm not talking about 'people' here. I'm talking about what you did. Was it decent? Was it decent of you to have this . . . man over to our house while I was away? Did you think about how that would make me feel? Did you think about me at all?"

"I thought about you every second."

"Well, Nat, you sure didn't act like it," Paul said. He felt hot saliva gathering in his mouth and he spat into the sink.

"I did a stupid thing," Nat said. "I was stupid. But I didn't do anything wrong. I didn't do anything with that man. He's a really nice person, a local person, and he just helped me out and fixed some things for me. I swear to you."

"I'm sure he was really nice," Paul said. "He sounds like just a wonderfully nice local person."

"Paul, please."

"Don't even worry about it," he said, raising a hand. He was shaking. "It's my fault. I should have known better. All the signs were there, and I ignored them."

"All what signs?" Nat asked in a small voice.

Paul stared into the sink drain, flecked with bits of food and soapy froth. "I tried to tell myself you were this pure and innocent girl, but I knew it wasn't true. I'm not going to be that stupid again. I was away and you acted like a hooker."

Nat sucked in her breath. Her eyes sparked tears.

"Listen," Paul said, in nearly a whisper. "We are never going to talk about this again. Do you understand? We will pretend that this never happened. And if you ever mention it, I will leave this house." He looked her in the eyes. "I will never be able to trust you. Do you understand?"

"Don't say that," she said.

"You will have to help me," Paul began.

"All right—" she said, almost eagerly.

"You'll have to help me pretend to trust you," he finished, and she turned away. "But do not ever talk about this."

"I never meant to—"

"Nat!" he shouted. "Shut up."

She was crying openly now. "I didn't do anything. You have to believe me—"

He grabbed her upper arms and she looked almost relieved. "Do you understand what I said?" he asked. "I want you to *shut up*."

He released her with a backward shove. The sick feeling kept gathering in his mouth. He spat one last time into the sink, and headed for the back room. His sparkling-clean khaki uniform dangled on its hanger in front of the closet door like a flattened man. He yanked it down and slung it over his shoulder and on second thought grabbed his coveralls, too. He strode past Nat in the hallway without looking at her, stepped carefully into his shoes and laced them as if he had all the time in the world, not wanting to seem rushed or erratic. He wanted her to know that his actions were solid.

Nat still stood in the kitchen, making unbearable sloppy weeping sounds and holding herself around the waist with one arm. He did not feel even the slightest bit sorry for her. He stepped into the freezing air and closed the door behind him.

The car started up after several tries. He drove away, through the deserted downtown, out across the Snake River Plain as fast as he could, as if the yellow line of the highway were his train of thought and the car, racing alongside, could catch up to where it began and erase it.

DEER EYES FLASHED GREEN in the fields, and the world beyond the road was dark. Paul felt the car skim eerily over a patch of ice and then straighten out. He felt disembodied. He did not want to go home.

Maybe he could go to Franks's house, but with the wife and four children around that could be embarrassing. They'd all be staring at Paul, wondering who this guy was and how he'd managed to screw up his life so badly.

Or he could stay with Webb. Webb had a roommate, but that wasn't so bad. Paul could sleep on the couch, assuming they had one, or the floor. Webb would be surprised when he showed up—he always seemed to think Paul had the perfect life, the perfect family—but he wouldn't turn him away.

He remembered that the night shift was beginning the restart, though, and that Webb was there, filling in for Kinney. He thought of dropping by the reactor to kill time with the guys, but knew that in his current state he wasn't capable. One minute of talking to him and they would think he had dynamite strapped beneath his coat. His thoughts were worse than an illness; he couldn't get past them. He wanted to shake Nat, throw her out of the house, tell *her* not to bother coming home. He wanted to find her kind local person and gut him like a fish. He wanted to keep away forever.

He was so deep in thought that it took him a moment to notice the ambulance heading toward him on the horizon. It arced up over the road, a starry flare growing larger until it met and then passed him. He watched it glide away, bright but soundless. A minute later came two fire trucks, also without their sirens, and the chief's station wagon. He eyed them in the rearview mirror until they turned east.

These vehicles could mean nothing or anything. But their eeriness in the dead of night, the fact that they were headed toward the testing station, gave him a premonition. He pulled a U-turn and followed them, hanging back a little, as they streaked down the highway.

He saw that they did not continue into the heart of the testing station but stopped at the pocket of yellow lights that was the CR-1. His heart tightened. *It's just a false alarm,* he thought. Just a false alarm like usual, from the furnace room or something; the firemen would make their inspection and grumble and gripe, and then they'd drive away and everything would be normal.

But it was the night of the restart, when they took that reactor from stone-cold nothing to full power, the riskiest night of the year.

There was no one at the gate. The fire trucks were lined up, some of the men bustling back and forth between them and the chief patrolling around, but no one came out of the reactor to let them in. Usually an operator hustled down as soon as the alarm rang so they wouldn't keep the already-pissed-off fire crew waiting. The guys were being slow out of embarrassment, maybe, or because of the cold—but that was unforgivably rude. Seventeen below with the wind, Paul had heard on the radio; you didn't keep the firemen waiting in weather like that.

Come on, guys, Paul thought. *Send someone down now.*

He ran through the crew in his mind: Sidorski and Slocum along with Webb. Screw Kinney for cutting out on them. He'd claimed to be on a ski trip with his family, but who went skiing when it was ten degrees at the height of day? Everyone had whispered that he was just dodging the restart. Paul had never liked Kinney and now he felt a spasm of downright hatred for the man, who always sucked up to Richards.

One firefighter—the most junior on the crew, who had to ride standing on the back of the truck through the subzero air—hopped down, blowing into his hands, and walked to the guardhouse to call up to the control room. Where the hell was Slocum? He was shift supervisor; he needed to get himself outside. Paul thought of Webb and felt gathering anxiety: *Come on, Webbsy, get yourself downstairs now and tell us this was all some terrific fixable fuckup, CR-1 style.*

The fire chief, Sechrist, left his car idling, stopped to check the guardhouse, then hunched over to Paul's window. His thick mustache flashed red and white in the spinning lights.

Paul rolled down the window. "Hello, sir."

"The nosebleeds up there aren't answering," Sechrist said, jerking his head toward the reactor. He squinted back at Paul. "Can't understand why you'd be out here when you could be at home."

"I was just driving by."

"This time of night?"

"I'm sure they'll be down in a second."

"When I get ahold of those guys, I'm going to tan their hides myself."

Another firefighter joined the first in the guardhouse, as if it took two men to work a telephone. Chief Sechrist went over to consult with them again and then stomped back to Paul's car. "Who's on security tonight?" he asked.

Paul thought for a moment. "Mullins," he said. "I forget his first name. He comes inside sometimes for a cup of coffee with us."

"That's sweet. Where's he at, you think?"

Paul said, "I'll go look for him." He put the car in reverse and headed out around the testing station. He'd worked the night shift a hundred times, but always stayed inside the building or its gate. It was odd to drive through the site now, bumping over frozen dirt, the world around him the kind of dark you didn't expect to see until you died. He drove with his chest nearly against the steering wheel.

A couple of miles later he spied headlights to his left and honked twice. The truck honked back. It pulled alongside Paul and its window rolled down.

"Mullins!" Paul called.

"Yeah?"

"It's Collier."

A flashlight blinded Paul for a second and then came to rest on his stomach. Mullins, a compact fifty-something man, leaned his balding head out the window. "What are you doing driving around?" he asked.

"Have you been by the CR-1?" Paul asked.

"No." Mullins thumbed in the opposite direction. "Pipe burst out by Materials Testing, so I was helping those guys. The goddamn cold. What's going on?"

"The fire alarm's triggered at the CR-1 and no one's answering." Paul realized that his hands were shaking a little and he gripped the wheel to steady them. "I'm sure one of the boys has come down and let the firemen in by now," he said, "but would you come back with me, just in case?"

"Sure," Mullins said and pulled out ahead of Paul, driving quickly. Two of the firefighters were shaking the chain-link fence when they pulled up, preparing to climb. "I'm sorry!" Mullins shouted, jumping from his truck and waving his keys over his head. "I'll get it."

He unlocked the gate and opened both sides, and the vehicles drove through, Paul last. They parked in the gravel lot. The firefighters gathered in a circle and Paul joined them.

"We'll pair up," said Sechrist. "Esrom, you're with me, we'll check the reactor floor. You two," he pointed at a pair of firefighters, "you take the furnace room, see if that goddamn light is blinking and if it is, get it turned off. If it ain't blinking, check Admin."

"The men won't be in Admin," Paul began.

"Collier, you can come with us," Sechrist said.

At the mention of Paul's name the young fireman spun to look at him, but Paul didn't have time to ponder this because the chief headed up the stairs.

The firefighter and Sechrist carried handheld radiation monitors, rectangular yellow boxes with meters inside. Paul could hear them clicking, their speed increasing with each step. Halfway up, the clicks accelerated into a choppy, propeller-like whirr.

"What the hell?" Sechrist snapped. "Esrom, is yours doing this?"

"Yeah, it's all revved up," the young firefighter said. He had the slight country twang typical of locals.

"They're both doing it," said Paul, listening. The sound made the hairs on his neck stand on end.

"Mine's reading two hundred R," Esrom murmured.

"Well, then," said Sechrist, "we'd better *hope* they're broken."

Esrom had been focused on the chief as if, for some reason, he could not bring himself to look at Paul. But now his eyes darted to Paul's in a quiet appeal. "What do you think?" he asked.

"I don't see how they could both break at the same time," Paul said.

Sechrist's disgust was palpable now. "It's the cold," he said. "Goddamn things." He shook his monitor and waved Paul and Esrom back down the stairs with it. "We've got more in the truck. Move it."

Down the stairs they went, faster now. Esrom jogged ahead to the fire truck and tossed his detector inside, rooting around for another one.

"See," the chief said, "of course they're gonna break, Ez, with you throwin' 'em around that way." He took another monitor from Esrom and both men clicked theirs on. The monitors were silent for a moment and then began soft, steady beats. "Fine," Sechrist said. "Good. Let's go." They all breathed heavily now, moving back toward the stairs.

"I want to go ahead," Paul said, feeling desperate, realizing he sounded like a little boy. He could not move past their bundled bodies on the stairwell. "Let me just check up there. Let me go first. I need to see the guys—"

The chief, partway up the stairs, raised his hand. The three men stopped. Their monitors were ticking faster, faster, until each click blurred into a steady drone.

"Two hundred," Esrom said. "They both say two hundred again." He and the chief looked at each other. Paul could see them going pale.

He knew now, for certain, that something had happened. He strained to move past the firemen. "Webb!" he called up the stairs. "Webbsy? Sloke? Hey! Answer us!"

"Collier, get back downstairs," the chief said.

"Fuck you," said Paul. He shoved through the firemen's thick, coarse jackets, stumbled, and righted himself, sprinting up the steps.

"Hey!" Sechrist yelled after him. "Hey!"

Paul took the stairs two at a time. His chest burned. He reached the landing and cupped his hands over his eyes to look through the window into the reactor room.

At first he couldn't tell what he was seeing: It didn't make sense. He wasn't looking into a room he had ever seen before. The materials were familiar, steel and concrete, but everything was in the wrong place, shifted and cut up and rearranged, like looking through a kaleidoscope. The room didn't even seem to be the right *shape*.

The entire reactor, he realized in horror, was blown out in the center. It looked as if a Tarzan bomb had cruised into the room and blasted a crater where the core had been. Man-sized chunks of concrete lay around the perimeter of the hole. Metal pieces had been flung to the walls—large, twisted hunks that looked as if a tornado had picked them up and thrown them, steel punchings and blotting papers scattered among the other debris like deadly confetti.

He saw two bodies. Both lay on the ground, one faceup and the other facedown. They were soaking wet, their coveralls clinging to them from so much hot steam and blood, as if the fabric were made of a much thinner material. Paul scanned frantically for the third man but could not see him, and that was when a movement from the nearer body, the one facedown, caught his eye.

He jerked his head, uncertain of what he had seen. For a moment he thought he'd imagined it. Then, suddenly, the man lurched up onto his side and reached out in front of him, and Paul saw his mutilated face. The sight hung Paul's heart in midair: The man's mouth was curled and immobilized into a strange openmouthed grimace, as if it had been blasted back into his face; his skin had peeled away in hot pink burns; his eyes looked terrifyingly dull and squashed, unseeing.

The man was reaching not to Paul but toward some apparition. He lay with his arm extended and torso slightly raised, as though his body had seized up on him and left him propped that way.

"He's alive," Paul said, and shot down the stairs. One flight down he collided with Sechrist and Esrom, who were thundering up. "A man's alive, one of them's alive," Paul said, and the chief's eyes widened. He turned around and led the way down the stairs, shouting to Paul that they would get a stretcher.

The brand-new Pontiac ambulance, previously idling near the back gate, had been pulled closer to the building, and a nurse sat in the back, staring into the distance. When Paul and Sechrist plunged out of the building she leaped in fright. Esrom pulled out the stretcher. At that moment they heard someone calling to them, and the health physicist, Charlie Vogel, ran up. He was dressed in plain clothes, his rectangular glasses askew, and his face was raked with worry.

"I'm calling a Class One," Vogel said. "We need backup. We need to set up a checkpoint. If someone is alive we'll need decontamination—" He stopped and held Paul by the arm. "I'll take over," he said. "You can't go back in there. You're not on the rescue crew."

"It's one of my men in there," Paul said, panicky. "We need to get him out!"

Vogel tried to look him in the eye. "Do you understand the radiation field in that building? Those men have been in there for an hour, maybe. There's no way," and he stopped. "I can't in good conscience let a healthy man rescue someone who—"

Paul snapped his arm away. "Do we have suits?" he called. Chief Sechrist was already in the truck and handing out protective suits, which they struggled into, breathing hard, steam blooming and retracting in the freezing air.

"These suits offer limited protection," Vogel was saying.

The chief pulled a mask over his face; he pushed one into Paul's hand and Vogel's. Paul yanked it over his head, turned, and grabbed the far end of the stretcher. A fireman held open the door, and Paul and Chief Sechrist rushed up the stairs, Vogel and Esrom behind them.

"We need to be as fast as we can," Vogel shouted as they ran. "Hold your breath in the reactor room. Don't breathe at all in there! Get him onto the stretcher as fast as you can and then get the hell out."

They got to the top of the stairs and the chief opened the door. He and Paul ran through, the door wheezing shut against the side of the stretcher and Paul shouldering it open again. "Hold your breath!" Vogel shouted again, just before pulling the respirator to cover his face, as they burst onto the reactor floor.

The steam fogged Paul's respirator instantly. He was running blind.

Without time to think, he lifted the respirator, tried clumsily to wipe it but gave up, and jogged to the side of the man he had seen move. He and Sechrist set down the stretcher alongside. The man was still now, lying facedown, his arm extended on the ground in front of him. He was such a long and slender person that Paul knew, with instant desperation, that this was Webb.

Paul looked to Sechrist, whom he could see blurrily through the face mask. The chief made a flipping motion with his hands. Paul nodded, his lungs straining. He had just run up several flights of stairs with a stretcher and it was difficult to hold his breath. He slipped his hands beneath Webb's legs.

The chief slapped the ground, and they turned Webb over. He was so badly hurt that for a moment Paul feared he might come apart in his hands. But his body was heavy, and its very human components—muscle, fat, tissue—held together in one piece. They got Webb onto his back. With one heave, they lifted him onto the stretcher. Paul fumbled for the handles, pushed to his feet, and they ran for the door.

His lungs were bursting as if underwater. He tried to hold out for the door, knowing that the air around him was a toxic soup, thick with radiation. There was no shielding. The heavy elements from the core had melded instantly with the air in the room, and every molecule a person inhaled would be laced with them, but he just couldn't make it. Jogging with the heavy stretcher in his hands, he was forced to exhale: a gagging, star-seeing loss of breath. He tried to run several steps on this exhalation, but just before the door he inhaled again. He staggered and dipped, nearly dropping the stretcher, righted himself.

Vogel had been kneeling by the other downed man; when they'd passed him he'd shaken his head *no*. So they bolted down the stairs, Chief Sechrist at the front of the stretcher, Paul at the back, Esrom behind him, and Vogel taking up the rear. Paul took deep breaths in the stairwell, stars dancing behind his eyes. When his vision cleared he thought Master Sergeant Richards, holding the door at the bottom, was a hallucination. Then he heard Richards's voice: "What the hell is Collier doing here?"

Paul elbowed past him. He and the chief rushed the stretcher into the back of the ambulance, where the nurse knelt, unwinding the lines to an oxygen mask. When she saw Webb's face, her eyes grew huge.

"His name's Webb," Paul blurted.

"Christ," Richards said behind him.

"This body, this man is highly radioactive," Vogel was telling the nurse. "Do you understand?" She didn't seem to be paying attention; she was trying to hold the oxygen mask in a way that would cover Webb's mouth and nose at the same time.

"I need to ride with him," Paul said.

"That's not a good idea," said Vogel, diplomatic even in urgency. "Do you understand how much radiation you've already absorbed?"

"He should have someone who knows him!"

"Don't be a fool, Collier," Richards said. "Don't die for a dead man." He was backing away, doing the smart thing: putting distance between himself and the radiation.

"Shame on you, Richards," said Paul. He climbed up into the ambulance and squeezed himself between the stretcher and the wall, which required him to kneel and hunch, his face just above Webb's. The nurse pressed herself against her own wall to make room.

"I can't let you do this," Vogel said. "Not in good conscience." But Paul, glancing back, could see in the physicist's eyes that this protestation was a formality. He was an understanding man. Chief Sechrist shut the hatchback door and the ambulance peeled out of the parking lot, spitting gravel. Paul and the nurse were left on either side of Webb's body, rocking with the car's motion.

"Webb," Paul said, forcing himself to lean over his friend's face. It made him want to cry. He tried to think of something that might snap Webb to consciousness, grow strength within him, some thought or notion that could bring him back. "Webbsy, we're taking you to the hospital now. We'll call your mom. Think how happy she'll be to see you when you get back to Michigan. And your dog"—what the hell was the dog's name? Webb had a photo of his childhood dog in his locker, next to Paul's, he must have loved that creature, which now resided with Webb's mom back in Michigan—"your little brown dog, the dog." He was repeating himself idiotically, the dog, the dog, hating himself for not recalling its name as if this mattered, as if this were the magical ticket that could save Webb's life. "Freddie!" he said finally. "Freddie will be so happy to see you."

The ambulance lurched onto the road, and the nurse and Paul reached out to steady the stretcher. Paul glanced back to see the reactor grow small through the tiny window, its chain-link fence swung open, rimmed with silently flashing vehicles. His eyes lit on the cloud of steam that puffed from its vent, flowering palely against the dark sky, spreading. A wind sock flapped from the top of a pole. Even when that cloud dispersed and became invisible it would swell, widen, and cover an area that didn't recognize the boundaries of the testing station, of Idaho. Paul thought of Nat and his girls fifty miles away in Idaho Falls, his newborn baby, her lungs the size of dried apricots.

"There's no pulse," said the nurse, and Paul jerked back to her. "I'm starting compressions now." She held herself over Webb's bloodied chest. It looked concave, his clothing so redly soaked that Paul could not see any specific injury. She pressed her hands to it and began pumping. The ambulance rattled and bucked, smacked her momentarily against the wall, but she regained her balance and continued, face steely. Bottles of fluid clinked above their heads but there had been no time to intubate, and the fact that no one had even suggested it made Paul feel that all was lost.

"We're almost there, Webb," he lied. "We're almost at the hospital now."

The nurse paused to reposition her slipping hands. "Come on, sweetheart," she whispered. "Come on, Webb."

Paul felt his eyes tear up gratefully, as if he and the nurse both loved this man. He tried to banish the thought that no one could survive those injuries and that time spent in a radioactive field of such proportions. Then he cursed himself, because even at this, the most critical of moments, he was incapable of having faith.

The nurse was counting to herself, quietly, her fingers on Webb's neck. She began compressions again, her arms locked, crimson. The ambulance made a sharp turn and she thudded against the wall, but didn't stop.

It seemed that she worked on Webb for several minutes. The oxygen mask kept sliding to the side of his crushed face, so Paul steadied it. He felt that he was holding it against some open hole, and that it wasn't doing any good, but it was the only thing he could think to do. The nurse sat back and took Webb's pulse again.

Her head jerked, and Paul's did, too, as Webb's chest gave a rattle and a rise. Paul allowed himself one split second of hope that the nurse had somehow restarted him and that he would begin to breathe on his own. "Come on, Webbsy," he choked. But Webb's chest lifted only that once, higher than a normal breath would raise it, and he let out one low, ghastly moan. Paul waited, but there was nothing else.

"I'm sorry," the nurse said. She wiped her eyes with the back of her hand. She reached for the handheld radio and spoke to the driver up front. "The patient has expired," she said.

"There's a checkpoint," the driver replied. "They've set up a checkpoint. I'm stopping up here."

The ambulance ground to a halt, and someone raised the back. The nurse climbed out. Paul took one last look at Webb, who stared at the ceiling. This was it for Webb at twenty; this was the story of his life, over and done.

"Get *out* of there," shouted a voice, and Paul scooted to the back of the ambulance and dropped to the ground. The man who'd spoken must have been a doctor; he wore plain clothes but a stethoscope was looped around his neck. As Paul stepped away from the ambulance he saw that a few cars had met them at the checkpoint. The circle of light they made in that freezing, pitch-black desert was disorienting, and Paul moved to the edge of the group alongside the nurse.

The doctor took Paul's place in the back of the ambulance but emerged within seconds, slamming the door shut behind him. "Time of death, 11:14 P.M."

"Did you even have time to feel for a pulse?" Paul said.

The doctor paused and looked at him with a flicker of disdain, then glanced down the road. "Someone's coming," he said.

They turned as a car approached. The ambulance driver let out a yell and bolted toward it, waving his arms over his head.

"Wait," said the doctor, "you can't ride with a Good Samaritan. Your bodies are toxic." This pulled the driver up short, and he slumped a little, still standing in the road.

Paul recognized the man behind the wheel. "It's Vogel," he said. When the car pulled up to them and Paul saw Richards in the passenger seat, thorns bloomed in his chest.

The driver's side door flung wide as Vogel hurried toward them. "How is he, Doc?"

The doctor shook his head.

"Oh, no," Vogel said. He pushed his glasses up on his nose and shook his head. "Goddamnit. Okay. Shit!" He looked to Paul and the nurse. "You all right?"

"Yes," Paul said.

Richards hung back, standing beside the car. He didn't seem to know what to do, and he was clearly avoiding Paul.

Vogel strode back to his car and grabbed a radiation detector. When he returned and waved it alongside the ambulance, it whirred and clicked like a small airplane taking off. He held the instrument in the circle of headlights. "The ambulance alone is at four hundred roentgens from that body. Driver," he said, pointing, "I need you to drive this thing off the road a ways. Park it and then run back as fast as you can."

The ambulance driver stared at him with an expression of dread.

"You'll be all right," Vogel said. "Just drive as fast as you can, and then run."

The driver fumbled in his pocket for his keys, strode to the ambulance door, and climbed inside. At the last second Vogel called, "Wait," removing a lead blanket from the back of the car. He ran it to the driver, who wrapped himself awkwardly under the armpits, like a lady in a ten-pound towel, and slammed the door. The ambulance started up with a roar, shifted gears, and lurched away from them, spitting gravel as it bounced off the road and into the brush. When it was far enough away that only its red brake lights could be seen, pinpoints in the dark, it slammed to a rough stop, the brake lights went out, and the driver was illuminated for one instant as he jumped down from the vehicle. He shut the door behind him, and he and the vehicle disappeared. Everyone standing by the side of the road waited. A couple of minutes later, Paul heard the faint slap of feet on the ground. The sound grew louder until the driver came into pale view, running as fast as he could, his arms pumping at his sides. He sprinted into the circle of headlights and collapsed, turning to sit with his knees up and his head between them, gasping for air.

"Well done," Vogel said. "Collier, Nurse Brenner, you"—he motioned to the panting driver—"get in my car, and I'll take you to decontamination."

"Where is decontamination?" the nurse asked in a small voice.

"I'm figuring that out," Vogel said.

Paul's teeth were chattering by now—he'd given the nurse his jacket—and he turned toward Vogel's car, gesturing for her to come also. He opened the door for her and was about to climb in after her when he remembered Richards standing across the road, watching, talking to Vogel. "Excuse me," Paul said, closing the door and ducking across the road.

"We need to get the body into a steel cask," Vogel was saying, "fill it with alcohol and ice. It can't be buried and the family can't have it." When he saw Paul approaching, he went silent.

"Master Sergeant," Paul said.

"Collier," said Richards, stepping back.

"Specialist Collier," said Vogel, "we're going to have to ask you to stay ten feet away. I'm sorry."

Paul froze, then nodded. "I understand," he said. He'd had the most exposure of anyone; he would contaminate any person he was near. Now that things were less urgent, people could afford to stay away from him. He saw Richards scoot further from Vogel, too, as if suddenly recalling that the health physicist had also been in the reactor building. Richards was the cleanest of them, untainted. They formed an odd triangle in the middle of the highway.

"I'm concerned about our families," Paul said. He had to raise his voice to be heard.

"Don't worry," said Richards. "You won't be allowed to go home until you test clean."

"Not just that. The cloud. The radiation. It's still pumping," Paul said. "It'll be going for days until they get that thing cooled and covered."

"We don't want to send everyone into a panic," Richards began.

Vogel glanced at Richards. "I'm not sure what steps they'll take," he said, meaning the site administrators. "If they think it's unsafe, they'll get the families out."

"I think it's unsafe," said Paul. "I think we should get the families out now. We should get everyone out."

"Everyone in town? Can you imagine?" Richards guffawed. "People scrambling for their belongings, flooding the highways, screaming?"

"Fuck you," said Paul. "They wouldn't be *screaming*."

"Collier," Vogel warned.

"I know you're upset about your friend," Richards said, and Paul's whole body flinched with the effort not to lunge at him, "but we can't send everyone into a tizzy. We can't have everyone thinking that it's not safe to live here by the testing station. We know it's safe. It's perfectly safe—"

"You're saying this now," Paul said flatly, disgusted. He willed himself to keep his bearing: If he went apeshit they wouldn't listen. He planted his feet shoulder width apart and measured out each word in doses. "I know that building. Its vents lead directly to the outside air. There's going to be a radioactive plume, and it's invisible, but it doesn't just go up into outer space. It follows the wind."

"We don't know if there's much radiation going out," Richards said, but Vogel nodded at Paul.

"The prevailing wind is to the southeast," Paul said. "That's where the plume will go, probably for hundreds of miles. It will drift right over the town. We *do* know this." He turned to Vogel. "This kind of thing doesn't affect people immediately, you know that. They won't be falling over in the streets. It's years from now, the blood cancers, lung cancers. Think of children. And the unborn—you *know* this, Vogel. Radiation before birth has ten times the effect."

Richards also looked at Vogel, who examined the ground.

"I have a newborn baby," Paul said. Then understanding bloomed suddenly in his mind, and he nearly laughed. "Oh, I see," he said. "*Your* families already know."

There was a pause. Richards shifted. "Yes. My family and I will be leaving as soon as they let me go. Which should be soon; I didn't ride in the ambulance."

"No," said Paul icily, "you didn't." He turned to Vogel. "And your wife?" he asked, trying, in the dark and from his distance, to look the health physicist in the eye.

"I told her," Vogel said quietly.

"What did you tell her to do?"

"I told her to take the kids to her sister's in Seattle."

"Thank you for being honest," Paul said. He turned back to Richards. "And what did you tell Mrs. Richards to do? Did you tell her to go on a little trip for a few days, a week? Or did you tell her to stay right where she was with your little girl, because it's so safe?"

"You're out of line, Collier. What my wife does is my own business." His eyes squinted. "I'm sure you wish you could say the same."

Vogel looked at Richards curiously.

Paul was so stunned by this cruelty that he stood rooted to the spot. He felt as if his heart and lungs and gut had suddenly been wrung out once, hard, and released some kind of poison in him.

"Can I call my wife?" he asked. His voice came out ragged and he struggled to control it. "Or can you? Can someone please at least tell the operators' families?"

Richards and Vogel waited, looking at each other.

"All right. We will," Richards said, suddenly generous. "We'll give you that, Collier. We'll call your wife."

"And the other operators'—"

"Don't go overboard." Richards's voice cut him off. "We said we'd call your wife."

"You will, personally?" Paul asked. "Or you, Vogel? Which one of you?" His voice was too loud and he found himself looking from one man to the other, his finger waggling back and forth.

"We need to get you to decontamination," Vogel spoke up, almost chipper. "Come on, now. The master sergeant will call your wife. Won't you?" He looked back at Richards.

"Yes," Richards said. "I'll call her."

Paul felt as if the tight strings holding his muscles together had suddenly been cut, and his shoulders sagged. "All right," he said, and he walked ahead of Vogel back to the car. He could see the nurse's face peering out fearfully and was ashamed that he had lost control. "He'll call her?" he muttered to Vogel. "He'll call Nat for me?"

"Yes," Vogel said brightly, climbing into the driver's seat. "He said he would. We're going to get you three all cleaned up."

"How are you going to do that?" the nurse asked, scooting aside to let Paul in. Her eyes flicked to Paul's face as if for reassurance, but he stared straight ahead, not wanting to give anyone anything. It struck him how ridiculous and erratic all these safety efforts were: Vogel tried to stay away from him outside, but was now sitting with him inside a car. Did anyone know what was going on here?

"Don't worry about a thing," Vogel said. "The sooner we get you clean, the sooner we can get you home."

"Will it be safe for us to be around our children?" the nurse asked.

"Yes, eventually."

"I was in the ambulance the longest," the driver blurted. "I'm worse off than either of them."

"But we were right next to the body," the nurse pointed out, which, Paul knew, was a bigger concern.

"Are you taking us to a hospital?" the driver asked.

"We can't do that," Vogel said, pulling out onto the highway as a police officer stepped aside to let him through. "We need to get you decontaminated and keep you away from the public for a while before we do anything else."

"My insides are sick," the driver said, his voice loud now, quavering. "I can feel them. They're melting like goddamn popsicles."

"Calm down," Paul said. "That's impossible."

"I'm going to die now, just because of that stupid man," the driver raged. "Why did we have to drive him anyplace? He was already dead.

Did you see his *face*?" He whirled on Paul, jabbed an accusing finger in his face. "*You* don't care if you die!"

The nurse looked at Paul, trying to determine whether this were true. Paul recalled the cigarettes in his pocket, found them, and shoved one toward the driver, who stared at it, strings of saliva quivering, finger still naming Paul. "*Take* it," Paul said, and finally the man did. Paul lit it and one for the nurse, also. The ambulance driver turned forward again and sat over his cigarette, sniffling. Paul gave him the dignity of pretending not to hear.

He *did* care whether he lived or died. It occurred to him that this had been voluntary, this mess he was in, though it hadn't felt that way in the moment. What he wouldn't give to be back at home with Nat and his children: his new baby, sweet as a bunny, swaddled in cotton; his goofy big girls springing from the couch and dancing at his homecomings. Nat, hurt eyed and angry; would she forgive him now? But he couldn't have left Webb, and his eyes burned over the thought of that fatherless twenty-year-old, a lot like Paul if Paul had been softer, less guarded, a better person. How could Paul have lived with himself if he'd abandoned him, left him facedown on wet cement to take his last breath alone?

He tapped the small, flat cigarette box in his pocket. It felt comforting there, a light weight. There were two cigarettes left. Though he craved one, he felt he should keep them for later. Suddenly this seemed very important, as if saving them were a test of some kind.

Paul took one glance back as they pulled away. The headlights of the small group of cars lit up a circle in the dark, and just beyond them, invisible, sat the ambulance, its lifeless passenger throbbing a sphere of radiation into the desert night.

Cold water poured over and around the bar of soap in Paul's hand. He shivered. He had stood in this shower for two hours now, and the bar was translucent, a flinty hole starting in the center. He pushed at the hole with his thumb.

A health physicist in a radiation suit peeked into the room, his head covered by a white hood that cinched almost goofily around his face. "Keep washing," he called. "I'll test you in ten minutes." His eyes lingered on Paul for a moment. Paul had spent much of his first hour sweeping his own vomit down the drain, and he seemed to make the doc nervous.

The ambulance driver, who stood next to Paul, jerked out of his lull and slapped his bar of soap against his chest, washing in wide circles. Paul placed his thin bar on his own shoulder. He was freezing. The bar hardly lathered. It was some kind of industrial-strength oil soap, yellow and stinky. Robotically Paul wiped it over his head, down his chest, armpits, balls, feet, up and around again, while the ambulance driver did the same. They swung through these motions without speaking.

The scrubbing, Paul knew, would remove only the scantest amount of radiation. The rest of it throbbed within their bodies, fading slowly in proportion to their exposure. He wondered bitterly if the main reason they were kept washing themselves was so that they'd have something to do.

Still, obediently, he washed. Sometimes it kept Webb's crushed face away. Other times there was nothing he could do: His mind lit there again and again, as if a path to that image had been greased in his brain and it was the only place his thoughts could go.

The door creaked open, and his head jerked up. In came a new health physicist, also in a hazard suit, leading three men: Chief Sechrist, the firefighter Esrom, and Master Sergeant Richards. Paul spied Richards and felt his upper lip rise. He turned back to his washing as if it were possible to ignore anyone when you stood naked in a big empty room, rubbing yourself like an ape.

"Clothes off," the health physicist said to the newcomers, unwrapping three bars of soap and laying them on a bench like gifts. "Wash until I tell you to stop." He collected their belongings, even wallets and keys, in a large garbage bag. "These will be buried," he added, watching them defiantly as if they might rise up in rebellion over lighters and ballpoint pens. Each man took his bar of soap and moved toward the showers. Then the doc gestured to Paul and the ambulance driver. "You two, over here."

Paul sloshed ankle-deep past the three clothed men and over to a sink, and the driver followed. The doc turned to them and switched on his radiation detector. It buzzed perkily over their bodies, up behind them, to the tops of their heads, down the front. Paul was shaking unabashedly now; the shower water had gone cold an hour before. He heard a yelp from one of the new men entering. "Christ, this is cold," said Richards. Paul wanted to grab the back of his boss's head and smash it into the floor. Instead he stared bleakly at the radiation wand, heard its busy chirps gathering speed. When the wand cruised over his hands and wrists it revved ecstatically, as if to announce that Paul were winning something.

"Do you know if they're evacuating Idaho Falls?" Paul asked, trying to keep his voice low, but the men in the showers looked over anyway.

"I have no information that they're doing anything of the sort," the health physicist said.

Paul glanced over his shoulder to Richards's bare ass, white and hairy. "Master Sergeant," he called. "Did you contact my wife?"

"What?" Richards shouted, his hands over his head, lathering soap.

"Don't step there," the ambulance driver warned Richards. "Collier puked there."

Richards glanced at Paul as if this were disgusting, as if Paul could have helped it. He turned his back, rinsing his hair.

The health physicist clicked off his monitor, set it aside, and produced a fresh bar of soap. He held it out until Paul, struggling to focus, took it. "Keep washing," he said.

HOURS LATER, CLEANER AND yet dirtier than he had ever been in his life, Paul found himself shuffling into a windowless waiting room. His hair was parted and combed and he was wearing a white dress shirt and black slacks, though he had no idea where these had originated. He felt like a little boy ready for church. His skin stung raw; it twitched when it rubbed against his clothing. Every minute or so his whole body would clench and spasm in a giant tremor, and he felt as if he would never be warm. He crouched in a folding chair, his hands in his lap. The floor was gray and the walls were gray and the ceiling was gray. There was no one else in the room.

"You," a man's voice said, and Paul nearly toppled out of the folding chair. He stumbled to his feet.

It was yet another health physicist, his white suit crinkling as he pulled a dosimeter from his hip. The docs kept changing so that no one in particular would take on too much exposure. "Roll up your sleeves," this one said, nudging his glasses up onto his nose with his wrist.

Paul followed him to the sink by the wall, rolled his sleeves to his elbows, and allowed the familiar, clicking monitor to roam around him.

"Where are we?" Paul asked. The ambulance driver was in the room now, pacing the far wall opposite.

"You're in the gas-cooled reactor facility," the doc said, without looking up. He seemed either sad or slightly bored. His dark eyes were magnified by the curve in his large, heavy spectacles.

"Why this place?" Paul asked.

He shrugged. "It was as good a place as any." He set the monitor aside and produced a large squirt bottle of bright purple fluid. "Potassium permanganate," he explained, shooting the liquid up Paul's forearms, through his fingers, swirling it over his wrists with a flourish, as if he were decorating a cake. "Rub," he said.

Paul watched the juice dribble down his fingers and into the drain. He was suddenly reminded of Nat, how she'd dig around in the garden and chat with him as she rinsed her hands under the hose, mud running rivulets off her arms. Always fussing with those tomatoes in the backyard. When he thought about Nat, his stomach wove into a knot. He shook his head, once, twice, hard, which the doc seemed to accept as some mild tic; he glanced at Paul but let it go.

Paul was trying not to talk too much. He knew he'd been attracting attention in those first hours after the accident, bleating his pathetic questions about evacuation and when he could call his family. He needed to shut up and look for some kind of an opportunity. He might be able to ask someone else to call Nat for him, someone who'd get to leave sooner than he would. The docs were not even letting him near a phone. They seemed to fear what he'd say, as if he were the sort to stir up trouble without reason. Paul was their most contaminated man, and they were keeping their eye on him.

"Throat," said the doc.

"Sorry?"

"Open up." He showed a tongue depressor, waved it in front of Paul's lips. "Let's take a look-see."

Paul opened his mouth, wondering what the doc could see in there that would possibly give him any information.

"Eyes." The doc switched on a thin flashlight. Paul flinched at first, then concentrated on looking slackly ahead, resisting the urge to blink. The light roved over his corneas, then flicked away.

"How are you feeling?"

"Fine."

"More vomiting?"

"Not for a couple of hours."

"Diarrhea?"

"No."

"You took your iodine and kept it down?"

"Yes."

"Good."

"I should be able to go home soon, right?"

"Not until it's safe for others to be around you."

Paul nodded. "But what about you? You're around all of us." The health physicist knew as well as Paul that the white suit only did so much.

The doc paused. "This is my job," he said. "And we're working half-hour shifts." He asked Paul to hold his hands out flat and keep them still. After a moment he added, "They found the third man."

"What?" Paul asked. His breath skipped.

"Not alive. Sorry." He turned on the faucet and motioned to Paul to rinse. "He was standing on top of the shield plug when it blew."

Paul flinched, picturing the long, thick metal plug, big as a pole.

"It went through his groin," the doc said with a brisk frown. "Shot him up to the ceiling, skewered him through his body and came out his shoulder. Pegged him into the top of the reactor like a pin in a corkboard, terrible."

"Which man was it?"

The doc squinted. "Polish name."

"Sidorski," said Paul, nauseous.

"That's him. Don't tell his wife," the doc added.

"I don't talk to his wife," Paul snapped. He took a breath to steady himself. The doc handed him a towel; he took it, roughed it over his raw, pink arms. Each hair felt like it hooked somewhere deep inside his muscles. He shuddered in segments, like a horse.

The doc bent for his detector, thumbed it on, swung it over Paul's limbs again. He clicked his tongue, stared into space as the detector roved. It was as if Paul had buried treasure beneath his skin, coy nuggets of gold, and they were waiting for the machine to suddenly tweet in discovery. Instead it just revved, a long *hush, hush* as though Paul disappointed it.

"We're supposed to be vague about the names," the health physicist said. "About who was where. The man, he's still hanging up there. Can't go in to get him because of the radiation field. They're building some kind of crane to pull him down. So they don't want word to get out to the wife. Not now, anyway."

"Right," Paul said quietly, but his voice stuck, and he had to clear his throat.

That meant the man who'd been dead on the floor was Slocum, he thought. Now, at least, they had everyone accounted for.

The doc glanced at him. The monitor scolded Paul's arms, hands. "They can't even bury the men," he said. "It's a real dilemma. They'll probably be buried out at the hot waste site, or parts of them anyway."

Paul felt his lips curl in disgust, but he knew better than to say anything.

The doc tilted his monitor and shook his head. "Not yet," he said. Then he motioned to the pacing ambulance driver. "You, next," he called. To Paul he said, "Try to get some rest."

Paul barely heard him as he shuffled back to his seat. He couldn't stop thinking that while he and the other men ran in and out of the reactor room—carrying Webb, feeling the motionless carotid in Slocum's neck—Sidorski had been right above them, dangling over their heads the entire time.

Hours later, Paul was still in a folding chair in the gas-cooled reactor building, and he could feel himself starting to lose it. It seemed he wasn't the only one: Esrom, for no reason Paul could understand, was staring directly at him. Each time Paul glanced up, he'd see Esrom jerk his gaze away, but a few moments later the young firefighter's eyes would wander back. It was starting to make Paul almost angry.

They were dressed identically now, Paul and Esrom, pink and scrubbed and waiting out their own bodies in opposite folding chairs. The nurse had been brought in from whatever place the health physicists found for her to shower; Paul wondered where, as none of these buildings had locker rooms for women. Maybe they had located some small chemical shower for her someplace, with a pull-chain, where she'd had to stand for hours all alone. He pitied her this, but it didn't seem appropriate to ask. The nervous ambulance driver was there, too, standing, sitting, muttering, and finally falling into a merciful and all-encompassing sleep, like a child.

Richards had been allowed to wander someplace else within the building. It was probably for the best, given Paul's state of mind. So the nurse leaned her head on a folded blanket against the wall, and the ambulance driver slept, and Esrom peeked weirdly at Paul as if hoping he might suddenly mutate or erupt, and they passed some time that way before Paul finally decided he was about to lose his mind.

"Enough," he blurted, a rough edge rising within him. "I'm going outside."

A health physicist materialized out of nowhere and twittered, "Mr. Collier, no, you need to stay in the building."

Paul stared down the man's gray-faced disapproval as if he could capture and eat it. "I am stepping outside for a cigarette," he said.

"You may smoke in here. By all means do. By all means—"

"By all means, shut up," Paul blurted. "I am going to stand outside this building for ten minutes and smoke one goddamn cigarette. You are not to follow me. You are not to come anywhere near me until I return of my own volition. Do you understand?"

This was the secret side to Paul that usually got its way. Paul felt the nurse looking at him; he suspected she wanted a cigarette and would ask for one imminently. He was surrounded by goddamn zombies.

The health physicist nodded. "Ten minutes, Mr. Collier. Then you need to come right back in."

Paul spun and stalked toward the exit, his hand shaking its way into his pocket. On the strength of one cigarette he would be able to get out of there. He'd grab his family and take them anywhere, take them north, for three days, a week, however long he goddamn felt like. The only thing was, he couldn't safely be anywhere near them.

Outside, the cold was blistering. Paul saw that it was morning, ten or so judging by the pale sun. The testing site stretched before him, flat, sparkling with patches of snow. Paul tapped out a cigarette with unspeakable relief. He patted his left pocket for his Zippo. Goddamnit. The Zippo! They'd taken it from him. They had taken his Zippo! Of course it was radioactive, but this decision seemed, suddenly, a breach of protocol so galling that Paul's brain shot lightning. You did not take a soldier's Zippo. You simply did not. If a man was dying, if his leg was blown off and he was stranded on some icy hill in Korea, he could grope into his pocket and have one last cigarette. It was the one thing everyone agreed he deserved.

He turned back to the building and was about to push the door open when his brain shadow, Esrom, stepped out.

"Christ," Paul blurted, startled. "What are you doing?"

Esrom pulled a cigarette from his own pocket. "Getting a ride home. I don't usually smoke," he seemed to feel the need to say, "but," and he mumbled something that Paul could not have cared about in the least. He might have whispered a recipe or recited a prayer; the words looped together and slid away. Paul's eye latched on to the book of matches Esrom removed from his pocket. Now it was his turn to stare so blatantly that there was no question what he needed.

"Of course," Esrom said, extending the match to Paul. In the cold wind they hunched over it as if it were an impossibly delicate thing, a baby hummingbird. The flame flickered, ducked, then snapped up just enough to get Paul's cigarette going. Paul placed it between his lips and inhaled, and it was like someone had reached inside his head and petted his brain.

Esrom coughed twice, bumped a fist against his chest. "Hey, there's a plane," he said.

Paul squinted. Esrom was right. In the distance, a small prop plane circled tightly. They couldn't hear it.

"What's it doing?" Esrom wondered. He screwed up his face, and Paul glimpsed crooked incisors, backward-leaning.

"Testing the air," Paul realized. He scooted away from Esrom. "I forgot. I shouldn't be near anybody."

"Doesn't matter much," Esrom said, forcing half a smile. He took a drag on his cigarette, watching the plane.

"You saw it," Paul blurted, and Esrom looked at him. "You saw it, the top of that reactor core. There was no containment. You saw the steam pumping out."

Esrom cleared his throat. "Yeah." He paused. "I'm no scientist, though."

"He didn't call, that bastard," Paul said.

"Sorry?"

"Richards. He didn't call. I could tell. I asked him to call my wife for me, tell her to take the kids out of town for a few days. He didn't do it. Nobody around here is letting me near a goddamn phone. They think I'm going to stir up trouble. They don't want people scared. Why the hell can't I just use a phone?"

Esrom seemed pained. "You really think it's not safe here?" he asked.

Paul made a disgusted sound. "People say the scientists, the operators, they're so highly trained. Do I know if it's safe for folks to be here right now? I don't. I don't know a goddamn thing. They have me helpless—" and here Paul's voice nearly broke with frustration. He was mortified. He glanced back, saw the health physicist's face worry past the tiny front window. "They have me helpless. Watching me. I can't even make a phone call." He turned to Esrom and looked into his startled blue eyes. "Would you call my house for me? Would you call my wife? Tell her what I've just told you?"

Esrom paused. "You want me to tell her that?" he asked.

"Without scaring her."

"Where would she go?"

"A hotel. Somewhere north. The wind is headed south now."

"Okay." Esrom nodded, thinking. "I'll call her for you." They heard a car approach, and Esrom glanced up. "Here's my ride," he said, starting toward the car. "You should go in. It's freezing out here."

"I didn't give you my phone number," Paul began. And that was when he looked up and saw the dark green Dodge Wayfarer coming toward them.

He froze, looking from Esrom to the car and back again. "Well," Esrom said, "good luck to you." He opened the passenger door and slid inside.

Seeing that car, something in Paul's head snapped. He marched to the driver's side door, grabbed the icy handle, and yanked it open. The driver was so unsuspecting that Paul reached in and hauled him out as if he were a child.

"What the—" the driver yipped.

"Who are you?" Paul shouted. "Why do you have this car?"

The man in his grasp was a greasy young thing, wearing unwashed work pants and a dingy collared shirt. He writhed under Paul's fists, terrified.

"What's your name?" Paul shouted.

The guy looked from Paul to Esrom, who had hopped back out the passenger door and jogged around to them. "Mine?" he whimpered. "I'm Russ. What do you want with me?"

"I want to know what kind of a person you are," Paul began.

"What?"

"What kind of person you are moving in on a man's wife when he's out of town. Making all the neighbors talk."

"I don't know what you're talking about," Russ bleated. "Ez, get him off me!"

Paul slammed the thin man back against the car and heard the air go out of his captive in one wheeze. It felt both good and bad at the same time. His brain buzzed behind his ears, finally alive, finally able to take action. How could he stop now?

"Listen, *Russ,*" he snarled. "You made me look like a fool. Was it some kind of a game for you? Just an entertainment?"

"Collier, cut it out," Esrom said.

"Did you feel like a big guy?" Paul shouted. "Bet you feel pretty good about yourself."

"Please," Russ squirmed, voice thick, "I don't have any idea what you're talking about."

"It wasn't him," Esrom shouted. "It was me."

Paul turned. He stared at Esrom for so long that the man seemed to change shape before his very eyes. Then he looked back at the panty-waist sniveling in his hands and pushed him free.

"You?" he said.

Esrom nodded. Paul took in with fresh bewilderment Esrom's hill-billy haircut, a farm-kid scar on his chin, deep; his teeth like things that had washed up where they were.

"You?" He pointed at Esrom and nearly laughed. "Neither of you"—and now he was chuckling, nauseous, feeling his stomach ball and twist like a sea creature bathed in acid—"neither of you is *remotely* the kind of person I pictured."

"Let's get out of here," Russ said, still flat against the car. "Ez, let's go."

Esrom raised his hands, palms out. "It was in good faith. I helped your wife with some things while you were away. The gutters. I loaned her a car. There was absolutely nothing—"

"The gutters?" Paul sneered. "The car. The gutters. You spent a lot of time at my house. People talked. Do you know what that does? Do you know what that does to a marriage? People talking. Have you heard how people talk?"

It was almost funny. All this time, he'd imagined someone like Richards, someone with money, nice clothes. His replacement was a man who had even less than Paul did.

Esrom stood, not moving away, not shirking, palms up. Saying it was nothing. Paul's wife, and it was nothing.

In the corner of his vision he saw the door of the gray building swing open. The health physicist moved toward him. *Collier, Collier. You'll need to come inside now.*

His vision pulsed and blurred. A sudden thought came to him. Esrom was about to leave: He was clean; he was free. Paul was stuck here, dirty, watched. He couldn't leave, couldn't help his family. But maybe there was another way.

Mr. Collier. You're going to need to come with me—

This was Paul's chance. It might ruin everything he had ever worked for, but if he didn't take it now, he might never get another one.

"Listen," he said, stepping up to Esrom's face. To his credit, Esrom didn't flinch. "I need to ask you a favor."

"A favor?" Esrom watched him, suspicious.

Paul cleared his throat in a long, dread-filled stutter. He gathered his courage. "Go to my house," he said. "Tell Nat what has happened, then take her and the girls somewhere for a few days. Can you do that for me?"

There was a pause. Then Esrom said, "No."

"I need you to."

"I can't do that."

"For the girls, you could do it."

Esrom looked Paul in the eye. "If you think people talk now, imagine how they'd talk then."

"She's going to be upset," Paul said. "Our car's at the reactor; they'll never let me near it. It's toxic and they'll destroy it. So she has no way to get out, and I'm a walking poison, and no one's even letting me near a phone. She's got the big girls and the new baby. But if you could take her and the girls out of town—she trusts you. She'll do it if she knows it's for the girls. Can you do this for me? Please."

"Mr. Collier," the health physicist was at his elbow now in his crinkling suit, "it's time for you to come back inside. Are you getting upset? Are you feeling disturbed?"

"One moment," Paul barked.

"Are you sure you mean this?" Esrom asked.

"Yes."

"This isn't some kind of trick? It's not some kind of—"

"It's the least you could do for me!" Paul snapped. "Please."

The doc fretted by his elbow. "Mr. Collier, I need you to come back inside." He addressed the other men: "Is Mr. Collier having emotional changes?"

For one moment Esrom, Russ, and Paul all stood, as if this question had finally silenced them.

"I'm getting out of here," said Russ, ducking back into the car. He pointed at Paul, his voice half-muted by the windshield: "You are a freak."

"Promise me," Paul said. "Promise me you'll do it."

"I'll do it," Esrom said, climbing in.

Paul watched the car turn and grow small. It seemed to take forever, on the flat plain, for it to leave his vision. How odd to think of Nat driving that car around town all summer, the girls in the backseat, singing her old Girl Scout songs. It was like watching a movie of his life taken by someone else, but he had been rubbed out.

"Let's go inside now, Mr. Collier," said the health physicist.

Paul turned and followed him back into the building, feeling like a trained bear.

He imagined the car collecting Nat from home. Esrom would explain the situation. He would be reassuring and protective. He'd reassure Nat that this was for the good of the girls; settle them in the car, adjust the baby's basket, ask if everyone was warm enough. You're so kind, Nat would say, you're so kind. Then he'd take Paul's family and drive away. It was a moment that had been in the making for a long time; it shouldn't have been any more horrifying than the ones that had come before. The worst step had already been taken long ago.

NAT

NAT DID NOT SLEEP. BY MORNING SHE COULD SEE THAT SOMEthing larger than an argument with her husband had taken place. Neighbors gathered in the street, trading misinformation. A prop plane circled low over the town. She called the dispatcher over and over and was told that no one could be put through to the CR-1—wives were *always* put through to the operators—and she did not know if Paul had gone there anyway. She felt pent in a bubble of quiet terror. He could have been anywhere, could have thumped off the icy road and frozen, unconscious, could be bunking with a friend from work with no plans to return to her, could have gone in to the reactor and been somehow involved with whatever disaster people assumed had happened there.

Nat paced the house while her heart simultaneously raced and dragged. She prayed with thoughtless desperation: *Please Lord, let Paul be all right. I'll do whatever you ask.* Somehow she made bottles and fed the baby. Triangles of toast appeared on the big girls' plates and were replaced with crumbly, butter-smeared parentheses, and the girls slid from their chairs and trotted away.

Her distressed isolation was finally broken by the sight of Esrom's pickup in front of the house. She laid Sadie down, shot out the door, and ran to him, gripping his forearms, trying to explain what had happened and ask him questions at the same time.

"He just drove away," she said. She felt cold air lift and inflate her nightgown; it was noon. Her legs were bare. From the corner of her eye she could see a small group of neighbors gathered in Edna's window; she knew she was in their line of sight but she didn't care.

Esrom held her shoulders and turned her around. "Girls, get back inside," he said. He had never spoken to them with anything other than a shy, joking affection, and they bolted back through the door.

Nat allowed him to move her into the house. "Sit down," he said gently, pointing to the couch. Sam and Liddie were around his knees, touching his pant leg, asking questions. He put one arm around them both and held them against his side, which quieted them immediately, and they stood wordlessly while he talked to Nat.

"Do you need your robe?" he asked her.

"No," she said, impatient.

"Okay, then." He cleared his throat. She watched him as he explained about the reactor, the deaths of the crewmen—poor Webb, she could hardly believe it—and how they were taken to the decontamination center. He told her about waiting outside with Paul. ("You talked to Paul?" she cried, in simultaneous relief and horror.) Esrom claimed the two of them had reached an understanding. He said Paul wanted him to take her and the girls away.

She stared, not knowing what to make of this. Paul was okay; Esrom had seen him and spoken to him. He was walking and talking and aware of what had happened. With this burden of fear lifted she felt her whole body sink against the couch, her muscles trembling as if she'd been under tremendous physical strain. Could Paul really have meant it when he asked Esrom to take her and the girls away? Did he really think she would do it?

After Paul's meanness, and knowing now that he was not maimed or killed, part of her felt thrilled at the thought of leaving with Esrom. An entire week with him after her self-imposed ban seemed like an incomparable gift. But she knew it was a sick sort of gift, too, with the price people had had to pay for it.

"Are you all right?" he asked.

"This is what Paul wants?" she asked.

"It's what he asked me to do." He frowned down at the couch, and then looked back to Nat. "Your husband knows a lot more about this sort of thing than I do. I think if he says this is the right thing, then it is."

"Where will we go?"

"My cousins have a hunting cabin up north."

"What about people here?"

Esrom shifted. "I'm not sure. On the radio they keep saying no one's in immediate danger. Maybe your husband knows more than they do. But he was worried about the girls, long-term stuff."

"What about the past few hours? Haven't we already—"

"Nothing we can do about that now."

"Are you worried?" Nat asked him.

"I am now, I think." His mouth twisted slightly. "But not about myself."

"What about your family?"

"I told them. They prefer to stay."

"Really?"

"The ranch," he explained. "That's how they are."

"What about you? If the girls and I weren't in the picture, would you stay?"

"Probably," he said.

Nat opened her arms and gathered Sam and Liddie into them, kissed their heads. Their little bodies were sweet and soft; she squeezed their hands. Then, getting to her feet, she went quickly to their bedroom where she gathered some of their little clothes, socks and pants and sweaters in pink and lavender, a small canvas bag each for Sam and Liddie. She filled another bag with Sadie's tiny gowns, cloth diapers, and safety pins.

Then she found some clothes for herself. She still had to wear a maternity dress, but at least she could belt it now. She paused by her own dresser. She'd once imagined what she would wear if Esrom invited her and the girls to his family's ranch for the day, a self-indulgent fantasy that had never come close to fruition, the silliest sort of brain game. (She'd planned to wear black slacks and a pale-green blouse with her hair in a mother-of-pearl clip. Those pants wouldn't even fit her at the moment.) But now she felt the surge of guilty power that had grown familiar over recent months, as if her ungovernable thoughts had somehow made this whole mess happen. *Are you happy now, Nat? Are you getting what you wanted?*

She headed back to the living room. Rounding the corner she saw that Esrom had the girls' coats on, their mittens and hats. This was startling and natural at the same time.

"We're going on a trip!" Sam beamed. "I hope the baby doesn't *cry*."

Nat settled Sadie into the Moses basket. Esrom leaned over it, smiling. "Hello, little baby," he said. He offered Sadie one rough finger; her spindly hand closed over it, and her feet jerked with the sensation. She looked so much more alert now, her little eyes taking in the room. Nat and Esrom both smiled at her for a moment. "Well," he finally said, to Nat, "you sure did a good job."

"I'm so glad you're here," she blurted.

Then she stood, wiped her palms on her skirt, and grappled with the heavy cardboard box that held cans of formula. Esrom got to his feet after her, took the box, and headed outside to load it into the truck; the cans clanked gently down to the curb. A moment later he came striding back up the walk.

"We'll have a good time, won't we, girls?" he asked, gathering an armload of blankets Nat had dug up. "I hope you like checkers."

"Who's Checkers?" Sam asked.

He smiled.

"Mama come, too?" said Liddie.

"Yup," said Esrom. "We're all going to just get out of town for a little while."

"This is a vacation, Liddie," Sam said, as if she knew of such things. "This is where people go and they have fun, and they have checkers, and beaches."

Esrom said, "There won't be any beaches, darlin'. Just trees."

"That's okay," Sam said. God, those girls loved Esrom; they'd be happy wherever he was.

"I'll take your bags," he said, collecting them into his free hand. He reached toward Nat: "You got your bag?"

She hesitated. She found it hard to catch her breath.

He stood expectantly.

"I didn't pack one," she said.

He stared at her a moment. He was puzzled and then his expression turned inward, hurt. He nodded, turned, and carried the bags out to the car.

Nat felt wretched. She stood, leaden, and finally forced herself into action. "Sam, Liddie, let's go." She gave Sam's shoulder a nudge. The girls traipsed ahead of her down the walk, the wind nearly blowing them sideways.

Esrom met the girls halfway, scooped them up, and carried them down the walk. He piled them into the truck, squeezed tight side by side. Nat nestled Sadie's basket at their feet.

"Stay on your seat, girls," she told Sam and Liddie. "Watch out for the baby." She closed the door and turned back to Esrom, who stood with his arms crossed over his chest.

"I had orders," he said.

"I know."

"What are you planning to do, Nat?"

She placed her hands on his crossed arms. "I need you to take the girls—"

He nodded. "Of course. They can't stay here. But you shouldn't, either. That's why your husband asked me—"

"And I'm going to need to borrow your green car back." She squeezed his arms. "Please."

He paused, staring at her.

"Please, Esrom."

He looked away, chewing the corner of his mouth, and finally nodded. His lips were chapped and his skin looked grayish, cold. She could feel the disappointment emanating from him, a silent devastation that slumped his shoulders and drained the color from his face in one fell swoop, as if she had just zipped a knife down his chest.

The part of her that wanted to go with him bucked in defiance: They wouldn't do anything wrong; they could just be near each other and live, briefly, in a daydream of affection and sweetness, feeling the rare joy of empathy: *Can I get this for you? Here, let me help you.* In a world gone mad, their makeshift family would be nothing but kindness and love. The one thing Nat knew about Esrom was that he would never, ever be cruel to her; he would never shout at her or make her feel ashamed. He wouldn't keep things from her just because he could, not if they were together a hundred years. She imagined them all at this hunting cabin of his cousin's, a fire in the fireplace, the girls tumbling around underfoot, all of them having dinner at some little local restaurant, an elderly couple smiling at what a sweet family they were, what a charming picture, gentle blue-eyed Esrom and Nat and her dark-haired girls.

But those girls were Paul's, and Nat was Paul's, too. And Paul was a good person; his anger at her was not wholly unjustified, as her thoughts about Esrom, seconds before, were proving. Of course Paul was hurt, drawing into himself like a skittish, muscular clam inside its double shell. He thought they could recover from all this by never speaking of it again, as if his dignity had spilled out, a tragic war wound, and he could shuffle around picking it up and packing it back in. *I'll have to pretend to trust you,* he'd said. Well, damn him, because she deserved more than his pretend trust; she deserved his real trust. She had faced a temptation and she hadn't strayed; she had endured his anger and she loved him still.

Esrom looked stricken. "Everything is just going to *hell,*" he blurted, avoiding her eyes, an unfamiliar catch of desperation in his voice. "Everything seems so ruined. Then I look at you and the girls and I think, *That would feel like a warm glow all of the time.*"

Nat stared at him.

"I'm sorry," he said, sounding disgusted with himself. "I shouldn't have said that."

"I know you'll be fine," she said, feeling the inadequacy of the words.

"I am," he said dully.

"You're a good person, Esrom. You're the best person I know. Do you see how much I trust you?"

"Thank you," he said. He pulled his arm gently away. "Please get in the truck. You'll freeze solid out here." He leaned around her to open the passenger door and she reached for his arm again.

"I'll take good care—" he started, but she leaned forward and kissed him, cupping his cheek with her free hand. His lips were cold and dry, and her heart lurched when she touched them. His whole body seemed to pound through his jacket. For a moment she kept her face against his, noticing the smell and feel of him, thinking *How strange, this could be my person, this could be the smell and feel that was familiar to me*. She would get used to it, see it every day, notice all its variations and changes, and over time it would just be another version of her own. But then eventually they would belong to each other, which was a miraculous kind of thing but a savage one, too.

"Nat," he said. She let go, and he opened the door for her, and when she'd climbed in beside her daughters he shut it and went around to his own seat. Neither of them spoke as he drove across town to his apartment. Nat leaned forward to stroke Sadie's belly through the blanket, Sam chatted happily about the snow, and Liddie stared out the window in thrilled, silent wonder. When they got to Esrom's place, the building seemed to have deteriorated even since Nat had last seen it. The brick was sleety and chipped and appeared to be crumbling into the snow. Esrom pulled up alongside a slanted carport.

"Girls," Nat said, turning toward them as much as she could in the cramped truck. "Mr. Esrom is going to take you to the cabin because I have to stay here. I wish I could go with you, but I can't."

Sam looked at her, surprised, and Liddie turned a moment later.

Sam said, "I want you to come, too, Mama—"

"I can't, sweetheart," Nat repeated. "But you'll still get your nice trip with Mr. Esrom. You'll be good for him, won't you?"

"Yes," said Liddie.

Sam said, "We're taking Sadie, too?"

Nat felt a jitter in her rib cage. "Yes, Sadie, too. But I'll see you very soon." She kissed each of their faces, tears blurring her sight, and looked at Esrom. "Take good care of my girls."

"Of course. I'll treat them like gold."

He handed her the key to the green car. Nat closed the door and stepped back, pressing the key into her palm, and watched Sam's and Liddie's heads and Esrom's profile as the truck groaned back down the snowy road.

PAUL

THE AMBULANCE DRIVER WAS ALLOWED TO LEAVE, AND THEN THE nurse. Paul sat in his folding chair in the corner of the room and watched them go. He surveyed the small group of new people who had just come in from the showers. Listening in on their conversation, he learned that some of these men were part of the search team whose task had been to sprint onto the reactor floor, spend thirty-five seconds scanning for Sidorski's body—during which they absorbed a year's allotment of radiation—and race outside again. One claimed to be the man who himself spotted the doomed operator. "I saw him, too," another voice said, "but I thought he was a clump of rags."

The next task would be to recover Sidorski. Operators from across the testing site were being called in. They would take turns snagging at the dead man's skin with hooks until they could pull him down onto a giant stretcher. There was some fear that if the body missed its target and fell into the core, the reactor could go supercritical again.

Paul shuddered, overhearing this. He had done the right thing in sending his family away, even if it felt as though he'd handed Nat to another man. When he pictured her and the girls riding in Esrom's car, jaunting off into the country as if they were going on some kind of vacation, he felt physically ill. He could not sit still. He could not concentrate. Some part of him always had to be moving—his foot tapping the metal chair leg, his arm adjusting against his body, his head giving a small twitch—to shake off the agitation he felt building in him. It crept up his shoulders and back like a thousand near-weightless insects, and only by moving could he reset it and feel, for an instant, relieved. Then it would crawl onto him again, and he could tolerate it only for a few seconds before he had to shake it off.

He saw Webb in his mind, not just the devastating close-range view he'd had of him in the ambulance, but the initial shock: Webb rising half up from the reactor room floor, moaning, reaching out for something he couldn't see; his clothes stuck to him like tissue paper, as though he were being découpaged. He had looked horrific, but he'd still had animation, if only a last gasp of it. And then there he was in the ambulance, the nurse dialing in the time, and Webb's face slack as if it might slide off sideways. Webbsy, good-hearted, twenty years old. What a waste.

The creeping feeling came up over his shoulders again. It built and built, slowly. He tried to hold still but felt as if a fist were squeezing his lungs. Finally he could bear the sensation no longer and he jerked his shoulders, squirmed in his seat. For a moment it dissipated, and he sagged in the chair with relief.

When Nat bolted through the door, he thought for certain he was dreaming. He didn't even move until he saw her stride toward him, break into a run. He sat up, completely confused. She shouted his name, and the next thing he knew her arms were around his neck. She kissed his forehead, his cheek, his shoulder, her lips like butterflies landing on him, lifting. He stared at her in wonder as she knelt before him, stroking the hair above his eyes.

"You're here," he murmured. The whole world had changed in one second.

"You look awful," she said.

"Ma'am!" came a shout behind her, and the health physicist bustled over, waving his arms. Nat turned, her cheek on Paul's forehead, staring down the doc as if she had no idea where he'd come from and was sure his role was irrelevant.

"You can't be here," Paul whispered. "You shouldn't be near me, you need to go."

She shook her head, pressed against his.

"Ma'am!" The physicist was frantic. "Ma'am, this is absolutely a closed area. This man has not been cleared."

Nat stood, gripped Paul's hand, and tucked his arm beneath hers. "I'm sorry. He's leaving now."

The man pointed, nearly hopping in his shoes. "You're holding his hand! These men's hands are the most contaminated parts of their bodies. Ma'am! Would you like me to show you on the detector? You'll see that—"

"I don't care," Nat said, and she tugged Paul's arm. Dazed, he stood. "We're going," she said.

Paul followed her across the room, weaving through folding chairs as men stared. When she got to the front door she pushed straight through.

The door of the green Dodge Wayfarer was open for him, and for a moment he pulled up short. But she tightened her grip on his arm and guided him into the passenger seat. She jogged around to the other side.

"I'm calling the police," the physicist shouted after them.

Nat set her mouth in a grim line and threw the car into gear. She stepped on the gas, and Paul's head thunked back against the seat. His heart filled with fear and relief and love for her.

"Where are the girls?" he asked.

"With Esrom."

He nodded. The road flew beneath them.

"I'm going to stay with you," she said. "We'll keep the girls out of the house until you think it's safe for them to come back, but I'm not leaving." Her voice tightened: "We will not be separated again, do you understand? We are *together*."

"I don't want to hurt you," he said.

"You won't."

"You don't know that. Every second you're around me, it's like you're getting X-rays."

"How bad are X-rays?" she dismissed with a wave of her hand. "They X-ray the girls' feet every time we go in for new shoes."

"Those only last a second."

She didn't answer this but shook her head. She reached for his hand

and squeezed it. "It's awful about Webb," she said, her eyes filling. "And the other two. Did you see them?"

"I did," he said. He had only seen one, but didn't have it in him to explain. He looked out across the testing station, barren and cold. A wind sock flapped on its pole. He could just make out the CR-1's silhouette on the horizon, enlarged by a crowd of vehicles.

Nat ran her thumb over the top of his hand, still holding it. "The whole drive here I was looking for some kind of sign," she said, almost to herself. "You know, giant flames, or a pink mushroom cloud, or something like that. A guard just waved me through at the gate when I told him I was coming to pick you up. All I saw were a few men in white hazard suits back on the highway and an ambulance off by itself in the bushes."

Images of the ambulance swarmed his thoughts: heading into the darkness, just the glow of taillights; the slapping footsteps of the driver racing back to them. He shuddered. Webb could still be in there, destroyed, alone.

"What?"

He shook his head. When Nat still looked at him he said, "I'm glad we got the girls out of here."

"Me, too," she murmured.

"Part of me wants to be there," he said. "At the reactor. I feel like I *should* be there, helping remove the men. I'm already shot, anyway."

"What do you mean, you're already *shot*?" she snapped, indignant.

"Sorry."

"Don't talk like that. You'll be fine now. You just need to rest."

Paul leaned his head against the car seat and closed his eyes. "Sidorski must have been working the rod," he murmured, trying to picture it in his head. "I'll bet it got stuck, so he was pulling on it. If it were really jammed in there, he might have yanked it up past four inches on accident."

"What's four inches?" Nat asked.

"We were always told never to lift the rod above four inches. People took it pretty serious even though we didn't know exactly what would happen if the rod went that high. Sidorski was new," Paul said. "He was called in as my replacement when I was in Greenland. He was twenty-two years old; he has a son. If I'd been there, I might have been able to stop it."

"Or you might have been killed," Nat said. "God was looking out for you."

"Why would God look out for me?" He'd never be able to convince Nat how absurd he thought this was.

She frowned, shook it off. "We need to be happy that you're alive," she said. "Just think: You get to go home. You get to hold your little girls again. You can't feel bad about that, just grateful."

Paul looked out the window. He felt thankful for this, he truly did. But he didn't deserve it any more than the other operators.

"You were there when it mattered most, Paul," she said. "Esrom told me. You couldn't have done any more."

His eyes welled, and he blinked. "Thank you," he said.

Esrom had told his story. This was an odd relief. But he knew that Nat wanted to hear it from him, too, the way she always wanted him to tell her things, and he feared he would not be able to do it. This was the common disappointment, and it should have been easy for him to overcome: Just talk, damn it! Just talk and make your wife happy! But he couldn't do it, and so she had found Esrom who, though he seemed nearly silent to Paul, apparently talked.

She fumbled in her pocket as if just remembering something and came up with a piece of light blue graph paper. "Paul, I forgot to ask. What is this?"

He could see even before he unfolded it that it was a page from the reactor log, but how it had come into Nat's hands was beyond him.

"Where did you get this?" he asked.

"It was left in our mailbox."

All the dates, he noticed, were from about a year and a half ago, when the rods first began sticking in earnest. He ran his index finger down the page and saw that Franks had taken the rare and bold step of recording that the number nine rod had stuck.

He looked at her. "Someone put this in our mailbox? Who?"

"Jeannie Richards, I think."

"Jeannie Richards?" he repeated, bewildered. "How do you know it was her?

"Yesterday, I was taking out the trash and saw Jeannie driving down the street. She'd put the flag on the mailbox up. When I checked it, I found this."

"So you're pretty sure it was her—"

"I'm almost positive."

"She couldn't have taken this from the reactor herself," Paul said. "She'd never go to the CR-1, or be in any position to handle the logbook if she did. Richards must have brought it home."

"Why would he do that?"

"I don't know," Paul said. Whatever his supervisor's reasoning, he felt fairly certain that Richards had hardly known what he was doing, either. It was a hopeless, almost childish move, taking a page from the logbook as if just erasing bits of evidence here and there could sanitize the history of a machine so fatally flawed as the CR-1.

"Was it some kind of a cover-up?" Nat asked.

"An attempt at one, maybe," Paul said. "Franks recorded here that the number nine rod, our most powerful control rod, had stuck that day. Richards and Harbaugh were pressuring him to leave any big glitches out of the written record, I guess in the hope that they both could coast until the new core arrived."

"But look what happened!"

"Well, yes. But if the reactor had lasted until the new core arrived, no one would have thought anything of it. No one would have looked, and the record would have been a little cleaner for Richards's efforts. I think he was hoping to promote one more time."

"He'd risk all that for a promotion?"

"I really don't think he grasped how much he was risking. He never worked the floor with us. And, yes, in his mind, it might have been worth it. There's a lot more pressure around promotion when you get to his level, far more than at my level." Paul shook his head. "People are going to go over every last line of the logbook, now. I'll bet they have DOE folks flying out from Washington as we speak."

"So it was true what Harbaugh said that night at the Richardses' party? Your reactor was having trouble this whole time? Every day when you went to work you could have been killed?"

"We didn't quite see it that way; we were making do. There's always an element of risk. We were waiting for the new core to arrive—they have one ordered for this spring."

"Paul, all that time, and you didn't *tell* anybody. You didn't tell *me*."

"It's hard to explain."

"But this is horrible. Three people have died!"

"I know," he said, feeling sick.

She shook her head but kept quiet, realizing the depth of his grief. They pulled out onto the highway, leaving the testing station and the reactor behind, and for one excruciating moment Paul felt desperate to leap out and run back to it; too much had happened, he belonged there, how could he leave? But Nat drove on steadily without stopping.

THEY SLOWED ON HIGHWAY 20 as the snowy fields fell behind them and the town approached, hunkered into itself, white-roofed and gray. If people were choosing to leave town, Paul could hardly tell. He had no idea what the official word had been on the reactor, what the average Joe had heard.

Then Nat pointed and said, "Look." Paul lifted his head from the window to see a heavily bundled middle-aged woman standing on a street corner holding a sign nearly as tall as she was. In red block letters it said TELL US THE TRUTH COMBUST. ENGINEERING. The woman pumped the sign at them, and someone from a truck yelled at her to go home and mind her own business.

Paul had seen protests and sit-ins on television and on the cover of *Life* but never in person, and it was riveting. He couldn't tell if it felt like watching something brave or irritatingly deranged. "Good for her," Nat said quietly, which surprised him on the one hand, but on the other didn't.

It was only a few blocks later that Paul spied Master Sergeant Richards's car in front of them. "Jesus Christ," he muttered. It shouldn't have been a shock; in this small town you couldn't drive anywhere without seeing someone you knew, and there was only one highway into town from the CR-1. Still, it was a slap in the face to see Richards's pearly Cadillac just cruising along ahead of them, the low flare of its tail fins and glow of brake lights against asphalt and snow. He recognized Richards's head of gray and brown hair, the pretty neck and curls of Jeannie beside him. Richards had probably figured he'd be released soon, with his low exposure, and had asked his wife to pick him up.

In that same instant Nat sat bolt upright. Her hands clenched the wheel. "Do you *see* them?" she said through gritted teeth. "Do you see them driving?"

"It's okay," Paul said. "They'll get what's due to them. He'll get what's due. There's a process—"

"It isn't fair."

"I know—"

"It isn't fair!" she raged. "He could have killed you! You, my *you*!" which he could hardly follow, but she kept going. "And those poor men! And look at him, just driving off to who knows where to spend the next few days in peace!" She banged the horn and Paul jumped. "Pull *over*!" she shouted.

"He can't hear you."

They were coming up to the bridge. Beside them the long, low falls hung immobilized, frozen as if a spell had been cast upon them; black water yawned at the base.

"He could have wrecked my *family,*" Nat said.

"But he didn't. We're still here, Nat. We're fine."

"And what's he going to get, an army hearing? What, dock him a month's pay?" She pointed at the car. "They have *persecuted* us for no reason ever since we got to this town!"

"What do you mean?" To his knowledge Nat had only spoken with Richards and his wife the once, at their dinner party.

With that she pressed her foot to the gas and the Wayfarer leaped with a clattery roar, like a mechanical door falling. In seconds she cleared the strip of road between their car and the Richardses', pulled up behind them, and laid on her horn again. Richards's eyes flashed in the mirror, his wife turned back to stare, and Paul felt the disdain in their eyes, the gaze of powerful and untarnished people upon someone unbalanced. He almost wanted to egg Nat on.

But he said, "Nat."

"I want to talk to them," she seethed, jabbing his hand away with her elbow. Richards was stopped at a light; he looked twitchily back at her as she rolled down her window and shouted into the freezing air, "Pull *over*! I want to talk to you."

Richards leaned out. "I see you've got your boyfriend's car again," he called.

Paul felt the color drain from his face . He sat tightly in the seat and said, "Let's just go home." In his head he said some other things. Then, before he could blink, Nat pressed the gas so that the tires spun and sent the Wayfarer run-and-jumping into the Coupe de Ville's bumper with a shockingly loud crash.

Paul's and Nat's heads thudded against the seat backs and forward again.

"Holy Christ," Paul said, leaning forward to see. The shiny steel was dented in around the license plate. "You smashed his bumper. Have you gone *crazy*?" he cried, more appreciatively than it sounded and also with a sinking heart, because there went Richards hollering out his window, saying Nat was going to pay for that, his car cost over five thousand dollars, she was a trollop who drove her boyfriend's car around town, and so on. He was still shouting when the light turned; Jeannie Richards, who seemed about ready to die on the spot, tapped his arm, and he jammed his foot onto the gas, speeding away from them, still turned back to jab a blocky index finger at Nat, his big face contorted with rage, the outer contours of his mouth winnowing rapidly from one oval into another; and, of course, driving in this manner, there was no way he could have seen the pedestrian.

The pedestrian registered first as just a shape, a moving shadow: a tall, thin man loping across the street in winter boots, crossing just in front of the bridge. He wore a thick flannel work coat and a hat with earflaps, and carried a canvas bag that appeared to be full of books. He stopped to shift the bag in his arms. Paul couldn't believe how long it took—how close Richards's car bore down, closer, closer—until the man turned to them, his face open with surprise, eyes wide, and dived out of the way.

Richards jerked his car across the opposite lane and off the road. It seemed to drop, like an optical illusion, over the edge of the riverbank. Paul stared. Nat slammed on her own brakes with a yelp and their car slowly spun, so that for a minute after the Coupe slid over the bank their backs were to it, and Paul could almost convince himself that he'd imagined it, that they'd turn around and find the cream-colored car still sitting on the road. Instead he and Nat were stuck staring at the few oncoming cars, which dodged them by delayed reaction, people honking, someone pulling over, the pedestrian in the corner of Paul's eye turning back to stare in confusion, his bag of books spilled everywhere, making splashes of brown and green and blue across the snowbank. Nat drifted the Wayfarer to the side of the road where she turned the key and sat for a moment in stunned silence.

"Are you all right?" Paul asked her, grasping her shoulder.

"I'm fine." She twisted around in the seat. "Paul, are they okay?"

He opened his door and crunched through ice-crusted snow toward the bank; she got out and followed. When he crested the ridge he stopped for a moment in surprise. The Coupe de Ville had skidded backward down the shallow riverbank and broken through, its tail end sinking, front half still clinging to land with weak traction. Beneath the chunky, ice-thickened water its rear lights glowed faintly red. Paul saw with relief the figures of Richards and Jeannie on the bank, Richards huddled by the car, Jeannie a short distance up the slope. She must have gotten out before the car slid all the way down.

Then he heard Richards shouting: enraged about his car, Paul thought. But Jeannie turned frantically to look up the bank, shrieking for help, and the terror in her voice registered with Paul as something more. Her eyes locked with his and she waved her arms in a panic: "My daughter's in there!"

Now Paul could see what was happening. Richards was trying to get back in; he climbed half over the front seat as the car groaned downward, quickly filling. Why, Paul thought, aghast, hadn't it occurred to him that the child might be in the car? It hadn't even crossed his mind and he was horrified, hoping the little girl hadn't been hurt in the car's thudding descent, hoping Richards would emerge any second, holding her up like a trophy. Paul bolted down the bank, instantly going down hard—the rocks were iced clean over—and crawled, then half-stooping-scrambled, to the car.

When he got there Richards was still struggling across the passenger seat. He'd grabbed the child by the hair and one arm and was trying to pull her up through the front. Freezing water poured into the car like a fishbowl.

"Take her," Richards shouted, and Paul squeezed in around him, the edge of the door pulling him slowly down as it sank. His feet slid over the icy rock toward the water. A wave sloshed into the car, washing once, to Paul's horror, over the girl's head; he elbowed past Richards between the two front seats and grabbed the girl under the armpits, heaving her head above the water. Slippery, desperate seconds passed as he shoved back against the passenger seat, one knee on it and the other foot outside the car, his shoes like useless flippers against the slick, iced-over rocks. Finally he dragged her onto the passenger seat, lurched back again, and got them both free of the car.

He went to his knees, clutching her cold trunk to his chest. She was terrifyingly silent and he slapped her on the back, hard and then harder. Jeannie was sliding toward him screaming, but though she was almost upon them the noise was all background, tinny and distant, until the little girl sputtered, choked out a vomity hiccup of water, and began to cry.

"Oh, thank God," Paul said. "Thank God," and felt his throat harden up. She was about the size of Liddie and all he could feel as he held her was overwhelming gladness and relief. He kissed her cold, wet hair the way he would have kissed his own girls' if they'd appeared before him, and strained up the bank to hand her to Jeannie.

"Here," he said. "I think she's okay."

Jeannie choked out a sob. She bundled the child into her fur coat and rocked her, weeping, pulling back again and again to look her daughter in the face and make sure she was okay.

Paul glanced back at Richards and saw him kneeling beside the car, his hands on his thighs, sides heaving.

"Is she all right?" Nat cried as she descended the bank. Paul wanted to remind her to be careful, but he wasn't quite able to speak. He saw that she had pulled an old blanket from the Wayfarer's backseat, and she and Jeannie wrapped it around the child, who was crying hard now. They closed in around her, patting and rubbing and shushing. Something about the two women with the child in the middle made the lump in Paul's throat larger, and he stood back, washed over with relief so strong that his knees nearly buckled, a spreading wet circle on his chest in the shape of the girl: This one he had saved.

"The police are on their way," someone called over the ridge.

Richards limped up the bank, teeth chattering, face blue-gray. "Angela?" he rasped. His rear foot slid out from him; he pushed himself hands and knees over a flat swath of boulder.

"She's all right," Jeannie called, not taking her eyes from the girl. "Not a scratch, just wet and cold." Angela was calmer now, resting against Jeannie's chest, sucking her thumb. Jeannie swayed, briefly closed her eyes.

"Thank God," Richards said as he reached them. He stood, wincing, and ran a hand over his face. His front teeth were outlined red as though he'd sucked blood through a straw. He spat onto the rocks and looked to each of them in turn, a little disoriented.

In the distance Paul could hear a siren wending toward them. Then, below them, there was the sound of suction followed by a terrific groan. The car trailed lower into the trough of river. The windshield slid under, then half of the hood, until just the grille showed like eerily grinning teeth. Around it a black oval in the ice widened, welcoming.

"Holy Moses," someone called, peeking over the top of the bank, "is that your *car*?"

There was another deep, grinding racket, and then the Coupe's headlights slipped underwater with the surety of something it had planned for all its life.

"Yes," Richards said finally, "that's my car."

Jeannie snickered softly. She rested her chin on Angela's bundled head. "Well," she said, rocking the girl from side to side, "it was."

Now the car sat in a shadow world just below the surface. Elegant belches of air rose from it one by one.

"That fucking car," said Paul, shaking his head.

"Her lights are still on," Richards whimpered.

And then, they went out.

V

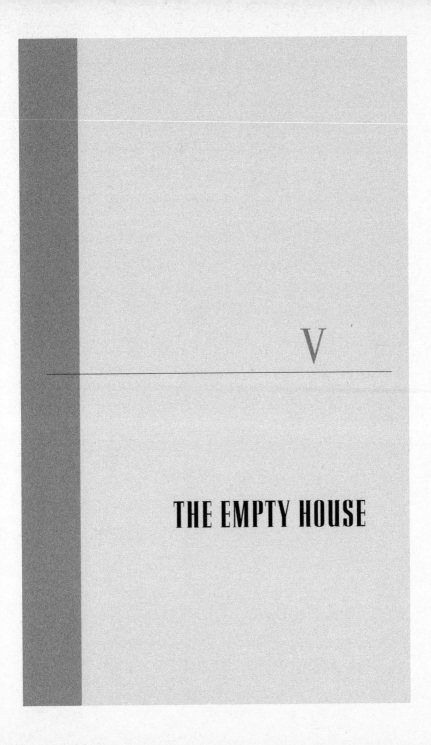

THE EMPTY HOUSE

NAT

January 1961

Paul was leaving the army. He'd decided it all at once, while Esrom was still at the cabin with the girls. Paul had just walked into the living room where Nat was sitting and said, "I think I need to get out."

She'd nodded, not questioning; for him to come to this decision was no small thing. She knew he had been grappling with it since the accident. He would take whatever discharge they gave him, but because of his role during the accident, he'd been told they would go easy. "What will you do instead?" she asked.

There were new power plants opening all over the country, he said, being approved every day; the nation was wild for nuclear energy, but the army program was slowing down. The CR-1, everyone was whispering, had been its death knell. Paul called the office at the brand-new civilian plant in Illinois, and was surprised by the eagerness of the supervisor there. So few people had real nuclear training that he'd been offered a job at well above his current salary. He'd proposed to Nat that they head east now, first to Michigan to pay their respects to Webb's mother and attend his funeral (which had been delayed because of the investigation and the decontamination of his remains); then they would drive to Illinois, poke around the town of Morris, where the Dresden nuclear plant was, and find a place to live.

For a moment Nat felt a pang: It would be strange to leave the army, despite her mixed feelings toward it; she liked their house; she was just getting used to Idaho Falls; most of all, of course, there was Esrom. Guilty little thoughts had slipped through her mind in previous days, oddly focused fantasies where she would occasionally bump into him in their small town (for if they stayed another year to finish out Paul's tour, surely she'd encounter Esrom from time to time) and the happiness she would feel, seeing him. Sometimes she allowed herself to consider standing outside his apartment, waiting for him to come out, and surprising him. The sudden jump of joy on his face would be something rare, something you didn't get from everyone. It seemed a waste to squander it and yet it was a thing you couldn't put back, either, once you picked it up.

If she couldn't stop such thoughts even after all that had happened, the hard truth was that she'd need to get herself away from Esrom entirely. She would just have to shut that door in her brain. It could close but maybe not latch, and when they left this town it would slowly rust over.

THE ARMY MOVERS CAME and packed up their things. Moving was always a two-day process: one day to pack up, sleeping that night among the boxes; the second day for the movers to load everything onto the truck. They would sleep one last night in the house before leaving for Michigan early the next morning.

And so, suddenly, the little house was empty again. It was painful how cute a house looked right before you moved; Nat glanced around and thought, *I'd really like to live here,* as if she never had.

Two days before they left, on her way home from getting a few items downtown, Nat spotted Jeannie Richards climbing off the city bus at the neighborhood stop. Jeannie was bundled in ankle-length fur with a matching hat, her high heels punching through snow; only she could make public transportation look so good.

Nat's first impulse was to try to avoid her, to stop the car (a used Chevy station wagon Paul had picked up for cheap because, after the accident, the Fireflite had to be destroyed). She could wait until Jeannie was out of sight, or make a U-turn, but either move would have been obvious. Besides, what did she have to lose now?

So she pulled over and rolled down her window. "May I give you a ride?" she asked.

Jeannie paused, hugging her coat around herself. Her red hair was bright against the gray snow and sky. "It's only two blocks," she said.

Nat pushed open the passenger door. "Please, hop in." She lifted Sadie's Moses basket around to the floor of the backseat; Sadie was sound asleep. "Try not to wake her, girls," she whispered to Sam and Liddie, moving their feet gently aside to make room for the baby.

Jeannie climbed in, lighting herself a cigarette. "Thank you," she said.

"Do you have any Cracker Jack?" Sam asked.

Nat turned, her finger to her lips. Good grief: Sam practically shook the woman down for Cracker Jack the moment she got in the car. She'd never forgotten it from that dinner party with the nannies.

"How is Angela?" Nat asked.

"She's good," Jeannie said, managing a quick smile. "They put her in warm water at the hospital and her color came right back. She was drinking broth half an hour later. The doctor said to look out for a cough, but she never got one."

"Oh, I'm so glad to hear that," Nat said. "I was worried about her. I'm sorry that she ever got . . . involved."

Jeannie paused. "We were lucky," she finally said, her eyes flashing to Nat. "Both of us."

They drove a few more moments, and neither woman said anything. What Nat wanted to ask Jeannie, more than anything, was why she'd put the page from the logbook in her mailbox. It was an action that might have been selfless, but altruism seemed out of character for Jeannie Richards. The question was nearly popping off Nat's tongue and yet she found it hard to get started.

"May I ask you a question?" she finally said.

Jeannie glanced at her warily. "Go ahead."

"Why did you put that paper in our mailbox?"

Jeannie paused. She gazed out the windshield, holding her cigarette at her shoulder, and eventually exhaled. "I was worried that Mitch was going to get himself into even more trouble," she said. "Removing pages from the logbook. Fixing documents, even. I thought maybe if Collier, if your husband found out—well, we both know his conscience would have eaten him alive. He'd have done something about it. I hoped he could stop my husband before it got too far. I put it in your box the day of the restart, but the accident happened that night, so I guess I was too late."

"You were kind of setting Paul up," Nat said, processing all of this. "Because you knew he would have taken action."

"I suppose so, yes. He's the only one who ever did."

Nat felt a little proud and sad at the same time. "I'm sorry about the car," she finally said.

Jeannie shrugged. "It was my husband's car. It had a rather poetic end. He'd probably prefer to see it go that way than to just be handed over to me in the divorce."

Nat froze.

"Don't look shocked," Jeannie said. "My goodness, you virginal young thing. It's legal now. I'm flying out to Reno on Thursday. Haven't you heard of the Reno Cure?"

"I have," Nat said, glancing back at the girls in her rearview mirror.

"Six weeks to establish residency and the divorce is yours, no matter the reason. I was going to do it here, but it was so much trickier. You had to establish wrongdoing; you needed hard proof. In Reno it's practically no-fault."

"Wow," said Nat.

"Mitch is being discharged." She scratched her head delicately with one finger, lowering her voice as if this were the word she didn't want the girls in the backseat to hear, the one they risked repeating rather than the two hatchet-blade syllables of *divorce*. "I thought he might get a general discharge but, mercifully, they made it honorable. Obviously they didn't know everything he was up to. Three years shy of his retirement, though—he won't get his pension. Isn't it a laugh to think of me hanging on all those years for a retirement that would never come?"

"But what will you do?"

"My brother still works at Boeing in St. Louis. They need secretaries, dispatchers. I talked to him last night and he said he could get me work. So Angela and I will drive out there eventually. Mitch plans to live nearby so he can see her when he likes."

"My goodness. You're so brave," Nat said, amazed.

"Well. Sometimes we have to be brave, right?" Jeannie turned to Nat and actually smiled. Then she opened her door, the fur of her coat slithering from the seat as she stood. Perfectly erect, her copper hair lifted by the breeze, she made her way up the snowy drive.

NAT

ELVIRA, MICHIGAN

THE SMALL FUNERAL PARTY HUDDLED AT THE EDGE OF THE cemetery, far from the sweep of gray headstones, in an unmarked spread of snow-covered ground. They were gathered around a wheeled crane that idled, blowing puffs of smoke into the air, and their gaze followed its gently quivering chain into a deep rectangular hole. At its bottom was a huge lead-lined casket weighing hundreds of pounds, looped by the chain.

Nat shifted Sadie in her arms, peeled black the blanket to peek in at her sleeping face, and then covered her again. Paul held Liddie, and Sam stood between them, solemn, red-nosed, and probably bored beneath her small fur hat.

There was a grind and a creak as the casket was pulled, slowly, to the top of the grave where it had been placed a few hours before; Webb's mother had requested it be lifted for the service. The two men from the Atomic Energy Commission who'd been sent to oversee the ceremony said the casket could be lifted for only five minutes because Webb's body was still emitting radiation. The rattling chain interested Sam, who peered forward on tiptoe.

Nat tried not to think about what Paul had said, through gritted teeth, one night soon after the accident (when he'd read yet another newspaper article speculating that Webb or Sidorski had purposefully lifted the rod too high on some sort of suicide mission): that they'd had to cut the most radioactive parts of Webb's body away, including his head and hands, and bury these separately in the hot waste site in Idaho Falls. As soon as he'd said it he'd looked to Nat and apologized with horrified eyes. *You didn't need to know that. I'm so sorry*. Nat had simply put her arm around him. She was grateful that he was not allowed back to the testing station to witness all these proceedings firsthand, that he only heard reports back from Franks. But it was hard, now, to press her mind away from the knowledge of what was actually in the casket—not the peaceful, handsome young man they were all trying to remember. She prayed to God that his mother didn't know.

"Can we cut the engine?" asked the priest, looking toward the crane. He motioned to the driver, trying not to shout, and made a slicing motion across his chest. "Let's cut that engine, hm?" When it finally silenced he smiled closed-lipped at the group of congregants and whispered, as if they had turned it off themselves, "Thank you."

Sam started to whine about something. Nat reached down to take her hand.

The priest read a Bible passage, his nasal, upper Midwest accent surprising Nat each time she heard it afresh. It sounded like a funny voice from the radio, someone who was supposed to be a grocery-store gossip or a nosy neighbor. Further throwing Nat off was that Webb's first name had been Johnny; every time someone mentioned Johnny she had to force the image of Webb's smiling face into her mind to keep from feeling disoriented. Paul said he'd been aware of Webb's name but then forgotten it because he'd never heard it said aloud.

Next to the priest Webb's mother stood, swaying slightly, her eyes closed. She was a slight, short-haired woman, no older than forty, her skin pitted here and there in gentle divots, soft folds of skin pouching her eyes.

"Being perfected in a short time," the priest was saying, "Johnny Webb fulfilled long years, for his soul was already pleasing to the Lord."

Sam raised one foot, shook it, set it down, and did the same with the other; her Mary Janes were too small and her toes must have been freezing. Nat squeezed her hand and jiggled it encouragingly.

It was time for Paul to read. He took a step forward; he'd already removed his gloves and he held a small handwritten piece of paper that bent damply in the moist, snow-flecked air. Mrs. Webb had asked him to choose a verse from a list the priest had given. Never in her life had Nat seen Paul read anything aloud, let alone a Bible verse, and it gave her the odd impression of watching a handsome, spiritual stranger. He shook the paper gently to stiffen it.

"Gracious is the Lord, and righteous," he read, stammering slightly as he found his rhythm. "Our God is merciful." He looked briefly at Mrs. Webb as if to make sure she was all right, and read on. "I kept my faith, even when I said, 'I am greatly afflicted'; I said in my consternation, 'Everyone is a liar.'"

In her blanket, Sadie made a snuffly cry, and Nat bobbed her, watching Paul. "O Lord," he finished, "you have loosed my bonds."

Mrs. Webb opened her eyes and smiled at him, and then she closed them again.

The priest read two more passages and led them with a honky, rhinal singsong through the twenty-third Psalm. Then he stepped back, and the instant he did so the two Atomic Energy agents, in suits and dark ankle-length coats, came forward from the edges of the group. They signaled to the driver of the crane, who snapped to attention and rumbled his machine to a smoky start-up. Webb's body in its layers of shielding swung softly to the bottom of the grave, and his mother knelt to scrape a handful of snowy dirt into her glove and toss it on top.

At this the suited men extended their arms, quietly sweeping the congregants forward. "This way, please," whispered the man closest to Nat. "Let's move across the field now." He turned back to wave in a cement truck parked out by the fence; it would quickly seal the coffin under eight feet of concrete.

The priest turned Mrs. Webb by the shoulders and walked her back the way they'd come, trampling their own overlapping footsteps through the snow.

"We made it," said one of the two men, looking at his watch. "Good work." They followed the gathering back to where the rows of regular headstones began and then stopped to make sure that no one, from reasons of sentimentality, curiosity, or absentmindedness, doubled back.

THE SMALL HOUSE SMELLED of coffee and dusty carpeting and old brocade drapes. Sharon Webb set cup after cup of shaking black liquid on the low table, refilling them the second they were drained, telling Nat and Paul she didn't mind at all. She brought out a plate of cookies and a bowl of potato chips and some crackers with pub cheese. Sam and Liddie watched television nearby, their feet swinging merrily from the floor up to their sprawled bottoms and back again as they kicked the orange rug, dug their toes into it, kicked again. Occasionally they lurched up to grab a handful of chips and then they flopped back down.

"It was so good of you to come," Sharon said, in her Michigander's inflection: "so" tucked into itself and shortened, "come" stretched out into a soft "a." "Johnny mentioned you. He said there was one of the boys on shift he really got along with, that you were like an older brother to him."

"Thank you, ma'am," Paul said.

"It was a lovely service," said Nat.

"A bit quick, though," said Mrs. Webb, her mouth pursed. She sighed. "I suppose I should sit down. Can't keep bustling about forever. I should probably put my feet up."

She finally settled onto the couch next to Nat, lit a cigarette, and watched them eat. Nat ate and ate, trying to show her appreciation. Then she worried that Mrs. Webb would get up again to replenish things, so she slowed down, nibbling a cracker, rocking the sleeping Sadie, looking around at the pictures on the wall: a couple of old paintings of flowers in vases and children sitting by white fences, a few family photos, a soft-focus profile of Jesus with blushed cheeks. Mrs. Webb began to reminisce, which Nat knew was healthy and useful, so she was glad to listen. She heard about Johnny Webb tussling with a much older boy in the front yard; Johnny, dared to eat a worm at three years old and doing it; Johnny, seeing a small brown dog limping by the side of the road in the eighth grade and climbing right off the school bus at a stop sign, luring the dog over with a peanut butter sandwich, bringing it home and naming it Freddie. Freddie still lived in the house, panting cheerfully on his side just a few feet away beneath the swell of a large fatty tumor.

"There was a fellow I dated awhile, when Johnny was eleven," Sharon said, exhaling smoke, flicking her middle finger against a hangnail on one thumb. She paused to nip off the strand of skin. "He had a little daughter, nine or ten. She and Johnny got real close. He wanted her for a sister bad, he hated being an only child, and when the fellow and I stopped seeing each other Johnny was so mad at me he hid in his room for days."

"Aw," said Nat, not sure what else to say.

"You've heard what people are saying, haven't you?" Sharon said. Her face hardened suddenly and she looked to Paul for reassurance. "That the explosion wasn't an accident, but it was caused on purpose?"

"That's rubbish," Paul said. "Don't believe a word of it."

Nat's gaze darted to Paul uneasily. Nothing made him angrier than these rumors, which were being reported in the papers with such persistence that people were taking them for true. The press latched on to Webb's recent breakup with his girlfriend to suggest that he'd knowingly pulled the stuck rod well above its limit. Others intimated that there'd been a love triangle at play, with two of the operators fighting over the same woman. The gossip drove Paul to distraction. "It's cruel," he'd said, back in Idaho Falls. "They're slandering his name. I need to get away from this goddamn town."

Sharon looked down at her hands and then back up again, her eyes glittering. "If it's not true, why's everyone saying it?"

"People don't want to believe that the reactor itself failed," Paul said. "That's what I think. Because if that's true, then nuclear power isn't as safe as we thought. But if folks can tell themselves it was just one crazy guy—I'm sorry, Mrs. Webb, you know I don't feel that way—then they can tell themselves it was a freak thing, human error, and that the machine was sound."

Sharon's eyes filled with tears, and Nat reached over to squeeze her hand. "Do *you* think it could have been prevented?" Sharon asked.

Paul looked pained. "I don't know for sure, Mrs. Webb. But I know that your son didn't do anything wrong. He would never hurt anybody else. And I will tell that to any person who ever brings it up."

She nodded and wiped her eyes. "Thank you."

Paul shook a small brown paper bag out of his duffel and handed it to her. "Here are the things from his locker. I'm sure he'd want you to have them."

"Oh," Mrs. Webb said. "How thoughtful." She fished out a photo of herself on the front steps of the house in a checkered apron, her hair tied up with a top-knotted scarf. "Oh, look at me," she said, "I look so young."

Sharon insisted that the Colliers stay the night; she wouldn't dream of sending them off to a motel. Nat felt they were too many people for the small, close house—it had only two bedrooms, and she wouldn't have felt right about sleeping in Webb's childhood room, which still held his baseball glove and Matchbox cars—but she and Paul didn't want to be ungrateful, and besides it didn't hurt to save the money. So after a dinner of lasagna a neighbor had left on the front step, Sharon brought out armfuls of blankets from some secret, blanket-stuffed closet, heaping them onto the floor: quilts and afghans and an old one of Webb's with baseball players all over it. Nat got the girls settled on the floor, telling them that of course these blankets were different from theirs at home and of course they would still sleep fine, and please don't repeat that the blankets are dusty, and in the morning they would be on their way south from Michigan to Illinois. Her mind flickered back to their early days in Idaho and she felt a stab of nostalgia. She remembered that summer night air, the toads trilling outside, the girls asleep on the floor of their then-new house and she and Paul on the back patio. It seemed a lifetime ago, like the days before the fall, when people were innocent and did such things.

With the lights dim and Paul dozing beside the girls on the floor, Nat sat up, giving Sadie her bottle. She loved these moments alone with the baby, no other demands. She could concentrate on Sadie's small moving fingers, the hearty suck and swallow, the way her dark eyes wandered the room alertly while she drank. Once the milk was done she would sag with sleepiness, but during her bottle she was fascinating to watch, tiny and observant, as if memorizing the angles of doorjambs and the tilt of curtain rods.

Nat thought Sharon Webb had gone to bed, but then she appeared in the living room in her nightgown and housecoat, her feet in ancient, flattened slippers. "Is everyone comfortable?" she whispered to Nat.

"Yes, we're perfect," said Nat. She patted the space next to her. "Here, have a seat."

"Oh," Sharon said, easing next to Nat on the couch and smiling at the baby. "Look at her. Isn't she just a wonder? Does she sleep the night?"

The bottle had drained down to a few slow bubbles so Nat swung Sadie up onto her shoulder and patted her tiny back. "Not yet," Nat said. "She takes another bottle around three or four."

"That's not too bad."

"No, I can't complain." Nat said this and then winced slightly, because of course she couldn't complain, not now or ever.

But Sharon just smiled. "May I hold her?" she asked.

"Of course."

For a moment in Sharon's arms Sadie perked up, registering something different, but the fullness of her belly soon won out. Sadie fell asleep with one fist up by her head and the other tiny hand resting delicately across her blanket-tucked belly, and Sharon Webb rocked and rocked her, smiling as if she could never tire of such a thing.

"It goes so fast," she said. "One blink and it's all gone by." She looked as if she might cry. "I remember everything about Johnny at this age. Every little thing. It does make me sad that I'll never have another one."

Nat reached out to rub her arm, not knowing what to say.

"Isn't it odd, though? How everybody was someone's child this way?" Sharon asked. "Every little old lady you see, every big, galumphing man, was once someone's precious baby just like this."

"I never really thought of that," said Nat, her eyes flicking to Paul with his mysterious unknowable childhood, his family dead and gone. Had his mother loved him like this, rocked him in the dark of night, watched his curious dark eyes? It seemed impossible but it had to be, just like anyone else.

"Did I tell you?" Sharon asked, suddenly bright-eyed. "Did I tell you about last summer?"

"I don't believe so," Nat said.

"Oh, I'm sorry. I don't want to wake the baby." She lowered her voice. "Well, it was last summer—not this recent one but the one before, just when you all started up in Idaho. And I hadn't seen Johnny since he went into the army, you know, not since he graduated boot camp. He left here with a little bit of a reputation—some partying and a couple of fist-fights. Elvira's a small town."

"Sure," Nat said.

"And so I was at work down at the Best Western. I've been there eight years, since I gave up drinking. Haven't touched a drop in all that time. That's why I drink a dozen cups of coffee a day." She smiled self-deprecatingly, and Nat, who loved a harmless confession, laughed. "So I was down there, cleaning rooms with the girls, and we go in on morning break to have a smoke and eat the leftover muffins from the continental breakfast. If there are extras we get them free. And we're sitting there and suddenly in walks this tall man, this *man,* in an army uniform. And I say to him, 'Can I help you find something?' And he says, 'I'm looking for Sharon Webb,' and he's grinning at me a little goofy, and I'm thinking did the girls put this poor fellow up to this for a laugh? And then Marcella says, 'Shari, that's your *son,* that's Johnny!' "

"Oh!" Nat said.

Sharon wiped her eyes. "He looked like someone who'd been born like that—born finished. Does that make sense? Not like he'd been a scabby-kneed little boy, ever. I couldn't believe I'd had anything to do with this man standing in our break room holding his hat."

"But you had everything to do with it," Nat said.

"Oh, it was wild. He brought a bottle of champagne and we all had a little in the break room. Even me! After how many years as a teetotaler. The girls just *loved* it. That was when Johnny was on his way from Belvoir out to Idaho. You all must have been going about the same time."

"I guess we were."

"Ah," Sharon said, passing Sadie back to Nat and then sitting a moment, her face glowing. "Just seeing him come in, I didn't recognize him. But on the other hand, I knew. From the minute I saw his profile I knew that was Johnny. I just didn't want to admit it to myself. I wanted to keep that moment where he was so grown-up and so perfect that I wasn't quite sure it was really him. I wanted to keep it like I could have it forever, over and over, that feeling of recognizing."

"You'll always have it."

"I will." Sharon stood briskly, rubbing her arms. She looked around the room, at Nat's sleeping daughters, and at Paul, who was now facedown on the floor, his head turned away from them. "You're all right here? Do you need anything at all?"

"Not a thing," Nat said.

"Good night, then."

"Good night, Sharon."

Nat laid Sadie in her bassinet, holding her breath as she lifted her hands to see if the sleep would stick. It did. So she took off her robe and climbed in her nightgown under the blankets next to Paul, turning over a few times on the floor. The carpet seemed ancient, dusty down to the boards, so she rolled onto her back again. Paul laid a sleepy arm over her. "I thought you were going to take the couch," he murmured.

"No," she said. "I'll sleep here with you."

"Okay." And he tucked her in close, his nose against her hair so that it lifted and fell with his breath. A clock ticked on the wall. In the bassinet, Sadie gave a small sigh; Sam pushed Liddie with her leg and Liddie rolled over with a grunt; Paul breathed beside her, up and down, healthy and safe, and it was as if Nat overheard her own body in five places at once.

SHE'D ONLY SEEN ESROM twice more since the day of the accident: first, the afternoon when, after five days at his cousin's cabin, he'd brought the girls home. Nat had nearly gone mad from missing her daughters. She'd longed for all three children, but especially for Sadie, on some visceral, hormonal level that defied explanation. When Esrom's pickup pulled in front of the house she felt as if her heart had been rocked by some small underwater explosion, a burst and reverberation. She raced down the walk as Paul watched from the doorway behind her. She kissed and hugged Sam and Liddie until they squirmed and trotted away, made shy by her tears. Sadie looked bigger; her satiny newborn arms had plumped and her eyes were more focused. "Oh," Nat kept saying, "oh," as if she hadn't before known the baby's sturdy, singular beauty.

"We had a good time," Esrom said, "but they missed you."

"I missed *them,*" she said, burying her face against Sadie's small body. She had missed Esrom also, but couldn't say it.

He had already stepped back toward his truck, his fingers twitching anxiously against the hem of his jacket. "Thank you for trusting me with them. Just leave the green car out by the curb in a day or two, with the key under the front seat. I'll come by and pick it up."

"I can find a way to bring it by—"

He shook his head. "No, that's not a good idea." Nat knew he was probably right; Paul wouldn't be happy to learn that she knew where Esrom lived, wouldn't like her driving the car over and getting a ride back. "I'll just stop by and get it," he said. "I won't come in."

"Thank you," Nat said, and, heart pounding, she'd turned back toward Paul. She couldn't stand having the two of them in such close proximity, with so much unbearable intensity sparking back and forth from them to her.

But Paul hadn't stayed to monitor: He had taken the girls into the house. Nat was surprised and grateful. When she opened the door he was sitting on the couch with Sam and Liddie, and while she could tell it was momentarily difficult for him to look at her, he wasn't angry. He seemed softer, somehow. She handed Sadie to him and he seemed instantly absorbed; and if he noticed the way Nat paced in the kitchen, wringing her knuckles and fighting back tears until she could calm herself enough to return to him, he never mentioned it at all.

SHE SAW ESROM ONE last time the afternoon before they left Idaho Falls. She'd dashed downtown alone to pick up a few last-minute items for the road: powdered milk, saltine crackers, Paul's cigarettes. When she got back in the car she sat for a moment, and then, instead of heading straight home, drove toward the auto body shop instead.

The body shop was located at the edge of downtown along with a couple of car dealerships, two other mechanics' shops (one European, one American), and a large feed store with a giant rooster statue outside, now wearing a mantle of snow that made it seem almost grave. It was a small shop with a handful of dirty cars on blocks out front, apparently held in the same limbo the Fireflite had been. The garage door was closed, and this was nearly enough to turn Nat around and send her home, but a greater urgency propelled her to the small side door.

She rapped on the door, and a moment later a bristly faced older man answered. He had watery eyes, yellow-red at the corners, and he looked gruffly at Nat.

"Is Esrom in?" Nat asked.

"You here about a car?"

Nat paused. What did she have to lie about? "No," she said.

He sized her up. "Then what for?" he asked.

She had not expected further interrogation and wished she had fibbed. "I just want to say good-bye," she said.

The man looked as if he were about to inquire her name and relationship to his nephew, and she braced herself, but instead, with a twist of annoyance around his mouth, he turned and disappeared into the shop. A moment later Esrom came ducking out, and there it was: the look on his face she'd both dreaded and hoped to see, a sort of simultaneous illumination and flinch. It pulled her heart open and made her feel awful at the same time, and she felt she should not have come.

"Is everything all right?" he asked, closing the door behind him.

"We're moving away," Nat said. She wanted to get it out of her mouth as quickly as possible.

"Oh," he said. "Okay. Yeah. I thought probably you would."

"To Illinois. We leave tomorrow."

"Illinois?"

"There's a power plant there that'll hire Paul."

"He hasn't had enough of those for one lifetime?"

"No," Nat said, her mouth pulling to one side. "I guess not."

"Well, thank you for telling me—"

"It's horrible to leave you," Nat cried, suddenly overcome, stepping forward to wrap her arms around him. Even through his cold and heavy jacket, the feel of his anxious, kind self made her heart turn over. She was tall enough that no hug felt sisterly, her face toward his neck. "I wish we'd always live near you," she said, "so I could see you every day." Then, feeling his body twitch, she wished she could take back those overexcited words.

He cleared his throat as if to say something, but it was too much for Nat to have come in the first place and for her to be there still. She'd said what she wanted to say. So she pulled herself away and headed for the car, pressing her fingers into her belly. She listened for the body shop's side door to open and close, but it didn't, at least not before she had climbed into the car and driven away.

THE DAY THEY LEFT Idaho Falls had been as cold as any of the ones before. It seemed darkly comical that their first destination was, of all places, Michigan in January. Paul got the car running and wedged a carpet square and a bag of road salt into the trunk. Nat had bundled the girls, wrapping Sadie in layers of blankets and tucking them tight, and arranged them all in the car, big girls in the back, Sadie's basket up front with her.

"Are we ready?" Paul asked, coming down the walk, a large suitcase in either hand.

"We're freezing!" Sam said.

He smiled. "Then we'd better hit the road."

Paul hoisted the suitcases one by one and tied them to the roof. He yanked on the length of rope, leaning back to test its sturdiness, then knotted the loose end and gave the suitcases a jiggle. Apparently satisfied, he bent down to peer in the window at the girls. "Time to head out, explorers," he said. He saluted Sam and then, catching Nat's eye, laughed almost bashfully.

Watching him, Nat felt her heart pull. Paul said he'd felt mostly fine since the accident, though he admitted to having what felt like a low-grade flu. He didn't want to see any more doctors. It made her uneasy. He admitted that back in reactor school a health physicist had told them the effects of radiation might not surface for years. And the human body was unpredictable—Paul might develop some rare cancer while he was still young, or never show any ill effects and live to be 105. He told her he wasn't losing any sleep over it. "That's kind of how life goes anyway," he'd said. "Right? Anybody could live to a hundred or die tomorrow." Nat nodded, and then decided that she would not ask about it anymore.

Later, over the years, they would hear of people—the nurse, the health physicist Vogel—developing rare, sudden cancers, malfunctions in their bones and blood, dying quickly and young. Nat would spend the years counting her time, watching Paul, as if she could spot the very instant that something went wrong. She would raise her hand, sound the alarm. But there was never any way to know.

He'd climbed into the driver's seat, adjusting the rearview mirror. Nat settled into the passenger seat and murmured down at Sadie, who waved her fist past crossed eyes and sucked on it.

Nat had taken one last glance at their little yellow house, empty now. She imagined that as this town grew over the years, the yellow house would begin to look smaller and plainer, as if it had shrunk, but really it was just that the world around it would have grown. Every few years a new military family would come into that house and leave signs of themselves here and there: a pot of flowers planted by the front step, a flag raised or lowered. These items would come and go with time, living brief lives of their own. People driving past might notice them or drift on without noticing, because the families inside were part of a long line of ghosts that the locals only partially remembered.

Paul backed the car down the driveway. Its tires bumped over the snowy gutter, grinding onto the salt-flecked road. Nat watched the girls in her side mirror, their fingers hooked against the edges of the windows, Sam's tousled dark hair and Liddie's short, shiny pigtails.

For an instant, as they passed the last downtown block toward the highway, Nat thought she saw a familiar silhouette by the barbershop: Stetson hat and canvas work jacket and boots. She managed to keep herself from spinning in the seat—moved just her eyes; but it wasn't him, of course. This man turned to look up as they drove past and his face was older, grizzled, not as kind. For all she knew he might be Esrom's uncle, some juniper-tough branch on the family tree. She'd think back to this moment days later, at Sharon Webb's house. It was only a reflex but it was still something: a pulse, a scrawled graffiti on the cellular level. She'd remember what Mrs. Webb had said: *I wanted to keep that moment when I wasn't sure it was really him.*

Her eyes darted to Paul; he was focused on the drive before them, his immediate task, his endless and careful responsibility. When they left a place, he kept his eyes straight ahead, but she would always be the one who looked back.

AUTHOR'S NOTE

WHILE *THE LONGEST NIGHT* IS A WORK OF FICTION, AN EXPLOSION at a small nuclear reactor called the SL-1 in Idaho Falls, Idaho, did kill three young operators on January 3, 1961. The explosion occurred after a control rod was lifted too high, causing the reactor to go "supercritical" in a fraction of a second. But the tragedy at the SL-1 has been allowed to fall away from our cultural memory, with Three Mile Island looming much larger in the American consciousness, because Three Mile Island's meltdown took place more recently, in a more populated area, and perhaps among a more skeptical society. It looms *so* large in our minds, in fact, that many of my peers were surprised to learn that, thankfully, no lives were lost at Three Mile Island in March of 1979.

In an effort to give a sense of what I considered the more fascinating aspects of early American nuclear history, I have conflated some historical events; for example, Camp Century in Greenland was actually completed a few months after I sent Paul there in the novel.

Anyone interested in learning more about the SL-1 accident and the National Reactor Testing Station in the 1950s and '60s should consider reading Todd Tucker's fabulous *Atomic America* and William McKeown's *Idaho Falls*. While the events at the SL-1 have always been open to more interpretations than is typical, given that all three participants were, sadly, killed at the scene, Tucker's and McKeown's books are—unlike my own novel—nonfiction accounts.

ACKNOWLEDGMENTS

THIS BOOK WOULD NEVER HAVE SEEN THE LIGHT OF DAY WITHOUT the efforts of my amazing agent, Sylvie Greenberg, who championed it from the start. Her instincts are pure gold, she somehow manages the impossible, and she's made this whole process more fun than I dared hope it would be. Thanks also to Jordan Carr for his early read of this manuscript.

It's been a pleasure and an honor to work with the lovely, talented Andrea Walker at Penguin Random House. Thanks to everyone there and to everyone at Fletcher & Company literary agency.

Gratitude to Aaron Gwyn, David R. Gillham, David Abrams, Siobhan Fallon, Celeste Ng, Nina McConigley, Molly Antopol, Frederick Reiken, Peter Molin, Vincent La Scala, Michelle Daniel, and Kaela Myers.

I owe a debt to my friends from the MFA program at the University of Minnesota for their encouragement, and for the example of their talent and hard work. Rob McGinley-Myers, you're the best first reader I could have asked for. Also Kate Hopper, Suzanne Rivecca, Alex Lemon, Richard Hermes, Kevin Fenton, Amanda Fields, Bryan Bradford; and to Valerie Miner and Julie Schumacher, my advisers.

Terri Barett, Britta Hansen (and Eric and Kenny), Dave and Anne Johanson, Alfred Faro (and Alexis!), Sarah Williams, Gail Buteau, Paul Wyman (my main character's namesake), and all of the Williamses,

Faros, Moneys, Baretts, and Johansons for their warmth and love. You can't know my gratitude!

Erin Wilcox and Lisa Crawford, you were my first writing teachers and the people with whom I shared my most meaningful love of books, imagination, and adventure. I could never deserve friends like you (and your wonderful families). Huge thanks to Erin for—thirty years later—working with me on my first manuscript as part of Wilcox Editing Services.

Big thanks to "the Alaskans," including (again) Erin Wilcox, Leslie Hsu Oh, Signe Jorgenson, and Shehla Anjum, for reading some of these chapters in an earlier form, and for all the evening Skype sessions.

Julie Shadford Odato, if everyone loved books as much as you do, writers wouldn't have a thing to worry about.

I've been lucky enough to have some wonderful literature teachers, especially Hilary Zunin and Justin Aaron. I've also been fortunate to have students who taught me more than I taught them: Pete Meidlinger, Andy Uzendoski, Matt Bruce, Jaz Roemer, Shawn Swanson, and the Steel Workers one and all.

They say a good man is hard to find, but I worked with three of them: Mark Schultz, Mike McMahon, and Adam Warthesen.

Thanks to the folks at the Bad Ass Café in Rancho Penasquitos, where I wrote nearly all the revisions for this novel—especially Danny, Nicole, and Savannah. Thanks to Becky Cardoso, Nancy Bergman, and my PQ book club.

From my early Navy days, when I was a stranger in a strange land: Meg Riley Hutchinson, Jane Hill-Gibson, Rachel Duncan, Tricia and Martin Walsh, and Nereyda Gonzalez.

To the military spouses out there: Thanks for holding it all together.

Dave Johanson, when you wrote out Ginsberg's "Song" by hand and taped it to my car's windshield in the high school parking lot I knew better than to let you get away. Nora, Soren, and Susanna, thanks for making life fun. I love you guys more than anything.

Last of all, I wouldn't be nothin' without my truly selfless, funny, and loving parents, Bob and Elaine Williams, and my brother, Nick

Williams. Mom, thanks for telling me it was okay to stay inside and write when the other kids were playing outside. You always got me. Nick, if you ever get put in time-out again, I will still sneak you chocolate.

Mom and Dad, you mean the world to me and I hope you know it.

The Longest Night

ANDRIA WILLIAMS

A
READER'S
GUIDE

A Conversation Between ANDRIA WILLIAMS and DAVID GILLHAM

Author's Note: David Gillham (author of the *New York Times* bestselling novel *City of Women*) and I are writers with similar interests: We tend toward historical fiction that explores the daily lives of women in tough situations. I loved his debut novel, *City of Women,* which focuses on Sigrid, an SS officer's wife living in Berlin during the Holocaust. With all the men away at war, Berlin has become a "city of women." Sigrid, though insulated as the novel opens, comes to realize the scope of the horror taking place all around her, which causes her to revolutionize—and risk—her own life in an effort to save others. I love big novels with women at the center: tough, thinking women who undergo such fierce upheaval that they are moved to change the world around them.

So I was thrilled to chat with David, one novelist to another, and answer his perceptive questions about my book: the historical event behind it, the fictional characters, and more.

David currently lives with his family in Massachusetts, where he is at work on another novel.

David Gillham: I loved this book, Andria. The characters, the setting, the friction, and the plot are all pitch perfect. But I'm curious, how did you first hear about the explosive events surrounding the military's SL-1 atomic reactor (styled as CR-1 in the book)?

Andria Williams: Thank you so much, David! I am a huge fan of your work, too. I'd read about the reactor accident in Idaho Falls long ago, while doing research for another project. Then, a few years ago, I came across a book called *Atomic America* by a former Navy nuclear officer named Todd Tucker. Tucker's book, which is nonfiction, focuses in large part upon the SL-1, a tiny reactor in the Idaho desert that mysteriously exploded on a freezing January night in 1961. The rescue crew who arrived at the reactor, not knowing whether the operators were dead or alive, had to decide whether or not to risk their own lives on the very slim chance that they could save one of these men. Remarkably, all of the first responders did take that chance, putting themselves in grave danger.

After the accident, rumors swirled about the operators who'd been working that night. Whether or not it was useful to the investigation or even ethical, their personal histories became central to the story of what happened at the SL-1.

I started thinking about who these characters might be, what sorts of men would work that job in the late 1950s and who their wives might have been. When your imagination starts running wild like that, you just feel in your bones that you have the makings for a good novel.

DG: Can you talk a bit about the rumors still orbiting the SL-1 meltdown and what made you want to dig deeper and ultimately create this terrific story?

AW: The 1950s was a time of boundless nuclear optimism. I can't think of many times in history when science and government alike have put so much faith in a single technology. So when the SL-1 accident occurred, it was much easier for people to see it as having been a human error rather than a mechanical one. No one wanted to believe that the reactor had just *blown up;* the operators had to have done something wrong. Taking it even further, many of the investigators claimed that the operator lifting the central control rod must have *knowingly* yanked it above the four-inch limit, which would have flooded the core with energy and caused the reactor to go supercritical in a fraction of a second, blowing the whole thing up. But why would someone do this?

The investigators dedicated a remarkable amount of time and energy to investigating the young operators' backgrounds, love lives, personal histories. One of the young men was known for having big drag-out fights with his wife in front of their apartment building, where she'd throw all his clothes out the window and the cops would be called and so forth, which apparently happened on multiple occasions. In fact, his wife had, that very afternoon, stolen his paycheck and filed for divorce. So the story started to be told that he was distraught and, working that night, had decided to end it all in a murder-suicide. Even the newspapers reported this story, and it stuck for decades.

Things got even more outlandish, with some rumors claiming that there had been a love triangle between this man and one of the other operators' wives. Never mind that the wife in question was Mormon and eight months pregnant at the time, and that there is no evidence she and the operator had ever even met. The rumors were much more salacious, exciting, and easy to understand, than the frightening and nebulous idea of mechanical failure, and they stuck—to the point that they are sometimes *still* used to explain the SL-1 accident.

But after reading about the accident, watching documentaries, looking up oral histories, I found myself agreeing with Todd Tucker's conclusion that the operators themselves had been blameless in the accident, and that mechanical catastrophe had been brewing for a long time. And this seemed even more poignant to me, even more the story I wanted to tell.

But because there's no definitive answer to what happened at the SL-1, I decided to tell the story in fiction form, taking composites of various characters described in the reports I'd read, and using this story to give an overview of this segment of our culture at the sometimes surreal-feeling dawn of the atomic age.

DG: In the book, there are several memorable scenes of break-room antics among the soldiers who work at the reactor. One of my favorites is the "Tic-Tac-Dough" scene in which the men play along with a popular game show. The banter between the soldiers is really wonderful. How did you go about crafting their language and the easy, authentic rapport you portray?

AW: Thank you! I really enjoyed writing scenes between soldiers. I've spent a lot of time around military folks by now and have enjoyed the certain shared sense of humor they often have. They spend a lot of hours together, so there's a lot of teasing, of course, a universal love of the prank, a gallows humor that comes with the job, and a predominantly masculine energy to it all. Putting soldiers in rooms and bars and on the beach together gave me an excuse to work in historical details—music and TV shows of the time—while also just letting them talk to each other, show a little bit of who they were.

DG: There's another scene in the book that I found very riveting. It centers around the men out for a night on the town outside of Idaho Falls. This is the Idaho Falls 1960 version of a red-light district. The boys head out to celebrate a birthday and one of them hires a prostitute, a local Native American woman. An incredibly uncomfortable scene follows—drunken men climbing behind the wheels of cars and, most heinously, the cruelty inflected upon the woman. Will you speak a bit about writing this scene and its importance?

AW: This is the flip side to those nice guys joking around in the break room: no group of people can be one hundred percent clever and charming. I needed to show what might happen when the group dynamic changed, when the boss-man was present and encouraging his guys to do some unsavory things.

Military installations often generate a market for alcohol and sex, and Idaho Falls in the late fifties was no exception. Most any report written about the personal lives of operators working the SL-1 mentions their occasional wild parties, including one where they hired a local prostitute to entertain the men for two bucks apiece. I found this an interesting counterpoint to the code of chivalry the men kept in place toward their own wives, who were supposed to be these domestic angels tending the home and hearth and waiting patiently for their soldier boys to return home. Women who were not their wives, who didn't fit this formula of extreme propriety, were seen as having signed away some of the right to manly protection that the housewives received. If you were nonwhite, or unmarried, or sexually loose—well, you didn't have to be treated with kid gloves like these upstanding housewives were.

So Paul finds himself in a situation where a woman is being abused and most of the guys are going along with it, and there could be repercussions for him if he decides to be the one soft-heart who helps her out. These strict gender expectations cut both ways, and Paul is trapped by his own need to be stoic and macho and to have a good time out on the town. But the woman in question is "just" a prostitute, right?—I mean, she's not one of their wives, because they would never treat a *lady* like that, for goodness' sake. The operators' fear of what will happen if one of their darling wives finds out allows the risky situation to carry on much longer than it should. Of course this is reprehensible, but it's something that happens all the time.

I wanted to show how one act of bigotry taints everything around it, so when Paul gets home, Nat, who's completely innocent in the situation, becomes the unwitting recipient of whatever disgust and self-loathing he is carrying.

DG: Jeannie Richards, the wife of Mitch Richards, who is the big boss at the reactor, is a wildly enjoyable character to read about, but probably not so enjoyable for the other characters to endure within the confines of their little coffee klatch. Jeannie's smart as a whip, and charming in her way, but also controlling and manipulative behind the perfect mask of her smile. She felt like a caged animal to me—a woman whose potential for good had been diverted and corrupted by snide neighborhood power struggles. Were you drawing on any particular example of the archetypical 1950s housewife in Jeannie's creation?

AW: I think you're right on target in seeing Jeannie as a "caged animal." She has that exact same snarling, frantic presence at times, especially when she is alone and can let down her façade of total control. And you're right, she is very smart—much more streetwise than Nat—but she's forced to channel her intelligence into social machinations and the losing campaign to promote her husband's sluggish career.

I loved writing Jeannie's sections because she serves as the perfect counterbalance to Nat, who is all sweetness and good intention. Sarcasm and sexuality are Jeannie's weapons of choice. Her sections came to me so quickly; they had the most momentum of any of the parts of the novel that I wrote. I could just *see* her setting the table for that party or sneering at Mitch across the room or tunneling madly through his desk drawers in an effort to gather intel on what fool thing he'd been up to this time.

Jeannie knows that undercutting other women is one of the quickest ways to get the things she wants, most of which have to come from men. The sad thing is, I think she and Nat are both trapped by their circumstances, and could probably have been friends of a sort if they had both just been honest with each other.

DG: Could you talk a bit about your research process for the Greenland section?

AW: I read a ton of oral histories, many of them found on a terrific website called thuleforum.com, moderated by the generous Steffen Winther. The experience of being at Camp Century and its support camps, TUTO and Thule, was such a unique and specific one that men seem to have sought one another out in subsequent years to share their memories. I sat and read scores of these personal stories and at times just laughed out loud, and at other times felt great sympathy for men serving at a base that was so isolated and remote that no one was allowed to serve more than six months there at a time because it was considered a psychological hazard. Sometimes, men would hallucinate; I remember reading reports that certain soldiers were convinced they had seen grazing cows and "medium-sized Midwestern cities" out on the polar ice cap. This was all before e-mail and Skype and whatnot, and these men must have felt very, very far away from not only their families but the rest of the human world.

DG: I have to bring up the cars. This book is full of fabulous vintage automobiles. Are you a car aficionado or did this come with the territory of writing about the late 1950s? Sometimes I felt as if you had a job similar to the producers of *Mad Men,* in your conjuring of a period piece, and to me the cars are at the very center of it all. But they're more than just set decoration. Will you speak to how you so skillfully wove these powerful autos into the plot?

AW: The designs of the 1950s are so instantly recognizable, so stylized. It's an aesthetic I find immensely appealing, from home décor to clothing typefaces to, yes, the cars of the day. Is there anything so striking as a big, shiny, shark-finned Cadillac from the 1950s? I don't think so.

In a more serious vein, cars played an important psychological role during the fifties, a boom time in which more families than ever could afford their own automobiles. The interstate highway system was built in large part during this decade, starting in 1956. Vehicular mobility came hand in hand with upward mobility. A car was a symbol that you were not just going somewhere, but *going somewhere.*

For Paul, just owning a car is a huge achievement; he grew up so poor that he had to steal his brother's boots to leave home. But then his new boss, Mitch, has this gorgeous Coupe de Ville that he throws in Paul's face any chance he gets.

For the women in the novel, particularly Nat, cars symbolize a freedom that is otherwise unavailable to them. Nat is a military wife who must stay put while her husband traverses the globe, so just being able to drive away from her house for an hour or two is immensely liberating. She and Paul have a notable argument over who gets to drive their family car, and it's when this car is wrecked that an opening is created for Esrom to slide into the family dynamic. Later, when Paul learns that Nat has been driving Esrom's car, it's tantamount to hearing that she's slept with him. He is horrified and betrayed.

DG: You very deftly highlight for the reader the significance of Idaho Falls in American culture. Of course there is the reactor meltdown, but there are many aspects of the town that I think are notable: the Native American history, the history of the Mormons, the town's role as a bridge between the West and Midwest. Once you finished the book, did you feel like you were leaving Idaho Falls too?

AW: I've always thought Idaho is beautiful, although the most time I've spent there was on a road trip in 1999 when I was twenty. The place stuck with me.

I think the West's severe natural beauty, coupled with its fascinatingly layered history, lends itself to fiction. For instance, by the time Paul arrives in Idaho, it's already been home to Blackfoot Indians for thousands of years, then white settlers, particularly Mormons. It's held a Japanese internment camp and a military proving ground, which has recently been turned into the development site for all major nuclear projects in the United States—and that's where Paul reports for duty and will be faced with his toughest choice.

If all that doesn't encapsulate the layered strata of history in the West—the land grabs, power struggles, religious migrations, manifest destiny, xenophobia, loss and ambition—I don't know what does.

QUESTIONS AND TOPICS FOR DISCUSSION

1. In an early scene, Paul and his family stop by a lake for a swim on their move to Idaho. Nat wants to go cliff-jumping, but it's obvious that Paul would rather she stay on the beach. Why doesn't Paul want her to join the group of young people on the cliff? Why do you think Nat disregards his fear even when she knows it bothers him?

2. After Paul's first meeting with his boss, Mitch Richards, Mitch drives off and leaves Paul stranded at work. Do you think this was a mere oversight, or was it intentional? Was Paul right to be so angry?

3. Paul is often worried about Nat and his daughters. Do you think his fears are justified?

4. When Nat first meets Jeannie at the dinner party, she's alternately impressed and frightened by her. In what ways does Nat attempt to be the proper 1950s military wife, like Jeannie, and where does she reject this? Do you think she wishes she could be a "better" wife?

5. Mitch's cream-colored Cadillac plays a large role in the novel. What do you think the car represents for Mitch, for Jeannie, and for Paul? Did you find its end fitting?

6. Paul, Jeannie, Nat, and Esrom all struggle with loneliness in various ways. Which character do you think does the best job overcoming their loneliness?

7. Were you surprised to learn of any of the historically based details in the novel, such as the National Reactor Testing Station or the Army base below the ice in Greenland? Had you heard of any of these things before, and what conceptions of them did you have coming into the novel? If you did, did knowing that the story was based in part on a real event make it more interesting to you, or less?

8. Should Nat have refused the car from Esrom? Was it all right for her to accept it?

9. Nat's friend, Patrice, is angry with Nat when she learns of her friendship with Esrom. Do you think Patrice overreacted, or was her frustration with Nat justified? Does her role as a fellow military wife give her particular insight into Nat's behavior, and if so, why don't you think she was more sympathetic?

10. Patrice's anger serves as a wake-up call for Nat. Was Nat naïve in hoping that she could keep her relationship with Esrom a secret from her friend, her neighbors, and, most important, from Paul? Do you think either Nat or Esrom were innocent in the situation? If not, is one of them more to blame than the other?

11. What do you think happens to Paul in the years following the close of the novel? Do you see him living a long and happy life, or does his involvement with the reactor accident catch up with him? If so, what do you see happening to Nat? To Jeannie? To Esrom?

PHOTO: © DAVE JOHANSON

A native of northern California, where her parents were public schoolteachers, ANDRIA WILLIAMS attended UC-Berkeley (BA in English) and the University of Minnesota (MFA in creative writing). She and her husband, an active-duty naval officer, have three young children. They have been stationed in Virginia, Illinois, and California, and are currently in Colorado. *The Longest Night* is her first novel.

andriawilliams.com

militaryspousebookreview.com

@Andria816

ABOUT THE TYPE

This book was set in Bulmer, a typeface designed in the late eighteenth century by the London type cutter William Martin (1757–1830). The typeface was created especially for the Shakespeare Press, directed by William Bulmer (1757–1830)—hence the font's name. Bulmer is considered to be a transitional typeface, containing characteristics of old-style and modern designs. It is recognized for its elegantly proportioned letters, with their long ascenders and descenders.

RANDOM HOUSE
READER'S CIRCLE
®

RANDOM HOUSE